They ran back to the car and stopped, aghast: both tires on the exposed side were flat, the knife slashes in them showing dark in the dim light. A slight noise behind them brought a cry to Vanessa's lips and they whirled around, their backs to the car. Out of the shadows a group of six figures loomed—they were young teenagers, and their leader, who towered head and shoulders above the rest, said something in their own tongue and then in English: "You don't understand—she's a friend, a friend of our people. She's here to help. Keep back!" Then to Vanessa, as they padded menacingly toward them, "Run! run for your life!"

DESPERATE MEASURES

Margot Arnold

FAWCETT GOLD MEDAL • NEW YORK

A Fawcett Gold Medal Book
Published by Ballantine Books
Copyright © 1986 by Margot Arnold

Library of Congress Catalog Card Number: 86-90872

ISBN 0-449-12877-6

Manufactured in the United States of America

First Edition: June 1986

To Sarah Elizabeth Ruth Cook. May all her days be blessed with joy.

Chapter 1

*I*t was while waiting to go through passport control at Orly Airport that Vanessa Hale first noticed him, though she was so keyed up by this, her first adventure abroad, that she was not in a very noticing mood. But there was something about him, a certain air, a certain inconsistency, that drew her eyes to him. Why, she wondered as her mother fidgeted impatiently in the line beside her, does a man with such an elegant suit have such an unruly mop of hair? Why, though he is obviously an American, does he have a funny-shaped black passport and not a square blue one?

"Come on, Vanessa, stop daydreaming—it's our turn," her mother said crossly, and jostled her up to the next desk so that she was elbow-to-elbow with the intriguing, curly-headed man. A dour-faced customs official was asking him in a bored voice, "And what is the purpose of your visit to Paris, Monsieur Bannerman—business or pleasure?"

"Oh, most certainly pleasure. Why else does one come to Paris?" he said, and grinned sideways at Vanessa. It was a most engaging, mischievous grin that revealed perfect strong white teeth, and though the smile appeared to make the passport official gloomier than ever, she found herself smiling back.

"*Do* come on, Vanessa!" her mother said, thrusting their passports at her. "Here, you take these, and for Heaven's sake don't lose them. We've still got to find the bags, and I'm simply *exhausted* already. I can't wait to get to our hotel and lie down." She was fumbling frantically around in her large shoulderbag for the tickets with the baggage claim stubs.

Vanessa sighed inwardly and followed obediently behind. Her mother was not going to let her forget for an instant what a sacrifice she was making in chaperoning her on this trip when she could be safely home in Larchmont with her bridge club, ballroom dancing classes, and, of course, the bereft Mr. Cross, on whom, Vanessa was sure, her mother's sights were most definitely set.

With all the cynicism of her twenty-two years, Vanessa realized that she would never have rated this expensive trip if her mother had not been hell-bent and determined to break up her own romance with Sam. Poor Sam! She wasn't sure what her mother hated about him more: the fact that he was a Jew or the fact that he was a penniless and temperamental musician. Temperamental he most certainly was, but what a violinist! If only she had half his talent, she thought wistfully, she would be so happy. If he weren't so thin-skinned and edgy, she would be with him now at the Tanglewood Festival, but they had had such a flaring row just before the end of the Juilliard spring term that she had allowed her mother to decoy her off on this European trip, figuring that her absence would make his heart grow fonder over the summer. When the fall semester started they could have a wonderful romantic reconciliation, and next summer, after graduation, maybe, just maybe, she'd become Mrs. Sam Goldberg, no matter *what* her mother said or did.

Her rosy dream was punctured again by her mother's insistent voice. "Oh, *do* pay attention, Vanessa—I'm sure that was one of our bags that just went by. I can't do everything, you know!" The chute of the baggage carousel was now spitting out an endless stream of luggage onto its steadily revolving metal surface, rimmed by anxious faces and clutching hands. Vanessa grabbed at the indicated bag, only to find it had someone else's name tag on it. She fought her way back into the crowd and dropped it back on the carousel as a gray-clad arm shot under her nose and seized a lightweight, expensive-looking wardrobe bag. "Oops, sorry! This is a real rat race, isn't it?" It was the intriguing Mr. Bannerman again, so close that she could smell his Brut after-shave lotion.

She pounced on one of her suitcases and jostled it off, trying to avoid crushing his toes in the process. "Yes," she said dolefully. "And we've got six more to go. You'd think we were going to settle permanently here instead of just spending the summer."

On closer inspection she saw he was older than she had first thought, with little laughter lines radiating from his vivid blue eyes that showed white against his tanned fair skin, and his clean-shaven square jaw already bluish with beard in the unmerciful light of early morning. Why, she thought with a pang, he must be quite old—in his late thirties, at least.

"We?" he queried with a slight frown.

"My mother and I." She indicated her mother, who was now poised at the edge of the carousel, scanning the bags with a grimly determined expression.

"Ah! Then you're going to need a porter to help you with all of these." He looked at the growing pile of bags at her feet. "Know the ropes?"

"No—it's our first visit," she said, feeling gauche.

"Want me to rustle up a porter for you?"

"That would be very kind." She glanced over a little helplessly at her mother, who had just pounced on the last of the bags with a snort of triumph.

"Right. No problem. He'll put you into a cab. Where will you be staying?"

"Er, the Hotel Lutetia on the Boulevard Raspail—I think that's on the Rive Gauche," she said, trying to sound sophisticated.

He grinned down at her. "I'll be back in a jiffy. Stay right where you are." He elbowed his way out of the thinning crowd.

Her mother advanced on her, bearing her spoils. "Who was that young man you were talking to?" she demanded suspiciously.

"A Mr. Bannerman, an American—he's gone to get us a porter. We can't manage this by ourselves." Her mother struggled between relief and disapproval but was saved the trouble of making up her mind by the reappearance of their broad-shouldered rescuer with a blue-coated porter in tow.

Anxious to preserve her "woman of the world" poise, Vanessa said, "Mother, this is Mr. Bannerman, who kindly offered to help us out."

The effect on him of this innocent remark completely took her aback. He literally froze in his tracks, the laughing blue eyes becoming cold and wary, and his jaw set in a dangerous line. "How do you know my name?" he demanded in a quiet, hard voice.

"Why, I was next to you going through customs—I heard the passport man call you by name!" Vanessa stuttered, trying to fight down a blush.

His tenseness disappeared as swiftly as it had come. "Ah, then you have *me* at a disadvantage," he said, looking at her mother, his well-marked, dark blond eyebrows raised in inquiry.

"I'm Clarissa Hale, and this is my daughter, Vanessa," her mother said, taking in the expensive gray three-piece suit with an appreciative eye. "It was most kind of you to find us a porter. We do have rather a lot of luggage. Thanks again."

He did not take this as a dismissal but proceeded to help the porter load the bags on the trolley. "John Bannerman. You are from New York?" "I live in Larchmont, out in Westchester, but my daughter goes to Juilliard, in Manhattan." Her mother was following him and the baggage out the automatic doors.

He eyed the violin case on top of the baggage and

smiled his infectious smile at Vanessa. "Ah, so you're the musician."

"And what part of the States are you from, Mr. Bannerman?" her mother persisted as the porter started to hurl their bags into a battered-looking cab.

"I live overseas," he said easily. "I'm with the State Department."

"Oh, a diplomat! How interesting." Her mother was visibly impressed.

He ushered them into the cab and stepped back onto the curb. "Well, it was a pleasure meeting you, and enjoy your stay," he called as the taxi shot away at breakneck speed.

Her mother settled back with a contented sigh. "What a nice-mannered man! You so rarely meet a gentleman these days—but then, if he's a diplomat . . ." she trailed off, yawning.

But Vanessa had not quite recovered from his sudden transformation. "Yes, he was very—interesting," she agreed softly.

The next few days were a frantic whirl of sightseeing. Since this was their first visit, her mother had wisely elected to take a series of guided walking tours to get the feel of the city. The guides were good and very energetic, so the two women walked and walked until their feet were ready to drop off. They saw everything there was to see in the medieval quarter of the Marais, the Latin Quarter, the Ile de la Cité and Notre Dame, the Trocadero with its museums and the Eiffel Tower, and so on and on and on.

"I swear at this rate we'll have walked every damned street in Paris," Vanessa grumbled, rubbing her aching feet. She was feeling thoroughly out of sorts because she had tried to do some practicing in their hotel room and the management had politely asked her to desist.

"I can't go a whole summer without practicing," she had complained. "My bowing will go to hell, and I can't afford to lose ground. I've got my senior recital to think of."

"It won't kill you not to practice for a while," her mother had sniffed. "Wait until we get to Italy—the Italians love music and are more understanding about these things anyway.

"Well, we've only got one more tour to go, and then we'll be on our own and can relax a little," her mother placated. "Maybe you can take your violin out to the Bois de Boulogne or somewhere like that and practice. Don't be difficult—there's more to life than music."

At this heresy Vanessa snorted, flounced off to her room, and wrote a long, complaining letter to Sam in Tanglewood.

But the very next day Sam was once more shunted to the outskirts of her thoughts. It was very hot, and they were sitting, resting their feet, and gazing at the cool depths of Monet's Water Lilies at the Orangerie when a voice behind them said, "Very cool and restful, isn't it? Just the place for a hot day like this." And they looked up to see John Bannerman watching them expectantly. He was incredibly elegant in well-tailored navy slacks and a white, open-necked silk shirt into which was tucked a colorful silk scarf.

Clarissa Hale positively lit up. "Why, Mr. Bannerman, how nice to see you again! Won't you join us?"

He dropped down beside Vanessa on the bench and eyed her. "So, how's it been going? Enjoying Paris?"

"A little exhausting," her mother replied before Vanessa could get a word out. "But very enjoyable. This is the last of our guided tours, so from now on we'll be on our own."

The intensity of his gaze deepened, but he said lightly, "In that case, I wonder if you'd take pity on a lone voyager and perhaps have dinner with me tomorrow night. I was thinking of taking in some of the musical nightlife of Paris, and it is so much more enjoyable when one has company."

Vanessa, who was already more than a little sick of the nightlife at the Hotel Lutetia, which consisted of eating dinner and watching French television, said quickly, "Why, that sounds lovely, doesn't it, Mother?"

"Well, yes—it's very kind of you, Mr. Bannerman," her mother fluttered. "But are you quite sure?"

"Quite sure. It will be a pleasure." He smiled, looking

so deeply into Vanessa's eyes that she felt tingles run up and down her spine. "I'll pick you up at your hotel at seven-thirty."

What to wear for this night out concerned her mightily, for she had brought little in the way of formal dresses and did not even own that many non-casual clothes anyway, Juilliard not being into dressing up. She finally settled on what she thought of as her toreador suit, in brown velvet, which matched the color of her dark brown eyes and brought out the red highlights in her chestnut hair. It had a short bolero jacket and a very full skirt that cinched into a tight cummerbund waist. This, with one of her ruffled white performance blouses, she decided, would constitute a snappy enough outfit to keep up with the elegant John Bannerman. I hope I don't roast to death in it, she thought, but the French summer weather, in its sudden, unpredictable way, cooperated beautifully by suddenly plunging the temperature into the low sixties.

John Bannerman turned up a little late but resplendent in a dark blue three-piece suit, white silk shirt, and Gucci tie of dark crimson silk. "Sorry I'm late," he apologized cheerfully, "but I had to wait for a long-distance call at the embassy." And he swept them off to dinner at the famous La Coupole in Montparnasse.

The huge, brightly lit, old-style restaurant had not gotten into its full nightly swing as yet, and they easily obtained a table by the window looking out over the busy boulevard Montparnasse. When they had settled the vital questions of what to eat and drink and were applying themselves to the first course of langoustines accompanied by a Pouilly-Fumé, Clarissa Hale began a gentle but persistent probing of their host. "I had not realized you were actually stationed at the embassy here, Mr. Bannerman. Have you been here long?"

"Please call me John," he said smoothly. "And I'm not posted here. I'm with our embassy in Pretoria, South Africa. Just getting back—or, rather, dawdling back—from home leave in America."

Vanessa contributed little to the conversation. She was too entranced by the kaleidoscope of people whirling by, inside and outside, and she loved it when an exotic high-fashion model made a scene because the doorkeeper would not allow her to bring in the two enormous, needle-nosed borzois that she had on golden leashes and that in some strange way strongly resembled their exotic owner. She tuned in on the conversation from time to time and learned, among other things, that John was a Second Secretary in the Economic Section, which sounded dull; that he'd been to Yale; that he had served in the Vietnam War; and that he had been married but was now divorced.

"You might say my marriage was one of the last casualties of the Vietnam War," he said ruefully to the relentless Clarissa. "My wife was violently against my going, and after it, when she was faced with the type of nomadic life diplomats must lead—well, she had a career of her own and she just couldn't face it. I don't really blame her."

"Nevertheless, going through a divorce is a terrible stress on *anyone*," Clarissa asserted positively. "I know; I've been through it myself. . . ."

Vanessa tuned out again, feeling a little sick. If her mother was going to launch into a detailed description of her marital traumas, she did not want to hear any part of it. It seemed her parents' long-drawn-out separations and divorce had lasted her entire adolescent life, its ills compounded by the fact that her father had dropped dead of a heart attack in Grand Central Station before the divorce had ever become final. In the shock of this, she had realized that she had never really known her father, who had always been too busy scrabbling to make money in the madhouse of the Madison Avenue advertising world to get to know her, but that she had loved him nonetheless, and that now it was too late and she would never have the chance to know him.

He had been heavily insured, so there were no money problems: there was ample for her schooling, for the house in Larchmont, and for her mother's modest suburban life—but there were some lacks that now could never be filled.

"Well, shall we move on?" John's voice penetrated her consciousness. "It's after ten, so things should be getting underway at the cabarets. I thought we might start off at Le Lapin Agile in Montmartre—they have some good French folk music." She looked up to see his eyes on her, gravely questioning. "You've been so quiet, Vanessa— are you bored? If so, we could do something else."

"Oh, I'm not bored at all—that sounds great!" she said quickly, her color mounting. "I find everything so fascinating and different that I'm just trying to drink it all in."

"She's such a daydreamer," her mother sighed, getting up. "Always off in a world of her own."

Le Lapin Agile, tucked away on the crest of Montmartre in the rue des Saules, was small, dark, and crowded, but the music *was* good, and they sipped the specialty of the house, dark cherries soaked in cherry brandy. The plaintive old French folk songs, with their themes of love and death, the darkness, and the cumulative effect of the wine and brandy unsettled Vanessa: she felt dislocated, floating in both space and time; her only anchor was the close physical presence of John Bannerman.

When the music took a more strident and rollicking turn and the rafters were echoing to the hunting song of "le bon roi Dagobert," John murmured, "Shall we move on? I thought maybe a discotheque and some dancing for a change of pace." She floated back to earth.

The discotheque on the boulevard St. Germain was jumping, in every sense of the word. Huge nude statues supported the low ceiling, their navels little green screens across which the decibel levels of the music danced in savage white zigzags. The noise level was incredible. Politely, John asked Clarissa to dance first, and she shrieked roguishly into his ear, "I'm afraid this isn't my kind of music—old-time cheek-to-cheek is more my style."

"Next time we'll have to find some of that," he roared back, and held out his hand to Vanessa. As she took it, it was as if an electric shock traveled up her arm and jolted her heart, and she glanced quickly at him to see if his face mirrored what she had felt. But he was too busy threading his way through the packed tables for her to see his face, and when he swung her into the rhythm of the music his eyes merely sparkled with laughter.

"I'm not too good at this," she shouted at him. "Haven't done it much since high school."

"Don't you like dancing?"

"Love it, but no time. We music students work hard, you know." She could scarcely explain that Sam was against anything as low-brow as dancing and that their rare evenings out were dedicated to string quartets or Pro Musica concerts.

John was a wonderful dancer, and soon she was happily immersed in him and the music. They returned after a couple of sets to find her mother literally flattened against the wall. "I'm sorry to be a wet blanket, but I find all this noise rather trying," she complained faintly. "Perhaps we should call it a night, John—it is getting rather late."

"Oh, not yet—there's one more place you just *have* to see," he said quickly. "We'll leave right away, and it's quite close by. Please come! It's not a place you could go by yourselves, and I'm sure you'll enjoy it."

The taxi dropped them on the boulevard St. Michel at the opening of a narrow, dimly lit street. "This is the famous rue de la Huchette," John murmured as he guided them down it. "Written about by the American Eliot Paul, who lived here before World War II. It's totally changed from his day, of course, because now it's the heart of the Algerian Arab quarter. Off it runs the narrowest street in Paris, with a name wider than it is—la rue du chat qui peche. This is it." They came to an incredibly narrow runnel at the base of which the river Seine glimmered faintly. "Our destination lies just beyond—we're going to hear some Arab music and see some belly dancing."

The harsh, wailing cadences of an Arab song came out to meet them as the swarthy proprietor greeted John like a long-lost son. He ducked and bobbed in front of them until he had led them to a low brass table at the side of the small stage and had seen them seated on piles of cushions. A veiled, dark-haired Arab girl, her lush form scantily concealed by swaths of blue chiffon and a-clink with gold coins, was doing incredible things with the muscles of her bare stomach as she gyrated slowly around the stage.

The dancing had cleared Vanessa's head, and she decided to keep it that way, so settled for Arab coffee rather than more brandy, while her mother and John had both. She watched with fascination as the dancer glided up, zeroed in on John, and proceeded to flip her hip coins individually in his face. "I wonder how on earth she *does* that! I'm sure I don't have that many muscles," Vanessa whispered to him, and he chuckled at both her and the dancer. Even her mother was entranced, and they had been watching for about fifteen minutes when the proprietor came up and whispered urgently in John's ear. He uncoiled himself and got up. "Excuse me. I'll be right back," he whispered. "Another damn phone call."

The blue chiffon dancer had been replaced with a gold chiffon duplicate, this one with an earthen water pot balanced on her head. As the girl sank full length to the floor, the water pot still incredibly balanced upright, Vanessa watched her distractedly. How on earth did anyone know he was here, she wondered, and at this time of the morning? And it was evident the proprietor knew him. For someone who was stationed in Africa, he certainly had a lot of contacts elsewhere. It was strange, definitely strange.

He rejoined them shortly with a rueful grimace. "Sorry about that! Even on leave they never let you alone in my business."

"I never knew the State Department was so long-armed," she murmured, eyeing him reflectively.

"Oh, you musicians aren't the only ones who work hard," he quipped. "It's just that we get better paid for it."

It was evident to both of them that the last brandy had been too much for Clarissa Hale; she was visibly sagging and had begun to nod off. John looked at Vanessa. "Time to call it a night?"

"Yes, I think so. Mother's had it."

"Come sightseeing with me tomorrow?"

She looked at him steadily. "Yes, I'd like that."

They got Clarissa up and out with the minimum of commotion, and as they piled her into a taxi she recovered enough to say, "Thank you so much. Such a delightful evening! Though I'm sure it will take me days to recover from it."

"All right if I take Vanessa off your hands for tomorrow?" he queried.

"Oh, certainly. Just delightful, delightful..." she muttered, and she dozed off again.

He looked down at Vanessa. "Then I'll pick you up about eleven, and we'll have lunch somewhere?"

"That'll be fine," she murmured, and sank exhaustedly back into her seat. As they drove back to the hotel, she realized guiltily that she had scarcely given a thought to Sam all evening. No matter, she told herself fiercely. This isn't real; this is just a midsummer night's dream, and John Bannerman is just an intriguing mystery, a mystery to be solved. That's all!

Chapter 2

"*So where would you like to go first?*" John seemed a little nervous at their being alone together, and this, for some reason, made Vanessa feel more at ease and sure of herself.

"I'd like to go back to Notre Dame and look at the rose window," she said positively. "These tours are all very well, but they do tend to rush you around, and I like to dawdle over the things I really like."

"Then Notre Dame it shall be," he said. "*And* the Sainte Chappelle, if you are into windows."

"*And* the Sainte Chappelle." She smiled at him.

"Do you know you have two of the most adorable dimples on either side of your mouth when you smile like that?" he said solemnly, and this threw her back into a state of confusion.

"Until I saw it, I never realized what a gorgeous honey color Notre Dame was. I always thought it was a grungy black," Vanessa said as they walked up to the massive carved central doors of the cathedral.

"Up until a few years ago it was, with eight centuries'

worth of Paris dirt on it. They did a marvelous job of cleaning it up," he said absently. "One of De Gaulle's pet projects for Paris that worked magnificently."

They strolled up to the huge rondelle of colors that the sun, shining through the multicolored panes of the great window, was projecting onto the gray stone floor. Entranced, Vanessa looked up, feeling herself bathed in rainbow radiance. "It's *so* beautiful," she breathed. "It's like . . . it's like Beethoven's Ode to Joy in glass—how wonderful to be able to create something like that!"

John was looking at her with an enigmatic expression, his blue eyes dark and solemn. "It must be so nice in that ivory tower of yours—life must be beautiful in there," he said softly.

She bridled at that. "I can see you've been brainwashed already by my mother. I'm not a hopeless, romantic dreamer, whatever you may think. Musicians live in a tough, competitive world where they have to produce their best or go under. There's no letup, no easy way."

"I stand my ground nevertheless." He relaxed into a smile. "I know music is a tough world, but at its core is a satisfaction, a beauty, to which you can always turn and which is closed to us mere mortals. You've always got something to retreat into."

"Now I think it's *you* who are being the romantic," she snorted, turning away. "Shall we go on?"

They inspected the less subtle splendors of St. Louis's symphony in glass in the Sainte Chappelle, and then John suggested lunch. "I know a nice little place on the rue de l'Odeon—we can walk to it up St. Michel, and maybe afterward take a turn through the Luxembourg Gardens."

"Sounds nice—is there anything else we can see on the way?" she asked.

He threw back his head and laughed. "You really *are* a culture vulture—take it easy, or you'll run out of things to see before the summer is done!"

"Oh, but I've only got another six days here," she said. "So it's now or never."

She could tell she had startled him. "But I thought you were going to be here all summer," he burst out.

"In Europe, yes. Two weeks here, a month in Italy, and then two weeks in Spain and Portugal—my grand tour," she said, an edge on her voice. "My mother's expensive solution to breaking up my 'unfortunate' romance—or so she thinks. I'm sure in all the confidences you shared last night, she couldn't have failed to mention *that*."

His response caught her off balance. "Is it serious, this romance, or is it just to bait your mother?" he asked as he guided her across the busy boulevard.

"Well!" she gasped, and tried to pull herself together. "She just doesn't understand what a brilliantly gifted violinist Sam is—to hear her you'd think he was some sort of way-out hippie, she's so out of date. I've tried to explain to her that there *are* no hippies anymore, that the world belongs now to the 'yuppies.'"

"And you don't like yuppies—is that it?"

She was back in balance. "No, that's not it at all. I've nothing against yuppies—God knows, without them we musicians couldn't even survive. After all, it's their money that supports the music world."

"I see." They had arrived at the little restaurant nestled by the ancient bulk of the Theatre de l'Odeon and settled at a table on the pavement under its shady striped awning, and in the interval of ordering drinks and lunch this uncomfortable subject was dropped.

"So when do you return to South Africa?" she asked, tucking into a delectable paté de campagne.

"Oh, not for a while yet—I've got lots of leave to use up," he said casually. "I'm off to Italy myself shortly. Where will you be staying?"

"Well, we'll be based in Rome, but we plan to take a lot of trips—Florence, Siena, Viterbo, maybe even Venice."

"Your mother's doing you proud," he observed with a faint smile.

"You think I'm a spoiled brat, don't you?" she challenged, her chin jutting defiantly.

"No, just a little overly antagonistic to your mother,

who, seems to me, is a very nice, well-intentioned person
with problems of her own," he said mildly.

"Don't we all have problems?" She flared back, then
softened. "Oh, dear. I *am* sounding like a brat." She gave
a little helpless gesture. "It's not that I don't like my
mother. I do. I'm very fond of her. But we get on a lot
better when we're apart—if that makes any sense. When
we're together, we just grate on each other, and it brings
out the worst in both of us. Anyway, this is a dreary
subject for such a lovely day—let's talk about something
else."

"Your wish is my command." He grinned, and they
talked about something else then, and later as well as they
strolled hand in hand through the Luxembourg Gardens
and all the way back to the hotel. He was, she decided
as she headed alone directly for her room, unwilling to
face her mother as yet, the most fascinating and charming
man she had ever encountered—and she did not understand him in the least.

"How did it go?" her mother, still subdued from her
hangover, asked later.

"Oh, very pleasant," she said airily. "He'd like to squire
us around again tomorrow, if that's all right with you."

"How nice!" her mother murmured, and, for once,
there was no inquisition.

This was the pattern of the next three days, lulling her
into a euphoric sense of continuing delight, so it was
something of a shock when, on the fourth day, he did not
appear, did not even telephone. The day of their departure
she looked for him at the airport, but there was no sign,
not even a bon voyage message, and she was disappointed
beyond all reason.

Her spirits sagged still further when they arrived at
their modest little Roman hotel to find Sam's response to
her voluminous letter. It consisted of a postcard of the
Berkshire hills, and its message read, "Tanglewood's great.
The conductor is an egomaniac and an idiot. Greta sends
regards. Sorry the trip is a bust. Love, Sam." Greta was
a cellist, also Jewish, who had been after Sam for some
time and who hated Vanessa's guts.

Listlessly she took in the ancient grandeurs of Rome, and she was so docile that her mother began to look at her with lively concern. "We don't *have* to do all these tours," she said anxiously. "If there's something else you'd rather do, we can cancel. Just say the word."

"No—it's fine with me, just fine," Vanessa said drearily.

But on the fifth day the world righted itself. They were just about to set out on their daily tour when the manager of the hotel intercepted them. "A gentleman to see you, Signora e Signorina." He whisked open the door of the tiny lounge, to reveal John Bannerman in profile gazing thoughtfully out the window. For a moment she was so overcome, her heart thudding so painfully, that she couldn't get her breath, but then he swung around and his enchanting smile revived her with its warmth. "If I had a hat, I'd throw it in the door," he said. "I came to offer my apologies for deserting you in Paris—some business came up. But now, if you can forgive me, I've come to ask if you'll come to the opera with me tonight. *Aida* at the Baths of Caracalla—it should be good."

"Well, thank you, John," Clarissa said. "But I find this Roman heat rather exhausting, and opera is not really my thing at all. But perhaps Vanessa would enjoy it...."

He looked at her pleadingly. "Say yes—please!"

She tried to be cool and calm. "I've never seen an opera in Italy—so, okay, I'm game."

She had fully intended to keep up this coolly distant façade, but the excitement of the evening soon broke down this pathetic subterfuge, and she found herself clinging to John's arm and gazing starry-eyed at the great floodlit ruins of the Baths, rose-colored against the midnight blue of the summer sky, and at the hordes of people that were scurrying like streams of ants into the towering magnificence.

John had managed to get seats on the wide central aisle facing the elevated stage. "You'd better watch yourself," he warned her. "Sometimes they bring some of the animals down the center aisle for the triumph scene, and you know how unpredictable they can be! Have you seen *Aida* before?"

"Only a Met production on PBS television," she confessed. "And I thought the staging pretty tacky—the enormous headdresses on the Egyptians made them look like top-heavy toadstools."

"Well, I think I can promise you a good spectacle here. They usually have the works—elephants, camels, and the hero arriving in a real horse-drawn chariot," he assured her.

The opera began, the magnificent Verdi music soaring to the stars, and the triumphal procession was everything he had promised—that is, until its climax, when the hero, a tubby little Italian tenor, slowly drove his chariot down the center aisle. Just before it reached their seats, a program fluttered into the aisle; the two white horses reared back and suddenly took off, thundering up the ramp onto the stage like racehorses. Attendants immediately seized and gentled them, and the tenor, a pasty green from fright, descended shakily from the chariot to begin his big aria. His eyes still bulging with terror, he opened his mouth wide, but not a sound came out as he glared helplessly at the audience; it was too much for Vanessa. Stuffing her handkerchief in her mouth, she fled up the aisle, John in hot pursuit. When she was safely behind a sheltering wall, she unstuffed her mouth and let the laughter out. She laughed helplessly until the tears streamed down her face. John was laughing almost as hard and they were reeling about like a couple of drunks, beating on the wall with their hands and holding their aching sides. "I've never seen anything as funny and ridiculous as that in all my life!" she sobbed. "Oh, dear, I wish I could stop, I ache so!" And she went off into another peal.

Gradually their laughter died away, and they were standing looking teary-eyed at each other. John reached out suddenly and pulled her to him, his lips seeking hers in a long, lingering kiss. She felt she was being slowly transmuted into fire and that in this moment her real life was beginning; she never wanted it to end. At length, he drew away, his blue eyes cloudy. "There!" he said defiantly.

"That's something I've been wanting to do ever since Orly Airport. Are you going to slap my face or let me do it again?"

She put her hands up to his flushed face and drew it gently down to hers. "Do it again," she whispered. "You left off just in the middle of a burst of shooting stars."

Afterward, back in the hotel, she could not remember whether they had seen the rest of the opera or not, but she did have some faint recollection of a horse-drawn carriage ride, a full moon, and a frenzy of kisses that had left her in an emotional daze.

She fought to get her feet back on the ground. "Damn it, you can't be in love with him. This is just a summer romance—it's nothing serious." To banish him, she tried to summon up her past loves: Peter, her high school steady; Sam—but she found she could not even remember their faces. All she could see was John's face, all she could feel was the strength of his arms around her and the tense virility of his body. Damn it, she *was* in love with him, she was forced to conclude with dismayed delight.

In the next few days it was evident, even in her bemused state, that he was vigorously courting her; their courtship helped by the temporary indisposition of Clarissa Hale due to a slight case of food poisoning. Vanessa gave herself up to it, not daring to think beyond the morrow, not wanting it to end.

The climax came one evening at an alfresco restaurant on the Via Veneto with tables set out in a garden trellised overhead with winking lights in every color of the rainbow. John was tense and jumpy all through dinner, and she drank an inordinate amount of Chianti trying to calm her own nerves.

When he was summoned away for another of his mysterious phone calls, she sat looking muzzily up at the lights, luxuriating in the sensuous warmth of the Roman evening and thinking how happy she was. On his return, John's jaw was set, his face grimly determined, as if some momentous decision had been made. He sat down and reached across the table for her hand. "Van," he said huskily, "I know I'm rushing my fences. I know this is not fair to you. But I'm fighting time, so I must say it. I love you and I need you—need you desperately. I want you more than anything I've ever wanted in my whole life. Will you marry me? Now, right here in Rome? If you love me at all, say yes." His grip tightened painfully on her hand.

She looked dazedly at him, her heartbeat thudding loud in her ears. "I do love you," she stammered, "but. . . ." Problems seemed to heave up into a tidal wave before her eyes. "Well, I haven't even finished college yet, haven't even started my career. I mean, *marriage* . . . !" She trailed off helplessly.

"Look, in a few short weeks I *have* to be back in South Africa. Then we'll be half a world apart and I'll lose you for sure. If I could give you more time, believe me, I would. But it's now or never for us, my dearest. I know I'm asking a lot, but for God's sake say yes." His face was desperate in its intensity.

She looked at this man, who was just as much an unanswered mystery now as he had been from the start, and she knew that he was everything she wanted, everything she needed. Nothing else mattered. "Yes, my darling," she whispered. "I'll marry you—but how will we ever tell Mother?"

"We'll face her together," he said grimly. "And let me do the talking."

Clarissa Hale was neither as surprised nor as shocked as Vanessa had anticipated, though she did put up some spirited objections. "This is all so terribly sudden—I really feel it would be better to wait. And then there *is* the age difference. Vanessa won't be twenty-three until December, and you're. . . ."

"Thirty-seven," John said tersely. "And if that doesn't concern Vanessa, I don't see why it should matter to anyone else."

"And she hasn't finished her education, and *that*, I think, is very important," Clarissa went on as if she hadn't heard.

"I realize that also, but I assure you I have no intention of blighting Van's musical career. I'll get her the best teacher in South Africa, and there'll be lots of opportunity for her to play. There's a symphony in Pretoria, another in Jo'burg, and both universities have lively music departments. Granted, they are not Juilliard, but then, what is? The bottom line is that when I return to South Africa I will have to remain there for two years. Vanessa and I love each other and we want to get married—*now*. We'd like to do it with your approval. . . ." He left the rest unsaid, but his meaning was as clear as if he had spoken the words.

"Well, if you are quite sure this is what you want. . . ." Clarissa looked a little helplessly at her daughter.

"I'm sure," Vanessa said firmly.

"In that case, I have no objections. But *how* it's all going to be fitted into the next few weeks I've *no* idea," her mother fluttered.

John was grim. "Just leave all that to me. When you want something badly enough, it can be done."

The next period was a nerve-stretching blur to Vanessa as she trailed with John from Italian bureau to Italian bureau for endless bits of paper and to the embassy for more bits of paper, all set against the relentless ticking away of time. Her mother complicated things by insisting on a church wedding, which meant that, as Protestants, they would have to be married twice: once by Italian civil law and again at the American Episcopal church on the Via Nationale. This meant more consultations and arrangements with the Episcopal clergyman, to whom, fortunately, Clarissa took a tremendous shine, so they left all that to her.

Vanessa and her mother had a lively row about her wedding dress, which made them both feel a lot better. She wanted a white suit that she could wear afterward; her mother insisted on a traditional white gown. They finally compromised on a short white traditional gown and a mini-veil with a wreath of white roses.

By the time the wedding day arrived Vanessa was numb—beyond worry, beyond tension. As she sat beside a white-faced and nervous John on the gilt and red plush thrones in the Campidoglio Palace, listening to a little bald man, the ribboned tricolor of Italy slung across his chest, gabbling incomprehensible Italian to the counterpoint of their own muted *Si*s, she gazed down at her traditional bouquet of orange blossoms and thought stupidly, over and over, I'm getting married, I'm getting *married*.

It was only when she was walking down the dusky aisle of St. Paul's, with Burne-Jones's pre-Raphaelite windows shedding their pallid light on her, that panic seized her. She glanced in sudden terror at the stranger to whose arm she clung. He was an American embassy colleague of John's who had been roped in for the occasion and whom she had never seen before. Why am I doing this? she thought. I must be mad!

But then they were at the altar and there was John, who took her hand in a firm grasp and smiled, and everything was all right again. "Love, honor, and cherish until death do you part," the clergyman droned as he bound their hands together with a white and gold stole, and she looked at John and tried to imagine him as an old man with white hair and dentures. She couldn't; to her they would always be as they were at this moment.

It was over. The register was signed, the over-hearty congratulations of John's colleagues, another of which had served as best man, were accepted, her mother, in traditional tears, was sniffing, "It's not at all the sort of wedding I'd hoped you'd have, dear."

Despite her protestations, Vanessa felt her mother's paramount emotion was one of relief: instead of the unacceptable Sam she now had an "establishment" son-in-law of the best kind and could retreat happily home to Larchmont with the sense of a mission accomplished and get back to her own pursuit of poor Mr. Cross. And why not? thought Vanessa, her own happiness bubbling up in her like champagne. Finally we are out of each other's hair for good, and she can get on with her own life.

They had a brief champagne lunch at the same restaurant on the Via Veneto in which John had proposed, for they were to catch the afternoon train to Venice. John had been such a whirlwind of efficiency that they were even going to be able to squeeze in a four-day honeymoon before flying off to South Africa. "After all," he said, grinning, "I've done you out of the rest of your European tour—the least I can do is treat you to Venice!" His colleagues said their good-byes and strolled back down the Veneto to the embassy at its bottom end; they collected baggage, said good-bye to her mother—in tears again—and were on their way.

As the train drew out of Termini station, an attendant brought in an ice bucket with a magnum of champagne and two glasses, opened it with a knowing grin, and went out, closing the door of their first-class carriage firmly behind him. John took her in his arms and kissed her tenderly. "Well, my sweet, we did it—indeed we did it!" He poured out two foaming glasses and held his up to her in a toast. "To happy ever after, my darling."

"To happy ever after," she echoed.

Chapter 3

"**O**h, a log fire, how nice! Brr! It's so cold outside. I never get used to this upside-down climate—cold in July and hot as Hades in December. Where is everyone, Mandy?" Eleanor Heitz looked a little aggrieved as she walked over to the fireplace and stretched out her hands to the blaze—as she was senior-ranking wife, her juniors should all have been gathered here ahead of her. But then, she reflected bitterly, if her husband never showed her any respect, why should she expect it from anyone else?

Amanda Drake, who had been fiddling with the coffee tray, assembling the Limoges cups so that their handles were all neatly aligned, looked up, her plump face a little uneasy as she observed Eleanor's handsome, haggard profile. "Rose isn't coming—she's on vacation. Bobby phoned to say she'd be a little late, but that she has some big news to tell us, and—well, you know Clara—she's never on time for anything."

As if on cue, the door opened to admit a statuesque platinum blonde, her considerable height augmented by three-inch heels, on which she teetered delicately toward

Eleanor. "Ooh, sorry I'm late, everybody!" she said in a high-pitched, little-girl voice that totally belied her over-blown Las Vegas showgirl figure. "I just couldn't find the car keys. Grant says if I don't clean up my act, he's going to make me wear them around my neck like dog tags."

Eleanor snorted gently, accepted a cup of coffee from Amanda, and subsided into an easy chair. Clara Zecco did the same, draping her shapely dancer's legs at a becoming angle. "I'm not *that* late," she announced triumphantly, looking around. "Rose and Bobby aren't here yet."

"Rose is away and Bobby phoned she'd be late," Mandy Drake repeated, and, settling herself, launched into a detailed account of two of her four children's current colds.

The door opened again to reveal a square-shouldered, tweed-clad figure who strode in and shut the door behind her with a firm click. She turned to the small group, her normal high color heightened to bright red by the cold and her excitement and her green eyes sparkling in her angular face. "Sorry for being late," she said perfunctorily to Eleanor, "but I simply had to stop by the embassy to see Robin for more details." She went over and helped herself to a cup of coffee from the gleaming silver coffee pot, then swung around, her eyes dancing. "You'll never guess what's happened. Robin called me from the office this morning in a state of shock—he'd heard from John Bannerman. John's just got married in Rome."

"I don't *believe* it!" Clara squeaked. "Dandy Jack *married*! Wowee! Wait till Grant hears that!"

They all looked at Roberta West, their eyebrows raised, their mouths round *o*'s of surprise. "Anyone we know?" Eleanor asked at length.

Bobby shook her shoulder-length black hair vigor-ously. "No, she's some young college kid he just met."

"That will certainly send a few shock waves around town," Mandy observed, getting up to put another log on the fire. "Not to mention closer to home, if you follow me."

"An Italian girl?" Eleanor asked.

Again Bobby shook her head. "No. American. Name of Hale—Vanessa Hale."

"As in Nathan?" Eleanor said drily.

"Yes—apt, isn't it?" They all tittered, with the exception of Clara, who looked blank.

"Robin didn't get many details, but apparently she's a musician of some kind. Oh, and there's one other thing." Bobby had seated herself, and her hands were smoothing down the pleats in her tweed skirt, her eyes lowered. "John was very insistent about it. She doesn't know about him, and he doesn't want her to, so he has asked us all to keep hands off for the time being. They'll be back next week."

"You're *kidding*!" Mandy burst out. "What is she— some kind of nitwit?"

Bobby shrugged. "That's all I know." She looked over at Eleanor. "What do you think?"

Eleanor ran a hand over her smartly styled, short gray hair. "He must have his reasons, I suppose. Let me see. She'd fall under Vera Watson's care as a new arrival in that section, wouldn't she?"

"God help her!" Mandy exclaimed with feeling.

"Yes, well, we all know about Vera. Maybe I'll have a word with Willy Watson—he's a reasonable man—and I'll pass the word to the Minister's wife, though she is so out of it these days, she probably won't bestir herself on a newcomer's account." Eleanor's finely marked brows knitted. "Since we don't know the first thing about the girl, it may have something to do with security, so we'd better go along with it until John says otherwise. If we play this charade, the brunt of it will fall on you, Bobby, Robin and he being so close. Think you can handle it?"

"No problem." Bobby's firm chin went up. "No problem at all."

Clara Zecco had evidently been pursuing her own line of thought. "It will be nice for you, Eleanor," she said brightly. "If she's young enough to be in college, she'd make a nice friend for your daughter to pal around with, and you won't have to worry about Betty so much."

The others looked uncomfortable, and Eleanor looked at her with cold dislike in her gray eyes. "I doubt whether anyone who would marry John Bannerman would be of much interest to my daughter," she said icily, "but we'll see. Anyway, let's decide to keep the Inner Circle out of John's affairs for the present. I think there's no use going on with further idle speculation now, so let's go on to what we should do about this benefit the Ambassador's wife seems so dead set on. . . ."

The conversation drifted into more mundane channels.

Vanessa hoisted herself up on one elbow and looked wonderingly down at her sleeping husband. In sleep, his hair tousled on the pillow, the lines of his face smoothed out and relaxed, he looked younger and somehow vulnerable. An overwhelming wave of tenderness welled up in her, and she had to blink away the happy tears that pricked her eyes; she loved him so much. . . . She leaned over and kissed his bare shoulder; he twitched and mumbled something but did not awaken. Their first night together had been so unbelievably wonderful, his ardent and expert lovemaking taking her to peaks of ecstasy she had not known existed.

She had been understandably nervous, not only because her experience was limited but also because she had experience at all. She had tried to put a bold face on it. "Er— I don't suppose it matters, but this isn't exactly the first time for me," she had managed to get out.

"Oh?" He cocked an inquiring eyebrow at her, but his eyes were twinkling. "The omni-talented Sam?"

"I had a steady boyfriend in high school also," she said, her color mounting.

"Ah, a woman of experience, I see—thank God for that!" He threw back his head and laughed. "Well, my dearest darling, having been married for seven years, and not having exactly been a monk myself either before or after, I wasn't really anticipating a blushing virgin bride. I'm not interested in being your first love—only your last." He drew her to him and kissed her hungrily, passionately. "What has been before for either of us is nothing and means nothing—our life starts now. Because I love you and need you beyond belief, I want to make you happy, happier than you've ever been, and I *will* make

you happy or perish in the attempt. Making love together
and enjoying it is important, but I'm old enough to know
it's not *all*-important in a marriage. Liking each other,
understanding each other, growing together—that's
every bit as important, and it takes work. And I intend
to work at it to the end of my days. So pleasure me, my
darling, and I will pleasure you." And indeed he had.

She leaned over again and kissed him on the neck. This
time he rolled over and buried his head in her breasts,
his mouth seeking and finding a nipple, on which he nib-
bled sleepily. It sent delicious little thrills up her spine,
and his left hand slid up her thighs to the other breast,
which he cradled, titillating the nipple with his thumb.
She could feel him hardening against her as his head moved
slowly up her breast, her neck, until his lips found hers,
and he rolled on top of her, seeking and finding entrance,
his hands quickening their play on her body. They moved
together, slowly and languorously at first, then with
mounting urgency as their ecstasy grew. As he came to
a climax, she cried out, arched, and clutched him to her,
wanting this oneness to go on forever as her whole body
pulsated to her orgasm. He relaxed upon her but stayed
within her, his hands gently brushing away her short brown
hair from her flushed face, his lips kissing the dimples by
her mouth as he murmured, "Well, my love, shall we stay
here and all the pleasures prove—which would be fine
with me—or shall we seek breakfast to fuel our energies
for further delights?"

She laughed and pushed him away. "Breakfast, and
then Venice—we've only got three days, remember?"

"All too well," he groaned, sliding out of bed and holding out a hand to pull her up. "Shower?"

They showered together to save time, which further
delayed them, since they got so excited soaping each other
up that they had to make love again and then take another
shower—this time apart. It was almost noon by the time
they finally emerged from their room in the Hotel Danieli
and found a disgruntled-looking chambermaid muttering
to herself in the corridor. She shot into the room, clat-
tering her paraphernalia noisily to vent her displeasure.

"Whoever said the world waits upon lovers obviously never stayed at the Danieli," John observed, looking at his watch. "We seem to have missed breakfast. What say we have an early lunch and then do our sightseeing?"

She felt as sleek and contented as a cat. "Sounds fine to me," she murmured, taking his arm and strolling out into the hot sunlight, which was turning the lagoon in front of them into a blinding sheet of molten silver.

They strolled along the quay to St. Mark's Square, stirring up the fat pigeons with their feet as they passed the ornate mosaic facade of the cathedral and settled at an outside table under the medieval clock tower, whose mechanical men on high thudded away with their hammers to announce to the world it was noontime, and the bells of the campanile tolled the Angelus. Vanessa found she was ravenous, and she ate her way through antipasto, then a linguini marinara, and then a very rich zabaglione for dessert. As she was spooning the last of its rich creaminess down she said gloomily, "You know, we've had so little time to talk of such things, but I really am miserably qualified to be a wife."

"Oh, really? I wouldn't have said that at all," he said with a wicked grin.

"Oh, I don't mean *that*!" she snorted. "I mean I'm just about as undomestic as one can be. I don't know the first thing about housework—beyond making my own bed and keeping my room picked up—sort of. And my cooking skills are virtually nil. At the apartment my roommates and I lived mostly on yogurt, spaghetti, and salad—which was about all we could afford."

"Then it's just as well I wanted a wife and not a cook-housekeeper, isn't it?" he retaliated, his cheerfulness undiminished. "If you are concerned about such things, luckily we are going to one of the few places in the world that still have servants galore, and if you've a mind to, you can learn it all secondhand. We, for instance, have three."

"Three! To look after an apartment?" she gasped. "Whatever for?"

"An *apartment*? My dear, you're going to have to get

over such lowly ideas. I have a three-bedroom house, complete with tennis court and swimming pool—a very *small* swimming pool, granted, but still a swimming pool."

"Good grief! What are you, a secret millionaire?" she said in awe.

"Far from it," he said ruefully. "No, actually the furnished house goes with the job, as it were, and since most people of my rank have families, well, that's the way it is permanently set up. I've been rattling around in it like a pea in a drum, but things will be different now. We'll turn one of the bedrooms into a music room for you."

"Sounds wonderful," she said doubtfully. "And I suppose I'll have to order the servants around?"

"Not really, unless you fancy being boss-lady. I have a married couple for the house—she cooks, he cleans. They're grateful for the job, because they have a couple of kids and they can live on the premises instead of in the native township outside of Pretoria. So they do a good job for me. The garden boys tend to come and go, but that's my bailiwick anyway. 'Gardens is men's work,' according to them," he quoted.

"And I suppose we'll have to do a lot of entertaining, and I've never done much of that, either," she said faintly. "Do you give a lot of dinner parties and cocktail parties and things like that?"

"You've been reading too many romantic novels about the diplomatic life," he said, standing up. "It's not that big a deal. Anyway, I refuse to discuss such trivialities on our honeymoon. Let's see St. Mark's."

They saw the cathedral and the Doge's palace and then took a romantic gondola ride up the length of the Grand Canal to Mostra on the mainland. They had a quick drink there and then decided to walk back through the islands that constituted the city to the seaward-facing Danieli. It was all so fascinating and so different from anything in her experience that Vanessa forgot all about her preoccupations with her future life and just gave herself up to drinking in all Venice's beauty, secure within her husband's arm encircling her waist. They crossed the Grand Canal to the Danieli side by the great Rialto Bridge, put-tering through its miniature shops and pausing at the parapet to watch the multitude of boats gliding up and down this main artery of the city. As she gazed dreamily down she gradually became aware that John's hands gripping the stone parapet were white-knuckled with tension, and, glancing over at him, she saw his face was rigid and white, his eyes fixed and withdrawn. In sudden alarm she grasped at his arm. "Darling, what's wrong? What's the matter?"

He came to with a start but didn't meet her anxious gaze. "Nothing," he said, turning away. "I just wish to hell that we didn't have to go back so soon, that's all. I wish we could just stay here—maybe forever."

"Lovely as all this is, we've got to come back to the everyday world sometime," she placated. "I think it's marvelous you managed to get us any honeymoon at all."

But he remained subdued and withdrawn all the way back to the hotel. They eschewed the ornate palatial splendors of the Danieli's dining room for the more informal atmosphere of an outdoor restaurant in St. Mark's Square, complete with an orchestra that seemed less intent on what they were playing than on drowning out a competing orchestra on the opposite side of the square. Amid the warmth of the lights, the music, and the busy nightlife of the great piazza John seemed to relax, the cloud on his spirits vanishing as fast as it had appeared. Only then did she dare go back to her own preoccupations. "You know, you haven't told me a thing about the people at the embassy—what they're like, who your friends are, what I must do to fit in—I'd like to know."

"Plenty of time for that when we get there," he said briefly. "And nothing for you to worry about. One thing you have to realize about diplomats is that they are all socially charming—it's part of their business to be, after all. But it's not a life where you have many friends—we move around too much, and it just isn't the nature of the game."

"I'd like to know about them all the same," she said with determination. "I'd like to know what to expect. Surely you've got someone there you're close to."

"Well, there are the Wests," he said almost grudgingly.

"Robin and Roberta, or Bobby, as she likes to be called. He's number-two man in USIS." His face softened. "Robin and I go back a long way. We were in college together. I expect they'll be in Jo'burg to meet us."

"There now," she said in triumph. "Great! And who else?"

He became firm again. "Look, I'm on my honeymoon, and all I want to think about is us. It's a long, dreary air trip back to South Africa from here, and if you're so inclined then, you can ask me anything you like during it. Until then, let's drop the subject. What say tomorrow we go to the Murano glass factory and buy some expensive doodad and then take a vaporetto out to the Lido and bask on the beach? And as for my immediate plans, my fair lady, I intend to go back to the hotel and love you to pieces."

And they did just that, to her unending delight.

Chapter 4

As the South African Airways jumbo jet lifted off from Leonardo da Vinci airport and circled out over the coast before turning to a southward heading, Vanessa looked down at the receding foam-edged land with a feeling equally compounded of regret and excitement: regret at leaving Italy, which, for her, would always hold her dearest memories, and excitement at the thought of the great continent that lay ahead—Africa! To her, Africa had been just a large land mass in an atlas, a place of which she had known little and cared less but which was now to be her home. She would have so much to learn, so much to find out, and the myriad questions and problems raging in her mind kept her silent as they crossed the serene blue of the Mediterranean, as they passed over the delta of the Nile spewing its vast fan of red African earth like life's blood into the azure sea, and as they followed its serpentine course beyond the fertility of Egypt into the sterility of the Sudan, where the shadow of the huge plane, reflecting off the sands, was diminished into a child's toy.

They had run into a business acquaintance of John's, some Englishman also bound for Johannesburg, at Leonardo, and after the takeoff John had gone back to talk to him in the smoking section. So absorbed was she in her thoughts that she was unaware of his return until he squeezed her hand and said, "Are you all right? You're terribly quiet."

With reluctance she came out of her reverie. "Just watching the world go by," she said briefly.

"Want a drink before we get to Khartoum? We'll have a fueling stop there, and then it'll be nonstop to Jo'burg, thank God! I don't think there is anything more boring than a long trip like this. I can't wait to get home."

A sudden spasm of irritation shook her. "Well, since it's the first time for me, I find it fascinating," she said tartly. "Particularly since *I* don't know what 'getting home' entails."

He looked at her in mild shock. "*Whoa* there, bosslady! I am yours to command. What do you want to know?"

"Whatever I'm supposed to. Why don't *you* tell me?" she was still sharp. "I know so little about anything, I don't even know what to ask."

He seemed nonplussed. "First order of business is that we'll be met and taken home by the Wests, so you'll get to meet them. We will probably be too busy to bother much with the rest of the embassy for a while."

"Busy doing what?"

"Some heavy shopping, for one thing—that ought to grab you!" he said with a faint smile. "Getting you set up with everything your little old heart desires."

"Shopping? For what?" It was not at all what she had expected.

"Clothes, for one thing."

"What's wrong with the ones I have?" she bristled.

"My dear addlepate, we are going back to midwinter in South Africa, and you haven't even as much as a warm jacket with you."

"But this is Africa!" she protested.

"Nevertheless, Pretoria sits high on the plateau, and it can be bloody cold this time of year. It can even snow on occasion. We've got to get you some warm clothes pronto."

"Oh," she said blankly.

"Also we have to get you your engagement diamond." He grinned. "We're going to where they grow them, so we'll hop on down to Kimberley and dig one out." Seeing her dazed expression, he laughed. "Just kidding! We have a jeweler who really does us proud at the embassy, and he's right in Pretoria. Then we'll have to get you some music—tapes, records, whatever—to go on with. I've got a good stereo system, but I'm afraid you'll find my collection definitely not to your highbrow tastes, and it'll be some time before your own things arrive, even if your mother ships them air freight. Then we'll have to rustle up a teacher for you, get the music room set up to your specifications, see what's cooking in the local music groups—"

"But will I have *time* for all this?" she broke in. "Won't there be things I have to do as an embassy wife?"

"We may have to go to a few receptions," he hedged, "but no; as you're a newcomer, and particularly as you're a new bride, they won't expect anything until you're all settled down, and really not even then if you haven't the taste for it. It's not like the old days—"

"But I'd *like* to do anything I can to help you and your career," she interrupted. "I don't want to be just some coddled"—she sought for the word—"appendage!"

He sighed. "Oh, Van, that's just it. You can help me most by settling into your own life, doing your own thing, so that when I have to go away, I'll know you're okay and happy."

"Go away?" she echoed. "Where?"

"Oh, I have to do quite a bit of traveling in my job— not long trips, but two or three days here and there."

"But that sounds great!" she exclaimed. "Can't I go along with you?"

"No, I'm afraid business is business, and the c—the embassy frowns on wives going along on official trips."

"Not ever?" She sounded so crestfallen that he consoled her with "Well, sometimes, of course, on longer trips, but as a rule, no. That's why it's so important that you get settled in your own world. I can get an official car most of the time, so you can have our car more or less exclusively for your own use."

"*Hmm*," she said doubtfully, and he looked at her in sudden alarm. "You can drive, can't you?"

"I have a driver's license, but I haven't done much driving—none at all in the past three years," she confessed. "A car is such a hassle in Manhattan. I did have a rattletrap in my last year of high school and in the eighteen months I was at the Hart School of Music in Connecticut, but I sold it when I transferred to Juilliard and found out they were going to make me start from scratch again. It's why I'm so late graduating—that eighteen months at Hart was a virtual write-off. And I never was a very enthusiastic driver...." Her voice trailed off.

"It'll soon come back to you," John comforted. "That's one thing that *will* be necessary. We live up in Waterkloof, and public transport doesn't reach those rarefied heights, I'm afraid. The only thing is..." He hesitated. "I've got a sports car with a stick shift—do you know how to drive a nonautomatic?" She shook her head ruefully. "Well, we'll work something out. Maybe we can pick up an inexpensive automatic secondhand for you."

"I'd certainly prefer that—and one with plenty of dents in it already. Then I wouldn't have to worry about putting more in it," she said. "Or about bashing up your car."

They were circling down over the yellow-brown desert, the Nile taking on more definition in milky-green contrast, a scattering of palm trees marking its course, and the dun-colored sprawl of Khartoum sprang like a gigantic mushroom bed from the desert floor. They emerged from the plane into blinding sunlight and heat that shriveled by its intensity.

Inside the transit terminal it was suffocatingly hot and smelly, and they were glad to escape out onto the red-tiled terrace, where at least the earth was fresh and there was a modicum of shade under the umbrellas that protected the tables. The Englishman joined them for drinks, so her catechism had to be forgone in favor of social chitchat.

When they reboarded the plane there was dinner to be eaten and a movie to be seen, and by the time it was over the sudden night of Equatorial Africa had fallen and there was only darkness beneath them. "Tell me something about the people at the embassy," Vanessa coaxed. "Who they are, what they do, what you think of them—please, John!"

"All right," he agreed. "A swift rundown and then I think we ought to try to catch a nap. It's a good hour and a half's drive from Jo'burg to Pretoria, and we'll be dead tired by the time we get home. Okay, then. From the top down. The Ambassador and his wife—George and Mary Hackett. Old-time Foreign Service, last posting before retirement, feet hurt—do the right things, but do not want the boat rocked one fraction of an inch. The Minister and his wife—Kyle and Margaret Kulman. He's looking to be an ambassador on his next trip out and so is an eager beaver. She's sort of switched off. Has had a lot of trouble with their son—a drug problem, I think—and it preoccupies her. The First Secretary on the political side is Mike Brown, expert on South African history, scholarly type—doesn't agree with either the Ambassador or the Minister but isn't pushy enough to gainsay them. His wife, Molly, is a nonentity, but nice enough. My boss on the economic side is Bill Watson—a very nice guy. Great golfer and likes to garden. His wife, Vera, is a bit of a witch but keeps it hidden—most of the time. Then there are the Heitzes—Armand and Eleanor. He's Chief of Intelligence. He's also got a very roving eye, and she resents it like fury. They have a daughter here, Elizabeth. Takes after dear old Dad and is a real wild one. She's about your age, but I don't think you'll have much in common. She's already been through one husband and is hunting number two. You *may* like the head of USIS and his wife, Herman and Violet Corby—they are our culture vultures, but also roaring snobs. He's Robin's boss. That's most of the top brass. Now, as to us underlings...."

"Stop!" Vanessa said faintly. "My head's spinning already. I had no idea there would be so many!"

"And I haven't even gotten halfway through yet." He grinned sideways at her. "There are all the military attachés and the trade people as well. As I said before, much better leave this till we're there, and you can take them all in in dribs and drabs." He put up the armrest between them and put his arm around her. He tilted her face up and kissed her lightly. "The important thing to remember," he murmured, "is that none of them matter a damn—all that matters is us." He cuddled her to him. "Now, let's get some sleep, my love."

Nestled against him, she relaxed, loving the feel of him, the scent of him. He's right, she thought; they don't matter, nothing matters but this. . . . And she drifted into sleep.

They slept a long time, wrapped in each other's arms like babes in the wood, and had to be shaken awake by the stewardess for the landing in Johannesburg. "Oh, my— I do look a sight!" Vanessa moaned, looking in her compact mirror and trying to brush her hair into some sort of order. "I hope the Wests aren't set into first impressions— what will they think of me?"

John was stripping off his coat jacket. "I'm far more concerned about you catching cold. Here, put this on, and I'll wear my raincoat."

She protested this but, when the chill air struck her as they deplaned, began to shiver and submitted to having the jacket draped over her shoulders as they passed drearily through customs and immigration.

They emerged into the outer terminal and to the usual crowd clustered around the arrivals entrance. "Over here, John," a voice boomed out, and Vanessa saw a very tall, thin, fair man waving energetically. Her first impression of Robin West was that his clothing did not go with his face: the tweed jacket, polo sweater, and casual slacks were all wrong for the long, ascetic-looking face with its blazing dark eyes and overly sensitive mouth; in her mind's eye that face should have been peering out of a monk's hood of Franciscan gray or Benedictine black. Her second impression, as the dark eyes clamped on her own, was that she had already been weighed and found wanting.

A tall woman with straight jet-black hair and angular,

slightly horsey features detached herself from the crowd and came rushing toward them, her hands outstretched. "John, dear, it's so great to have you back! Welcome home. And this must be Vanessa—welcome to Africa, my dear!" She clasped both of Vanessa's hands in a strong, bony grip, her green eyes alive with curiosity. "I'm Bobby West, as you probably know already, and that's Robin lagging in the rear, as usual. You must both be dead after the trip, but not to worry; we've got the station wagon parked just outside the door, and I see you've got all your bags, so follow along and we'll have you home in no time at all."

She continued her lively chatter until everything was stowed, and—since John showed no signs of relinquishing his hold around Vanessa's shoulders—she showed only a moment's hesitation before shooing them both into the back seat. Her husband seated himself behind the wheel and took off; except for the usual greetings, he had not said a word. "You mustn't mind Robin," Bobby said to Vanessa, craning around to talk to them over the back of her seat. "He never talks when he's driving. So if you want to catch up on any news, I'm going to have to be your town crier."

"So what's been happening while I've been away?" John asked. "Anything interesting?"

As if to gainsay his ebullient wife, Robin's deep voice answered, "Nothing—it has been extremely quiet, thank God!"

"Well, we'll have to put a stop to that and stir the pot a little, won't we?" John said easily. "All quiet on the home front, too, Bobby?"

"Yes, I checked the house. I can't guarantee the rest of it, but at least your bedroom is clean," Bobby said with a slight emphasis. "Even good servants tend to goof off when the master's away, as you well know, but everything seemed to be more or less in order. I know how they force-feed you on these long air trips, so I didn't tell Ben to have any food ready for you when you got in, but I did tell him to leave out a drinks tray and not to wait up.

I always get off a plane feeling like a stuffed goose and with a most terrible thirst."

"We all could use a drink after this tedious trek," John returned. "Damned nice of you to meet us this late and not just send an office car. I know what a bore this drive is."

"Our pleasure—we've missed you."

Vanessa had been watching with fascinated awe the huge gold mine slag heaps that towered like miniature volcanoes by the roadside, but they had now plunged into a suburban area of large houses and gardens that could have been the outskirts of any city anywhere in the western world, so she transferred her attention to the moonstruck heavens, where the stars looked somehow unfamiliar. "Oh!" she exclaimed suddenly, clutching John's arm, "Is that the Southern Cross?" A perfect diamond crucifix blazed out of the sky.

"Yes—so now you know you're 'down under.' You'll have to take your bearings from that now and not the Big Dipper," he said.

"When Vanessa's all settled in, we'll have to make an expedition to the Jo'burg Planetarium," Bobby said quickly. "It's one of the best in the world, I'm told, though I'm not into stars myself. That's more Robin's bag."

As they shook off the outskirts of Johannesburg and sped through the dark, flat expanses of the veldt even Bobby fell silent, and Vanessa drowsed against John's shoulder until the sky brightened with a city's lights and they were speeding through the outskirts of Pretoria. They flashed through the faceless and deserted downtown area and were once more in the suburbs. The car's engine changed rhythm as it climbed a steep hill. Finally, there was a crunch of gravel under the wheels and the engine died.

"Home, sweet, sweet home," John sighed as he helped Vanessa out before the long, low sprawl of a house in which only one set of lights showed through the barred windows. He handed his keys to Robin with a grin. "Do the honors, will you? I have to carry my bride over our threshold." Effortlessly scooping Vanessa up in his arms, he carried her into the lighted, red-tiled hallway, kissing her soundly before he put her down. "Welcome home, my sweet."

He and Robin went off in search of the bags and Bobby led Vanessa into the long, low-ceilinged living room, which ran the entire depth of the house, and toward a bar trolley that stood temptingly by one of the deep couches. "Help yourself," she invited.

"What can I get *you*?" Vanessa asked, asserting herself. "You've been terribly kind meeting us like this, and at such an ungodly hour."

"Oh, I think I'll take a raincheck for tonight. I know how spacy one feels after a long trip like yours. We'll get together very soon—that is, if John will let me." Bobby flashed her a quick smile. "In any case, call me if you need anything, anything at all." She pecked her quickly on the cheek and went out to the hall, where the men were in low-voiced conference. "Come on, Robin, let's fold tents," she ordered, and kept right on going.

As they drove back down the kloof to their own house in Lynwood she said, "Well, what do you think of her?"

Her husband shrugged. "Too soon to tell—seems a quiet little thing."

"Little is right. I had no idea she'd be so small—can't be more than five foot two at most, and about a hundred pounds wringing wet. At the airport, with John's coat drowning her, she looked like a poor little orphan in a storm. Still, she's attractive—not pretty, exactly, but— well, cute. Lovely eyes, don't you think?"

"Yes, she looks intelligent enough," Robin said quietly. "Which may not be all to the good in the long run. I think she'll bear watching."

Chapter 5

"**W**hy, *John, a real fountain—how lovely!*" Vanessa exclaimed with delight as they stepped from the long French windows of the living room at the back of the house onto the stone-paved patio beyond. The fountain stood in the middle of the patio and consisted of a single spout ending in a gape-mouthed fish from which the water spurted into a small upper basin and then cascaded into a low-curbed large basin beneath which a few goldfish were languidly swimming.

"Yes, it has its uses." He grinned at her. "There's a gizmo on the side here where you can control the flood of water—see?" He fiddled with a knob and the jet increased in height and volume, filling the air with the noise of cascading water. "Out here I can murmur all sorts of obscene suggestions into your shell-like ear and no one would ever hear."

"What a weird thing to say!" She laughed a little uncomfortably, looking directly ahead at the wire enclosure of the tennis court that occupied most of the back area. "Where's the swimming pool?"

"Around here." He led her to the side of the house. "It's empty at the moment, because of the season—and, as you can see, it's not exactly colossal." The blue-tiled pool was edged by a cement walkway all the way around and was of a uniform depth of six feet with a small shelf at one end. He pointed at it. "My favorite spot on a hot day for cooling off after work. Drinks tray at elbow, of course. Maybe we should get a Jacuzzi as well and set it against the wall of the house, and we could bubble away together like crazy."

"They are fun," she retaliated. "I went to the summer music festival in Taos one year, way up in the mountains, and we spent most of our free time sitting in Jacuzzis and drinking Chablis."

"Ahha! More of your lurid past coming out, I see." He looked at his watch with a groan. "Oh, lord! I've got to check in at the office, and we simply *have* to get you a coat or jacket. Tell you what. I'll drive you downtown, then you go shopping, and I'll sneak out at lunchtime and drive you back."

"No need for that. Aren't there taxis? I don't have to be carted back. I'll find my own way," she said with spirit. "I'm a big-city gal, remember? If I've learned how to survive in New York, I surely can handle a small place like Pretoria."

He threw back his head and laughed. "All right, my fair, independent friend, but at least let me show you where the embassy is, so that if you get into any difficulties you know where to run for cover." They settled on that.

Even though he had given her a large wad of money, with instructions to blow the lot, she shopped carefully, inured by a lifetime of having to watch price tags. She purchased a lightweight blue wool suit, a long-sleeved dress, a pair of warm slacks, several sweaters, a casual suede jacket, and a raincoat, and decided that that would be ample until her own winter clothes caught up with her. She had a quick cup of coffee and a sandwich—neither very good—in a small fast-food restaurant, and as she ate she listened intently to the strange, harsh sounds of the Afrikaner tongue and the funny, lilting accents of the few English speakers she heard. Too laden to do anything else, she went through several drivers at a taxi stand until she found one who spoke decent English, and she set off for home. She was a little dismayed on arrival to see the amount of the fare: Waterkloof was farther from the center of things than she had imagined.

She changed into her new slacks and a sweater and proceeded to unpack and stow away her things, for Ben had evidently already taken care of John's. At the back of one empty drawer in her bureau she came upon a small vial of Arpege perfume, which caused her a momentary heart flutter and a pang of unease. She banished this firmly. Good grief! she told herself, she knew already she'd married a very sexy man, and she'd be lucky if there weren't bigger jolts than this ahead.

Greatly daring, she took her first step as mistress of the house and asked Ben, who had been going about his work eyeing her as warily as she had been eyeing him, to help her start on the music room. She had selected the smaller of the two spare bedrooms, the one that lay directly above John's small downstairs den and also looked out onto the patio. "What you want done, missus?" Ben said cautiously.

"I want all the furniture out except for that chest of drawers and a chair, the rug taken up and the curtains down. It's going to be a music room," she explained.

"Well, if you say so," he muttered. "What you want done with the furniture?"

"Put it all in the other spare room for the moment." The likelihood of guests seemed to her a little remote.

He went off to seek the sullen-faced garden boy, and under her watchful eye they had the room cleaned out in no time at all. "That's great!" she announced, surveying the almost empty room with triumph and setting up her music stand. "Thank you both very much indeed." They looked a little surprised.

"Er, you want something special fixed for dinner?" Ben inquired tentatively. "Miz West brought some stuff over yesterday, but Reba got to know how you want it fixed."

This took her aback. "Oh, anything Reba wants to do is fine with me," she said hastily. "Just make it like she usually does."

"Master don't like desserts," Ben volunteered.

"Neither do I most of the time—fruit and cheese will be just fine," she assured him. Looking relieved, he went on his way.

She soon found it was well nigh impossible to deal with Reba directly, for the cook's English was minimal and all communication had to be through Ben. "I have never heard anything so extraordinary in my life," she confided to John on his return. "Their language sounds like corks popping."

"That's the Bushman click you're hearing," he informed her. "They're Xhosa, one of the Bantu tribes that intermixed with the Hottentots and inherited the click. Even most of the Africans can't reproduce it, let alone the whites."

"I've so much to learn," Vanessa mourned. "It's really quite frightening."

"I'd say you were doing just fine," John comforted. "So how do you like your new home?"

"I think it's great—that is, apart from those." Vanessa indicated the intricate wrought-iron bars that masked the downstairs windows and doors. "Do we have to have them? It makes the place look so . . . sinister."

"I'm afraid so, my love," he sighed. "It's a very necessary protection. To give you a for instance—one American couple at the embassy were so incensed about 'living in a cage,' as they put it, that they had their bars removed. In one year they had had twelve break-ins; on the twelfth their insurance company canceled their policy, and they had to have the bars put back before they could get another."

Vanessa was appalled. "But everything seems so quiet and orderly!"

"Seems, but isn't." His tone was grim. "South Africa is a smoldering volcano, and sometimes it erupts. Oh, we don't see much of the violence here—not in this exclusive neighborhood—but it's always around, just below the surface, and unfortunately one can never let one's guard down. Everyone here has a gun, and a lot of people keep guard dogs. Would you like one for company when I'm away?"

"No," she said firmly, "I don't believe in living like that. Not with fear. Anyway, I'm a cat person—I'd rather have a cat for company."

"You should get on fine with the naval attaché's wife, then, when the mob returns." He grinned. "She keeps a couple of cheetahs as pets. It's quite an adventure going to their house."

"You're *kidding*! What next?" she exclaimed. "But what do you mean, when the mob returns?"

"Oh, they are all down in Cape Town until the end of the parliamentary session—most of the embassy, that is. They don't get back until the end of this month. That's the way the government here is set up—six months in Cape Town, six months here. Weird, isn't it?"

"I'll say! But why aren't we down there, then?"

"The economic, intelligence, and USIS sections don't move. We stay here permanently. Makes life a lot easier," he said smoothly. "Now, let's go do some shopping."

He was as good as his word, and for a while her life settled into a pattern of putting her house in order by day and rushing madly around shopping as soon as John appeared. In short order she acquired a magnificent one-carat blue-white diamond engagement ring and, to her delight, an old, very battered, bright red Volkswagen Beetle, which liberated her from incomprehensible cab drivers and enabled her to scuttle around—albeit somewhat erratically—at will.

Outside her own domestic circle the sole contact she had had with the rest of the world was one phone call to Bobby West, who had proved a mine of information on where to buy groceries and domestic items. Beyond a vague promise to get together soon, though, Bobby had shown no signs of cultivating her further.

John had even found a teacher for her, but at this she had balked. "I'm not ready to try out for anyone yet," she said firmly. "I'm hopelessly out of practice and out

of shape, and I don't intend to make a fool of myself."
She didn't add that she had never even heard of the puta-
tive teacher, Hans Haupman, who was the concertmaster
of the Pretoria symphony and who, according to John's
enthusiastic description, was "a first-rate world-class violinist."

When she did take up her violin again, she was appalled
by how much her technique had slipped, but after some
long practice sessions she was impressed by the improve-
ment in the quality and tone of her playing. "I've never
sounded this good before," she told herself. "Maybe it's
because I'm so much in love; maybe it's because I'm so
terribly happy." Whatever it was, her new expertise so
engrossed her that she immersed herself in her music, and
this was aided by her mother's prompt dispatch of her
own stereo, tape collection, and sheet music, which were
all duly stashed in the music room for immediate and
constant use. So immersed was she that John would sometimes return from work and catch her still at it. Far from
upsetting him, her absorption in what she was doing
appeared to delight him, although he kidded her unmercifully about her music-filled ivory tower.

For all her avowed interest in the embassy and its
personnel, it came as something of a shock to her when
John arrived home one afternoon to announce, "The Watsons have invited us for drinks tomorrow evening, just to
say hi and see how you're getting along. It'll be just the
economic people—no big deal."

When the time came for them to leave for the Watsons'
home at the base of the kloof in the small suburb of Bai-
ley's Muckleneuk, she realized that for the first time since
their arrival, John was jumpy and ill at ease. Was he
worried that she wouldn't measure up to diplomatic standards? she thought uneasily. "Do I look all right?" she
demanded, having donned her new long-sleeved dress,
which was an attractive shade of jade green. "Not too
much eye makeup?"

"No, you look lovely," he said absently. "We'll only
have to stay an hour. Then we can go and do something
more interesting."

Bill Watson was big, bluff, and a little over-hearty in his greeting. Vera Watson, by contrast, was very small and thin, with a set smile that seemed permanently engraved on her leather-tanned, wrinkled face but that never reached her small, dark eyes. The only other guests were the Louds, Stephen and Sandra—Stephen was a Third Secretary and assistant economic officer—and two secretaries—one South African girl, who was introduced as Bill's secretary, and the other a rather hard-faced American redhead, Dilys Gold, who was introduced as John's. She found it a little puzzling that Bill should have a local girl and John an American, and more puzzling that both secretaries regarded her with definitely hostile eyes. A possible explanation did strike her, but she got close enough to both of them to establish that neither was using Arpege perfume—not that that ruled them out entirely.

The conversation was general and predictable: how did she like Pretoria, the climate, the shops; did she play tennis, bridge, golf; what did she do with herself all day, and so on. When John gave her the high sign to leave after an hour or so of this harmless chitchat, she felt obliged to say to Vera, "I'm really quite settled in now, so if there is anything I can do to help you, I hope you will call upon me."

The set smile never wavered. "Oh, yes, if anything does, I will." Then, almost reluctantly, "Also, if you need anything, I hope you'll call on me."

"Thank you very much, but I don't intend to be a bother. Roberta West has been very helpful in guiding me to shops and things like that."

The claws that had been smoothly hidden all evening showed at last. "Oh, I see. You're friendly with the Wests, a case of to each his own. Well, so long as you're being taken care of, that's all that matters, isn't it? It's of no consequence to me."

For some reason she had apparently put her foot in it, but she couldn't for the life of her see how or why .

John seemed to expand as they got back into his Alfa Romeo and took off along the jacaranda-lined avenue.

"Well, like to live it up a bit and go dining and dancing? Get the taste of official life out of your mouth?"

"No, stop it, John!" She was nettled. "I'm not a child who has to be fed a lollipop after a visit to the doctor's office. I'm all grown up—honest! I don't expect everyone to fall on my neck and be my friend at the first moment of meeting. I don't expect to be amused all the time. I am quite prepared to go anywhere, do anything, and put up with a lot worse than tonight's little wingding, so long as I am with you, doing what's expected of us, and helping you all I can. Now, is that quite clear?"

He was silent for a moment, then took one hand off the wheel and reached over and squeezed hers. "Sorry, hon," he said quietly. "I suppose it did sound a bit like that. It's just that I so desperately want you to be happy—for both our sakes. So let me put it another way. Will you give your old man the pleasure and the honor of taking you dining and dancing?"

"You know that I'm happy—happier than I've ever been in my whole life." She squeezed his hand back. "And yes, if you want to, I'd like it very much."

They went to the rooftop restaurant of one of Pretoria's plusher hotels, and after a lengthy dinner they danced languidly to the small band on an even smaller dance floor. "This place would suit your mother to a T," John murmured, cuddling her close to him. "Nothing but cheek-to-cheek music."

"One wouldn't want it as a steady diet, but it does have its advantages," she whispered back, nestling up to him, her cheek against his, her eyes closed. "In fact, I can see how one could become addicted."

His lips brushed her cheek lightly. "Glad you feel that way, because this, alas, is going to be our first farewell. I'm going to have to take off on a trip tomorrow night."

Her eyes opened in surprise, and she drew away from him. "You are? For how long?"

"Oh, about a week, maybe less."

"Then what are we wasting our time here for?" she demanded, smiling up at him. "Let's go home and make love—then maybe, just maybe, I'll last until you get back!"

It proved to be a memorable night.

Chapter 6

The house seemed large and intimidating without John's comforting presence. The first night of his absence she found difficulty in sleeping. She wasn't nervous, exactly; Ben and Reba and the garden boy, in their little cement house at the side of the main house, were in easy calling distance, if the unlikely need arose. It was simply that— and this she realized with shock—for the very first time in her life she was completely alone. There had always been someone—her parents, her roommates—but now there was no one, and it gave her a strange feeling—a feeling equally compounded of apprehension of the unknown and a certain awed realization that she was, for the first time, faced solely with herself. To blot out this disquieting thought and the strange, anonymous creaks and groans of a house at night, she tried to think what it must have been like for John in all his long years alone. How many of those had there been? Again she was shocked to realize she had no idea and that she still knew so little of him and his past. This thought inevitably led her back to the hidden vial of perfume. He had not always been alone—that was certain—but how many had there been? How many had passed briefly through his life, leaving him alone, as she was now? With them he had not had, nor evidently had wanted, a permanent commitment, and yet he had wanted one so desperately with her. Why with me? she wondered, but she was glad that it had been so. Maybe that was why he was so solicitous, so unwilling to share her, even a little, with the outside world—because he had finally found someone with whom he wanted to share his life exclusively. As sleep finally overcame her the thoughts jumbled together in her tired mind, and her dreams were of John, sitting hunched over, his face buried in his hands as faceless shadows flitted by him and touched him briefly on the shoulder.

She awoke late, and to a small domestic crisis. She went downstairs to the kitchen in search of coffee, to find it empty of life and her entire household staff in a small gaggle by the tennis court looking at something on the ground. Throwing her jacket over her shoulders, she went out into the thin, chill sunshine to see what was up.

Mewing pitifully, crawling around on the winter-sparse grass, were two tiny kittens, one a solid bright orange, the other a riot of black, orange, and white. Ben looked up as she approached and said, "Omuru says someone threw these over the hedge last night onto the tennis court, missus. Do you want he should drown them?"

Vanessa let out a horrified yelp. "Certainly not!" She leaned down and scooped up the two downy balls, which promptly arched and hissed. "They're adorable! We'll keep them. I was going to get a cat anyway, so now I've got two. When you bring me my coffee, bring a couple of saucers as well."

In the dining room, under his disapproving eye, she poured two saucers of milk and set them down on the table before the kittens, who cowered back on their haunches, looking at her with frightened blue eyes, but cautiously began to scent the air and investigate the saucers. Their hunger prevailed over their fear, and with wary sideways glances at her they began to lap up the milk ravenously. She refilled the saucers, and when they had lapped through the second lot, they both stretched luxuriously, yawned, and looked at her expectantly.

"That's enough for now," she said, and ventured to stroke their tiny heads. The orange one began to purr like a rusty clock; the calico had a more subdued tone. "Well, Tweedledum and Tweedledee," she said, "I guess the first order of business is to get you taken care of." She scooped them up and took them up to the music room, where they both promptly scuttled under the chest of drawers. "Good!" she approved. "Just stay there till I get back." She went off in search of litter, litter boxes, and cat food of all varieties.

She returned to find them sound asleep under the bureau, curled up tightly together, but a saucerful of cat food brought them wide awake in an instant and they scoffed it all down. The calico retreated again, but the orange kitten investigated the litter box and promptly used it, mewing triumphantly; the calico reemerged and, after some timorous smelling around, did the same thing. They then had a spirited fight in the box, scattering litter across the bare parquet floor. "Well, I can see this had better be your home for the time being, you clever things," Vanessa told them, "because here I can keep track of you. Also, if you're going to make messes like this, you are not going to be very popular in the rest of the house."

She settled down to practice, putting a music-minus-one tape on the stereo and getting out her violin, but it was quickly established that she had acquired one music lover and one music hater. The orange Tweedledum scrambled up on top of the stereo, purring loudly, eyes blissfully closed at the vibrations, and settled cozily down to sleep; ears flat, Tweedledee retreated under the chest of drawers.

She kept to her resolution to keep them immured in the music room until bedtime arrived, by which time they were frisking about, completely at home with this food provider who had been stuffing them all day. She put out the light, shut the door of the music room, and went off to have her bath, but on her return she heard a frantic scratching and pathetic mewing going on inside. "What's up?" she demanded, opening the door, and they scuttled out mewing and swarmed up her bathrobe, for all the world like two children frightened of the dark. "Oh, very well, we'll just have to see if this works out. If not, back you go!" And she carried them off with her to bed. They prowled around, investigating their new surroundings, then marched back and forth on her for a while before settling down, one on each side of her, and promptly going to sleep. She looked fondly down at the two warm little balls. "You're very cute, you know—and you're just what I need at the moment." And she fell into a sound and dreamless sleep.

The next day, feeling revivified by her long sleep, she took the plunge and phoned Hans Haupman for an appointment. His English on the phone was heavily Germanic, but he sounded very affable. "Ja, Mrs. Bannerman, I was looking to hear from you. Today at four I am free. You can make it for then, yes? At my studio at the university, perhaps? I teach there alzo."

She could indeed make it, and he turned out almost exactly as she had imagined him: bald, with a tonsurelike fringe of white-flecked, gingery hair around his bare pate; short, with a formidable beer belly and twinkling blue eyes. After a few generalities about her training and her former teachers, he heard her audition through in silence, his round head cocked to one side, his small hands with their extremely long fingers folded across his ample stomach.

When she had finished her orchestral excerpts, he nodded his head briskly. "Ah, yes, good, very good. Not great, you understand? But good." She sighed inwardly, for that had been the theme of her musical life. "Your tone is excellent," he approved. "Your technique"—he see-sawed his tiny, plump hands—"not so good. Your interpretation could be better alzo. But I would be most happy to have you for a pupil, and, I think, very quick we make a place for you in symphony. Always place for good violinist."

This had been something that had been worrying her, and she blurted out, "I'd very much like to study with you, Herr Haupman, but about the symphony...That would be difficult. Because of my husband's position at the embassy, I cannot take paid employment in a foreign country—it constitutes a conflict of interest—and I am too much of a professional to play as an unpaid volunteer. It would take the position away from another musician who needs the money. So is there, perhaps, some smaller group I could play with? A string quartet, or a wind and string ensemble?"

"Ach, zo." He nodded. "I see your difficulty, and I approve your thinking. How about if you rehearse with symphony but do not play in concerts? Would that suit?"

"That would be great!" she agreed.

"As to other matter, I put you in touch with another colleague, for I do not do much like that anymore. She is first viola for symphony, but has several little groups. Very active woman." He sounded faintly disapproving. "One thing only. Is very liberal lady. Groups are mixed. You would object to that?"

She looked at him in puzzlement. "But I've always played in mixed groups!"

"No, no, no—you do not take my meaning, I think. *Mixed* groups, racially mixed—Indians, blacks, coloreds—like that." He cocked an eye at her.

So that was it! "As I said, I've always played in mixed groups," she said dryly. "And it *certainly* doesn't bother me. Why should it? It's the music that counts, is it not?"

He chuckled grimly. "Spoken like a good American democrat—I can see you haf not been in South Africa long. Well, then, I fix you up with an appointment with Gerda Baum, and you make arrangement with her."

They settled on a weekly afternoon lesson, he set her some work for it, and they parted amiably.

Feeling elated and eager to get started, she drove home to find the inevitable scatter of litter over the floor of the music room and some sheet music she had left out in tumbled disarray; the two kittens ran to her and looked up with innocent eyes. "I wish you two would have your fights somewhere other than the litter box," she scolded, cleaning up the mess as they twined around her ankles, purring. She had just settled down to practice when Ben tapped at the door. "Miz West on the phone for you, missus."

"Oh, tell her to hang on. I'll be down in a minute." She put away her violin, mindful of her mischievous companions, and carefully shut them in before going to the extension in the bedroom.

"Well! I've been trying to catch up with you all day," Bobby reproved. "You're quite the gadabout."

"I've been fixing up my music lessons," Vanessa said briefly.

"Oh. Well, the reason I called was to invite you for dinner tomorrow evening."

"I'm afraid John is away," Vanessa explained.

"All the more reason for you to come, then, and banish the solo blues," Bobby persisted.

A spasm of irrational irritation shook Vanessa. "Won't that be awkward—a single woman at a dinner party?" she returned. It had been one of her mother's most continuous plaints after the divorce: that in married circles no one wanted the odd woman out, but the odd man out was always welcome.

"Not at all—it's just family. Two couples from the embassy and Robin's secretary, so we'll be nicely balanced—it's quite informal. Everyone's dying to meet you, and it'll do you good to get out," Bobby urged. "Seventhirty. And would you like Robin to pick you up?"

It seemed churlish to refuse. "Thank you, but no. If you give me directions, I'll find you," Vanessa said, wondering who "everyone" was. Bobby provided detailed directions and rang off.

She was delayed the next evening by the untoward escape of Tweedledee, who was finally run to earth tucked away under the bed, and so she did not arrive until fifteen minutes after the appointed time, having further delayed to tell Ben that if John happened to call she would be at the Wests.

"We were just about to send out a search party," Bobby informed her gaily as she answered the door, clad in a flowing, heavily embroidered caftan. "Everyone else is here."

"Sorry I'm late," Vanessa muttered, eyeing the caftan doubtfully and wondering if she was underdressed in her velvet suit. "A small domestic crisis at the last minute."

"Everyone" turned out to be the Corbys, the Heitzes, and a middle-aged, extremely plain American woman who was introduced simply as "Maggie" and who had to be the secretary.

The Heitzes were a handsome couple, tall, gray-haired, and stately, with similar long, aristocratic, high-nosed faces. The difference lay in their eyes: Eleanor's were a cold, icy gray, and Armand's were a hot brown that frankly ogled. She had had a teacher at Hart with eyes like that, and he too had been a chaser, she reflected as she shook Armand's hot, unpleasantly moist hand. "So this is our little bride, eh?" he said, leaning forward and planting a wet kiss on her cheek. "How delightful to meet you at last!" Eleanor's eyes got icier.

The Corbys, by contrast, were very undistinguished-looking: he, medium-sized, plump, sandy, and placid; she, thin as a rail, dark of hair and eye, and all of a twitch.

"You've got time for a drink before dinner, Vanessa," Bobby said. "We are all way ahead of you. What'll you have?"

"White wine, thank you." Vanessa accepted a glass from Robin.

"I *said* we ought to have champagne tonight," Bobby told him triumphantly. "To toast our bride. Vanessa's a wine drinker."

"Perhaps we should keep that until the groom is here," Vanessa said quietly, and lifted her glass in a toast to the expectant group.

At dinner, she was relieved to find herself next to the placid Herman Corby rather than the hot-eyed Armand. She was seated in the middle of the table, opposite Maggie and between Corby and Mrs. Heitz, who was at Robin's right hand and who continued to ignore her. This was fine with her, for she had decided to be seen and not heard, but in this she was thwarted by Herman Corby, who started in on what amounted to a personal quiz. At the magic name of Juilliard, he positively beamed, and his wife, who had been listening avidly across the table, broke in. "Do you play the piano as well, Vanessa?"

"Yes, after a fashion. We all have to have it as a second instrument, but I'm not an expert by any means."

"Why, that's wonderful!" Violet Corby gushed, looking over at Eleanor Heitz. "Now you'll have someone to play for your Christmas choir, won't you? And, my dear, you'll be in *such* demand at all our parties."

This did nothing to cheer Vanessa.

Herman Corby took up the inquisition again. "I believe your maiden name was Hale—any relation to *the* Hales of Connecticut?"

"If you mean the descendants of John Hale of Hartford, yes, that is my father's family—and my mother was a Van Schuyler of New York," she added, to forestall the inevitable next question.

"Ah, I see you are into genealogy as well," he approved.

"Not really, but my mother belongs to the DAR, and so I know a certain amount." It was a subject that had always bored her to extinction.

However, it was evident that she had said all the right things, for the Corbys in counterpoint gushed out their own family trees and went on to expatiate on all the wonderful cultural opportunities that abounded in South Africa and how lucky she was to be here when so much was going on.

"Yes, I intend to take part in some of the musical activities—as an amateur, of course," she added defensively. "I hope to join one of Gerda Baum's groups."

There was a sudden electric silence, which was broken by Robin, who said, "Indeed? She's a very interesting woman, Gerda."

"You know her?" Vanessa asked in surprise.

"Oh, yes, I've worked with her several times. Did John put you on to her?" he said casually.

"Why, no, he knows nothing about this as yet. Does he know her?"

"I'm not sure. I hadn't thought so, but John knows so

many people..." Robin murmured, and turned the talk into other channels.

They had gotten to the coffee stage when the maid appeared and murmured in Bobby's ear. "A call for you, Vanessa," she said, inquiry writ large on her high-colored face.

"Oh, that must be John," Vanessa exclaimed, jumping up. "I left word I'd be here. Please excuse me." And she rushed out after the maid.

John's voice sounded strained and edgy over the phone. "So sorry I haven't called before, darling. I just haven't had the chance. Are you all right? Nothing wrong, is there? Is that why you're at the Wests?"

"No, nothing at all—everything's fine. Bobby insisted I come to a dinner party."

"Oh, who's there?"

She told him and there was a small silence. "Enjoying yourself?" he asked in a tense voice.

"Without you? Not very much," she confessed. "But I've been very efficient...." She went on to describe her activities, omitting the kittens, which she was keeping as a surprise for his return. "You don't sound too hot yourself," she concluded. "Is anything wrong?"

"Oh, tired and missing you like crazy, that's all. I can't wait to get home," he sighed. "I hope to be back in three days, and each one will seem an eternity. God, I love you so much, Van!"

"I love you too, dearest," she whispered. "So hurry home. Now I really ought to be getting back to the others."

"Wait!" His voice was urgent. "There's something I've got to tell you, something I should have told you before, but the time didn't seem right—not that now is very good, either, but—"

Bobby poked an inquiring head around the door. "Everything all right?" Vanessa smiled and nodded. "Be right with you, Bobby." The head disappeared. "Sorry, darling, what was it?" she said into the phone.

The silence at the other end made her think they had

been cut off, but then he said in a strangled voice, "Nothing—it's better we leave it until I get back. Just remember how much I love you." And to her utter mystification he rang off.

Chapter 7

*J*ohn's mystifying behavior and a chance remark of Violet Corby's at the end of the dinner party unsettled Vanessa. They had been gathering up their coats to leave when Violet had said to Eleanor, "I suppose Vera Watson will have us all at it like beavers before the Ambassador's wife gets back next week. Has she been after you already?" And Eleanor had nodded grimly.

"What was all that about?" Vanessa whispered to Bobby, who was saying all the right things to her departing guests.

"Oh, it's a big Red Cross benefit Mrs. Hackett is bent on having as soon as the Cape Town contingent returns," Bobby said offhandedly. "Terrible bore, but one of those things everyone has to pitch in on. Since Bill Watson is pro tem acting in charge here, it falls on Vera to round up the herd."

As she drove home, Vanessa wondered uneasily what she ought to do about this. She had made the offer of help to Vera very clear, and if John was Bill's chief assistant, it followed that she should be one of the first to be roped in—and yet she had heard nothing from Vera Watson. A panicky thought struck her: so engrossed had she been in her own affairs that since John had left, she had not even bothered to pick up the mail that came to the embassy. Maybe there was an imperative message there. She made up her mind to go and check the very next morning.

But from this excellent resolve she was sidetracked when at breakfast the phone rang. It was an enthusiastic and insistent Gerda Baum on the line: Hans Haupman had evidently wasted no time. "Ah, Mrs. Bannerman— could you possibly come this morning for an audition? My wind and string ensemble has just lost its first violin, and from what Hans Haupman has said, you would make a very good substitute. If you could come to my house, perhaps, this morning? I live in Brooklyn. Do you know it? I am sorry to rush you like this, but we have a full rehearsal tomorrow afternoon, and there will be one or two other new people, so if you could possibly manage it—"

"Well, I . . ." Vanessa stammered. "Couldn't we make it this afternoon instead?"

"I'm afraid not. This afternoon I teach at one of the local schools, and then I have lessons this evening. It would be of great help to me if you could make it."

Vanessa did not want to get off on the wrong foot, so with some reluctance she agreed to meet at ten o'clock. She put in some hasty practice to limber up and rushed off.

Gerda Baum's voice on the phone had been young and vibrant, so it was something of a shock to find her white-haired and stooped, though her dark eyes sparkled with energy, and the hand that grasped Vanessa's was strong and sinewy. Her house was large and richly furnished, and there was an eye-catching collection of brass menorahs in one of the cabinets. Gerda followed Vanessa's gaze. "Ah, I see you are looking at my husband's prize collection! Poor Joseph. He collected them from all over the world. We were both from Johannesburg originally, but he practiced as a doctor in Pretoria for many years, and so here I have stayed." She sighed softly.

"All alone here?" The question popped out before Vanessa could stop it.

Gerda's hands spread out in an age-old gesture. "It was our home, but now the children are grown and gone, of course: a son in Israel—a doctor, like his father; a daughter in England—a musician, like me. But I do not lack for company, praise be! I have many friends." She led Vanessa through to a large, well-equipped music room and got down to business. She explained the makeup of the ensemble, their schedule of concerts, and the repertoire. "You sight-read, of course," she stated.

"Oh, yes—quite well," Vanessa returned.

"So, perhaps, if you try this piece?" It was an excerpt from Mozart's String Quartet in G Minor, with which Vanessa was very familiar, and she played the haunting second theme with everything she had. "Why, that was just marvelous!" Gerda beamed. "Such feeling, my dear! How happy you must be." Vanessa could feel herself blushing under Gerda's knowing eye. "You are newly married, perhaps?" the old woman asked.

"Six weeks ago," Vanessa confessed.

"Aha! No wonder you play so well. We also play modern classical, so what would you like to try—Hindemith or Schoenberg?" Vanessa opted for Schoenberg.

"My dear, it will be a joy having you with us," Gerda confided at the end. "We usually rehearse in the afternoons, but the concerts are often on weekends, for nearly all of our players work full-time jobs, but I promise not to take you away too much from that new husband of yours. Music is important, but there are other things more important."

Vanessa was so delighted with herself and with Gerda that she drove all the way home before she remembered her errand at the embassy, and she decided that that could wait until after lunch.

She had only been down to the embassy a couple of times—once for a general show-around with John and once to pick up her new diplomatic passport—but she remembered the way to his office and so marched boldly in past the Marine guard and the reception desk. She went upstairs to the third floor, continued past Bill Watson's office, where the door was open and she could see him in conference with Stephen Loud, and on to the double office at the end of the economic section, which housed Dilys Gold and John.

The redheaded secretary was seated at her desk in the outer office, and as Vanessa came in she looked up. There was no mistaking the hostility in her eyes. "Yes?" she said in a tone that verged on the insolent.

"Good afternoon, Dilys," Vanessa said with firm politeness. "I came in to pick up our mail."

"It's all on John's desk," Dilys said, looking down again.

"Then would you please get it for me? I presume his office is locked," Vanessa said, a harder edge to her voice.

Dilys flounced up and made a great clatter of keys as she unlocked the door and reappeared with a bunch of mail done up in a rubber band, which she handed over, and she sat down again without saying a word. Vanessa calmly sat down in the other chair and leafed through the bundle, but there was nothing for her—merely a couple of personal letters for John, some bills, a few circulars, and one letter addressed to them jointly. She opened that, to find an invitation to a reception at the Ambassador's residence to celebrate the return of the Cape Town contingent. This left her in a quandary. "Er—there hasn't been any message left here for me by Mrs. Watson, has there?" she ventured.

"No." The smoldering eyes clashed with hers. "Why should there be?"

"About the Red Cross benefit—about what we're supposed to do for it."

"If you want to know, why not ask Eleanor Heitz?"

"Eleanor? What's she got to do with it?"

Dilys snorted. "Oh, really, now! I'm John's secretary, remember? No need to play any silly games with me. I'm part of the company, too. If you want to know what's going on, ask John's boss's wife, not Vera Watson."

"What on *earth* are you talking about?" Vanessa blurted out in amazement.

Dilys looked up suddenly, her eyes narrowing, an

expression almost of triumph appearing in them. "You really *don't* know, do you?" she said softly, and chuckled. "Well, I'll be. Then the plain fact is, *Mrs.* Bannerman, that John's position in economics is simply his embassy cover. Willy Watson isn't his boss; Armand Heitz is. John is CIA—a spook, a spy. I'm not sure what term you *young* people use for it nowadays."

The shock was so sudden and savage that Vanessa was thankful she was sitting down so that her sudden trembling could be disguised; her knees felt like water, her head like an overfilled balloon. She tried to hide what she was feeling from those triumphant eyes, and finally she managed to get her vocal cords to work. "I wasn't sure how far the cover went," she lied. "Naturally, now that you've explained it, I will contact Mrs. Heitz." Somehow she managed to get herself out of the chair and out of the office without collapsing, but by the time she got down to the street and back to the car she was trembling so violently that she had to sit behind the wheel, grasping it until her white knuckles ached as she fought to get back her self-control.

She drove home in a daze. Why? why? why? hammered at her temples. Why had he done this to her? What kind of witless fool did he think she was? Her face flamed as she thought of what a fool she had made of herself, what a fool he had made of her—at the Watsons', at the Wests', and now before that obnoxious Dilys Gold. How *could* he, she thought as her shock started to turn into a furious anger. How could he do this to me, if he loves me? How long did he plan to continue this charade? Until the whole embassy was rocking with laughter behind her back? It was then that the import of their last conversation finally hit her. Was that what he had been trying to tell her? But even so, it was still unforgivable.

Her anger kept her fired up, even through her first rehearsal with the ensemble the next day, although she was only dimly aware of the others in the group as Gerda introduced her around. If it was a mixed group, it certainly was very lightly mixed—one turbaned Indian who played bass viol and one nervous black, a newcomer like herself, who played the flute though there were two other sad-eyed, sallow-skinned women who may have been "colored." She didn't know, she didn't care; her inner anger seethed and roiled. She plunged into the music with an almost savage intensity, so that by the end of the rehearsal she felt drained and exhausted. Afterward, as the others filed out, the sharp-eyed Gerda put a restraining hand on her arm. "My dear, is there anything the matter? You look so different from yesterday—so white and strained. Are you in any trouble? Anything I can help with?"

"No, just a personal problem that will soon be resolved," she said grimly. "I hope it did not affect my playing."

"No, you played very well," Gerda said, withdrawing her hand. "But just remember I am here, if you need someone to talk to. It is not always easy when you are in a new land so far from home."

When she got back home, she was so tired that she lay down on the bed and fell into a restless sleep, only to be awakened by Ben's persistent tapping and his announcement that dinner was ready.

She pecked away at it without appetite, and when Ben cleared it away, his face concerned, he ventured, "You don't like what Reba fixed, missus?"

"It was fine," she said wearily. "I'm just not hungry." She helped herself to a large bourbon and soda and settled in front of the living room log fire, which Ben had coaxed into a cheery blaze. She sipped her drink and thought her dark thoughts.

Ben came in and made up the fire. "Anything else I can get for you, missus?"

"No, that's all for tonight, thank you," she said, and after a moment's hesitation he went out, and the house took on its empty, nightime silence. She tried to cry, but found she couldn't: her heart was aching so much with the hurt that the tears simply would not come. She wandered restlessly about the room, seeing it all for the first time with unveiled eyes: it was all a lie; everything had been a lie. . . . She had been introduced into the middle of an elaborate charade of which she knew nothing, not even the part she was supposed to play. She went and fixed herself another drink and sat down again before the dying fire, until suddenly the sound of the front door crashing open brought her to her feet with a frightened cry.

Then John's voice. "I'm home, darling! Couldn't bear another moment without you, so...." He rushed through the door, grinning happily, then froze as he saw her face, all color and expression draining from his own. "Oh, dear God," he whispered. "So you know.... Who told you about me?"

"What does that matter? The fact is I do—and what I want to know is *why*. Why did you do this to me?" She tried to keep her voice from quavering but was not entirely successful.

"Because I love you and need you...." He advanced toward her, his arms outstretched, his eyes pleading and agonized, but she held up her hands to fend him off. "No!" she choked out. "Don't come near me. Don't touch me. Just answer me."

His arms fell to his sides and he gazed at her helplessly. "Anything I say will sound ridiculous and weak to you, because you are angry—and with reason. And it will sound so, because I guess it *is* so. At the start your mother assumed I was a diplomat, though I never actually *said* I was, and somehow it seemed easier to let it go on like that, because I was terrified that if you knew the whole of it you would not marry me. I was afraid I'd lose you—"

"But that was before we were married!" she cried. "We've been married over six *weeks*! What happened to two being as one? What happened to *trust* between a man and his wife? Why make me this ridiculous laughing-stock?"

"Nobody is laughing at you," he said, looking wretched. "If they are laughing at anyone it is I, because I was so insistent that they keep silent until I got up my own nerve to tell you. You had so many adjustments to make in such a short time, I wanted you to be at ease and happy before I told you the rest of it. I've tried to get it out a dozen times, but we were so happy, I just couldn't bring myself to risk tainting that happiness in any way."

"Why? Are you so ashamed of what you do?" she flared.

This stung him. "No, of course I'm not!" he returned hotly. "I think what I do is important and necessary, and I enjoy it. But I also know that a lot of people don't like the CIA. It's had a lot of bad publicity, and so many young people, especially, have the wrong ideas about it—"

"But of course it never occurred to you to ask *this* young person how she felt about such things, did it?" she said bitterly. "Did you think my love was that shallow? Did you think it would have mattered a *damn* to me whether you were a garbage collector or a hit man—" She stopped, appalled, as a new thought struck her. "You aren't, are you?" she whispered.

"Oh, for God's sake, Van! Do you see any cloaks and daggers lying around the place? Of course I'm not a hit man. That's just what I was afraid of—all these crazy notions about what the CIA does. The gathering of intelligence is nowhere near as exciting or as dangerous as people who have been raised on a steady diet of James Bond suppose. But you are right to be angry, my love; I have been selfish and thoughtless in my own desire to preserve the enchantment we had. If you only knew what these past few weeks have meant to me, what *you* have meant to me...." He gathered himself together with an effort. "The thing is, now that it's out, what are you going to do about it? Whatever label I wear, I am still the same man you married and whom you have loved. Where do we go from here?" He looked questioningly at her.

Now that it *was* out, she didn't know; she felt completely at a loss, and the tears that she had vainly sought to release began to rise. "I don't know," she sobbed, the tears beginning to stream down her cheeks. "I'm just so confused and *hurt*."

With a single bound he was upon her and cradled her in his arms. "Dearest, I know," he choked, his own tears mingling with hers. "Oh, God, I know how I've hurt you by trying not to hurt you, but please, Van, please, let it not make any difference. I love you, I need you, and I swear to God nothing like this will ever happen again."

His mouth sought hers, and the feel of his lips on hers and of his arms around her soothed the raging hurt within her like a balm as they clung together. Her storm of sobs died away and she leaned exhaustedly against him. "I'm so tired," she whispered. "But we have to talk. You have to tell me what this is all about—but not tonight."

"No, not tonight," he murmured, gazing deep into her eyes.

They made love almost frenziedly, their passion driving out—at least for the moment—the tormenting thoughts, the wounded feelings. When he lay at last in exhausted sleep, she became dimly aware of the frantic scratching and mewing going on behind the closed door of the music room. "Good God, I had forgotten all about them," she chided herself, and slipped gingerly out of his embrace and liberated her bedmates. She tumbled back into bed and into instant sleep.

When she awoke in the morning, she looked muzzily over at John, who was still sleeping. Curled tightly around his neck, for all the world like a multicolored fur collar, were the kittens, their heads nose to nose under his chin, also fast asleep.

"You traitors!" she whispered fondly.

Chapter 8

They had slept so late that there had been no time for discussion before John had had to leave for the embassy to hand in his report on the trip. Vanessa was glad of this, for it gave her time to sort out her thoughts and her feelings.

So much that had mystified her about him was now clear: the odd phone calls that had punctuated their courtship, John's overzealousness in keeping her away from involvement with embassy personnel, even the sudden cattiness of Vera Watson. She wished that she was not so ignorant, but politics and government had always bored her, and she had never run with a crowd that was politically involved or interested in anything save the odd antinuclear protest or ecological campaigns of the more esoteric sort; Sam, she recalled, had been a dedicated save-the-whales man. But of the CIA and its workings she knew virtually nothing save—as John had said so bitterly—through television and the movies. The more she thought about it, the more intriguing it became: certainly the life of a spy had to be more exciting than the life of the economic officer she thought she had married. It explained also the maverick air that had so puzzled her about John. On the surface he had seemed so establishment in his elegant dress and his savoir faire, but there had been those other little anomalies: a certain recklessness, a certain disregard of some establishment norms that set him apart from, say, Bill Watson or Stephen Loud. He was truly an undercover man in an establishment world, which made her, she supposed, an undercover wife. This thought tickled her fancy—she would be leading a double life, just as he did. She wondered how many others, apart from Bobby West, there were in this position. Suddenly, she was eager to know more.

As promised, John came home early, a little tense and edgy, though the warmth of her greeting banished the doubt in his eyes. He had found her at work in the music room. "Put on a coat and let's go outside," he suggested, absentmindedly detaching Tweedledum, who had conceived a violent fancy for him and was swarming determinedly up his trouser leg. "It's quite warm on the patio, and we can have drinks out there and talk."

"All right," she agreed amiably, stowing away her violin.

Before they settled in the white iron chairs by the fountain, he carefully turned up the cascade, then turned and grimaced at her. "Welcome to the world of paranoia. It's probably safe enough inside, but I haven't had the time to check the house out for any recent listening bugs, so we're better off out here."

She looked at him in mild shock. "You mean the South African government knows about what you do?"

"Not me in particular, no. They just tend to keep a general eye on embassy personnel. For one thing, all our phones are tapped. The South Africans tend to be pretty paranoid themselves, so we play little games with each other."

"Good grief!" she said faintly. "Have there been any bugs around since we arrived?" He shook his head. "No, I checked the house as soon as we got back, and it was clean." He sat down and looked at her uncertainly. "Well, Van, the ball is yours. Where do you want me to begin?"

"First I'd like to know who the others are at the embassy, beside the Wests and the Heitzes, and just what the setup here *is*," she said. "After that, I'd like to know how you got involved in the first place, and why."

"The setup here is a pretty standard one. Armand Heitz and his assistant, George Drake, are the accredited intelligence men at the embassy—in other words, the South African government knows about them and their own intelligence services interact with them. Robin and I are 'deep cover,' which means we *do* work legitimately for our respective branches, but we also do our own work under their umbrella. There's another deep cover man in the trade section—Grant Zecco—but he operates on his own." His face tightened for a second. "Then there's a deep, deep cover man here who isn't connected with the embassy at all but who interacts with all of us: an American who manages a travel agency in Pretoria—Joe Ferraro, a nice guy, but a bit of a wild man. You'll meet him when it's my turn for our poker night, which is coming up quite soon." This time he grinned.

"That sounds very macho," she said mildly. "What do you do, turn the house into a smoke-filled gambling den for the night?"

"It's a good excuse to get us all together in an innocent-seeming way," he explained. "Every week we go to a different house."

"And are all these people married? Do they have families?" Vanessa was pursuing her own line of thought.

"Oh, yes. Well, you know the Heitzes already. Besides their daughter here, they have two married children stateside and recently became grandparents—which infuriated Armand, I might add."

"I can imagine," she said absently.

"The Drakes have four kids—teenage on down. Amanda Drake is a very dedicated mom. The Zeccos have one, a boy, who's a bit of a mess. Clara Zecco is an ex-showgirl and a real bubblehead. The Ferraros—his wife is Rose, by the way—are good Catholics and so have a vast tribe—six or seven—I've lost count."

"But the Wests don't?"

John shook his head. "No. Bobby either can't or won't—I'm not sure which—and Robin isn't exactly the paternal type."

"Any more than you are," she said.

"Why do you say that?" His tone was sharp.

She looked at him in some surprise. "I just didn't think your interests lay in that direction. You mean you are interested in having a family?" It was something she was very ambivalent about herself. As an only child, she had never had much contact with other children or with the give and take of a larger family, and the thought of a child of her own intimidated her.

Put that bluntly, her question seemed to throw him into some confusion. "Not right away, perhaps, but someday. Yes, someday I'd like us to have children." He looked at her questioningly. "Wouldn't you?"

"Like you said, maybe someday, but not now," she evaded. "Anyway, we seem to be getting off the track. Why did you pick the CIA as a career?"

He was silent for a while, gazing moodily at the splashing fountain. "I'm no longer sure whether I picked it or it picked me," he said at length. "They tried to recruit me right from Yale—both Robin and I were political science majors and had vague ideas about going into government and saving the world. But I had just gotten married and was going to be called up, and somehow the war seemed a far more exciting prospect at the time." He grimaced. "A very mistaken notion on my part, even though I had it a lot easier than most of the poor devils that went. There again, I'm not sure whether it was just happenstance or I was already being steered, but they put me in Army Intelligence. I didn't get out of the States until 1971, but then I was all over the war zone until everything collapsed in '75—Cambodia, 'Nam, and all places east. I got back as dislocated and as disillusioned as most of my peers, and what with the dreary economic conditions then and the fact that my marriage was rapidly going sour—well, when the CIA recruiters approached me, it seemed a more exciting prospect than being stuck behind some desk in Washington. They can be pretty persuasive—the money is good, the prospects bright, and it's a damn sight more interesting than most jobs."

"Then it wasn't being in the CIA that broke up your first marriage?" she asked.

"Let's say it was the last straw. We had been apart too much; too much had happened to both of us. Mary had her own career going in real estate, and she was a pretty ardent women's libber. She just couldn't see giving it all up to trail around the world after a man who was more or less a stranger and who worked for an organization she didn't like. We got divorced in '76, the year after I went in. My first assignment overseas was in Paris, then here—end of story." He looked at her questioningly. "That enough?"

"You still haven't told me what you actually do here," she persisted. "Nor what I can do, now that I'm in the picture, to help you."

He stood up, as if terminating the discussion. "Look, there's no need for you to know. It's best for both our sakes that you don't. So far as you are concerned, I go to the office, do my job, and come home again, just like any other working man. The best help you can be to me is to fill the house with your music and my life with your love."

She looked up at him and smiled. "That's a very pretty speech, but there must be *something* I can do that's a little more practical than that," she said dryly.

He threw back his head and laughed. "You're a hard woman to convince, Van. All right, if you're so dead set on it, you can keep your eyes open for workmen, meter readers, or the like that come to or near the house—then we'll know when to have a bug hunt. And if you've the taste for it, you can interact with the other wives and fill me in on all the juicy gossip that goes on in our little charmed circle. Now, the sun's going in, so let's go in ourselves before we both freeze to death. What do you say to some more cheek-to-cheek dancing to celebrate my return?" They celebrated.

She was satisfied because she wanted to be satisfied, although there were dozens of questions that still swarmed in her mind. There would be plenty of time for those—the rest of their lives, in fact. She would do as he asked simply because she loved him, and she realized that her ivory tower, her bulwark of music, was as important to him as it was to her. With this knowledge she faced her obligations as an embassy wife with added confidence.

Not that it was all smooth going. The first big reception at the residence after the Cape Town contingent's return was an eye-opener for her. Although she stuck closely to John, and everyone was polite or gushing, according to their natures, she was well aware of undercurrents, of the curious glances and the whispered asides as they wandered from group to group in the crowded reception rooms. They ended up, as seemed inevitable, with the Wests, and the two men wandered off by themselves, leaving her and Bobby to their own devices.

"So how's it going?" Bobby asked.

"Oh, pretty well, though I must say a little of this goes a very long way with me." Vanessa smiled.

"Get used to it!" Bobby charged. "This is only the beginning of an unending season. By the way, I gather the need to be discreet is past. Welcome to the club and all that. Hope it wasn't too much of a shock. If I'm not being too nosy, how did you find out?"

"John's secretary," Vanessa said, without elaborating.

"Oh, that bitch! I should have known. Probably wasn't all that nice about it, either. As you have no doubt deduced, she had hopes—vain ones, of course—of becoming the new Mrs. B. Lesson one for you, my dear: when the chance comes, be sure you get to set your seal of approval on his next secretary. I always do."

Which explained the plain Maggie, Vanessa thought, for she had already noted that Robin was never allowed far from Bobby's possessive eyes. "She did seem overly hostile," she murmured. "Not that that appears to be all that unusual—half the women here tonight have been looking daggers at me. Don't tell me they were all after John, too!"

Bobby snorted with laughter. "No, John may be attractive, but he's not *that* attractive. Half of them probably hated you on sight because you're half their age and are an attractive young thing; the other half just because you're one of us."

"But why should that matter?" Vanessa protested. "Surely we're all on the same team."

"Not the way they look at it. Some 'regular' State people have always resented the fact we are given cover as bona fide diplomats within the embassy. It goes all the way back to the fifties, when State was devastated by Senator McCarthy and his witch hunters, and the CIA got its foot in State's door. They think it shouldn't be allowed to continue, that it puts them in danger."

"Does it?" Vanessa demanded.

Bobby shifted uneasily. "Most of the time, no. Occasionally you get something dire happening, as in Iran, when the host country used us as an excuse to do something inexcusable themselves, but, God damn it, most of the time *we're* the targets, not the diplomats, so they have no beef."

Their tête-à-tête was broken up by the arrival of Clara Zecco, whose spectacular cleavage had to be seen to be believed and who towered over Vanessa like an Amazon. "My turn to have the group, I believe," she squeaked in her little girl's voice to Bobby. "I hope you can come, too, Vanessa."

"Er—when is it?" she said cautiously.

"Thursday morning at my house. Eleven o'clock. We live in Brooklyn. Bobby could show you the way—I'm no good at giving directions."

"I'm afraid I have a rehearsal at three," Vanessa said.

"No problem!" The large, heavily made up, slightly vacant eyes widened at her. "It's just for coffee and things. We always break up by one, don't we, Bobby?"

"In that case, yes, I'd like to."

They were joined by Grant Zecco, whom Vanessa had only seen from afar as John had steered her around. From a distance his stocky, thick-set figure had appeared undistinguished, apart from his aggressive Marine crew cut; close up he gave a different impression. As introductions were made and he shook Vanessa's hand with a painfully hard grip she was both fascinated and repelled by his eyes. They were a peculiar shade of amber, had very small pupils, and reminded her of some large, wild cat. His heavily muscled frame also gave the impression of suppressed intensity, of something savage and dangerous coiled to spring. After the briefest of pleasantries, he turned to his wife and said in a loud voice, "Let's go—a bunch of niggers just arrived, and I'm damned if I'm going to stay around with them here."

The small groups around them stirred uneasily and seemed to draw away, as if from something tainted, and a glint of satisfaction appeared in his feral eyes. Vanessa was silent with shock. "All right, dear," Clara said. "See you both on Thursday, then," she added, and she teetered away by his side, overtopping him by some three inches.

"I see our charming Grant has made his usual impression," Bobby said acidly, looking sideways at Vanessa's shocked face. "I'm always expecting him to turn up one of these days complete with white sheet and hood. I don't know why Armand lets him get away with it. Though maybe he's just too plain scared of him—I think the man's a psycho. How Clara stands him I don't know, and that poor kid of his . . . !"

"Did he really mean it, or was it just to shock people?" Vanessa asked, looking at the people around them, who still had their backs resolutely turned.

"Oh, he means it right enough. It's not just blacks he's rabid about. To quote him, 'kikes, spics, and wops' are every bit as bad in his neo-Nazi worldview. Needless to say, the Afrikaners love him and think he's great. Robin can't stand him."

They were rejoined by their husbands and shortly after made their own farewells. "I finally met Grant Zecco," Vanessa told John as he drove home at breakneck speed like a man newly liberated.

"Poor unlucky you!" he returned lightly, but would not

be drawn further on the interesting subject. Vanessa, who had been mentally making plans for their first dinner party, hastily revised her tentative guest list. She could not see the Zeccos and Gerda Baum under the same roof. Come to that, she couldn't see Grant Zecco under their roof at all. She hoped that that would be all right with John, but she didn't much care if it wasn't.

Chapter 9

*H*er proposal for a big dinner party met with such a tepid response from John, as well as the glum Ben and Reba, that she quietly shelved the idea until such time as she felt more competent to command its operations. John had been almost testy about it. "It's really not necessary, and I've never had any here," he kept repeating.

"Yes, but now it's different. And anyway, you must have done *some* reciprocal entertaining. How did you manage?"

"One big bash here once a year in the summer season that I had catered by one of the local hotels, and a few parties where I had guests for drinks here first and then took them out to dinner."

"But that's so expensive!" she protested. "At least if we had them here we'd save some money."

"I'm less interested in saving money than in not being bothered," he had returned, and it was then she had decided not to pursue it further until she had acquired some expertise in matters culinary and social.

Her life was settling into a pleasant routine. Her lessons with Hans Haupman were enjoyable without being very stimulating, but when she started to rehearse with the symphony, she realized he was a far better concert-master than he was a teacher, and they became more amiable with each other in jointly tearing their conduc-tor—whom she thought decidedly inferior—to bits in cozy, catty tête-à-têtes after the rehearsals. Gerda Baum did stimulate her, and though the personnel in the ensemble appeared extremely volatile, for there was always some-one coming or going, they managed, through Gerda's unflagging energy and enthusiasm, to pull through some-how as a group, even though there was very little inter-personal contact between them.

Her first meeting with the inner circle of CIA wives had been pleasant and uneventful enough, although she was conscious of undercurrents and tensions within the group and could not put her finger on the source of these. To her surprise, Eleanor had been very affable to her, and she wasn't sure whether this was due to the fact she was now a known and accepted entity, or if it was just happenstance because Armand was away on an official trip and Eleanor was relaxed. On the other hand, Amanda Drake had seemed obscurely worried and ill at ease, her eyes constantly flickering around Clara's far-from-impressive decor as if taking inventory, and she had asked Vanessa some pointed questions (which to her had seemed pointless) about how she was getting along with John's friends. Amanda had been rather abruptly turned away from this by Eleanor and had lapsed into a sulky silence.

Rose Ferraro, whom she had met for the first time, was very dark and very Italian, and it came almost as a shock to hear a flat Boston accent emerging from that Mediterranean face. She was a thin and very nervous woman—a circumstance Vanessa ascribed to the vast family John had credited her with—and it was plainly evident that she and Amanda both disliked Bobby West, to whom Eleanor naturally seemed to turn for support. Their hostess bubbled and babbled, and Vanessa could not help warming to her, for nothing seemed to upset

Clara's amiable good humor—not Amanda's barbed little comments nor Bobby's evident impatience with her slowness.

Part of Eleanor's new affability was undoubtedly due to the fact that after having the entire distaff side of the embassy in a hubbub for a week, Mrs. Hackett had finally decided to postpone the Red Cross benefit until the weather was warmer and the spring rains had passed, and all of the feverish plans were promptly shelved in favor of a later garden party. "So, much ado about nothing, as usual." Eleanor had smiled wryly at Vanessa. "Now we can all relax until the next ambassadorial brainstorm."

Somewhat to her own disappointment, Vanessa had missed out on John's first poker night at the house, for it had coincided with her first concert with the ensemble. In one way she was glad, for it meant he could not attend the concert, and she was afraid that her debut as first violin might be far from spectacular and that he would be disappointed. She performed creditably enough, although not up to her own high expectations, and so was in a good mood when she returned to the house.

She tiptoed to the door of the den and listened to the dull rumble of male voices, an amused smile on her lips. "Raise." "See you." "Get me a beer while you're up, Joe." "Damn these cards, haven't had a hand all night. Let's have a new deck, John." This last she recognized as Grant Zecco's voice, and her smile faded. John had impressed on her that on no account was she to interrupt these stag sessions in any way. "If there are any phone calls, take a message; if the house is burning down, call the fire department"—he had grinned—"but *don't* interrupt."

"Not even if you are losing your shirt and all our worldly goods?" she had shot back.

"No, because I never do. Grant and Joe are our big plungers, but we play for such small stakes that the worst they can do to each other is about fifty bucks' worth. Robin and I usually break about even, George is always a little ahead, and Armand—when he graces us with his presence, which isn't all that often—usually walks away with the whole pot."

"Always the same cast of characters?" she asked.

"Oh, occasionally we have a gullible stranger," he said evasively.

As she listened tonight, isolating the individual voices, she realized there were no outsiders. She wondered how long these sessions continued but, feeling pleasantly exhausted, decided she would not stay up to find out. So, collecting the kittens, she went to bed.

She awakened to feel John slipping in beside her and cursing softly. "Damn these cats!"

"What's up?" she muttered.

"I just sat on Tweedledum and he bit me."

She giggled sleepily. "That'll teach you to wear pajamas. Good night?"

"Nothing that can't be improved on." His lips sought hers and his hands caressed her breasts. "Particularly now you're awake."

"Mmm." She put her arms around his neck and moved against him as he slipped off the panties of her shortie pajamas. "Insatiable brute!"

"Isn't that the truth," he breathed, his tongue driving deep into her mouth as he entered her, his hands grasping her buttocks and pulling her to him. His tempo quickened and they came immediately to a gasping climax, her nails digging hard into his bare shoulders. He rolled sideways, keeping her clasped to him, his hands continuing their play on her body underneath the sheer fabric of the pajama top. "Now I have bloody wounds on both ends, you hot wench, you!"

"Serves you right for attacking me," she murmured, exploring the inside of his ear with her tongue and then gently biting him on the neck. "We cats have to defend ourselves."

He groaned softly and hitched her left leg over his hip for deeper penetration as he began to move against her languidly, and wave after wave of sensuous pleasure washed over her as she came slowly and tantalizingly to another climax. "Happy?" he whispered after the pulsations of their joint orgasm had passed.

"So happy!" she murmured. Their heads close together,

they lay looking into each other's eyes. A small, furry orange head inserted itself firmly between them, quickly followed by a multicolored one. "I think we're being told to sign off for the night." John's voice came muffled through the fur. "Good night, my love."

"Good night, my dearest," she breathed.

At her insistence, they entertained the Wests, although John stuck to his old pattern of drinks at the house and dinner out. It was the first time she saw a side to Bobby that John had remarked on acidly and that had led to some sharp words between them. "She's a pusher," he had stated. "She's always pushing Robin about something or into something, and it just isn't his style. She should leave things alone."

On this occasion, over the pre-dinner drinks at the house, Bobby was complaining long and loud about the Corbys. "They just don't appreciate how much Robin does for them," she said hotly. "Always piling things on his shoulders, as if his own job wasn't hard enough. I honestly think Armand should intervene. Robin is exhausted all the time."

"Then take some leave," John said tartly. "I'm sure you have plenty coming, and there's nothing going on I can't handle by myself for a while."

"It's all very well for you to say that, John," she flared. "You have a pussycat like Willy Watson, who lets you go anytime you like, but between Herman and Armand they never want to let Robin off the hook for more than a few days at a time."

"Bill has Stephen Loud for backup, but Robin is all Corby's got," John pointed out. "But if it's a case of needs must, he'll have to let him go."

"Oh, I'm all right," Robin interrupted wearily. "Bobby always fusses so."

But Vanessa was inclined to agree with Bobby. Robin did not look at all well; his normally pale face seemed more haggard than usual, and he had developed a nervous tic under one eye. He always put Vanessa in mind of a dormant volcano, calm and rigid on the outside but seething inside with unseen fires. He was still as much of a mystery to her as he had been at their first meeting. Although he had thawed a little toward her, she still felt a tremendous barrier of reserve between them, as if he was weighing and watching every move she made. Of the two, she much preferred the outgoing Bobby, although she had never admitted this to John.

"I do all I can to help him with things and further his career," Bobby went on in an aggrieved tone. "But as you well know, there's a limit to what I'm *allowed* to do."

This awoke a fresh pang of guilt in Vanessa, for she had lapsed into an easy round of her own and neither knew or did anything along these lines for John. He apparently wanted it that way, but she knew, for her own peace of mind, that she would have to raise the subject again before too long.

She had almost nerved herself up to this when he suddenly announced he was off on another trip. "A week again, I'm afraid, honey lamb" he told her. "But this time I'll keep more in touch, I promise."

"Do I get to know where?" she said evenly. "Though I suppose I mustn't ask why."

"Oh, no deep secret!" he exclaimed. "Bloemfontein first, then on to Durban and some other places in Natal, then Jo'burg and back home. Just an information-gathering expedition, and I'm picking up stuff for Bill's annual railway report at the same time."

She asked nothing further and got the impression that this rather irked him. Maybe this is the way to play it, she thought—the less he thinks I really care about knowing, the more he may tell me.

This time, also, she was not as unsettled as she had been at that first separation, but two days after his departure she received a jolt that unsettled her considerably. She had gone to fetch the local mail that was delivered to a box in their stone gatepost at the end of the drive, and found, sitting on top of a couple of bills, a single sheet of folded paper with the typed superscription "Mrs. Bannerman." Opening it, she read the typed message. "So your new hubby is off to visit his little friends in Durban again. You poor thing—out of sight, out of mind. Not that that stops him. Ask him when he gets back about the interrogation room. Hot Heitzy isn't the only one!" It was unsigned and obviously hand-delivered. Feeling a little sick, she folded it with a hand that trembled. Damn! she though miserably. Damn, damn, damn! She knew she could not bring herself to burn it, so put it out of her mind; she knew she would have to show it to John.

Fortunately, her music was keeping her very busy, and she was thankful for that. The spring rains had begun, and on coming out of a rehearsal at Gerda's into a downpour she had seen the black flute player, Tom Mbeni, racing desperately after a receding bus. The bus did not heed his frantic waves, and he ducked his head into the driving rain and started to walk disconsolately after it. On an impulse, she drew the car up alongside him and rolled down her window. "Can I give you a lift to the bus station, Mr. Mbeni?"

He looked up, startled. "Oh, thank you, but no. There will not be a bus for another hour and I must get back."

"Then I'll drive you home," she volunteered.

He looked shocked. "But I live in the native township. I could not ask you to go out there."

"Why? How far is it?"

"Four miles outside Pretoria."

"Well, you certainly can't walk all that way in this downpour!" she exclaimed. "You have no raincoat. You'll be drowned, and you'll ruin your suit. Come on, hop in. I insist!"

He hovered a moment in agonized indecision, then ducked his head and, running around to the passenger side of the car, scrambled in. "This is really most kind," he muttered, staring straight ahead. "And I'm afraid I don't even know your name. I do not know anyone in the group besides Mrs. Baum, you see."

"Vanessa, Vanessa Bannerman," she said, starting up the Volkswagen. "And I know you are Thomas Mbeni, right?"

"Right," he agreed with a sudden flash of white teeth. "Tom Mbeni."

"You are going to have to direct me," she said, and he nodded eagerly. "Oh, yes, that I can tell you very well."

After a flurry of directions, he stated, "You are not South African, I think."

"No, I'm American." Vanessa smiled over at him. "My husband works at the embassy here."

"He is a most fortunate man." It was an ambiguous statement, and she did not know how to interpret it. "I am a Sotho and a teacher at the school in the township," he went on, "so my life is there, but my music gives me means to escape—occasionally." His tone was bleak. He peered through the cascades of rain and exclaimed, "Here we turn off the main road, and then it becomes complicated."

They left the tarmac of the main road and turned onto a narrow, unpaved road full of potholes and awash with water; on both sides huddled squat, one-story, flat-roofed cement boxes, some semidetached, some built in rows, but all of the same uniform, drab grayness. Nothing moved; nothing stirred. It was like a city of the dead. They bumped and lurched left, then right, then left again through the warren, until Vanessa was totally disoriented. Suddenly he said, "At the end of the road here—that is my house." And she drew the car to a shuddering halt before a semidetached house at the end.

The one he had indicated had a path edged neatly with whitewashed stones that led up to its brightly painted door, and in the minute patch of garden in front was a flower bed, now empty of life, also edged by whitewashed stones. The bright color of the door was picked up by the fresh, floral-patterned curtains that hung at the small window. By contrast, its semidetached neighbor showed no such individuality; its garden was a riot of rank, dead weeds that barely screened an assortment of rubbish ranging from decayed tires and tin cans to sodden cardboard boxes. Its door was of peeling gray, showing rotting wood beneath, and one of the panes of the window had been replaced by a filthy, battered square of cardboard. Tom Mbeni followed the direction of Vanessa's gaze and said softly, "Some of us still have hope, still have belief, but with others the hope is gone, and so they do nothing. You cannot blame them." She did not know what to say.

After a little hesitation, he went on timidly, "I share my house with my sister, who is a nurse at the native hospital and is still at work. After all your kindness, I should ask you in, but she would be very cross with me if I asked an honored visitor in when the house was not picked up as it should be. I hope you will forgive me and perhaps will come and take tea with us some other time."

She was both embarrassed and flattered. "Why, that would be very nice," she said. "Yes, I would like to meet your sister very much. Now I'm afraid you'll have to give me directions to get back to the main road. I'm completely disoriented."

He shook his head. "No, please wait here and I will guide you out. It is too difficult, and it is not safe for you to drive here alone."

"But you'll get all wet again if you do that," she protested.

He smiled at her and got out of the car. "No, this time I prepare, and I insist." He let himself into the house and shortly reappeared, sporting a raincoat and brandishing an umbrella. "You see?" He smiled. "Now I shall be quite all right."

As they drove slowly out she noticed more, particularly this mingling of houses that were well kept and even had, on occasion, a car as battered as her own standing outside, cheek by jowl with others that had the same look of hopeless squalor and abandonment of Mbeni's neighbor's house. They were taking a different route, and they passed a larger building before which an expanse of beaten earth with sagging goalposts at either end defined a playing field. "That is my school," Mbeni said with a touch of pride, "and that is our soccer field. Now we go past the cemetery where my parents lie." They went by an enclosure surrounded by whitewashed mud brick walls inside which a few markers, mostly of wood, were visible. "All this I show you when you visit us," he said.

One more turn and she felt tarmac under the wheels again. "Here we are," he announced. "Please drop me here. And perhaps, after the next rehearsal, if the weather is fine, you will take tea with us?"

She stopped the car. "Yes, thank you very much, Tom."

"Thank *you* very much," he said, getting out and stooping down with another flash of white teeth. "We shall look forward to it."

She watched him as he opened the umbrella and, using it as a shield, marched off into the driving rain. In a very thoughtful mood, her heart a conflict of sadness and anger, she drove slowly back to the suburban splendors of Waterkloof.

Chapter 10

This time she saw no reason to wait for John's return to spring their latest problem on him. When he called, and after the usual loving exchanges, she zoomed straight to the point. "Darling, we've got a problem. There is someone close to us who either hates you very much or me very much, and I think as soon as you get back we ought to have an air-clearing session so that we can decide what to do about it." She read him the contents of the anonymous note, and he reacted, as expected, with disgust and anger. "God! How come you didn't throw that into the garbage, where it belongs?"

"And keep it from you? We're back to the old problem of trust, aren't we? Whoever is doing this is playing on the fact that I know so little about you or the setup here and is banking on me getting upset. We've got to put a stop to that, and the way to do it is for me to know the *whole* picture so I'll have nothing to wonder about or fret about. Surely you can see that."

There was a long silence and then he said, "Yes, I can

see that, although I still think what was before has *nothing* to do with what is now."

"And I agree, but knowledge is power, and it will help me deal with any further filth like this."

"Well, I'm talking from a public phone, so now is not the time—" he began.

"No, of course it isn't, but as soon as you get home," she said, then added cautiously, "one thing did occur to me. Do you think it could be your secretary, Dilys Gold?"

"Dilys! You say it was hand-delivered and not through the mail? Then no. Not unless she altered her plans. Because of my absence she was going to take some leave down in Cape Town, and she left the day before I did."

This really startled and confused her, so she changed the subject. "Oh, just one more thing. I'm going out to tea in the black township next week. I hope that's not likely to make any waves at the embassy."

"No, none—but how did that happen?" He was curious.

She explained and then exploded, "I still haven't gotten over that awful place. I've been feeling guilty ever since because of having so much and they so little. How can the Afrikaners do this to them? Have you ever seen those places?"

"Plenty of them." His tone was grim. "And the one in Pretoria is a king to most of them, but try saying that to a South African and they'll quickly point out that Harlem and Watts are a damn sight worse."

"But that's different—entirely different," she protested.

"Yes—and no," he replied. Then he said, "Darling, I have to go. I love you." And rang off.

His return, a day late, coincided with another torrential downpour, and it was not until he had dried off and they had dined and installed themselves before a fire in the living room with coffee and brandy before them that she produced the note and handed it to him. He read it with a disgusted look and tossed it on the fire. "So," he said heavily. "Where do we begin? You know I was single for almost nine years before I met you, and, as you also know,

I am a man of hearty appetites, so I'm not sure what any of this is going to prove or do except to upset you further."

Vanessa leaned over and squeezed his hand. "I know all this and I don't relish it any more than you do. I don't want a list of every woman you have taken to bed or even been romantically involved with. I just want to know what I'm dealing with *now*. For instance, let's start with the first item—the 'little friends in Durban.' How about them?"

"Yes, there are a couple of girls down there," he said uncomfortably, "but I swear on anything sacred you care to name that since our marriage there has been no one and there will be no one—"

"And I believe you," she cut in, "and you're going to have to believe me, just as I believe you. Now, are you still seeing them?"

He looked even more uncomfortable. "Yes, but only in the line of business. They do work for us down there."

"And they understand the new situation?"

"Of course."

"Then that's all there is to that." She was trying to be as pragmatic as possible but found it was not all that easy. "Now, what's this about an interrogation room?"

He grimaced. "That's something that seemed like a good idea when it began, but now is a royal pain in the ass. The company decided it would be a good idea to rent a room away from the embassy where we could meet contacts in private and maybe even hide people for a while. Unfortunately, Heitz, being what he is, started to use it for his little extramarital flings, and a lot of the embassy personnel jumped on the bandwagon for theirs as well, so now it's become a bad joke. But I have *never* used it for that. Why should I, when I have a perfectly good house?"

"But not anymore," she said quietly.

He looked at her, his brow furrowed. "I always tried to keep my private life well away from the embassy and did so with one exception, which I may say I have bitterly regretted ever since."

"That exception being your secretary, I suppose."

"Except that she *wasn't* my secretary when it happened, and it was a very short-lived thing. She was Robin's—I inherited her from him."

She looked at him in astonishment. "Dilys was *Robin's* secretary?"

"When she first came out, yes. The one I had at the time had developed a bad alcohol problem, so she was shipped out, and Robin and I shared Dilys. Then Maggie came and somehow she ended up with Robin, and I was stuck with Dilys. But all this is ancient history. If you *have* to know everything—just before you came into my life I was getting it on with two girls: one a South African working for the British embassy, and the other a junior secretary at the French embassy—who just got married herself, by the way. And neither of them knew anything about me or what I really do, so it can't be them. And this latest incident can't be Dilys, either—she is away; I checked. And yet it has to be someone at the embassy who knows a lot. . . ."

They both worried at this in silence. A sudden thought came to Vanessa. "It couldn't possibly be Amanda Drake, could it?"

"Why on earth should you think that?" he asked in amazement, and she related the odd little remarks at Clara's coffee party.

"Amanda tends to be insecure. She has this fixed idea that Robin and I are out to get George, who is the same rank as we are but quite a bit older. It's nonsense, but she keeps this 'mother bird defending her nest' thing up constantly. But . . ." He shook his head. "Catty remarks I can see—she makes them about everybody—but not this. No, Amanda isn't that kind of psychotic bitch."

"We don't seem to be getting very far," she sighed. "The thing is, I'm sure it's not going to stop here. If I don't appear to react to this, whoever is doing it will probably try another tack, and I would like to be prepared. I don't want state secrets, but can't you just tell me what you do, particularly when you go off on these trips? Then perhaps I'll be strong enough to burn these things as they arrive, put them out of my mind, and avoid this unpleasantness for both of us."

"Nobody's been here since I left?" he asked.

She shook her head. "No one. I always check with Ben if I've been out."

"Then I guess it's safe enough to talk." He turned on the stereo and came and sat close by her. "Robin and I work in tandem," he murmured into her ear. "Our job is to keep the black freedom movement active and agitating and to see its leaders don't start looking to the Russians for assistance. That way we keep a prodding finger on the spine of the government here. We supply money and what help we can to the black activists and do a certain amount of orchestrating of strikes, protests, and the like, as well as keeping an eye on what they are planning. Robin mainly deals with the local area, including Jo'burg, which is very important, and particularly with the intellectuals—his cover job gives him entree to those circles. I have more of a roving commission to keep things going in the rest of South Africa, with the exception of Cape Town, where we have another special agent."

"So where does Zecco come in?" she asked.

"Oh, he's quite separate," he said quickly.

"Yes, but what does he do?" she persisted.

"Well, mainly he works with the Afrikaner secret police to prevent subversion by the Angolans in Southwest Africa and to stop the pro-communist Mozambique government from running guns to the dissidents in South Africa."

She looked at him, stupefied. "But surely that's the direct opposite from what you and Robin are doing. That doesn't make any sense! He's working against the black movement and you are working for them!"

"We're all working for the interests of *America*," he retorted grimly. "And you'll just have to take my word for it that we know what we're doing. In any case, he has nothing to do with my activities, which you say are your only interest in all this." His voice had taken on a hard edge and she could feel him tensing up, so she thought it politic to let the subject drop, even though she still could not see the sense of it.

With John home again she was so fully occupied that the day of the proposed tea party with Tom was upon her before she realized it. It was a day of pale sunshine, so she supposed that that meant the party would be on and agonized over what she could take without appearing ostentatious. She settled on a bunch of spring flowers and a small box of chocolates. The only thing John had had to say on the subject had been a warning. "This is quite an honor this Mbeni is offering you, but don't try to reciprocate by asking them back here—not because I don't want them but because you'd embarrass the hell out of them, not to mention our own domestic staff." This left her in even more of a quandary, though during the rehearsal an idea germinated in her mind that she thought might solve the looming problem.

Tom Mbeni was evidently in a state of high excitement and nervousness as they drove back to the township after the rehearsal; he chattered and giggled the whole way, adding to her unease. This time, as they lurched over the dry potholes, there were signs of life in the streets— people sitting on their doorsteps and children playing in the dirt—but when they saw the color of her skin the smiles on their faces vanished and were replaced by expressions of blank hostility. She was mildly thankful as she parked the car in front of his house that his dilapidated neighbor's showed no such signs of life.

He opened the door and almost tripped over a bicycle parked just inside. With a shrill apologetic giggle, he seized it. "Please excuse! My sister did not put it away. We have to keep them inside, you see. So many thieves!" And he wheeled it quickly into a room off to the left.

The small living room was extremely clean and neat and very crowded; every available inch of space was used. In the center stood a Formica-topped table simply loaded with foodstuffs, with three plastic chairs around it. Along one wall was a couch that evidently doubled as a bed and over which were several shelves full of books—many dog-eared with use—and a series of small, native flutes— some wooden, some bamboo, some aluminum—in a neat row. Tom's reemergence coincided with the rattle of the bright beaded curtain in the rear of the living room, which parted to reveal a grave-faced woman visibly older than

Tom and still clad in a gray and white nurse's uniform, who eyed Vanessa with wary reserve as he introduced her proudly. "My sister Monica—Vanessa Bannerman."

Vanessa hastily presented the flowers and chocolates, which the black woman acknowledged, saying, "Thank you. Please be seated, the kettle is almost boiling." And she disappeared again through the curtain.

"I see you have noticed my 'quela,' my pipes," Tom said eagerly. "All these I show you after we have eaten." He had just seated himself but immediately jumped up again. "Oh, I forgot. You, being American, would probably prefer coffee; that I know." He produced a very small jar of instant coffee from his pocket and held it out triumphantly. "See! I must give this to my sister."

"No, please!" Vanessa said a little desperately. "I like tea just as well."

"You're sure?" he said anxiously as Monica Mbeni appeared with a steaming teapot. "It would be no trouble, no trouble at all."

"Quite sure," Vanessa said, her eyes roaming over the enormous array of food, among which she recognized some petits-fours from Pretoria's most expensive bakery. He must have spent a whole week's salary on this, she thought dismally, and tried to force herself to eat some of the things he was pressing upon her with such enthusiasm.

Under the warming influence of the tea and the food, his sister thawed somewhat. On finding out where Vanessa lived, she said surprisingly, "We lived there, too, when we were young. My mother was a cook for a family from the British embassy. The lady there was very good; she used to tutor me. It helped me to get into nursing school. She helped Tom, too. It was a great change for us when our mother got sick and could work no more and we had to come here."

"But you keep this place so beautifully," Vanessa said. "It's really very attractive, and so cozy. It must be annoying for you that your neighbors do not keep their place as well."

Monica froze up. "They kept it well enough until the

police locked him up for something he didn't do. She gave up after that. Now she just sits and waits."

"For him to come back?" Vanessa said, aghast.

"No. To die. He won't be coming back." Monica stood up. "Now, if you will excuse me, I have a program that I must watch." She went into her room and closed the door.

"We have a television," Tom explained proudly. "And my sister always watches one of your programs we have here: *Kojak*—a very fine man, my sister says. You'd like me to play some quela for you?"

"That would be very nice," she said with relief, and sat listening intently to the sweet, sad notes of an African lullaby, punctuated by the scream of car tires and the crackle of gunfire from the adjoining room. She would gladly have gone on listening for the remainder of the visit, but after a little he put it away with an apologetic grin. "That's how I started in music. Mrs. Baum, she came to teach in our school and heard me, and it was she who gave me my real flute and encouraged me to go on. Now, would you like to see something of the township?"

"Perhaps a short tour." She looked at her watch. "I really should be home before my husband gets back from work."

"Of course," he approved. "But let me show you the school and the cemetery."

When they drove to the school, a soccer game was in progress, with a crowd of onlookers. Noticing his sudden hesitation, she said quickly, "Why don't we just go to the cemetery? It is later than I thought," and they drove on. At least within the confines of its walls, she thought, they would be screened from all those hostile eyes. As they walked the dusty path between the rows of graves she felt a mounting sense of sadness; so many of them seemed to be of children, the small mounds marked with tiny wooden crosses. On other graves she noticed broken crockery and various other small household items, also broken, and remarked on this to Tom. He appeared a little embarrassed. "Old superstition." He shrugged, indicating a broken teapot and cup and saucer on the grave adjacent to the more substantial monument to his parents. "Many people here are not Christians. They often leave the favorite things of the dead on their graves so that they may still have the comfort of them."

Vanessa duly admired his parents' grave markers, the plot surrounded by the inevitable neat outline of white-washed stones, and with silent accord they both turned back to the exit. "I will see you back to the road," he stated firmly, and she did not argue.

As they reached the main road she said, "I've so enjoyed this. I've been thinking of giving a little informal party at my house for the whole ensemble after the next concert, and I hope you will bring your sister."

"My sister does not go out much," he said quickly. "But perhaps this time she will come. I shall look forward to it."

He got out of the car, and she started to drive away. There was a rattle of stones against the back of the car, and when she looked in the rearview mirror she saw a small gang of children hurling stones and hooting at her. Tom continued on his way without looking back, his head down, his shoulders hunched.

She decided that a Juilliard-style party would be just the thing with which to launch her entertaining career, to indicate to both John and her domestic staff that the old order had indeed changed and a new state of affairs had arrived. She would make it a very simple beer and wine party, with the cold cuts, cheese, and snacks that were the standards of her youth, unlike the more rarefied feasts of the diplomatic world. She did not intend to invite anyone other than her fellow musicians. She was a little nonplussed to get a firm turndown from Hans Haupman. "No, my dear Vanessa, I never go out to parties, so do not be offended. Life is much simpler that way," he proclaimed.

She was even more nonplussed when John informed her that he'd invited the Wests and they were coming. She could hardly forbid him to invite guests to his own party, but she tried to head them off at the pass by under-playing the whole thing. "It's just a musicians' get-together," she explained to Bobby over the phone. "Just a wine and cheese affair; nothing elaborate."

"That'll be fine," Bobby said airily. "It'll make a nice change."

Vanessa was pleasantly surprised on the night of the party to find a new, gregarious Robin she had never seen before. Far from making her fellow musicians, most of whom were evidently a little awed by their surroundings, uncomfortable, he was the life and soul of the party, putting people at their ease, chatting animatedly away, and getting them into groups with an enthusiasm she had never before witnessed. That everyone, even the solemn Indian bass player, had a good time was in large part due to his efforts, and it was only at the end that Vanessa noticed he had stopped circulating and was deep in conversation with Gerda Baum. Everyone was so glowing in their thanks that she patted herself on the back and began to plan bigger and better things.

Her euphoria was not destined to last long. After the next rehearsal, Gerda Baum signaled for her to stay, and when they were alone in the echoing music room the older woman looked sternly at her and said, "I had not realized until the other night with whom you were connected, and I want to make one thing very clear. What I do or what I may be asked to do is one thing, but I will not have my musicians approached, however good the cause. I hope you will remember that, Vanessa. If you are here for any other purpose than the music, I will ask you to leave."

"But that's all I am here for," Vanessa stammered.

Gerda looked at her searchingly. "I hope so. I certainly hope, for all our sakes, that that is so. Life is difficult enough for most of them as it is."

Chapter 11

It was then that Vanessa began to feel the stirrings of fear. She had been proceeding, like a mounting musical progression, to gain control over her new life, and she had been satisfied with its development; now it seemed to her that the more she knew, the less secure she felt, as if there were hidden forces at work over which she had no control and of which she had little knowledge. She tried to banish this uncomfortable feeling by plunging even more resolutely into the superficialities of her surroundings.

The party season was now in full swing, and she was beginning to feel positively guilty at the number of parties and dinners they had attended without making the least gesture in reply. She had been very firm with Ben and Reba over her first party, but it was evident that they had neither the taste nor the aptitude for anything more elaborate. They would do well enough if directed, but she herself would have to get more skills in order to direct them. To this end she brought her problem to the inner circle at the next coffee party, which was being held at

Bobby's. "Do you know where I could go for cooking classes?" she asked. "Particularly for party cooking. I really could use some help and instruction."

It was Amanda Drake who immediately perked up at this and said warmly, "Why, you don't want to go to that kind of expense and hassle. I'd be more than glad to show you. I love party cooking and party giving! We're having one in a couple of days' time, and I do most of it myself. Why don't you come to my house on the day and learn on the job?"

Vanessa immediately seized on this. "If you're sure it won't be a bother, I'd love to," she said, thinking that this might indeed serve more than one end.

Clara, who had been following the exchange with more attention than she was wont to bestow on her fellow wives, squeaked, "Ooh, lovely! Could I come too, Amanda? I'm not very good at these things either. Not that Grant minds—he *hates* entertaining."

This was no news to any of them, but Amanda was evidently a little put out by the request. "Well, you've got to understand, Clara. I'm not *teaching* cooking; I'm just going to show Vanessa how I do things."

"That's all right with me," the blonde assured her, and so perforce she had to be included.

In her own kitchen Amanda was a different person from the rather dull, sharp-tongued woman of her public image. She positively glowed with confidence and expertise and was a surprisingly good teacher. Things were helped along by the fact that the obviously bored Clara dropped out after the first two sessions, using as an excuse her son's "problem."

"What exactly is his problem?" Vanessa asked Amanda, who was intent on icing a very decorative cake.

Amanda gave an indignant snort. "The kid's eleven years old and is still a bed wetter. Poor kid's just a mass of nerves. He's terrified of his father, and, of course, Clara is such a dimwit that she's as much use to him as a sick headache. Grant's very heavy-handed with both of them. I've seen her with more than one bruise she couldn't hide."

"Surely bed-wetting is easily cured nowadays," Vanessa said.

"*If* the kid gets the right sort of help, but you know Grant! 'Be a man, my son,' et cetera...and Clara just does what Grant tells her," Amanda said with venom. "Kid'll be a basket case before he's a teenager, at this rate. Now my Timmy, when he was four, had a bed-wetting problem when we moved posts, but we cured that in a jiffy...." She went on into a long dissertation about the care and handling of children, which Vanessa quietly tuned out.

After a few of these sessions she felt confident enough to have her first small dinner party at the house, consisting of the Corbys, the Watsons, the Heitzes, and the Wests, all of whom she and John owed, and even John was impressed by the smooth way in which it went off. To Vanessa's surprise, the only sour note of the evening was struck by the Wests: Robin was back to his morose, nervous self, and Bobby was unusually sharp-tongued and aggressive. They were among the first to leave, and instead of the glowing praise that Eleanor, for one, had bestowed on her young hostess, Bobby snapped, "I never put you down for a brownnose, Vanessa. Life is full of surprises. Still, I suppose it's one way to promotion and pay."

It both jolted and hurt her, and John, who had overheard the remark, said when they were once again alone, "I warned you that Bobby was not all sweetness and light. It's nothing to worry or get upset about, you know. She'll be as sweet as sugar next time you meet, you'll see. She just can't bear to see anyone mounting the slightest threat to her beloved Robin or, more important, to his career. So long as you stuck to your own thing you were no contest, but now that you've entered the ring, she sees you as a contender and a threat."

"But that's so childish!" Vanessa exclaimed.

He gathered her in his arms and tipped her face up to his. "Just because we are all so much hoarier in years than you are, my sweet, does not necessarily make us any smarter or wiser—in fact, quite the opposite. You, my love, have strengths already that few of them will ever have, which is *one* of the reasons I love you so much. Now let's forget the damned embassy and everyone in it, and let me show you some of the other reasons I love you." It was an offer she enjoyed too much to refuse.

But the buried fear surfaced again on the very next poker night. This time she was at home and finally got to meet Joe Ferraro, a large, dark, round, and red-faced man who was as bluff and blustery in person as he sounded. She quickly made herself scarce, and the men moved off into the den. She felt disinclined to practice that night, so she drove into the city and took in a movie—*Amadeus*, which she had seen in New York but wanted to see again. She was two thirds of the way through the movie when she remembered with a pang of guilt that she had left the music room windows open to the balmy spring air, so the kittens, now almost full grown, had an escape route to the outside world.

The difference in their respective growth rates had startled her: Tweedledum was now huge, with a beautiful orange plume for a tail that was a constant menace to all lamps and knickknacks. He had been well named, for he was anything but smart, with a tendency to fall backward off the furniture onto his back and with a placid, always amiable disposition. Tweedledee, by contrast, was small, dainty, highly excitable. She had an almost fiendish penchant for mischief and danced rings around her slower-witted, slower-moving brother. John had been warning Vanessa for some time that she should take them to the vets to be fixed "before we have a houseful of incestuous kittens," but she had put this off, since so far Tweedledum had shown no obvious interest in his smaller sister. Over the past couple of days, however, she had noticed Tweedledee rolling and giving provocative little mews every time he came near her. These he had ignored, but that open window might prove an irresistible lure to his more precocious sister. Tomorrow, she promised herself, she'd take Tweedledee to the vet, but tonight she had better get home and see that the worst had not already happened. As Salieri leaned over Mozart on his deathbed she slipped quietly out of her seat and drove home through the wind-swept night.

Going directly to the music room, she was further dismayed to find that the door had blown ajar and, switching on the light, was greeted by Tweedledum, who roused himself from his favorite perch on the stereo with a huge yawn and came purring to greet her. Of Tweedledee there was no sign.

With a sinking heart she began a frantic search of all the favorite hiding places throughout the house, with no result. She went out into the back yard and called the cat, rustling a box of kitty treats that normally was a certain lure to bring them out of hiding. Then she noticed that the French windows of the den also stood ajar, though the curtains inside were closely drawn; had the gregarious Tweedledee slipped in and joined the poker players? She went quietly over to the window and stood listening to the usual rumble of voices. "I'll see you and raise you ten." "I fold." "I'll see you." "Full house, aces over tens." "Damn, that beats me, eights over twos." This last was John's voice. "John," she called. "One of the cats got out. Is she in there with you, by any chance?"

The voice continued unheeding, and she could hear the click of poker chips. "Your deal, Robin." "Get me a refill, will you, Grant?" She began to feel a little annoyed; the least John could do was answer her! "John!" She pushed open the window and stepped inside, pulling the curtains apart, and stopped, transfixed. Tweedledee sat in the middle of the poker table, batting with a neat paw the multicolored chips one by one onto the floor; otherwise, the room was completely empty. The only other sign of movement was the slowly turning tape on the tapedeck that stood on John's desk, from which the voices droned inexorably on. She stood dry-mouthed, her heart pounding with anxiety. Where were they? What was this all about? What should she do?

Tweedledee tired of her private game and came over to her, purring invitingly. She picked the cat up and started to stroke her absentmindedly, her thoughts churning. She reclosed the curtains, leaving the door as it had been, and took Tweedledee upstairs to join her brother. Then she returned to the den and sat down, looking vacantly at the littered table. Was this always the way of it, or was there something special in the wind? Suddenly she was seized with panic that the curtains would open and they would discover her like this. She knelt quickly and gathered the scattered chips off the floor, putting them back on the table and hoping the men, when—or if—they returned, would put the disarray down to the rising wind that was now sending the curtains billowing into the room. The voices unnerved her as they continued their ghostly conversation, and she fled upstairs, trying to shut out the sudden fear. She went to bed but could not sleep; she lay staring up into the darkness wide-eyed, wondering and worrying. A small eternity later she heard footsteps on the stairs and, as they reached the door, sat up and snapped on the light, her heart pounding. She felt weak with relief when John, in his shirtsleeves and with his hair more than usually tousled, came in looking surprised. "Hello, there! Sorry, did I wake you up?" He looked more closely at her strained face. "Is something the matter? You look upset."

She gulped and stretched out her hands to him. "Yes, I am. Where were you all tonight?"

He stood looking at her steadily. "You went into the den," he stated in a flat voice.

"Tweedledee got out. I was hunting for her. . . ." She found herself gabbling out explanations like a guilty child.

"So you found out one of our little tricks. I'm sorry if it upset you, but I *did* ask you never to come in," he said.

"Is that always the way of it?" she whispered.

He made a brushing-away gesture with his hand. "No—most of the time we are there. This time, knowing the room was bugged, we thought it was a good opportunity to take advantage of it."

"But how—" she exploded.

"Oh, the other day when you were at a concert a 'termite inspector' called. When I checked afterward, I found the bug he had planted by the window and decided to leave it for the moment to suit my own purposes."

She nerved herself to say, "John, I find all this very hard to handle. I was so terrified for you tonight. If only I were more involved, if only I knew more. Can't I help? Can't I be in on some of this, so that at least I'll know what *not* to worry about? After all, it's evident that Bobby knows what Robin does, so why can't I?"

"No!" He was adamant. "What the Wests do is their business. I will *not* have you involved. If it's my safety you're worried about, *don't*. I'm not in any danger, and I'm well equipped and trained to handle any risks there may be. You are *not*. Let's not fight about this, because, as I've said before, the less you know, the better it is for both of us."

He would not even discuss it further and so, perforce, she had to let it go, but from that night on she was always anxious, always felt a vague knot of worry in the pit of her stomach when he was not literally by her side. Other undercover wives had to deal with this situation, she reflected, and she determined to sound them out on how they did so.

Her first opportunity arose at her next learning session with Amanda, and she waited until her self-appointed teacher was at her most relaxed, putting the finishing touches on a succulent-looking platter of hors d'oeuvres. "I wonder if I could ask your advice on something," she stated, knowing this was a sure way to grab Amanda's attention.

"Why, surely, dear." Amanda glanced up briefly. "What about?"

"I find I worry a lot about John's job. I know it's not quite the same as George's—at least, not here—but you must have been in situations in the past like we are in now. How did you handle it?"

Amanda looked up again, a slight frown on her plump-ish face. "George has never allowed what he does to intrude into our family life," she said stiffly. "He shoulders his own burdens, and I wouldn't want it any other way. I have enough of my own, keeping up our home and dealing with our family. That's *my* job. You ought to be firm with John so that he doesn't burden you."

"Oh, but he doesn't!" Vanessa protested, feeling guilty. "It's just knowing how secret and devious everything is, I still can't help worrying about him.

"Then don't think about it." Amanda's tone was sharp. "I don't. I put it out of my mind and get on with my job, and that's that."

Vanessa reflected as she drove home that if she had stopped to think about it beforehand she could have deduced all that for herself. She was certain now that underneath, Amanda was as confused and uneasy as she was but had succeeded in keeping her fears at bay by the endless domestic minutiae that constituted her life: the spotless house, the pampered children, the almost compulsive straining after perfection in all aspects of her daily routine. But that particular solution, she also realized, was not for her.

An unexpected opportunity to pose her question to the most senior member of the group, Eleanor, came on the day of the long-threatened Red Cross benefit, which was being held on the grounds of the ambassador's residence. She had been designated as Eleanor's assistant in the booth selling boxes of doughnuts (made by embassy wives with varying degrees of expertise) to unwary diplomats at highly inflated prices "for the cause." It was a beautifully sunny early summer day, and the gay red and white striped booths scattered about the emerald lawn gave a festive and informal air to the occasion. Eleanor was evidently in an amiable, relaxed mood also, for she sang softly to herself as they piled their wares on the counter and the benches behind it in the sweet, yeasty-smelling confines of the tent.

Vanessa used the same approach as she had with Amanda but this time added, "You've had so much experience. Would you mind telling me how you handle all the stress?"

Eleanor looked at her appraisingly, a grim smile on her firm mouth. "Once upon a time in the long, long ago, yes, I remember feeling as you say you are feeling now, and I'm sorry for you, I really am, but everyone has different problems and different solutions to those problems, and

I am not sure that I can be of any help to you with yours. All I can say is that in my own case, I am sorry I ever lost a wink of sleep or a moment of happiness thinking about Armand's job or, for that matter, Armand. Neither of them was worth it. To paraphrase Rhett Butler, frankly, I don't give a damn about either of them anymore. It was only when I came to that conclusion that I finally managed to find some happiness for myself. Is that frank enough for you?"

"Oh, Eleanor, I'm so sorry—" Vanessa stammered.

"Don't be!" Eleanor cut in. "I'm no longer sorry for myself. Perhaps the best bit of advice I can give you is to put a guard upon your heart and keep something of yourself for yourself. That way you may avoid some of the bitterness...."

A new voice interrupted them. "Hello, Mother, I'm back! Just dropped by to say hi." And Vanessa looked up to see a handsome, dark-haired girl eyeing her curiously. Eleanor's face lighted up. "Why, Betty! How lovely! I didn't think you'd get home for another week." She turned animatedly to Vanessa. "Betty has been visiting her brother back in the States, so you two haven't met. Betty, this is John Bannerman's bride, Vanessa."

Betty leaned over the stall and extended a languid hand. "So I heard—surprise, surprise!" she drawled. "Welcome to nothingsville, Vanessa." Her eyes were mocking.

As Vanessa took her hand, she recognized the heavy aroma of the perfume that Betty was wearing: it was Arpege.

Chapter 12

When, *shortly thereafter, John proposed that they* take a short trip together, she had to fight down the disloyal thought that the offer had not been unaffected by the return of Betty Heitz, or rather Betty Newman, as she preferred to be called. They had been to several parties that the Heitz family had also attended, and to see Armand and Betty, who so closely resembled each other, working in tandem was a real eye-opener. While he cut out the wives, she zeroed in on the husbands, and if it hadn't been so obvious and sickening it could have had its amusing side.

Not that Vanessa was at all amused when it happened to her, nor had John looked overjoyed when Armand had swept her off to the dance floor leaving him with the eager-eyed Betty. Armand danced uncomfortably close, breathing standard romantic cliches into her ear: how exciting she was, how attractive, how young. . . . She tried to keep a smile on her face, but her lack of response must have galled him, for suddenly he took her hand and guided it to his crotch, pressing it against the black cloth of his tuxedo so that she could feel the hard, rigid column of his erection. This was too much for Vanessa. She tore her hand away and stopped dead in the middle of the dance floor. "I really do not appreciate that, *Mr.* Heitz," she said with quiet venom. "In fact, I find you very pathetic." And she stalked off. She was so angry that she didn't much care about the consequences of upsetting her husband's boss, and she hoped that John would feel the same way.

The offer of the trip was timely, even if John had qualified it by saying, "I'm afraid I will have to do some business on the side, but you won't mind that, will you?" She had begun to feel increasingly claustrophobic tied into the closed circle of embassy life, with but few outside contacts. The only nonofficial South Africans she ever met were in connection with her music, and even there, since her confrontation with Gerda, she had felt hesitant about trying to better her acquaintance with any of them. Occasionally she still drove Tom home, and he was always warmly appreciative, but there had never been any further offer of hospitality, and she was quietly relieved at that. Recently he had been even quieter than usual in the group, and she felt he was worried about something; but, aware of Gerda's vigilant eye on her, she did not dare to pry.

"We might do some Christmas shopping while we're in Durban." John grinned at her as they set off in the Alfa Romeo under the blazing sun. "Got any ideas, my lady love?"

"I can't think of a thing I either want or need," she confessed, luxuriating in the warmth and the feeling his physical closeness always brought her. "Surprise me."

"I'm always trying to do that," he returned lightly.

"We ought to get something special for Mother," she went on, for she had recently received a jubilant letter from Larchmont with the news that Mr. Cross had been brought to a satisfactory boil and that her mother was planning to remarry "very quietly" just after Christmas. "No doubt Mr. Cross, who is a thrifty man, wants her for a tax deduction this year," Vanessa had commented dryly, but she was delighted nonetheless for her mother's sake, and also partly because it allayed her own sense of guilt at being so far away and so happy.

"How about a real live ostrich?" John said. "We're going to ostrich farm country. Now *that* would be a real conversation piece for her Larchmont neighbors!"

She punched him fondly on the arm. "I was thinking of something really nice in topaz or amethyst. I don't think a diamond would be appropriate; it might put Mr. Cross to shame."

"In that case we're heading in the wrong direction," John said. "All the good stuff like that comes from Southwest Africa, and the further away you get from there the more the price goes up. We'd better stick with our friendly neighborhood jeweler in Pretoria."

"Doesn't Grant often go to the Southwest?" she asked.

His face tightened. "I'd just as soon not ask any favors of him. He's becoming even more difficult than usual. Privately, I think the bastard is going off his rocker."

"Oh, dear!" she said faintly. On her own quest for information she had recently had a very revealing talk with Clara, who had started to drop in on her occasionally for a cup of coffee and a chat. Vanessa had gotten the impression that for all her bubbly good humor Clara was, in fact, rather lonely, as the other wives evidently had little time for her, and Grant's obsession about not having outside people in their home precluded her reaching out to a wider circle.

Vanessa had posed her usual question to the big blonde and had been astonished at her reply. "Worry about Grant?" Clara had said wonderingly, and then she had chuckled. "I can tell you've never lived in Las Vegas. If you think what our husbands do is dangerous, you should see what goes on there for a spell. Compared to some of the guys I used to pal around with, Grant's a pussycat. I don't know how dangerous his job here is, nor do I want to, but so far as I can see it's not half as rough or as violent as what goes on in Nevada. Those babies are *tough*."

"So you don't worry at all?" Vanessa asked.

Clara's face had suddenly taken on a pinched, haunted look. "Not about that, no. Grant's a good provider, and he's well insured even if something did happen. . . ." She had stopped then and bitten her lip as if she had said too much, then added, "No, I don't worry about things like that."

In this case Vanessa was prepared to believe it. Clara undoubtedly had worries, but they were not connected with the hidden machinations of the CIA, and her own sympathy for the fading showgirl grew. She also realized that she herself had come full circle with little result: the only one of the wives close to her left untapped was Bobby, and in her Vanessa hesitated to confide. Not that Bobby was at all unfriendly; as John had predicted, on their next meeting after the dinner party she had been as affable as ever. But Vanessa was nevertheless reluctant to give her any inkling of her own vulnerability. Besides, she knew how Bobby resolved her problem: she *was* involved in Robin's work, and that particular door John had closed for her.

"Will you be gone long on business?" she asked casually as they sped eastward toward the coast.

"No, just an hour or two here and there. In Durban you'll find plenty to amuse yourself with in my absence. In Mafeking and Ladysmith you can bone up on the Boer war, and in Bloemfontein—well, there you may just have to admire the flowers." He grinned.

She was amazed and delighted by the difference in atmosphere in Durban. In English-speaking Natal there was none of the surliness and suspicion that inevitably greeted the English-speaker in Pretoria, and it was as if the sparkling Indian Ocean that rolled lazily against the wide, white sandy beaches lent some of its own sparkle to the spirits of the inhabitants. Even the blacks—from the grotesquely garbed "Zulu warrior" rickshaw pullers who catered to the tourists to the ordinary black worker— seemed more relaxed and amiable. She scarcely minded at all when John left her to her own devices, and she would stroll contentedly along the wide promenade or gaze with fascination into the enormous tank tower of the Durban aquarium that housed everything from the tiniest brilliant-colored reef fish to the enormous sand shark that basked unopposed in its domain at the bottom of the tank.

Only one little untoward incident shook her. She had strolled over to the fun fair on the front, with its small Ferris wheel, to watch the children as they screamed their enjoyment on the various rides, when suddenly a vision of Coney Island and its amusement park—and herself with a crowd of Juilliard friends whooping it up—super-imposed itself on the image in her mind, and she was swept by an overwhelming wave of homesickness and longing. The vision vanished and she came to, gripping the edge of the stone parapet desperately. Damn! she thought savagely. Stop this nonsense at once! This is ridic-ulous; you are perfectly happy, perfectly content. But it disturbed her, and only John's return to her side served to banish it to the hidden recesses of her mind.

They drove out into the rolling and beautiful Natal countryside, inspected ostrich farms, dallied on sunstruck beaches, and danced under the stars in one of the open-air nightclubs—and in each other's arms they reaffirmed their love.

This idyll was ended on the sixth day of their stay. John had been summoned from the breakfast table for a phone call, and when he returned, his face was tight with anger. "All hell's broken loose," he said. "Peter Luluba's body was found on a Jo'burg dump this morning. He had been badly beaten, then shot in the back of the head. They are expecting black uprisings in the townships. You're going to have to go back to Pretoria by yourself. I'll get a consulate driver from the Consul-general here to take you back in an official car, and then I'll have to get busy. I don't know when I'll be back."

She looked at him in shock, miserably aware of her own ignorance. "I don't even know who Peter Luluba is," she confessed. "Why is he so important?"

"After Bishop Tutu, Peter is—was—the most impor-tant and most vocal of the blacks fighting for an end to apartheid. A damn sight more moderate and reasonable than most of them, too, *and* pro-West, which is more than you can say of many of them."

"Can't I come with you?" she pleaded.

He shook his head. "Whoever did this has upset the apple cart in a big way, and things may get very nasty from now on. There's going to be violence, that's for sure, and I don't want you near any of it. And that's final."

On the long, dreary drive back she listened to the news broadcasts—a thing she usually didn't do—on the car radio. Even though the official news releases were guarded and low-key, there was no disguising the fact that violence was erupting on a wide scale. Riot police were in action in all the Johannesburg townships; there had been violence in Cape Town, Port Elizabeth, and Bloemfontein, and there had even been a protest march in the Pretoria township, where tear gas had been used to disperse the crowd.

As she let herself into her darkened home in the early hours of the morning, her spirits at a very low ebb, she found herself worrying about Tom Mbeni, and she resolved to get in touch with Gerda first thing in the morning to see if there was anything she could do.

Her good intentions were thwarted when call after call to Gerda's house went unanswered. Throughout the long day she continued to listen to the news broadcasts, the tenor of which gradually changed. The violence was under control, though there had been some casualties on both sides, numbers unspecified. A full inquiry into the murder of Peter Luluba was being instituted by the government, the announcer intoned, but early indications were that it might have been the work of "foreign agents anxious to stir up trouble among the people of South Africa." What did that mean? Could that mean *us*? she wondered uneasily, and was more worried than ever about where John was and what he was doing.

Two days later, when the body of Peter Luluba was buried with great pomp and circumstance and to the counterpoint of fresh violence in the townships, she had still had no word from John and had also been unable to contact Gerda. Desperate for the sound of a friendly voice, she finally took up the phone to call Bobby West, only to find there was no answer there, either. It was as if her entire world had ceased to be, she thought drearily, and she returned to her lonely vigil.

When things did start to happen, they happened all at once: a call from John to say there had been some trouble and he would not be back for another week, a call from Gerda to say that Monica Mbeni had been arrested and spirited away by the secret police and that Tom had come to seek her help in finding his sister, and a call from Bobby West to ask her over "on a rather urgent matter."

Heartsick about Tom's news, she had put Bobby off and gone rushing over to Gerda's, to find a wild-eyed Tom pacing the floor like a caged animal. "Was she arrested during the protest?" she asked the troubled Gerda.

Tom answered her, his voice vibrant with anger. "No, it was before that. The night of Luluba's murder. They came and took her out of the hospital—'for questioning,' they said. When she didn't come home that night, I went to find her. The hospital people knew nothing; the local police post knew nothing. *Nobody* knew anything. I have been everywhere and I can find out nothing. I need help. I *must* find her."

Vanessa looked at the old woman, who was silent and withdrawn. "What can be done?" she asked.

Gerda shrugged. "At this point, I don't know. I've tried all my contacts, without any result. Perhaps your husband could find out for Tom from *his* contacts, or from one of his colleagues. Would you be willing to ask him?" She stared steadily at Vanessa.

"I don't even know where John is," Vanessa confessed, "but of course I'd be willing to do anything to help. I'll do my best. May I use your phone?" She called the Wests and said she'd be right over, then she tried to comfort the hopeless-eyed Tom. Her well-meant efforts met with little success, for he stared at her stonily and merely repeated, "I must find her."

At the Wests' she was greeted at the door by an anxious-eyed Bobby, who ushered her into Robin's study where the inevitable stereo was playing at loud volume. Robin sat behind his desk, an expression of deep dejection on his mobile face. "We are in one hell of a *spot*," Bobby hissed in her ear. "And since I've heard through the grapevine you wouldn't mind getting into the action, now is the time. What news have you had from John?"

"Very little," Vanessa admitted. "I don't know where he is or even when he'll be back. But before we get into this, there's something I have to ask Robin. Would you be able to find out where a person who has been arrested by the secret police has been taken and what is happening to her?"

Robin roused himself. "Possibly. Anyone in particular?"

"Yes, a Monica Mbeni. She's a nurse at the black hospital. She was apparently taken away the night Luluba was killed, and her brother's half frantic with worry. He's gotten nowhere with the authorities."

Robin's gloom increased. "Another one of mine," he sighed, looking at his wife. "Well, I'll see what I can do."

"The thing is, Vanessa," Bobby broke in anxiously, "that we're afraid we've got a pro-government mole somewhere in our own operation. As if Luluba's death weren't bad enough, there's been a spate of arrests following the protests in the townships, and we don't think it's any accident that these have included *all* Robin's and John's contacts in the Jo'burg area. Their entire network has been wiped out overnight. It'll mean starting from scratch again to build up links to the black nationalist leaders, and that's where you could be of great help to us. You, we know, can be trusted, because there is no way you could have been involved in this debacle. How about it?"

Vanessa's feelings were compounded equally of excitement and fear. "But what could I do?" she stammered.

Bobby nodded briskly at Robin. "You tell her," she commanded.

He cleared his throat awkwardly. "We'd like you to extend your musical activities to Jo'burg. There are several mixed ensembles along the lines of Gerda's there, and it'll all be arranged for you to get into them. If the driving is going to bother you, I can arrange for that, too. Once in, I want you to approach the blacks in the groups, very much on a cash-and-carry basis. We need a new group of couriers between us and the nationalists. I don't think you'll have any trouble recruiting. Once recruited, it'll be your job to act as go-between. You'll be carrying money to them and bringing information back. You'll be given the details after the contacts are set up. Would you be willing to take this on?"

She was silent for a moment, thinking about it. She had wanted in on the action, and now she was being given the opportunity with a vengeance. She only wished she knew how John would react to it. Finally, she said quietly, "I'll do it, but on one condition. I'll do it if you find out Monica Mbeni's whereabouts and get her out of any trouble she is in. Is it a deal?"

Robin looked at her with grudging admiration in his dark eyes. "It's a deal," he said after a pause. "When can you start?"

"How about right after you find her?" Vanessa said grimly. "Then I'll be ready and willing. How able I'll be remains to be seen."

Chapter 13

*S*he had heard the term "towering rage" but had never believed in its literal truth until John returned and she told him what she had done. Tower over her he most certainly did, and there was no doubt about the rage—if his own physical shape had been better, she was certain he would have hit her. As it was, he had returned minus the Alfa Romeo, with his left arm in a sling, and with the remnants of two black eyes spreading like a yellow-green mask across the upper half of his face. His story about a slight accident in the car she took with a large grain of salt.

When she told him, his eyes flashed vivid blue through the mottled mask. "You did *what*?" he yelled. "You had no right; Robin had no right...." And the battle was joined.

It was bitter, and they both said things that rankled and hurt long after the rage had passed, but while it left her exhausted and sickened, she stuck to her guns. Robin had kept his end of the bargain; now she was determined to keep hers.

How he had done it she had no idea, and all she knew

of it was secondhand through Gerda. Monica Mbeni was home again, dazed and broken, for her interrogators had been unmercifully thorough. She had lost her job at the hospital, and her stony-faced brother had told Gerda he was dropping out of the ensemble because he would have to find another job to make up for that and to pay for his sister's care; he would not be back.

"Oh, God, what a mess!" Vanessa said drearily. "But I swear to you, Gerda, I had no hand in recruiting her. I had no idea that she had even been recruited...."

"I believe you," the older woman sighed. "For whatever that is worth. But the damage has been done all the same. It's no more your fault than it is anybody's with our color skin in this whole damnable situation."

"I think perhaps it would be better if I, too, withdrew from the group," Vanessa said, trying not to look guilty.

Gerda did not look at her. "Yes, perhaps so. I heard you were going to a group in Jo'burg, and probably it is better so."

"I shall miss you all." Vanessa felt miserable.

This time Gerda did look at her. "We'll miss you, too, and I urge you to be careful. I don't know how West did it—I don't want to know—but if he has recruited you now, be sure of what you are getting into. The Jo'burg blacks tend to be a lot more sophisticated and streetwise than the ones here, and they know what they are doing. Watch out for yourself at all times."

It did nothing to lift her spirits, and only her own pride and John's opposition kept her firm in her determination. Robin's powers of persuasion were evidently more effective on John than her own, because he had returned from his confrontation with Robin in a much more subdued and amenable frame of mind. "I never wanted this, but it's your choice," he said, a hard edge on his voice. "And I don't want to know about it or hear about it. Just remember, you don't *have* to do any of this."

"I'm not competing with you, John," she said tartly. "We're both on the same side, remember? I'm only doing it to help, just like Bobby."

"And that probably accounts for the great shape Robin is in," he sneered, but they left it at that.

Relations remained strained up to the summer solstice and Christmas, when he surprised her with a brand-new car—a glittering Ford Escort. "Can't have you breaking down in that old heap of yours on the Jo'burg road," he said, with a brief return of his former jaunty self.

Though she pretended surprised delight, she was secretly dismayed. She had felt so anonymous and safe in her battered Volkswagen, particularly since she was now driving to areas where a new car stuck out like a beacon. But on this she could not disappoint him, and she tried not to feel badly when the faithful little Beetle was collected by a hard-eyed used-car dealer.

What mainly dismayed her in her new life was the slow rate of progress, which disturbed her but did not appear to faze Robin. Any guilt feelings she had had were soon allayed by the blacks she encountered in the groups, who tended to be hard of eye and abrasive in character, and as different from the gentle Tom as it was possible to be. When she made her first approach she was literally sweating with fear, but she was surprised by how easily it went off. She had picked as her target a rather vocal young violist who worked as a clerk in the Oppenheim conglomerate. He was quick on the uptake—and the take.

"How much?" he demanded as soon as she had stated her case. She followed Robin's instructions and named a figure far below what they expected to pay, then allowed him to bargain her up almost to the higher figure. "Okay," he had said laconically. "I'm in. But if they get to me, don't expect any heroics. I'll spill my guts."

It was easier after that, but the small size of the ensembles meant she had limited opportunities and so, perforce, had frequently to change groups. This unsettled her and had a devastating effect on her playing, which did not go unnoticed.

"What has happened to you, my dear?" Hans Haupman fussed. "Your playing is going backward. Where is the verve, the soul? Your technique now is much better, but the rest you have lost. Zis is terrible!"

"Maybe I just need a break," she said wearily.

"Maybe you need a new teacher," he said gloomily. "Maybe I am no good for you."

"No." She was firm. "I don't want a new teacher. I'm just going through a bad patch." He was all she had left from her bright beginnings in a new land, and she did not want to lose him.

The opportunity for a break came from an unexpected quarter. For some obscure financial reason, her mother's nuptials to Mr. Cross had been postponed until Easter, and her mother had written rather pathetically that if it was at all possible, she would like Vanessa to come home for the event. She even volunteered to pay the fare, which signaled to her daughter that she really did need her there. After consultation with John, she wrote back, eschewing the fare offer but saying she would come for a ten-day stay, most of which would coincide with one of John's projected business trips. She found herself looking forward to it with an enthusiasm she would not have dreamed possible a few months before.

But before she could take wing, another ugly shadow reached out again and touched her life. It was a Saturday, and they had risen late and dawdled over breakfast on the patio until Ben had brought in the small bundle of mail. She had only one letter, an invitation to a party for musicians from the leader of one of her groups, and she was debating whether it would be worth the effort of an extra trip to Jo'burg when John let out an angry exclamation. She looked up as he tossed a letter toward her, an expression of disgust on his face. "Our long-silent friend again."

She took up the typewritten, unsigned single sheet. It read, "So now it's your turn, Dandy Jack. Like mistress, like maid. They do say blacks are better in bed. So it's follow-the-leader for little Miss Music now all the way to Jo'burg. She's a quick study. Lucky they've got a doctor on hand for any little 'accidents,' isn't it? Serves you right for cradle-robbing!"

She read it through several times in deepening puzzlement. "But this is quite insane. I don't even understand it! What's this about 'like mistress, like maid'? And a doctor?"

John snorted angrily. "There's no reason you should know. I'd have said Eleanor has been as discreet as it is possible for anyone to be."

"Eleanor?" she gasped.

He nodded. "Robin passed it on to me some time ago, but there was no security involved, and we both figured it was none of our business. Armand had it coming, anyway."

"I still don't understand," she faltered.

"Eleanor's been having an affair with a black doctor in Johannesburg. They appear to have gotten together over this 'Buns for Bantu babies' setup she's involved in. Twice a week she goes over there for this soup kitchen—cum—clinic for the poorer blacks. He runs the free clinic. A really great guy—cream of the crop. Works himself into the ground for his people and is totally politically uninvolved, though everyone has had a go at him, including me."

"But how do you know for sure they're not just friends?" she queried.

"I do know. She has stayed overnight in his house too many times—when Armand was away, of course. The doctor is a widower and lives alone."

The full implications of the letter finally sank in. "And I'm supposed to . . ." She couldn't finish. "Oh, this is worse than sick! Isn't there any way we can stop this? Isn't there any way you can find out? It *has* to be someone within your group. Someone who knows about Eleanor, knows where I go. Can't you test it for fingerprints or find the typewriter it's written on or something like that? For all we know, this poison pen might be at work on everyone else, too; for all we know, he may be so unbalanced he could be the mole Bobby was talking about who blew the whistle on your people."

He took the letter back and sat staring gloomily at it. "Easier said than done. I'm no detective, and chances are the typewriter would not be the poison pen's, nor would there be any fingerprints. And it's not exactly the sort of thing that one would take to an Afrikaner police lab, is it? And you say 'he,' but it is even more likely to be a 'she'—in the main, poison pens are women."

"Well, we've got to do something," she said desperately. "Can't you get together with someone you trust and make a quiet investigation on your own? I mean, if what Bobby says is true, there has to be one going on right now."

"And whom would you suggest that I trust?" He looked at her with an even stare. "Dirty tricks are part of our normal business, and they aren't always played on the bad guys, you know."

She looked at him in horror. "You think *Robin* might be involved in this?"

He looked down. "Not consciously, no, but what he knows, Bobby knows, and I wouldn't put it past her to keep the pot stirred to keep us off balance."

"But that makes no sense at all!" she cried. "Why should she shoot down Robin's operation?"

"You are presuming that these two things are linked. They are probably *totally* unrelated," he returned. "I've got my own ideas about what happened after Luluba's murder, and about his murder as well. Ideas I can't prove, but I'm sure I'm on the right track, and this sort of thing"— he tapped the letter—"wouldn't be his style at all. He doesn't have that sort of mind."

"Who?" she whispered.

"Grant. But as I say, up to now I've no proof, so you haven't heard what I just said. I think Grant has snapped, and if I can get this across to Armand, I might be able to get him out of here before he does any more damage."

It left her more confused than ever. She still could not bring herself to believe Bobby was behind the poison pen. John's own prejudice against his friend's wife blinded him to the fact that, domineering and self-seeking as she probably was, Bobby was not sick-minded—and the writer of the letters was. But then, she couldn't believe the sadistic Grant had written them, either; his sickness was evident enough, but it was not of the right sort. She could see him pounding an enemy to a pulp in a dark alley, or even terrorizing his family, but not writing those letters.

When her plane lifted off from Johannesburg Airport, she determined to put all these worries behind her and to relax and have a good time on her visit to the States. To this end she took a sleeping pill after they had made their refueling stop in West Africa, and she slept soundly across the vastness of the Atlantic, arriving at JFK Airport fresh as a daisy and raring to go. She was as delighted to see her mother as her mother was to see her, and they chattered away throughout the traffic-jammed journey back to Larchmont as if they had been separated ten years rather than ten months.

This euphoria lasted through the day and the dinner hosted by the smug-looking Mr. Cross, who coyly urged her to "call me Bob." Neighbors who dropped in to greet the prodigal exclaimed on her chic hairstyle and clothes, on how well she was looking, how slim she was, and how thrilling it must be to live abroad. It was all very predictable and soothing.

It was only after she went to bed in her old room, still hung with music festival posters and the framed minor triumphs of her youth, that its familiar ambience suddenly stifled her, and she found herself lying wide awake, staring at the ceiling and thinking of South Africa, which already was assuming the quality of an insubstantial dream. Eleven months ago she had lain awake like this, torn between anger at her mother and Sam and excitement at the thought of her first venture abroad, and now. . . . So much had happened that she felt she had lived and aged as many years as the months that had gone by since she had left this room. She was no longer the starry-eyed, naive, and impractical student; she was someone completely different. The only trouble was, she was not sure who that someone had become. A sudden wave of longing for John's voice, for his arms about her, swept over her. The need for him became so great that she almost crept downstairs to the phone to call, until a little mental arithmetic told her it was now past noon in South Africa and he would still be at work. "Stop it," she told herself firmly. "You're on vacation. You're going to enjoy yourself and forget

South Africa. Go to sleep." Her tired body finally obeyed her last command.

In the days that followed, although both she and her mother were on their best behavior, old patterns quickly began to develop and they started bickering about minor matters. She had become so used to the life of ease that she found the everyday realities of American life irritating and restricting, and her mother's obsession with them—which put her forcibly in mind of Amanda Drake—precluded any serious conversation. She had come back with the firm resolve to tell her mother about John's real job and her own involvement, but as they rushed around fussing about flowers for the wedding, rehearsals at the church, and the endless minutiae that go into even a simple American wedding, her resolution faltered and dimmed. She was convinced that if she said, "Mother, I didn't marry a diplomat; I married a spy, and I am now recruiting spies myself," her mother would smile vaguely and reply, "How nice, dear. Did you get back to the caterers about the cake?"

It was arranged that after the wedding and the departure of the newlyweds on their honeymoon (the predictable Mr. Cross was taking his bride to Niagara Falls), she would return to the house and see it shut up and things shut off before taking off herself the following afternoon. On the eve of the wedding her mother seemed in an unusually pensive mood, and Vanessa said, half joking, "Not getting cold feet about taking the plunge, are you, Mother? Too late now, you know."

Her mother looked at her seriously. "No, dear," she said quietly. "I know enough not to expect too much, and life with Bob, whatever its limitations, is better than loneliness. I think we'll be happy enough—at least, I hope so."

Vanessa was taken aback. "You aren't in love with him?" was all she could think of saying.

"I'm very fond of Bob, as he is of me, and we've a lot of interests n common," her mother replied. "Maybe that's better than love: it brings less hurt."

So it was with decidedly mixed feelings that she watched

her mother walk down the aisle the next day on the arm
of the family doctor who had brought her into the world.
I hope she's right, she thought, watching them plight eter-
nal troth, but she could not begin to imagine what it would
be like to marry someone you didn't love. She loved
John—that was one thing she was certain about—and as
long as he loved her that was all that really mattered.

Returning to the empty house after the reception and
automatically going about the closing-down process, she
felt a growing sense of withdrawal: her life was not here;
she no longer belonged here.

This feeling was reinforced the next day when, in order
to kill the hours before the plane left, she dropped in at
Juilliard. It was Easter recess, but there were still a few
people about—none of whom she recognized—and as
she walked through the familiar halls and studied the
crammed bulletin boards she felt like a visitor from outer
space peering at an unknown world. She no longer
belonged here, either.

Her heart lifted with the plane as it took off into a
clouded sky. She was going home—not to poison pens
or furtive exchanges in darkened hallways with wary
strangers or paranoid spies or meaningless parties with
unhappy women—she was going home to John. She could
hardly wait to see his smile as she came through the barrier or to feel his arms around her.

It was good to be going home.

Chapter 14

*J*ohn wasn't at the barrier; he wasn't even at the airport. As she searched the crowd with growing anxiety
and disbelief a voice said in her ear, "Hello there, Vanessa.
Had a good trip?" and she swung around to see Robin.
Her first reaction was one of terror. "Something's happened to John!" she gasped, "Oh, Robin, what is it?"

His eyebrows arched upward in surprise. "No, he's
fine. I was coming into Jo'burg anyway, so I offered to
pick you up. Thought it would be a good opportunity to
have a chat about ongoing plans as I drove you home."

"Oh, I see," she said flatly, her terror replaced by an
overwhelming sense of anticlimax and disappointment.
"Well, my luggage is all here, so I won't hold you up."

Robin gave her a quick sideways glance, his sensitive
features registering uncertainty. "That's an awful trip, isn't
it? You must be dog-tired."

"Oh, no, I'm fine," she said tartly. "I'm one of the
lucky ones who can sleep on planes. Shall we go?"

They drove in silence until free of Johannesburg and
its suburbs, Robin driving, as always, with nervous con-

centration, but when the traffic had lightened and the flat veldt road stretched arrow-straight ahead, he relaxed a little and began to talk. He was treading very carefully, but the gist of his talk was that now that she had recruited a certain number of couriers, he wanted to change her role. "I'd like you to accept all invitations to musical parties that you get, and for both of you. The winter season is about to swing into action in Jo'burg, and that's always a good party time. The thing is that word gets around quickly among the blacks, and it wouldn't be beyond our Russian and Cuban friends to try to slip some of their people onto our payroll. It's a continuing problem, and one you're not equipped to deal with, but John is. So far, I think the ones you've brought in are straight enough, but now that the operation is spreading, the danger is going to get proportionally greater. John can take over the actual recruiting from now on, but I'd like you to continue as contact with your group so far as payoffs and exchanges of info go. John may want you to do the same for his, but that's up to him."

"Orders received and understood," she said laconically.

His hands gripped the wheel in a nervous spasm. "They're not orders," he said, an irritated edge on his voice. "You don't have to do any of this, but you did volunteer, you know. If you want out, just say so."

"No. It's nice to be useful for *something*," she murmured, and went on to talk about her trip.

When Robin dropped her off at the house she half expected to see John at the door, but he wasn't there, either. She went through her domain with a critical eye, sharpened by her own inner disappointment, and found that things in general did have a neglected air: the cats' litter boxes stank; their food was scattered over the music room floor. As the two cats twined themselves around her in rapturous greeting she saw that Tweedledum's magnificent plume of a tail was matted with burrs. "Well, at least you two are glad to see me home," she said, stroking them fondly, and marched off to raise hell with Ben and Reba over the sad state of the house.

Venting her righteous anger, which sent them scuttling about their neglected tasks, calmed her down, so that by the time John did get home she was ready to return his enthusiastic greeting with equal ardor. When it came time for dinner, a little of her rankling resentment popped out. "Don't get too comfortable," she warned as he settled before the drinks tray. "We're eating out."

"Oh?" He looked up in disappointment. "Why aren't we eating dinner here?"

"Because Reba tells me there is nothing in the house; that you haven't done any shopping since your return, and I didn't feel like doing any, either," she returned. "One more night of eating out won't kill you, will it?"

"No, of course not," he said hurriedly, taking in her tenseness. "Sorry about that. It just slipped my mind. Where would you like to go?"

She chose the most expensive restaurant in Pretoria and felt a lot better for it. He may not have missed her as much as she had missed him, but the ardor of his lovemaking that night reassured her that at least in this aspect of their life he had missed her, too. That, indeed, was something to be thankful for, she consoled herself.

Two days later she received another unsigned, typewritten letter through the mail. This one read, "While the cat's away, the tom will play. Such a coincidence Dandy Jack and Betty Newman being in so many places at the same time! Hope you had as much fun on your trip as he did on his." This one she shredded into very small pieces before burning it in the ashtray. She made no mention of it to John. What would be the use? she reflected bitterly.

Her life quickly settled into its old pattern: the trips to Jo'burg, her coffees with the inner circle, her lessons with Hans Haupman. The embassy staff made its annual move, and the tempo of partying tapered off as Pretoria settled into winter. Even the tempo of the black protests seemed to slacken with the waning sun, though nothing was changing; nothing had been done about finding Luluba's murderers.

She mentioned these phenomena to Hans Haupman, who was the only person she felt she could talk to freely, although he could rarely be drawn into talking about anything but music. On this occasion he was more expansive than usual. "Ja"—he shrugged—"zis is part of the unending circle of life here. Ven my wife and I first came here in the early sixties, she hated zis place. She vas convinced that the whole system vas about to blow up, just like the Belgian Congo, and ve'd all be murdered in our beds. It vas just after that terrible business at Sharpesville and all the massacres. But I told her then vat I tell you now: nothing here vill change, or, if it does, it vill be very, very slow. What South Africa has, the rest of the world still wants—the gold of the Rand, the diamonds of Kimberley, the ports for shipping. So long as they have those, the rest of the world vill sit on its hands and do nothing. Your government vill talk about human rights, the Russians vill talk about 'savage fascist repression of our black brothers,' but neither vill do anything drastic to upset ze status quo here, even though they are right, the government here *is* fascist, but"—again he shrugged—"it is vone the whites here vill support, so long as they enjoy the highest standard of living in the world—higher, I think, than even your own rich country. So I say to you as I said to her, 'Relax, enjoy, shut your mind to vat cannot be changed; nothing is going to happen here'—and nothing has."

"So does she like it here now?" Vanessa demanded.

"No," he said, "she has never liked it, but she is used to it."

She thought about that conversation often as she waited in dark doorways or in phone booths, clutching thick packets of money that were exchanged silently and swiftly for thin envelopes containing she knew not what. What was it all about? she wondered. Was she doing good or ill by all this?

John was accompanying her to all the Johannesburg parties now, for which she was doubly thankful—both for his presence on the long journeys, which kept away fear and doubts, and for the fact that recruitment was no longer her responsibility, her guilt.

Nothing had happened about Grant Zecco, and when she questioned John about it, he was not forthcoming. "I said my piece to Armand," he said tersely. "But he doesn't want anyone rocking the boat at the moment. Grant's got valuable contacts with the Broederbond and can get information no one else can. We're all just having to be a lot more wary of him, that's all." So Grant continued to pad around like some great predator, with his implacable amber eyes, carousing with his Afrikaner friends and disappearing for long periods of time. And when he would reappear there would be a satisfied gleam in those dangerous eyes, and the papers would record some new atrocity on the frontiers—or beyond.

For their first anniversary, John took her to the wildlife sanctuary in Kruger Park. "The only place in South Africa you'll see any wild animals," he said with irony. "The Afrikaners have shot all the rest."

She enjoyed seeing the kaleidoscope of African wildlife in the flesh, even if the lions at their kills did remind her uncomfortably of Grant; but it wasn't Venice. She and John were used to each other now. They had explored all the paths of passion, and if the first flaming fire had now settled down to a steady glow, it was still an area of their lives that was completely satisfying. Vanessa was not so sure about other aspects. Sometimes she felt she knew John no better now than when she had first met him, that their relationship was in stasis, that there had been no growth of understanding. On the trip, she nerved herself to ask, "How long are we going to be staying in South Africa? Any idea where we may be going to next?"

He had appeared disconcerted by her questions. "I don't know. We don't have fixed overseas tours like State does, though we try to take home leaves at regular intervals for appearance's sake. Unless our cover is blown too badly or something drastic happens, we tend to stay as long as a particular situation seems to demand it. Though the company doesn't like any operative to get too attached to any one place; seven years is about the outside limit."

"Seven years!" she echoed. "And you've been here four?" She tried not to sound as doleful as she felt.

"Why? Are you tired of your life of ease already?" he teased, with a little edge on his voice. "Do you yearn for the snows of Russia or a nice border post in Thailand? Not enough action here for you?"

"It's not that. I just wondered how—to borrow one of Bobby's favorite phrases—you 'got on' in the CIA. I mean, do you stay in a certain niche a certain length of time, like the armed forces do, or what?"

"Oh, I'll get a station of my own before long," he replied loftily. "The CIA isn't as bureaucratic as most government outfits. They know what their operatives can do and usually use them to their best advantage."

On this Vanessa had her private doubts—doubts that were reinforced on their return, when she went for her next cooking class at Amanda's. The target for the day was to initiate her into the mysteries of beef Wellington and a particularly delectable vegetable dish composed of potatoes, mushrooms, and cheese, but when she arrived, instead of being shown into Amanda's immaculate kitchen by the maid, she was ushered into the living room, to find the mistress of the house curled up on the couch, red-eyed and staring blankly at the smoldering log fire, a wet, wadded-up handkerchief in her tightly clenched hand.

Amanda waited until the maid had gone out and closed the door, then burst out, "I'm in no mood for cooking today, but for God's sake sit down, Vanessa. If I don't talk to someone I'll go out of my mind."

"What on earth's the matter?" Vanessa said, sinking into a chair. "Has something happened to one of the children?"

"No, thank God, they're all right." Amanda gulped and mopped at her eyes. "No, it's George. Armand's getting rid of him and it's *so* unfair. We're being sent home."

"Oh?" Vanessa said cautiously. "Well, that's not so terrible, is it? You were saying only the other day how you wished your eldest boy could finish high school in America, and now he can."

Amanda went on as if she had not heard her. "It's all that damn Zecco's fault. He's behind it; you mark my words. He's got something on Armand—I'm sure of it— and he's calling the shots around here now. He's after George's job, that's what."

"Oh, surely not! After all, it would blow his own cover, and that wouldn't make any sense," Vanessa protested.

"I tell you it's him," Amanda shrilled, her grammar going to pieces. "Just because George had the guts to protest to Armand about Zecco leading everyone around by the nose, this happens—almost overnight!"

"But Armand is so open about his activities, and nobody seems to mind," Vanessa pointed out. "So what could Zecco possibly have on him?"

"Armand's a dirty old man," Amanda said darkly, "and dirty old men can get into some peculiar situations. He can't be depended on. John and Robin had better watch out. If you ask me, Zecco wants this place all to himself."

It did nothing to ease Vanessa's own fears, and these were augmented rather than soothed by an unexpected visit from Clara Zecco shortly thereafter. She had not seen much of Clara since her return from the States and so was rather surprised when the big blonde dropped in one morning with something on her mind that she had difficulty getting out. After a lot of aimless and inane chitchat, Clara said abruptly, "I wish you didn't spend so much time in Johannesburg, Vanessa. Isn't there something you like to do here? I mean, it's a long way, and it's a lot more restless and dangerous than Pretoria."

"Are you trying to tell me something?" Vanessa looked at her inquiringly.

Clara's eyes met hers briefly, then flickered away. "No, of course not," she muttered. "It's just that we never get to see you anymore. I've heard of this neat aerobics class that meets three times a week. Wouldn't you like to come with me to that? It'd make a nice change for you, and I'd love it."

"Well, thanks, but I really am rather tied up with my music at the moment. Maybe later, when there's not so much going on."

Clara looked at her with anxious eyes, but she got up to go. "I do wish you'd change your mind. You can join in anytime, you know," she urged. "Think about it, will you? And call me anytime."

"I'll think about it," Vanessa said, but at the door Clara

turned and impulsively clutched her hand. "Do be careful, Vanessa," she whispered, "very careful." And she rushed blindly out.

Vanessa related both conversations to John, who did not seem overly impressed. Over Amanda's outburst, he snorted, "Oh, that's a lot of bull! George has been here five years, and it's time he went home anyway. And, as I've said before, we're all keeping a very sharp eye on Grant. He knows very little about what Robin and I are up to these days, so there's nothing to worry about."

She really tried to believe that, but it wasn't easy. The months passed by; the Drakes left, to be replaced by a younger, very reticent couple, the Lyle Browns; and nothing untoward happened.

It was only when spring returned, the magnolias in bloom and the jacaranda trees filling the Pretoria avenues with breathtaking vistas of purple blossom, that her hidden fears surfaced. Everything had been going so smoothly—the drops, the pickups, the contacts—that she had become almost nonchalant about her role, but on this particular spring evening things started to go wrong from the very beginning. John had promised to accompany her to a Mozart concert given by her current ensemble, but he called at the last minute from the office to say that something had come up and he would not be able to make it, so she had to take her own car and go alone.

She had arranged to meet her initial contact, the violist, backstage before the concert to hand over a considerable sum of money previously agreed upon. She did not know the purpose of the payment, only that Armand had okayed it. She was dismayed on arrival to find no sign of the violist, and she tackled her current contact in the ensemble, a cellist, who was a known friend of his. "William Kula?" he said. "Oh, he won't be here tonight. He's sick. Why? You wanted to see him?"

"I had something for him," she said cautiously.

"That's okay. I'll take it to him."

"No, I'm afraid I have to give this to him in person," she murmured. "It's quite important."

He shrugged. "Give me a lift home after the concert and I could take you to him."

"In the township?" she asked.

"Sure—where else? No problem. I'll take you in and out," he volunteered.

She hesitated. She didn't much like the idea, but then she equally hated to bring the money back, her mission unaccomplished. "All right," she agreed reluctantly. "But we'd better not go right to his house."

"Sure, I understand." He grinned. "I know a good place to park nearby."

As they drove through the dimly lit outskirts of the township, with its weird mixture of dilapidated tin shanties mixed in with more substantial houses, her unease grew, but she parked at his direction in a dark, dusty lot, close by a gutted house on a deserted street. "Kula's place is just around the corner," he said, and led her to a modest one story house with a battered car parked in front of it. The house was dark, and constant pounding on the door brought no response. Her escort turned to her, suddenly uneasy. "I don't like this. We'd better get out of here," he muttered. "I'll take you back to the main road."

They ran back to the car and stopped, aghast: both tires on the exposed side were flat, the knife slashes in them showing dark in the dim light. A slight noise behind them brought a cry to Vanessa's lips and they whirled around, their backs to the car. Out of the shadows a group of six figures loomed. They were teen-age blacks, and their leader, who towered head and shoulders above the rest, said something in a soft, venomous voice to her companion, who shouted something in their own tongue and then said in English, "You don't understand—she's a friend, a friend of our people; she's here to help. Keep back!" Then he yelled at Vanessa as they padded menacingly toward them, "Run! Run for your life!"

The leader reached him and felled him with one blow from a wooden club; then he turned toward her. She came out of her paralysis with a shrill scream and fled up the street, screaming at the top of her lungs.

She could hear the thud of running feet behind her and

then she was seized from behind and whirled around, a club thudding against her right leg with a sickening crunch, and, as she fell in a wave of unbearable pain, they were upon her, pummeling, kicking, and tearing at her clothes. As her consciousness slipped away she heard in the far distance the shrilling of a whistle and a voice shouting something incomprehensible in English, then the crack of a gunshot. As the darkness closed around her, her last thought was, What a ridiculous way to die! And then there was oblivion.

Chapter 15

She was staring up at the golden, haloed globe of the sun that resolved itself into a round light fixture embedded in a stark white ceiling. She was conscious of figures around her swathed in swirling veils of mist. A face loomed over her, breaking through its misty cloud—a hard face of a man she did not know. "Mrs. Bannerman," he said in a thick Afrikaner accent, "can you hear me? What were you doing in the native township? What were you doing there?"

The veils lifted and she saw the small room and its occupants with startling clarity: the mustached man above her in the uniform of the South African police, another man—very English-looking with his sharp, delicate nose, lean features, and short, slicked-back dark hair—who was also a stranger, and behind them a young doctor in a white coat hovering uncertainly as the policeman repeated his question.

Time, she had to play for time. "Where am I?" she muttered, her tongue feeling like a woolly balloon in her bruised mouth. "You're in the University of the Witwatersrand hospital," a very cultured tenor English voice broke in, and the dark man came forward and surprisingly took her hand and gave it a little warning squeeze. "Your husband is on his way. I phoned him. I'm Richard Morse of OXFAM. I found you. Drove off the blighters that were attacking you. Even managed to recapture your bag they had stolen." Again there was a gentle pressure on her hand.

She closed her eyes as a wave of relief washed her clouded mind. John was coming; John was on his way—she only had to stall until he arrived. The policeman gave an irritated growl. "That's enough from you, Mr. Morse. You keep quiet. Now, Mrs. Bannerman, what were you doing in the native township at that hour of the night? Answer me!"

A new voice broke in, diffidently. "Officer, I don't think she is in any fit state to answer questions."

"She's conscious, isn't she? You keep out of it, doctor."

She kept her eyes closed as long as she dared, trying to put her thoughts together, then opened them as she felt a rough hand on her shoulder shaking her. "What?" she muttered stupidly. The policeman repeated his question.

"Concert," she stammered. "University. Gave cellist lift home. Makuba. He's hurt—help Makuba."

"That must be the poor chap you found with his head bashed in on the vacant lot, officer," the English voice interrupted, and she let out a little groan of despair. Poor Makuba! Tears welled up and slid down her numb cheeks. "She's answered your question," the English voice continued on a rising note of anger. "Now why don't you leave her alone? Can't you see what a state she's in?"

The policeman started to snarl a reply when the door burst open and suddenly the room was full of people: John, and behind him the Consul-General for Johannesburg, flanked by two hefty Marine guards from the Pretoria embassy. She gave a little cry and John was at her side in a single bound, his arms around her protectively. "Darling, it's all right. Everything's going to be all right." His face became livid with anger as he glared up at the

Afrikaner. "What the hell do you think you are doing?" he hissed. "How dare you badger my injured wife like some criminal, when she is barely conscious! My God, your government is going to hear about this! Don't you oafs know what diplomatic immunity *means*?"

"Just doing my job. Your wife was in a place she had no reason to be," the policeman stuttered.

"And Mrs. Bannerman has explained—very clearly, in the circumstances, I think—that she was giving a fellow musician a lift home," the Englishman cut in suavely.

"Then get out!" John roared, "or, by God, I'll have our men throw you out. And there'll be one of them posted at her door to see that nothing like this happens again."

"You can't do that," the policeman growled.

Surprisingly, the young doctor, evidently emboldened by the new arrivals, spoke up. "This is a private hospital, officer, private property. Mr. Bannerman is within his rights."

"We'll soon see about that!" The policeman, seeing the Marines edging toward him, shouldered past them and turned at the door. "Diplomatic immunity be damned—this is going to be looked into thoroughly."

"You'll take care of it?" John looked inquiringly at the Consul-General, who was not looking any too happy but who nodded and went out with the Marines.

The doctor reasserted his authority. "Now, Mr. Bannerman, I'd like to give your wife some more sedation. Her right leg is broken and she's been badly beaten and bruised, but so far as I can ascertain there's no internal damage. If you give me a few minutes, you may come back for a little afterward."

John and her rescuer went out together, and the doctor busied himself checking her blood pressure and her heart before giving her a shot. He opened the door and beckoned, and as John came in again he said, "Only five minutes, Mr. Bannerman. She ought to be much better by morning, but she'll be here at least ten days," and went out himself.

John cradled her in his arms, kissing her with light

butterfly kisses. "Oh, my poor darling! I'll never forgive myself for this, never."

Because of her weakened state, the sedative was already beginning to take effect, and she had to fight to keep her mind working. "John, my bag—the Englishman must have given it to the police—the money—they'll find the money!"

"Don't worry," he soothed. "Morse gave them the bag, but he took the money out before they arrived. I've got it. You said just the right thing—all you have to do is go on repeating it."

"Who *is* Richard Morse, and what was he doing there?" she murmured as the mist started to close over her senses.

"I haven't the remotest idea," he said, and it was the last thing she heard.

When she finally awoke, it was the afternoon of the next day and her room resembled a miniature greenhouse: there were flowers everywhere, in pots, in vases, in baskets, even in jugs, and covering every available surface. The uncomfortable thought came to her that it somewhat resembled a funeral parlor, and this put her in mind of poor Makuba. She wondered miserably how many flowers remained for him. Although her body was one big ache and her leg a throbbing flame, her mind was clear, and she carefully went over the events of the night to prepare herself for the possible return of the police. The only flaw she could see in her story was that the car had not been anywhere near Makuba's house, but that, she thought, could be explained away by saying they were dropping in on their sick musician friend Kula. Thanks to the mysterious Mr. Morse, the police would have found nothing untoward in her handbag, but . . .

The door opened to admit a nurse, who smiled cheerfully at her and then said something to someone outside. The head of one of the Marines she had seen the night before appeared around the door. "You okay, Mrs. Bannerman? I'll call Mr. Bannerman now and let him know you're up. He stayed in Jo'burg overnight." She smiled and nodded as the nurse advanced on her with blood pressure paraphernalia and a thermometer. "What gorgeous flowers," the nurse said, looking around at the greenhouse. "They've all got cards from your friends. Want me to collect them so that you can read them?"

"Maybe later," Vanessa murmured, feeling delightfully lazy and secure. Her eyes strayed to a gorgeous African violet of deep, velvety purple and gold. She loved violets. "Perhaps you can get me that one." She pointed. "It's probably from my husband." The nurse plucked the card out and looked at it. "I don't think so. It seems to be in Italian," she said doubtfully. "It just says, 'Arrivederci, bella signora, R.M.'"

"Oh!" Vanessa said blankly. There was only one person she knew who bore those initials, and she did not expect to see him again.

When John did appear he was clasping a huge bunch of long-stemmed red roses, and she laughed a little at the sight of them. "They're lovely, darling," she giggled, "and if you can find a place to put them, be my guest! The embassy really seems to have outdone itself, doesn't it?"

"Well, it's not every day we get one of our own injured in the line of duty," he returned, a little grimly. "Everyone is feeling almost as bad about it as I do."

"And to think it was nothing more than a stupid coincidence," she murmured. "A group of teenagers venting their spleen on a bright new car and then finding an enemy in their midst to get even with: a classic case of being in the right place at the wrong time."

"Let's hope that's what the police continue to think." John was even grimmer. "Myself, I'm not so sure."

She looked at him in surprise. "But there's no way it could have been anything else! No one knew what I was going to do—it was a spur-of-the-moment thing."

"Granted, but I'd feel a lot easier in my mind if I knew where Kula was. He's disappeared. We've no idea if the police have him or if he's gone off for reasons of his own. The gang may have been watching his house, and you just happened to come along."

"Did they catch any of them?"

He shook his head. "No. By the time the police arrived

they had all scattered except for the one Richard Morse shot, and he was dead."

"One was *shot*?" she exclaimed in horror.

"Yes, a large youth of about eighteen—Morse claimed he was about to rape you. He shot once over their heads, and that sent most of them running, but this one didn't go, so he shot again."

"What was a man from OXFAM doing with a gun?" she whispered.

John looked at her, his eyes worried. "We'll probably never know. Morse has already left South Africa. He gave a statement to the police in which he claimed he carried the gun because his work often took him into dangerous places, and he had a permit for it. He apparently satisfied them, because they let him fly off to Kenya this morning. Anyway, let's not talk about this anymore—you're looking tired. I want you to put all this out of your mind as much as you can and concentrate on getting better fast." He took her hands and kissed them. "I'll be staying in Jo'burg until you can leave the hospital—it'll give me a good excuse to do some snooping around on the local scene." She didn't know whether to be flattered or annoyed.

The visitors came in droves, not only the inner circle but all the embassy personnel who were still around, and she became more than a little weary of recounting the standard lie she had composed. Even Hans Haupman came for a brief visit, and he left with a typical remark that amused her greatly. "Thank God it was your leg they broke and not your arm! At least it will not interfere with your playing."

But one visit was memorable—and frightening. It was the day before she was due to be discharged, and she was already hopping around her room, trying to get used to the cast on her leg and grimacing in the mirror at the unsightly yellow bruises that blotched her whole face and body. John had just left when the door opened cautiously and she was amazed to see Robin's secretary, Maggie, her eyes wide and wild, peering in. "Come on in, Maggie," she called with false heartiness. So far none of her visitors had been from what Bobby was wont to call "the lower echelons" of the embassy, and she was particularly surprised to see Maggie, who was seen at every embassy function but literally never heard: Vanessa had not exchanged more than a dozen or so words with her since her arrival, and these had been the merest banalities, since the plain woman appeared completely withdrawn and inarticulate.

Maggie crept around the door, her eyes still wild and fixed, and she revealed a small bunch of very wilted flowers drooping from one tightly clenched hand. Vanessa hopped over to the bed and eased herself up on it, waving a hand at the single chair in the room. "Sit down. It's so nice to see you, so nice of you to visit me."

The secretary, whose face was curiously mottled with dull red patches, ignored the invitation and came right up to the bed, thrusting her face within inches of Vanessa's. "Got to talk," she muttered. "Got to explain." She leaned heavily against the bed, emitting an overwhelming odor of gin, her head shaking visibly.

Vanessa felt faintly alarmed. "Of course," she soothed, "but why don't you sit down? You'll be a lot more comfortable, and then we can have a nice chat."

The woman looked at her dazedly but shuffled obediently over to the chair and slumped into it, her disconcerting stare still fixed on Vanessa. "Never meant this to happen," she mumbled. "Not this. All my fault—all mine—but you gotta understand. . . ." She closed her eyes and let out a deep, quivering sigh, and the flowers dropped from her hand and lay scattered on the floor. She began to talk in a queer, high-pitched voice, a rambling, incoherent jumble of words—about her unhappy childhood, her loneliness, an unhappy love affair, her joining the CIA—that Vanessa had difficulty following and that made little or no sense. "They shouldn't have done that to me," Maggie suddenly shouted. "I was meant for him, not them. I should have been his—that was all I wanted—and he didn't have anybody, but they wouldn't let me. And then you took him from me, and I had nothing left. Don't you understand that? *Nothing!*" Her voice was a high-pitched screech.

Vanessa looked at her, a cold feeling clutching at her heart. "Maggie, did you write those letters?" she muttered through stiffened lips.

"Wanted to hurt. I was hurt, wanted to hurt back," Maggie mumbled. "Hurt them, hurt you, hurt him. Showed you all—hurt you all. Damn people, never caring 'bout me, never even seeing me. He was the only one who ever listened, ever was kind. . . ."

"John?" Vanessa whispered.

Maggie gave an ugly bark of laughter. "Dandy Jack never has any time for anybody but his lousy self—but I fixed him, fixed everyone. Tol' my friend all 'bout their lousy little schemes."

The cold about Vanessa's heart intensified. "Is Grant your friend?" she asked softly.

Maggie suddenly broke into loud sobs. "Not anymore!" she wailed. "Nobody's my friend anymore. He tol' me I was just an ugly old lush and to keep my trap shut or he'd get me. He said that, after all I did for him! Jus' because I couldn't find out 'bout everything, 'bout you. Not my fault! I could tell plenty 'bout him, too. . . ."

She was making such a racket that the door flew open and a nurse rushed in, an alarmed expression on her face as she demanded, "What's going on in here?" Maggie's mouth snapped shut in mid-sentence, and she crouched back in her chair like a frightened animal, then staggered to her feet. "Gotta go now," she mumbled, suddenly truculent. "You get outta my way, you young bitch, or I'll fix you, too." And she stumbled past the nurse and out of the door. The nurse hovered uncertainly, taking in Vanessa's ashen face and the scattered flowers. "I'd better see to her," she gabbled. "Are you all right, Mrs. Bannerman?"

"Yes—see to her," Vanessa ordered, "but also call to the consulate and get my husband back here immediately. Tell them it's urgent." The nurse nodded and fled.

Vanessa sank back against her pillows, shaking, her feelings torn between cold revulsion and pity for the crazed woman. It had been right under their noses and no one had seen it. No one had seen it because no one ever saw Maggie; she had merely been part of the office furniture.

By the time John rushed in, his face creased with worry, she was in control of herself again. "Well, I've found our poison pen and your mole, who are one and the same person," she said tersely, and went on to give him the details.

"Good God!" he whispered, his jaw set and grim. "It's unbelievable! Well, first things first. I've got to find her and get her shipped out quietly as soon as possible. This is going to hit Robin hard. We never even suspected. . . ." He rushed out in search of the nurse.

When he returned it was to report that Maggie had simplified matters by passing out cold in an elevator, and the hospital had her in another room under restraint. "That'll make it a lot easier to get rid of her with the minimum of fuss—we can ship her back directly from here."

A little chilled by his callousness, Vanessa asked, "What will happen to her?"

He shrugged. "Oh, the CIA will get what they can out of her and see she gets treated. After that, who knows? Let's hope this will help Robin get Grant."

"What about you?" she said in surprise.

He looked at her uncertainly. "I wasn't going to tell you this until you got back home, but we're going to be leaving South Africa very soon. The government here just presented the embassy with an ultimatum. Either I go back home immediately or they will declare me persona non grata."

"What?" She was thunderstruck. "Was this because of what happened to me? Because of what you said to the policeman?"

"Only partly," he sighed. "They picked up one of my operatives in Durban—one of my direct contacts—and he cracked under questioning. My cover is blown. The embassy will use your injury to get rid of us gracefully. Do you mind?"

"Only if you do," she said, but she was quietly thankful. "Will we be going back to Langley?"

"For a while, until they decide where to assign me next." He grinned ruefully. "It'll mean quite a cut in our standard of living—none of these lovely unquestioned expense accounts we all enjoy overseas. We'll have to tighten our belts a bit. Back to grim reality, in fact."

"After all this," she murmured, "grim reality will be a delightful change."

Chapter 16

*T*heir going was magnanimously delayed by the powers-that-be until the cast was removed from her leg, and when they went, they did not go alone; the Wests went with them.

This was a greater shock to Vanessa than their own enforced departure had been, for there seemed no concrete reason for it. Even John was at a loss to explain it, though he still pooh-poohed Amanda's original idea, which Vanessa again put forth, that Grant Zecco was clearing the decks for nefarious reasons of his own. The Wests themselves were silent and tight-lipped, although there were vague rumors of a loud-voiced row between Robin and Armand, subject unspecified, and speculation ran wild that it was connected with the precipitate departure of Maggie, now penned, according to John, in some stateside mental hospital, awaiting evaluation.

The Cape Town cohort had returned and there was the inevitable round of farewell parties where, Vanessa was wryly amused to note, everyone was a lot more affable to them than they had ever been before. Not that she cared; the only people she regretted having to say good-bye to were the single-minded Hans Haupman and Gerda, to whom she paid a farewell visit and who was forthright in her farewell. "I am thankful you are going, my dear. This country is no place for a sensitive, caring person such as you. It would do you no good, or your marriage any good, and I should hate to see anything happen to either. Sometimes I despair myself, and I wonder if I would not be better off joining my daughter in England, but I am old and I am used to it, so I suppose I shall stay and do what I can for as long as I can. With our own holocaust so fresh in our memories, we cannot stand by and see unarmed blacks shot in the back by policemen because they have dared to protest the intolerable conditions under which they are forced to live. We have to do something to help, little as it may be. I hope that wherever you may go next you will be in far happier circumstances."

Vanessa had not dared think that far, for she was still wrestling with the guilt of the present, and what irked her was that both John and Robin had apparently already put everything behind them and no longer seemed remotely interested in the fates of those they had suborned and who had believed their promises.

She found her inner irritation bursting out in minor matters, as when John protested her decision to take Tweedledum and Tweedledee along with them. "Oh, come on, Van! What's the sense of trailing two cats back to a continent that's crawling with pets needing homes? Anyway, we'll probably be renting an apartment, and it'll be difficult to find one in the Washington area that allows pets. Why not leave it until we go overseas again? Besides, it'll be damned expensive—the company draws the line on some things, so it'll be out of our own pocket."

"I don't care," she flared. "They're my cats and I want them—in fact, they are the only things I care about taking. If it's the expense that worries you, sell my damned car and keep the proceeds—I can well do without it."

"But they'll be such a nuisance at the other end! What'll

we do with them until we get settled? Be reasonable!" he pleaded.

She was unmoved. "I can leave them with my mother, if necessary," she snapped. "But they are going with us." And with considerable uproar they did, particularly the vocal Tweedledee, who kept up an earsplitting howling all the way to the airport.

The Wests were booked on the same flight home, and Vanessa was a little intrigued by an interchange that took place in the departure lounge between Robin and Joe Ferraro, who, as their travel agent, had come to see them off. Joe's face was unnaturally solemn as he pumped Robin's hand. "Sorry to see you go," he growled. "And when you are ready, give the word and I'll see it gets done."

"Oh, I'll give the word at the right time," Robin replied with quiet venom. "You can be sure of that."

On the long flight back, after the refueling stop in West Africa, John swapped seats with Bobby West, who joined Vanessa with a relieved sigh. The last few months seemed to have taken their toll on her usual exuberance, and her normally high-colored face was pale and almost gaunt; she had a permanent, worried crease between her green eyes. "God, I so hate these in-between states," she volunteered, accepting a drink from the stewardess. "It'll be so nice to be settled back in Langley for a while."

"Have you got a place to live?" Vanessa asked anxiously, since this was high on her own list of priorities.

"Oh, there are always scads of apartments going." Bobby was offhanded. "Washington is such a volatile community that it's never any problem so long as you don't have a family. I don't expect to be a busy little homemaker, so the smaller the place the better, as far as I'm concerned."

"What are you going to do?" Vanessa demanded.

"Try for something in Langley itself. My girl Friday skills aren't bad, and they tend to give a break to wives because of the security angle. Besides..." Bobby hesitated, her worry lines deepening. "I'd like to stay close to Robin. He's not taking this move at all well, and I don't want any further upset."

Vanessa opened her mouth to say something and then shut it again; after all, it was none of her business. "I suppose I ought to get a job, too," she said doubtfully. "Though I'm not sure what."

"I thought you'd be starting a family," Bobby said. "Not a bad idea when you're stateside—better doctors and so on."

Vanessa looked at her in surprise. "Whatever made you think that? I hadn't even considered it."

Bobby gave her a quick glance, her color heightening. "Oh? Well—nothing. I just got the impression that John didn't want to wait much longer for a family—but forget I ever mentioned it. With the forties looming up so close for the rest of us, I keep forgetting how young you are." And she went on to talk about matters domestic until John returned for the last leg of the flight.

After much wrangling it had been decided that she and the cats would retire temporarily to Larchmont while John proceeded to Washington for debriefing and for a preliminary scout around for a place to live. When he had found a likely prospect, she would join him to put her seal of approval on it before they moved in. Her mother received the cats warmly enough, but Bob Cross was less enthusiastic, and after a few days of his fussing about having them declawed in case of damage to his somewhat humdrum furniture and his complaints about the festoons of orange fur that the longhaired Tweedledum liberally bestowed on the carpets, Vanessa solved that particular problem by boarding them with an old friend, Nancy, who had married straight out of high school and who was now housebound with two small children in Larchmont; her husband commuted into Manhattan. After a long layoff, he had only recently been rehired as a computer programmer, so Nancy was glad to have the liberal boarding fees Vanessa offered.

She had reached a state of near-suffocation in the claustrophobic suburban cycle that now comprised her mother's life when John phoned with the welcome news that he had found something that might do. He did not sound any too happy about it, for his find was in Falls Church—further away from Langley than he had wanted to be, and it did not have any of the conveniences (like a swimming pool or a tennis court) to which he had become accustomed. The problem, he informed her testily, was the cats—this complex was the only one he had found that allowed pets.

"It sounds just fine to me," she said laconically. "And as you say we can't afford a house, I doubt whether we'll do much better. Anyway, I'll come down tomorrow and take a look. How are things at Langley?"

"Oh, all right," he said gloomily. "They've tucked me away in the North African section for the present, but I don't think it's going to last."

"How about Robin?"

"They've got him in some sort of crash language program—again, object unspecified. He's not too happy about that. I saw George Drake, and *they're* on the move again—off to the Caribbean soon. He's quite pleased with it. And he passed on an interesting bit of gossip: Eleanor Heitz is back in the States, and she's filing for divorce. I must say that surprised me."

"Well, yes and no," Vanessa murmured. "Anyway, darling, see you tomorrow. Love you."

"Me, too," he muttered, and rang off.

She liked the small two-bedroom apartment at first sight. It was on the ground floor of an older brick apartment complex, built in the '50s, and was on a tree-lined avenue adjacent to a row of small houses, all liberally supplied with children, judging from the litter of go-carts, bikes, and strollers that adorned the small front lawns. "It has absolutely nothing in the way of extras beyond one's own parking space," John complained. "But the only other place I've found is way out in Culpeper, and I don't feel like commuting that far every damned day."

"Then let's take this," she soothed. "After all, it may not be for very long, if they reassign you. Cheer up, darling. We're in the center of things now, not in a penal colony, you know." It did not seem to cheer him.

The settling-in process was every bit as exasperating and exhausting as she had anticipated. John's share of his former household goods came out of its long storage with the drab air of things long unused and out of date, and she found herself fully occupied trying, for the first time, to be a housewife, cook, and lover. Only at the last was she at all confident of her skills; at the other two she soon realized she was woefully inadequate, and she found herself spending inordinate amounts of time muttering over cookbooks and reading the instructions on spray cans and appliance manuals. Her violin lay on top of her music in the spare room closet, gathering dust.

Only one thing cheered her long domestic days: she had found a friend, a thin-faced, harried, dark-haired girl a year or two older than herself, who occupied the small house closest to the apartment and who was the mother of a rambunctious pair of towheaded three-year-old twin boys. They had met when the boys had rammed their tricycles into each other at full tilt, and as the mother had scooped up one howling toddler Vanessa, who had been passing by, had scooped up the other. The cuts bandaged, the boys scolded and turned to less destructive play, Chrissy Davis had proffered an invitation to coffee, and the friendship had begun. They had a lot in common, for Chrissy had been a pianist, studying at the Manhattan School of Music, and had dropped out without finishing to marry her husband, a Treasury agent, and she was as hungry for someone who talked her own language as Vanessa was for someone outside the rarefied circle of Langley.

The few social get-togethers she had been to with John had quickly opened her eyes to the fact that compared with headquarters, the inner circle of the Pretoria embassy had been an amiable group of pussycats. The amount of back-stabbing, malicious gossip, and one-upmanship that went on at these affairs was so unnerving that she quietly applauded John's retreat into a strong, silent role, utterly different from the charismatic, gregarious persona he had displayed overseas. He said little, listened a lot, and looked profound, and she did her best to imitate him. "Are the men like that in the office as well?" she asked, appalled, after one more than usually virulent party.

"Pretty much," he said grimly. "But it's no different from what goes on in the rest of Washington. This is where the main action is, so this is where the infighting goes on to get the plum spots overseas. Survival of the fittest, nature red in tooth and claw, et cetera. My own role may seem a little passive to you, but I've been around long enough to know that when the fighters lie bleeding on the ground it's time to step in quietly and make off with what they've been fighting for. It doesn't always work out, but it's not a bad tactic."

"I don't see how you can *stand* it!" Vanessa cried. "Surely you don't enjoy this kind of thing. Oh, John, isn't there some other kind of work you'd prefer to do?"

He sidestepped the question. "You find this sort of infighting everywhere, you know—other government branches, business—it's become part of the American ethic. I still feel what I'm doing is important, even vital, so it's worth the struggle."

She was far from convinced herself and wondered how the sensitive Robin was coping with Langley, but on this she received little enlightenment. They had seen very little of the Wests since their return, for Bobby had achieved her goal of being a girl Friday in the biographical section of the CIA, and to get away from it all they had bought a small house in the country beyond Culpeper and so were too far removed for casual visiting. Vanessa had been to see the Drakes, who owned a permanent house in McLean, several times, but Amanda was gearing up for her next move in her usual efficient fashion and so had little time for social niceties. Increasingly, Vanessa found her most peaceful and pleasant moments were spent with Chrissy Davis when, with the boys tucked in for their naps, the two musicians would open a bottle of chilled white wine, put on a classical tape, and relax back into their own world in friendly silence.

She was anticipating just such a pleasant afternoon one day in late summer when the phone rang, and on answering she found a distraught Amanda Drake on the other end, her voice so choked with sobs as to be virtually incomprehensible. "Have you heard the terrible news?"

A spasm of annoyance shook Vanessa. "Don't tell me your posting has been changed!" She was in no mood to listen to another tale of woe about George and his career. "Get hold of yourself, Amanda. I can scarcely hear you. What is it?"

There were audible gulps and sniffles on the line before Amanda said in a stifled voice, "No. It's Clara Zecco and her boy. They're dead. Their car exploded in their own garage—dynamited, sabotaged. They were blown to bits." There was a fresh flood of sobs.

Vanessa went cold all over. "Oh, my God!" she whispered as terrible thoughts crowded her mind. "Did he do it? Was it Grant?"

Amanda got control of her voice again. "No, it was *meant* for Grant. Oh, it's all so tragic! You know how flaky Clara was about losing her keys—well, she had to take the kid to the doctor's and she couldn't find the keys to her own car, so she took Grant's. And the minute she stepped on the gas pedal..."

As Amanda's voice droned on, Vanessa closed her eyes against the image of Clara's beautiful showgirl legs disintegrating in a wave of flame. "When Grant got the news he went berserk. Screaming that it was Luluba's followers getting their revenge, he got hold of a machine gun and was going into the Jo'burg township, spraying bullets as he went, before the police managed to catch up with him and restrain him. They've got him in protective custody, and of course they're saying a full investigation will be made, but you know what the South African police are...."

"Oh, yes, I know what they are," she agreed woodenly.

"At least it'll mean the company will have to pull him out now, even if they do the usual cover-up." There was a slight edge of satisfaction to Amanda's voice. "He's completely flipped out."

As soon as she could get Amanda off the phone Vanessa called John's office, only to be told by a sullen-sounding secretary that he was out and not expected back, and she had no idea where he had gone. Canceling her date with Chrissy, Vanessa went back to the phone, willing it to ring, willing him to call her as the doubts and fears raged in her mind. But it stayed stubbornly silent as the hours dragged by past his usual homecoming, their dinner hour, on through the long, dark evening hours into the small hours of the night. By the time she heard the Alfa draw up in the parking spot beneath their front window, she was almost beyond terror; she was completely numb.

As he came through the front door with his shoulders sagging like an old man's, his face aged into creases of strain, all she could force out was "Where have you been?"

He stared at her, his eyes agonized. "I've been at the hospital with Bobby." His voice was husky with weariness. "Robin tried to commit suicide—he didn't quite succeed. They think he has about a fifty-fifty chance of pulling through."

All her worst fears crystallized. "So you know about the Zeccos?" she whispered.

He slumped into a chair and with a shaking hand wiped at his reddened eyes. "Yes, I know."

"But it wasn't anything to do with Luluba, was it?" she kept on, half hoping he would contradict her.

Something between a groan and a sob escaped from him. "No. Robin arranged the hit on Grant. He thought it was the only way. And by a thousand-to-one chance it misfired. O, my God, *what* a mistake." He covered his eyes.

She forced herself to ask the ultimate question. "And were you in on it?"

He looked up at her. "If I had known, I would have stopped them. I didn't know a thing about it, Van. You've got to believe that. If you never believe anything else, please, you've got to believe that!"

Chapter 17

The miracles of modern medicine had snatched Robin back from the oblivion he had sought, but he was in complete nervous collapse, and the CIA quickly whisked him out of the hospital into a private nursing home under their jurisdiction in southern Virginia. Bobby had quit her job, rented out the house, and moved down south to be near him.

Carless—for John had taken her at her word in Pretoria—Vanessa could only phone her support and friendship before Bobby left, but she met with little encouragement. Bobby did not want to talk about what had happened and had retreated into a bastion of protective optimism. "Robin's been overworked for so long, it's a wonder he didn't collapse before," she affirmed. "But he'll be fine once he's rested." But of the attempted suicide and its cause she said not a word. Vanessa did not press, for she was having enough problems with a morose and troubled John, whose depression remained a constant in their lives for several months and was only partially lifted by his promotion to a more substantive job in the

Near East section. There was still no word or sign of an overseas assignment.

By this time she was feeling more than a little restless herself. She had mastered enough housekeeping skills so that running the small apartment was no longer a problem, but it did not satisfy her. She despised housework, was bored with her own cooking, and yet could think of no practical means of escape. She was playing again, but her skills had slipped so much that the prospects of any kind of paid employment were nil, and she had no other salable skills. She had long discussions with Chrissy about this, because her friend was now looking forward to the twins' starting nursery school, which would liberate her to find a job, but she was in the same boat as Vanessa. It was she who came up with the bright idea of a night class in music calligraphy. "I've checked into it," she said eagerly, "and there's quite a demand for skilled notators around here."

"But aren't all the scores printed already?" Vanessa pointed out.

"Yes, but they're horribly expensive, and schools and colleges particularly are in the market for hand-done band parts because they are cheaper. Greg's agreed to babysit the boys and he says I can have the car, so we could go together. What's more, if we get any good at it, it's something we can do at home."

"Sounds okay, then," Vanessa agreed cautiously. "I'll talk it over with John." Next to music, art had always been her strong subject, and the idea of using her artistic skills on something other than decorating food platters strongly appealed to her.

Their third anniversary was fast approaching, and she thought that this might be a good moment to bring up the subject, since John had, up to now, been very negative about any job plans. He would usually turn them aside with a barbed quip. "Don't I keep you in style?" or "I thought I married a nonprofit, deductible musician! Whatever happened to your dedication to the arts?" This time she was determined not to be thwarted.

To celebrate, he took her to the most fashionable restaurant in Washington, and for a while she was swept away by all the glitter and glamour that surrounded them. In his arms on the dance floor, dancing to sleepy rhythms, she felt a little of the old magic returning and hated to break into its sweetness. John appeared more like his old self than she had seen in months: charming, amusing, tender, and loving—everything she most cherished in him—and he was so captivating that she let her opportunity drift. It was he who jolted her out of her euphoria. When they raised their champagne glasses to each other and she said, "Here's to us," he replied softly, "Here's to the Bannerman *family*." He reached swiftly across the table and took her hand. "How about it, Van? Let's start a family—preferably tonight," and he grinned his enchanting grin. "I want to be a father. Must be all those kids underfoot in the neighborhood. Puts ideas into one's head."

It took her so much by surprise that she handled it badly. "Not yet," she blurted out. "I'm not ready yet."

His grin faded and he looked uncertain. "But why, Van? After all, it's been three years, and I'm facing my fortieth birthday. There'll never be a better time—and I know you're restless. A baby would be good for us both, good for our marriage."

"I'm sorry," she stammered. "But I'm just not ready. With things as uncertain as they are, I don't know when I will be."

"What's so uncertain?" He was nettled. "My career is going fine, and you've known me long enough to be sure I don't turn into Mr. Hyde every full moon. We're healthy; we love each other—what more do you want?"

"I think I want peace of mind," she managed to get out. "And as long as you work for the CIA I'm not sure I am ever going to get it. I've tried to shut myself up in my ivory tower, which is what you seem to want me to do, but it doesn't work anymore, John. Too much has happened."

His face closed up and he frowned. "So that's it. Well, on that I'm afraid I can't accommodate your whims. I'm not going to throw up my career, the work I believe in, just to satisfy your tender conscience about things you should never have gotten involved with in the first place."

"That's unfair, John," she said quietly. "And besides, it's not my conscience that worries me as much as yours. I don't like what the CIA does to people, and I'm not sure I'd want a child of mine growing up within its clutches."

His jaw set grimly. "Then there's nothing more to be said—for now. Let's drop the subject and salvage what we can of the evening."

"There is one thing," she went on rather desperately. "I've been thinking of taking an evening course at the University of Virginia's local branch. Is that all right with you? I won't need the car; I can go with Chrissy Davis."

He shrugged and looked away. "If that's what you want to do, but you may not be able to finish it."

"Why not?" she said in surprise.

"Because I may be posted overseas in the near future."

"Then why on earth didn't you say something sooner?" she flared.

"Because it isn't in the bag yet."

"How soon?"

"Within six months."

"The course only lasts three—I'm going to take it," she said firmly.

"Do as you please," he said savagely, draining the champagne bottle. "Let's drink to that."

She took the course, enjoyed it, and was good at it, but she was also aware of the gulf that was slowly widening between John and herself. They no longer squabbled over minor matters as much as they used to; they were both a little more reticent, a little more careful with each other, as if guarding a secret inner segment of their selves from each other. He no longer talked about his work, nor, for that matter, did she probe for answers. She had learned her lesson in Africa, she told herself; she would not get involved again. But somehow that did nothing to calm her inner fears and worries.

She and Chrissy had just finished their first paid assignment—a series of band parts for the local high school band—and were gloating over their joint paycheck when John announced the long-awaited news. Their posting to Ankara, Turkey, had been confirmed. "It's going to be a two-part deal," he told her with evident enthusiasm. "The Turks are such a suspicious, paranoid lot that the company thinks it best to ease me into this one. I'll be going to the embassy to start with, as their oil expert, then eventually down to Iskenderun, where I'll be running my own station with my own operatives, which will have further-flung ramifications."

"And that's just what you wanted, isn't it?" she said, trying to mask her own lack of enthusiasm.

"Yes, indeedy. Running my own show with no interference!" He was jubilant. "And it's back to the gilded life for us, my sweet. No more toiling over a hot stove for you; no more of this damned daily commute for me."

"How soon?"

"Six weeks. A pity we'll be hitting Ankara at the beginning of winter, because it's damned cold on the plateau, I believe, but then maybe we won't be staying that long. However, there's a big European colony there, so maybe you can get into some musical groups for the time." He was so happy that she hadn't the heart to dampen his enthusiasm.

This time she was determined to be prepared, so she read everything she could lay her hands on about Turkey, the Turks, and the Near East situation, but this did nothing to cheer her.

Chrissy's reaction was doleful. "Oh, damn! I'm going to miss you so much. Just as we were getting our partnership off the ground, too! Oh, well, I expect it'll be a lot more exciting and interesting for you than Falls Church."

"But not too exciting, I hope," Vanessa murmured.

One thing she decided for herself, and that was that she would have to give up the cats. It had been one thing to leave them in unfriendly hands in Africa, but to take them to Turkey, where domestic animals were unwelcome and generally ill treated, would be doing them no kindness. So she would leave them in Chrissy's dependable hands, and they could live out their lives in peace, for they were long since inured to the Davis twins and, indeed, spent more time in the Davis yard than they did in the apartment. "I shall miss them terribly," she confided to Chrissy, "but I know damn well they won't miss me. That's one of the great strengths of cats—absolute independence. Pity we humans can't be as self-contained."

John was visibly relieved when he brought the subject up and she told him of her decision, and he even went so far as to say comfortingly, "Well, when we finally get to Iskenderun, I'm sure we can find you some substitutes."

"Only if they are gifts from God, as these were," she said obscurely.

But before their departure there occurred an incident that hurt her more than anything that had happened before, and, to make it worse, the unwitting bearer of these ill tidings was a friend.

It was just a couple of weeks before their departure, and she was busy separating those things they were taking with them from the remainder that was destined to go back into storage, when the phone rang and Eleanor Heitz's distinctive voice came on the line. "I know you are probably frantically busy," she said, "but could I just drop by for a little to catch up on things? I have a message for you."

"Why, of course, Eleanor, anytime." Vanessa was surprised; Eleanor was not the dropping-in type.

When she opened the door on her visitor, she was amazed at the transformation that had taken place. Before her stood a serene, smartly dressed woman with peaceful, happy eyes and a radiant smile. "So sorry to barge in on you when you're so busy," Eleanor said, seating herself tranquilly among all the clutter, "but I knew it was now or never. I'll be off abroad myself soon—I expect you've heard about the divorce."

"Well, yes," Vanessa said awkwardly, not knowing whether congratulations or commiserations were in order. "Er—are you going back to South Africa?"

The twinkle in Eleanor's eyes grew more pronounced, but she shook her head. "No. South Africa liberated me, or rather I should say a great and good South African liberated me, but we both know that that would never work. He cannot come to my world, and it would only compound unhappiness to try and cross into his. He finally opened my eyes to the unhappy waste my life had become and gave me the courage to do something about it. No, I shall never return to South Africa, but I *am* returning to my roots. My parents were missionaries in Turkey way back in the thirties and forties. They are both long dead, but I am returning to the fold, for a while at least, and will be teaching English at the mission's girls' school in Izmir."

"Why, what an extraordinary coincidence!" Vanessa cried. "We're off to Turkey, too—to Ankara. Maybe we can get together there. Let me see. Izmir is down on the southern coast, isn't it?"

"Yes, and if you get there, I'll always be happy to see you, but..." Eleanor smiled wryly. "I intend to keep as far away from the diplomatic world as I can get, so don't expect me in Ankara! Anyway..." She appeared to draw herself together. "That's enough about me—it's not why I came. I've just been to visit Maggie, and I feel there are some things I should explain. If I may say so, I think you handled the pressures you were under in Africa extremely well, but there must have been a great deal of hurt for you to deal with, and what I have to say might alleviate it."

"Oh?" Vanessa could not imagine what was coming, so she temporized. "How is Maggie doing?"

"Well, they've dried her out successfully, though I'm not sure that isn't a cruel kindness. She's a manic depressive and is probably too far gone to do much about it. I doubt whether they'll ever let her out of that ghastly place she's in. She is wallowing in guilt about all the poison pen nastiness she inflicted on you, and to ease her mind I said I'd see you and clear things up. She told me everything, you see." She paused as if undecided on how to proceed. "All that business about John's girlfriends on his trips was just pure spite on her part, based on his premarital dalliances. The same goes for her accusation about you acting like me." She grimaced. "It's amazing, really—I thought I was being so damned discreet, and yet . . ." Again she paused, then said, "But I feel I have to explain about Betty. That's another thing I had been blind about. I just didn't want to see, didn't want to think, that she was tainted with the same unfortunate drives as her father. It was a thing I could only bring myself to accept after I found my own peace. Betty is a nymphomaniac, pure and simple. She is incapable of love or commitment or anything that is real and lasting. For her, sex is the only reality. I am sure John had the good sense to tell you that she and he had had a fling before you were married, and that it meant nothing. And that later episode was entirely her doing—when you were in America, she chased after him on that trip and, I'm sure, pestered him so much that in sheer desperation he went to bed with her to get her out of the way. It was all she wanted, you see. She came back as sleek and contented as a cat, and that was the end of it. Obviously, you handled that as well as you handled the rest of it, but it must have been upsetting and difficult for you, and I just wanted to be sure that you understood how meaningless it was to him."

"I see." Vanessa felt icy cold and very queasy. "Thank you for taking the trouble."

"Well, I've held you up long enough. I must be on my way," Eleanor said breezily, standing up. "I'm sure you are going to find Turkey a lot less traumatic than South Africa, and I hope you'll be very happy there. If you come down to Izmir, be sure and look me up. The best of luck, my dear."

"Oh, I will, indeed I will," Vanessa muttered, seeing her to the door. "And good luck to you, too, Eleanor."

When she had closed the door, she slumped into the nearest chair and stared vacantly into space, the hurt raging in her heart. What was it he had said so many times and in so many ways since their marriage? "You are my last and only love; there will never be anyone but you for me." And yet already there had been, for whatever paltry reason, someone else. If he had lied to her about that, what else might he have lied to her about? The thought was so terrifying that she slammed that door in her mind firmly shut. She could not think like that; she could not afford to think like that. Yet she realized, with something like despair, that irreparable damage had been done. Again it was a question of trust, and the trust was gone. Where she was going from there she just did not know.

Chapter 18

*S*he said nothing to John of Eleanor's visit, either then or later, for it would only have exacerbated a situation that was tense enough. They were facing another fresh start, and she needed to put what was past behind her; it was not going to be easy. Was this going to be the pattern of their lives, she wondered, a series of new starts in new places, but with all the old problems, the unresolved situations stretching behind and ahead of them? Did she really want to live the rest of her life like that? And for the first time she allowed to herself the possibility that the marriage, however much they loved each other, might have been a mistake for both of them.

A brief good-bye visit to her mother further unsettled her, for on checking around with many of her peers she found a dismaying number of them divorced or in the process of getting divorces. Nancy, her former cat custodian, was suing her erring husband for divorce because of an office romance. Sam and Gerda had tied the knot, only to untie it six months later when Sam had flown the coop, declaring that his career was being stifled. There were many, many others. Maybe we are a spoiled generation, she reflected, maybe we expect too much, for, by contrast, her mother's companionable marriage to the far-from-perfect Bob Cross seemed to be working very well.

Her sad good-byes to Chrissy and the cats said, she and John flew off to Istanbul via London, where, in their brief stopover, John insisted on getting a fur coat for her and a fur-lined raincoat for himself. "By all accounts, we're going to need them in frigid Ankara," he assured her. And the first omens certainly bore that out, for they landed in Istanbul in a blinding snowstorm—so blinding that their onward flight to Ankara was canceled—and so they had to settle for the train instead.

She was glad of this, since it gave her time to recover from her jet lag and from the window of their cozy, overheated first-class sleeper she watched with fascination as the endless, snowclad waste of the high Anatolian plateau, encircled by its threatening ring of snow-capped mountains, slowly unfolded while the train chugged doggedly on. "Will you be doing much traveling in this job?" she asked, trying to sound casual, for John was as keyed up and excited as a small boy and was continually on the jump, consulting maps and dipping into stacks of reports in his briefcase as if the future of the world depended on his assimilating all the information before they arrived in Ankara.

"While we're in Ankara I'll be doing a certain amount," he muttered, still concentrating on the report in his hand. "After all, I'm supposed to be an oil and minerals man, so I'll have to take a look at the oilfields in the southeast— Raman and Garzan. North of that is where a lot of the minerals come from, so I'll probably have to look at the iron mines at Divringi, the chrome works at Guleman, and the copper mines at Ergini."

"It was a surprise to me that the Turks had any oil," she commented.

"Oh, yes, they've been prospecting like mad for more since the oil crunch of the '70s, and there's a pipeline now from Raman to Iskenderun—hence it's a logical place for me to settle." He looked up and grinned. "Not to mention that oil and mineral prospecting will make a good cover for some of my operatives. Once we are down in Iskenderun, though, I'll be staying put. I'm afraid you're going to be in for a lot of informal entertaining, because a lot of the boys will be passing through. I hope you don't mind."

"No, not as long as you're there and I have someone to do the cleaning-up." She smiled at him faintly.

"That's my girl!" He leaned over and kissed her. "That's the right answer, and I'll see you get the best darned help available."

"Any idea how long before we'll be going down there?"

"Hard to say, since this is an entirely new setup. It may be six months or even longer. The sad fact is that most of our top operatives and most of our high-powered network were demolished with the bombing of the American embassy in Beirut, and it has taken a long time to pick up the pieces. Beirut is still out of action, for the most part, and most of what's been done lately has come out of Tel Aviv and Cairo. But that's awkward. Too far away from Syria, Iraq, and Iran to make it easy to get information in and out, so it's up to me to make this new center work."

"So there's no one there at all now?"

"None of our people. Only a few locals, most of them feeding information into Cyprus."

"And what if the Turks find out? You say they are terribly paranoid."

He shrugged. "They tend to distrust all foreigners, period. But we have a lot of things working for us. For one thing, their main paranoia is about communists. The Russians have always been their number-one enemy. For another, they're in NATO, and that suits them very well. So long as we're not blatant about what we do and we don't do anything to get them in Dutch with their neighbors, they're liable to turn an accommodatingly blind eye. So far as I can see, our main danger here will be from double agents, which is why I intend to use as many of our own people as I can."

The early winter's darkness fell and there was nothing more to watch, so to break the monotony they spent a very long dinner hour in the dining car, where Vanessa studied the menu with marked attention, since it was conveniently bilingual. "I can see I'll have lots of new dishes to bone up on. At least 'sis kebab' I know, and this 'kofte' seems to be a souped-up hamburger. Ugh, look at this one! 'Calve's brains in batter'—I think I'll skip that! Here's one that looks interesting—'Yumurta ispanak'—spinach, hamburger, and eggs."

"This wine is pretty good, too—and cheap!" John said, examining the label. "Kavaklidere—better make a note of that, too, while you're at it. Let's have another bottle." They did, and they arrived in Ankara in a suitably mellow mood.

She found Ankara full of surprises, most of them good. She was taken aback by how large and modern it was: larger than Pretoria and, but for the dark, round-headed and round-faced Turks that thronged its wide, snow-covered boulevards, indistinguishable from any modern American city, with its high buildings, public transportation, and modern shops. They had been allotted a small furnished villa near the center of town on Mesrutiyet Caddesi, so she was within walking distance of practically anything she needed. She was absolved from housekeeping cares by a married couple, Ali and Selima, whose English was minimal but whose gifts were many. It was Ali who, in good middle eastern style, was the outside man, for he did all the shopping and all the outside errands; but it amused her to see that he was far from ruling the inside roost, for Selima would descend on his purchases like a ravening eagle, examine them critically, and give him hell if the vegetables were not fresh enough or the meat not of the right cut or the cleaning materials not exactly to her specifications. Outside, Ali may have been Mr. Macho; inside, he was undoubtedly Mr. Milquetoast.

With great delight, Vanessa found that Ankara boasted a flourishing music conservatory. When she timidly approached it, she was pounced upon with every appearance of enthusiasm and enrolled in their string orchestra.

Most of her colleagues were incomprehensible to her, but music is a universal language, and in no time at all, it seemed to her, she was accepted as part of the group. Grateful for this, she immediately enrolled in a crash course in Turkish, and within a very short time she was way beyond the limits of her Turkish phrasebook. "Once you catch on to the idea that they say practically everything in the form of a verb, it's not all that difficult," she informed her amused husband, who was delighted with her enthusiasm.

She was helped toward her own goals by the fact that the American embassy was in a state of suspended animation: the old ambassador had departed, the minister was on home leave, and the new ambassador had not yet arrived, so partying was at a minimum. Even Henfield, the CIA head of station, was newly arrived and only just settling into his job. "Not that we have to bother much, anyway," John assured her. "There's a young Foreign Service officer who does all the work for State in the oil section and then there I am as titular head of it, but we're separate and we really don't have to get involved."

For this she was duly thankful after she met Henfield, who was as different from Armand Heitz as it was possible to be. He was a slight man, with an overwhelming aura of grayness about him: gray hair, grayish skin, and a pair of the coldest, flattest gray eyes she had ever seen. His face was completely expressionless, and he seemed a man devoid of any human emotion. "Boy, where on earth did they ever find him?" she exploded after their first meeting.

"I believe he came here from Iceland," John said.

"That figures—he looks like an arctic wasteland himself."

"Yes, not very charismatic, is he? But they say he's very able," John said doubtfully.

"He's not your boss on this job, is he?" she asked with grave misgiving, for she had taken an instant dislike to the reptilian man.

"No, I'm an independent, but naturally we're supposed to cooperate," he assured her. "Oh, and guess what— with the new ambassador we are getting a female CIA agent. Haven't seen one of those in quite a while, and I gather Henfield isn't too pleased. He's a dedicated bachelor and doesn't have much time for career women."

"That also figures," Vanessa murmured, but she was intrigued by the news: maybe from a female CIA agent she could get some of the inside answers to her unresolved questions. This was one person she was eager to meet.

When John went off on the first of his survey trips, she was determined not to sit around and mope over her problems, and she made a concerted effort to explore the city. She enlisted the help of one of her fellow musicians, a large, buxom, and blond English girl, also a violinist, who worked for the British Council in Ankara and who bore the rather unfortunate name of Hope Thinne. "No, of course, it won't be a bother," Hope assured her. "I'd love to go around with you. I don't dare go to a lot of places by myself." She sighed resignedly. "Turkish men can be such a pain when you're by yourself. You're lucky to be small and dark. When you've my size and coloring they really give you a hard time. The Turks really go for heft—I wish Englishmen did." She sounded so forlorn that Vanessa couldn't repress a smile, and Hope laughed with her.

Together they explored the old village of Ancyra, set high above the modern city behind its mighty medieval walls. "The only place you get any real atmosphere, I think," Hope said. "Old Ataturk waved his magic wand and decreed that Ankara should come into being, because it was central and he wanted a fresh start away from Istanbul and all it stood for—but like all these 'created' cities, it has always been a bit lacking. Canberra is the same way."

"Washington, too, come to that," Vanessa said with feeling. They passed a huge bastion that, by its overwhelming smell, they identified as a urinal for the nearby market. "But then there's atmosphere and atmosphere," she added, wrinkling her nose.

Hope laughed. "Oh, you'd better get used to that, particularly if you travel around much. The Turks are true children of nature and don't give much thought to sanitation. You should smell some of their prisons—ugh!"

"I hope I never do," Vanessa said, thankful for once for her diplomatic shelter.

They visited the small Roman temple in whose wall rested the tablet of Augustus' decree, issued on a visit to Ancyra, that all the Roman world should be taxed after a census had been taken; tradition had it that it was this census that had sent a certain Jewish couple on the road to their native town of Bethlehem, and to a birth that had changed the world. "When John and I were in Rome," Vanessa told her companion, "we went to see the church of Santa Maria Aracoeli, where they still have the altar Augustus dedicated to the 'Unknown God' his soothsayers said had come into the world at the time of Christ's birth. I've always thought that such an amazing coincidence."

"Hmm. I've never been much into religion myself," Hope said. "You want to see Ataturk's tomb?"

"Not much," Vanessa confessed. "Let's have some tea."

She was more than a little irritated when, on John's return, he seemed displeased with her new-found friend. "British Council, eh? Well, be very careful you don't let anything slip about what I do or where I go. You never know with the British; they like to keep their finger in the pie."

"Oh, for God's sake, John!" she cried, "we met in the orchestra, and all she knows is that I'm married to someone in the embassy. I've better things to do than gossip about you. You really *are* getting paranoid!"

"We've got to be careful," he grumbled. "This is too damned important to have any slipups. Isn't there someone in the embassy you can pal around with?"

"Judging by Pretoria, *that's* no guarantee of anything," she parried, and they remained at cross purposes.

She knew virtually no one at the embassy, for John's assistant was unmarried, and she was glad to have it that way, content with her new life. It was only after the arrival of the new ambassador that the receptions began, and this forced her into a more active role.

At the first welcoming reception, hosted by the senior political officer in the minister's absence, she was duly impressed by the new ambassador's physical appearance. He was a commanding figure, tall, broad-shouldered, with a weatherbeaten, high-colored, beaked-nosed face under a helmet of tight silver curls. "Russell Owen is a political appointee," John murmured in her ear. "Very cozy with the present administration. Rich. Oklahoma oil. Very keen on archaeology and hunting, in both of which Turkey abounds. Hence this appointment, which normally goes to a career man. I gather the State people are a bit wary of him."

"Where's Mrs. Owen?" she asked, for the ambassador had appeared alone.

"Back in the States. Some long-standing physical problem. She isn't planning to join him, except for the occasional visit, I hear."

"Bit awkward for the minister's wife, isn't it?" she murmured back. "Will she have to do all the official entertaining?"

"Not really." He grinned sideways at her. "We're lending a helping hand—our new gal is going to be his social secretary and take care of that. Very useful."

"Where is she?" Vanessa said, with quickening interest.

"Over there. She's quite a looker," John said with evident appreciation. "Let's angle over and meet her casually. That's our number-two CIA man, Vern Wolf, talking to her now—another bachelor. This embassy is crawling with 'em. She's called Kim Garland—missus, though what happened to mister I've no idea."

They sidled their way through the chattering crowd to where the redheaded, chicly dressed woman was visibly scanning the crowd as she paid but scant attention to the rotund CIA man by her side. Her gaze clamped questioningly on them as they came up to her, and her wide mouth fixed in a faint smile. As they came face to face, Vanessa saw that her strikingly handsome, irregular features were marred by a pair of rather hard hazel eyes set too close together. By the faint lines around her mouth and eyes Vanessa put her down as in her early forties. "Mrs. Garland, I'd like you to meet my wife, Vanessa," John said heartily.

The smile widened. "Why, how do you do, Vanessa— delighted to meet you," she said in a deep, velvety contralto. "But please call me Kim—you, too. It's John Bannerman, isn't it?" A twinkle appeared in the hazel eyes. "Our oil man, I understand."

"Right," he agreed with an answering grin.

To Vanessa's surprise, Kim firmly put her hand through the younger woman's arm and said, "I'm going to steal your wife for a little to get the lowdown on you lot. We girls have to stick together. Have fun!" And without further ado she towed her firmly toward the bar, where, having supplied herself with a bourbon and soda, she turned on Vanessa, who had hurriedly recharged her own wine glass. "Now, let's find a quiet seat somewhere and you can fill me in on what's what and who's who."

"Oh, dear!" Vanessa exclaimed in dismay, "I'm afraid you've come to the wrong person. We're fairly new here ourselves, and I know practically no one at the embassy."

"Ah, an uninvolved wife—what a refreshing change!" Kim continued, unabashed. "No matter. Just tell me all about yourself and what you do."

A little mystified by her warm interest, Vanessa allowed herself to be corraled into a tête-à-tête. She found herself faced with a skillful interrogator, and almost before she knew it she had told Kim most of her personal history, to which the redhead appeared to give rapt attention.

"How romantic!" she cooed. "And how fortunate for John to have found such a young, attractive wife—and talented, too."

"Well, not very, I'm afraid—" Vanessa was muttering when they were interrupted by a deep voice saying, "Ah, there you are, Kim! I was afraid you'd run out on me." And she looked up to see Russell Owen towering over them.

Kim surged to her feet and said smoothly, "Mr. Ambassador, I'd like you to meet one of our young wives, Vanessa Bannerman. John Bannerman is your oil and minerals man. Like us, they are relative newcomers to Turkey."

Vanessa's hand was seized in a firm grasp, and Russell Owen's dark eyes appraised her as Kim went on. "Vanessa is a musician and already active in the cultural life here, so you see all your fears about entering a cultural waste-land are needless! We have talent among us."

"Indeed? Delightful! We must see a lot more of you," he boomed. "Now, I hate to tear you away, but I need help, Kim—so if Mrs. Bannerman will excuse us . . ." And he turned away.

But before she followed him, Kim put a confiding hand on Vanessa's arm. "Let's get together very soon," she whispered. "Lunch. Whenever you're free. Give me a call. I hope we can be friends, good friends."

Vanessa watched her go, feeling somewhat confused by the rapidity of events, and she jumped a little as John's voice said in her ear, "So what was all that about? I see you got a private chitchat with the ambassador. Lucky you!"

"Well," she said thoughtfully, "I certainly appear to have made a friend—I think." But there was a niggling doubt in her mind.

Chapter 19

Divided in her mind, she did nothing for two weeks about Kim Garland's whispered invitation, but then, thinking it might seem ungracious to wait longer, she phoned her office at the embassy. With quiet relief she discovered Kim was off on a trip with the ambassador, who was inspecting the consulates in his new bailiwick and would not be back for another week, and she left it at that. John was preparing for another of his own trips, and paramount in her own mind was the house he was going to pick out for their future home in Iskenderun. Thus it was that Kim eventually phoned her, a harder edge on the velvet voice. "I hadn't realized you'd be so busy. I've been hoping to hear from you."

"I did call," Vanessa said hastily, "but you were away with the ambassador."

"Oh, I didn't get your message." The voice sounded mollified. "Then how about lunch tomorrow?"

"Fine. Would you care to come here?"

"No, this was my idea. Lunch on me. I've already

found a couple of good restaurants. Do you know Serge's? Can you meet me there at one?" Vanessa said she could.

Throughout the luncheon she was beset by the uncomfortable feeling that her companion knew a lot more about her than she had at their first meeting; she seemed so knowledgeable, so sure of herself. Not that she was at all unpleasant; on the contrary, she was almost gushing in her flattery, and that only increased Vanessa's unease. What was she after? Had she conceived a fancy for John, who obviously found her attractive and interesting? Was this some elaborate dust-throwing in the unsuspecting eyes of his wife? Or was she trying to worm her way into Vanessa's confidence to find out what John was up to in his independent kingdom? No explanation seemed to fit, for Kim asked no questions about John at all and, in fact, appeared to steer the conversation away every time Vanessa mentioned him.

Nor did she seem disinclined to talk about herself, and during the course of the luncheon she revealed that her husband, or rather her ex, had also been a CIA man. Emboldened by this, Vanessa determined to try to get some of her own questions answered. "Do you find a great difference between your former role as a CIA wife and your present role as an operative?" she asked. "I mean, is your present job more stressful, or less?"

Kim looked at her calculatingly. "I'm not sure I understand your question," she evaded. "There is stress in any job these days. It's just that the stresses are different."

"And that's just what I mean," Vanessa said. "As an operative you may have the stress of danger or responsibility or whatever, but you know the whole picture; you know what's going on. As a wife, you only know *something* is going on, but you don't know the whole of it, and it makes for great insecurity, never knowing what to expect next."

"And that bothers you?"

"Yes it does," Vanessa said frankly. "Particularly when a lot of it doesn't seem to make any sense. I can't say I like what the CIA does to people. I'm not sure I even like what the CIA *does*, and yet here I am and it's something

I have to deal with. I'd just like to know how best to handle it, and you've seen both sides of the coin. How did you do it?"

"I'm not sure I'm the best person to ask." Kim's tone was dry. "After all, my marriage didn't last. But it didn't fold because of the CIA; it folded because my husband and I just grew in different directions. And, obviously, I wouldn't still be around if I didn't believe in the company and what it does. The best advice I can give you"—her voice became decisive—"is to live your own life, do your own thing—which you seem to be doing—and find more interesting avenues to explore. If you're up to plenty yourself, you don't have to worry so much about the plenty your husband is up to, do you? After all, if you had wanted a quiet, tranquil life, you would not have married a CIA man in the first place, would you?"

It had not been quite like that, but Vanessa was in no position to tell her so. "Oh, and I gather John is going off on another of his trips," Kim went on casually, and she tensed, wondering if this was where the probing would begin. "Yes," she said tersely.

"Good—then you'll be free this weekend. How about coming over to the residence on Sunday? Very informal— buffet and drinks. The ambassador likes to relax with a few congenial companions on his day off, and he indicated he'd like to see more of you."

"I'm afraid I've already got an engagement on Sunday," Vanessa said quickly. Kim's smoothly plucked eyebrows raised in silent interrogation, so she felt obliged to go on. "Now that the weather is warmer, a friend of mine and I are going off for the day and she's going to show me around Boghaz-koy—that's the old Hittite capital north of here. I'll be gone all day."

"How fascinating!" Kim purred. "The ambassador adores things like that—mind if we come along?"

She was taken aback. "Well—" she gasped, "I don't know. My friend only has a small car . . . and we're not *experts*, you know!"

"Oh, my dear!" Kim waved this aside. "Naturally we'd go in his limousine. We could make a day of it—champagne, picnic lunch and all. It'll be *perfect*! Please ask your friend—I'm sure she wouldn't mind a couple more rubbernecks."

"But what about the ambassador's other guests?" Vanessa said weakly.

They too were waved aside. "Oh, they can come some other time. He'd much rather do something like this. Will you get back to me on it? I'll take care of the other details."

Feeling she had boxed herself into a corner, she had to say yes, and later she put it to Hope, almost wishing she would negate the whole affair. Instead her large friend was thrilled. "Oh, my! What glory! Certainly, I'd love to. I'll have to do some quick brushing up on what we're going to see."

When the day came and they drove north in the warm magnificence of the official limousine, its flag fluttering proudly in the brisk breeze, through the bleak countryside where patches of snow still lay on the bleached grass, Vanessa was not pleased by the fact that Hope was so impressed by her distinguished companion as to be almost incoherent, and she found herself babbling extensions of the English girl's laconic explanations. Russell Owen was totally at ease and visibly amused by all this, and when they arrived at the scattered gray ruins of the ancient city he insisted that they have their lunch before embarking on their explorations.

Under the thawing influence of the Veuve Cliquot champagne he produced from the cooler and the gourmet luncheon the picnic hamper contained, Hope lost her shyness. To Vanessa's vast relief, all went well from then on.

When they had gone on to the nearby religious sanctuary of Yazilikaya and Hope was showing the ambassador through the stiff lines of Hittite figures carved on its rocky gray walls, Vanessa, who was strolling behind with Kim, said impulsively, "He's really *very* nice. Hope was scared to death, and now she's chatting away with him like an old friend."

Kim, who had been unusually silent, looked sideways at her. "I'm glad you think so. Yes, he's quite a man, and one who will need many outlets like this to ease the pressures on him."

"This must be an interesting job for you—not at all like the usual run of CIA skulduggery," Vanessa went on cheerfully.

Again Kim looked at her with quick suspicion. "Well, yes and no. I've done this sort of thing before, but it does have its problems, like everything else. It's good to have someone like you around. Maybe I can share them with you eventually." But she did not elaborate.

On the journey back they had more champagne, and by the time she was dropped off at the house, Vanessa was feeling quite lightheaded and totally relaxed. As she let herself in the phone was ringing, and there was a rather peevish John at the end of the line. "Where on earth have you been? I've been trying to get through to you all day."

"Cavorting around the plateau with the ambassador," she giggled, and went on to give him a blow-by-blow account of the day.

"Well, just be sure you don't let anything slip to Kim about what I'm doing or where I am," he charged her. He went on to say that he thought he had found a house that might do in Iskenderun. "It's in the hills a little above the town," he explained. "Not large, but with a lovely view of the Mediterranean, and sufficiently removed from its neighbors so that we can be completely private, which is a definite plus."

"Sounds great," she said muzzily. "Want me to come down and give it my blessing?"

"No." He was almost abrupt. "I think I'll go ahead and take it, if you've no strong objections."

"None that I can think of. When will you be home?"

"I don't know," he said. "Soon, I hope. Take care." And he hung up.

But it wasn't soon, and she didn't hear further from him. This irked her, but she tried not to worry about it, and when Kim phoned a dinner invitation a few days later she accepted it as a welcome break from her solitude. She took a taxi to Kim's apartment, which was located near the residence in a modern block of flats, and she was a little surprised on arrival to find they were eating in and not out. "Don't worry," Kim assured her with a grim smile. "I'm not going to inflict my cooking on you. I have a deal with the embassy caterers, and they run a first-rate send-out service. They should arrive before too long, so let's get down to some serious drinking—I've had a hard day." They drank and chatted and drank some more, and still there was no sign of food. By the time it did arrive Vanessa was definitely muzzy; the rest of the evening was clouded and her recollections vague. She woke up the next day in her own bed with a terrible hangover and the shock of knowing she hadn't the vaguest recollection of getting home.

Guiltily, she tried to remember what she had talked about—certainly it had not been about John's work, but she had hazy recollections of talking about her marriage, about older men, even about her father, and she seemed to recall Kim talking about her own life, but she couldn't bring the details into focus. She was tempted to call Kim and by apologizing find out more, but decided against that; if she had made a fool of herself, the less said the better.

When John arrived out of the blue the next day, he was so tense and edgy that he did not notice her own edginess. Although he told her nothing, things had evidently not been going smoothly, and he was only home to pick up a fresh supply of clothing before going off again. During their one quiet dinner together she managed to bring up the subject of Kim and her own reservations about her unrelenting friendliness. "You say she doesn't ask questions about me?" John said. "Well, then, have you considered that it may simply be that you're the only game in town? There *are* no other CIA wives of any heft on the scene at the moment. You're the only one she can relate to." But somehow she had the feeling there was more to it than that.

How very much more was revealed to her, like a thunderbolt, at her very next encounter with Kim. She had been out at an orchestra rehearsal and on her return found an incoherent note left by Ali on the phone to the effect that Bayan Garland had called and wanted urgent touch. She had tried calling the office, only to find that Kim had

gone for the day, but she was saved further searching by
the appearance of Ali, who announced, "Bayan Garland
is now here," and stood aside to let the redhead by.

"Hope you don't mind me dropping in like this, but I
gathered from your man you'd be here after rehearsal and
I wanted to talk to you." Kim appeared keyed-up and
nervous, and it flashed across Vanessa's mind that she
had already been drinking.

"Why, no, of course not." Vanessa was a little uneasy,
wondering if she was now going to learn the extent of her
evening's indiscretions firsthand. "May I get you a drink?"

"Yes, I'd love one," Kim said promptly, but after she
had been provided with a hefty bourbon and soda she
seemed in no hurry to reveal what was on her mind.
Instead she began to talk generally about the difficulties
of her job, the problems of an ambassador in a new post,
the need to make a good public image, and what a wonderful man Russell Owen was. It all seemed totally aimless
until she leaned forward and said earnestly, "You do like
him, don't you?"

"Who? The ambassador? Why, yes, I think he's
extremely charming."

Kim gave a satisfied nod. "Good. Because I need your
help." Again she took a long swig of her drink and appeared
to go off on a tangent. "It makes it very difficult for me
with a married ambassador on my hands and with no hope
of his wife joining him. The security angle is *so* important,
and yet we have here a healthy, dynamic man with normal
drives who will have to have an outlet for those drives—
and soon. The thing is to find an outlet that is *safe*; I'm
sure you can see that. That's my problem—that's part of
my job—so how about it?"

"How about what?" Vanessa was at a loss.

Kim leaned forward and said earnestly, "Look, dear,
I realized the other night how unhappy you are, so this
could be a solution for both of us. Apart from the fact
that he'd be tremendous fun to be with, he could do you
a lot of good. I mean, he's got everything—money, power,
position. He could *really* help you. And it would all be

handled very discreetly, I promise you, and you'd be perfect. I know he finds you attractive."

Vanessa looked at her with dawning horror. "You mean you're asking *me* to go to bed with the ambassador? You want me to be his *mistress*?"

Kim flushed faintly, but her wide mouth was set in a tight line. "Yes, that's about the size of it. We'd keep it nice and safe right here in the family, and there'd be no security problem, no scandal."

Vanessa was stupefied. "Why—" she gasped, "why, you're nothing more than a female pimp! Is *that* what the CIA uses you for—to pimp for official whores? Is that your *job*?"

"Oh, don't be so naive!" Kim said crossly. "This is a very special job, a very special assignment. And why are you so shocked? Don't you know that most major embassies keep a girl on the staff specifically to oblige visiting dignitaries? This isn't like that, of course; it's more important, it's vital. You'd be doing a real service for your country."

Suddenly Vanessa was so furiously angry that she could not see straight. She leaped to her feet and pointed a quivering finger at her guest. "You get out—right now!" she hissed. "I don't know where you come up with your sick ideas, but get *this* straight once and for all. I'll have no part of this ugly little scenario. I don't even want to *see* you again, and the minute John gets back I'm going to tell him everything about this and I'm sure he'll take some action. I've never heard anything so outrageous in my life!"

Kim sat looking up at her, her face a mottled red, her eyes slitted. "You're making a mistake, a serious mistake," she muttered, gathering up her things. "John knows the score better than you do. After all, unfaithful husbands expect unfaithful wives. You're angry now, but when you simmer down I think you should think this over—very carefully. If you sensibly change your mind, let me know; if not, I'm sorry I wasted my time on you. I hadn't realized you were so immature." And she was gone before Vanessa could think up a stinging retort.

Her anger continued to seethe and boil so that when John reappeared two days later she let it out in one scalding flood of pent-up frustration. "God knows, I thought I'd seen enough of the way the CIA operates, but this is the limit!" she panted at the end of her tirade. "What are you going to do about it?"

He had heard her out in tense silence, then answered quietly, "What do you want me to do about it? Punch the ambassador in the nose? Punch Kim in the nose?"

"*John!*" she cried, tears pricking her eyes. "This isn't a *joke!*"

"I know it isn't, but what do you expect me to do about it?" he repeated.

"Well, surely you're going to do *something*. Take it up with the CIA, at least. What if she puts pressure on somebody else who wouldn't dare to say no?"

"You seem to forget the CIA sent her to do this. She was only trying to do her job—mistakenly, perhaps—but she's under orders, just as I am. Nothing has happened, has it? Am I supposed to complain to them because another agent has put an improper suggestion to my wife? They'd think I had flipped out." His tone was weary.

"I see. So you're not going to do anything. You don't want to hear about it. Is that it?" she said bitterly. "Maybe Kim was right about some things—unfaithful husbands do seem to expect unfaithful wives."

"What's that supposed to mean?" he barked. "I thought we'd settled that long since. I'm not an unfaithful husband and have no intention of being one."

"Oh, really? Why lie about something that is obviously so unimportant to you?" she flared at him. "I know about Betty Newman—have known for some time."

It shook him. "Maggie? My God, she *did* do a job on you!"

"Yes, Maggie. But the cream of the jest was that I didn't believe her—it took Betty's *mother* to set me straight, to let me know how *unimportant* it all was to you. That I *did* believe."

"Oh God, darling, I'm sorry!" he muttered wretchedly.

"But it *was* unimportant—it made no difference to the way I felt, will always feel, about you."

"I wish I could say the same," she whispered.

He looked at her with agonized doubt. "Oh, hell, Van—what's happening to us? Whatever it is, we can't let it. We've got to make a fresh start, and now is the time. It's why I'm back so soon. Everything's ready to go. We can go down to Iskenderun the beginning of next month, and then we'll really be together. No more separations, no more of these damn trips, no more foul-ups or misunderstandings. We can put all this behind us; we can start again."

"Oh, yes, that's always a solution, isn't it? Brush everything under the rug." She sighed. "We can always start again."

Chapter 20

*H*e was evidently sincere in what he said, and she did make a conscious effort after the move to make this new start meaningful; but each time, she realized, it was becoming more difficult, less effective—her inner unhappiness simply would not dissipate. She left Ankara with mixed feelings: thankful to get away from the embassy and everyone in it, but loath to leave her musical circle, which, even in the short time she had been there, had given her the meaning and warmth she had needed. She knew she would not find its like in the smaller confines of Iskenderun.

Hope had tried to comfort her. "We're all going to miss you, too. Offhand, I don't know of anything musical going on down there, but I can give you the addresses of a couple of Turkish students who were in our BC programs and who speak excellent English. Be sure and contact them—if there are any musicians around they'll probably know, and they'll be good sources for where to go and what to see. They'll be delighted to practice their English—it's one of the biggest complaints of our ex-students outside of the main cities that they never get enough people to talk to. In any case, keep in touch, and if there's anything you need, shout!"

Iskenderun was a surprise to her. It bore the bewildered air of a sleepy provincial town that had suddenly been jerked out of its peace and quiet into the industrial twentieth century. Its heart still bore the imprint of more leisurely times; there were wide, palm-lined avenues, a boulevard along the seawall, and an impressive central square patterned in the French style—a legacy of its brief colonial heritage. But around this tranquil nucleus all was abustle and the streets thronged with uniforms, for it was a Turkish naval and army base, and not only did it have the pipeline terminus with its attendant large oil storage tanks, but it also boasted a brand-new steel processing plant that fed on the mines to the north and belched its fiery breath into the sunny sparkle of the Mediterranean air. Although she was impressed by its unexpected size, Vanessa was thankful when they climbed above the plain into the hills behind it and bumped down an unpaved road to the villa that clung precariously to their seaward-facing flanks, embedded in a grove of wattle and eucalyptus trees.

John looked at her hopefully as he showed her through it, flinging open the closed shutters of the upper rooms to reveal the sparkling vista of the sea. "Do you like it?"

"Oh, yes, it's lovely." She leaned on the wide window-sill, looking down into the small, enclosed garden where exotic flowers she could not name rioted about a small, green tile pool into which a spindly fountain dropped a tinkling spray. "I see we've got a fountain."

He grinned at her a little nervously. "Yes, but this one doesn't have a gusher. The Turks aren't into bugs—they rely on human ears. Our home here should be just that— a fine and private place."

"What's that?" She jutted her chin at a small white stucco building that stood to the right of the house, nestled up against the surrounding wall.

"That's the guest house. It has its own entrance from

the outside, too. We may be having a lot of guests, but you won't have to have them underfoot all the time."

"That's convenient," she said evenly. "The less I see, the less I have to worry about—right?"

"If the furnishings aren't to your taste, we can probably have some made locally," he went on hurriedly. She had taken careful note as they had wandered through the rooms, and though the Turkish furniture was sparse it was also tasteful. Many of the pieces, heavily inlaid with ivory and mother-of-pearl and ornately carved, looked antique to her. "No, I think it's fine. With our own bits and pieces added to these, what more do we want?"

He put his arms around her and drew her gently to him. "What I mostly want is for you to be happy here, for *us* to be happy here. I'm sure we can be, if we both try. So if there is anything you want, anything at all, I'll do my damnedest to get it for you."

"Oh, I know," she murmured. "You've always been very generous."

He drew away in sudden anger. "Oh, for God's sake, Van, what *do* you want?" he blazed. "You want me to *bleed* for you?"

"No, that I most certainly do not want," she returned quietly. "There's been too much of that already." She turned back to the view. "How about servants? I could certainly use some of those."

He got himself under control. "The old man who was caretaking this place for the owners—who live in Antakya, by the way—says his daughter and her husband are looking for a place. The husband works in the steel plant, but he'd be free enough to keep up the grounds and do the shopping, and she would take care of the house. She's a good cook. Iskenderun has grown at such a fast clip that there's a serious shortage of low-priced housing, and they'd be interested more in having a roof over their heads than in the actual money we'll be paying them. I said I'd let him know after you were here. The snag is that they *only* speak Turkish and a little French, but if you thought you could cope with that—"

"Yes, that sounds good. I'll go on with my Turkish

lessons with one of Hope's ex-pupils," she returned. "And it'll keep me in practice at home. Better all around, come to think of it. If they can't speak English, there'll be less worry about security, won't there?"

Thus Mehmet and Guzel Cilli joined the household: young, black-eyed, and gracile, with thin, long faces and heads that bespoke Arab rather than Turkish origins. They were very quiet and reserved, but also very efficient and evidently thankful for a solid roof over their heads. Mehmet would put-put off to work every day on his little Vespa motorbike and return in the late afternoon, his saddlebags bulging with household purchases. Unlike the redoubtable Selima, Guzel was appreciative of her husband's efforts, and it did Vanessa's heart good to see them in the evenings, sitting outside their own quarters to the left of the villa, holding hands and murmuring to each other, their dark heads close together.

The remoteness of the villa might have presented a problem, save that she was now once more in possession of her own transportation. Forewarned about the vagaries of Turkish roads, John had sold the low-slung Alfa in America at a vastly inflated price and had bought a high-clearance four-wheel-drive station wagon for himself. As soon as their move south was definite, with the remaining cash he had snapped up a small Ford Escort for her from a departing embassy family. The main hazard of driving down the winding mountain road into the city, she found, was not in the volume of traffic but in the livestock one tended to meet en route: the heavily burdened, slow-moving donkey, the occasional ox cart, and the even more occasional (and frightening) herd of camels driven by wild-eyed Bektashi nomads. It all tended to add a sense of adventure to every trip and made the mad taxi drivers of the city seem mild in comparison.

She had quickly contacted Hope's students, feeling that the busier she kept herself the less occasion she would have to get at cross purposes with John, who was still very much on the jump and prone to flare defensively at the slightest hint of criticism.

Her first contact was a plump, sullen girl whose English

was excellent but whose overall personality was so negative that she appeared deliberately unhelpful. Her second was a young man, Ahmet Ozguc, who by contrast was a ball of fire, although his English tended to disappear entirely in moments of stress. He knew nothing of music or the music world, but in no time at all he contacted her to say he had found an amateur group that got together to play chamber music and could always use fresh blood. Was she interested? She was.

It was a very mixed group: the French consul, who was a cellist and extremely suave; a Turkish army major as large and solid as the bass-viol he played; an elderly, bespectacled secretary from the British consulate who was a violist; and, surprisingly, a tugboat captain, Turkish by name but Greek by descent and looks, who was the principal violinist. The erratic demands of his job made his attendance always questionable, so Vanessa was welcomed with open arms, not only for her skills but for the more cogent fact that she could always be there and on time. With this outlet, and amid the unrelenting beauty of the Mediterranean climate and scenery, she began to hope that at least for a while, they had come to safe haven and that all would be well.

John was being extremely careful about keeping her uninvolved. Occasionally she would see lights in the guest house at night and John would be late to bed; more rarely there would be guests for dinner, some American, others of no discernible or announced nationality, and all ostensibly "in oil"; but so long as she was present, no word was said of their real mission, and in the morning they would be gone. He had set up a little office in town, separate from the American consulate and manned only by himself and a young agent, Dick Fortescue, who was a combination cryptographer, radio man, secretary, and general gofer. He was a tall, thin man, very quiet and equally enthusiastic, with a tendency to stutter if he got excited. Initially she felt quite motherly toward him, until she found he was six years older than she was, and then she began to wonder about his evident lack of maturity.

Nonetheless, she was glad she did not have another Dilys— or, worse, a Maggie—to keep her eye on.

Their contacts with the American consular staff in Iskenderun were correct but minimal. The American consul and his wife—both plump, elderly, unambitious, and cheerful—had had them to dinner, and they had had them back, but there had been no attempt on either side to develop the relationship, and for this she was quietly thankful. By contrast, their vice-consul was a young Italian-American, Jim Valducci, who was sharp of eye, aggressive, and rather overtly hostile to John and the unassuming Dick Fortescue.

As spring waxed into hot summer, activity in the guest house also stepped up, and she was more amused than alarmed when one of their overnight guests appeared on her doorstep one morning with a solemn warning on his lips. He was a small, balding man with nervously darting dark eyes, and he whispered, "I'm going now, Mrs. Bannerman, but I just wanted to alert you to be careful about what you throw away in your garbage for the next week or so. They follow after me, you know, and the first thing they go for is the garbage—so a word to the wise. You take care!" And he glided away.

"Who in heaven's name was that?" she chuckled, after she had related the incident to John that evening. "Or maybe I should say *what*."

He smiled grimly. "Oh, that's poor old Dunkerfeld. He's been in Libya for a couple of years, and they get that way there after a time. He's not mine, thank God! He's one of Henfield's, though why Henfield bothered to send him down here is beyond me. He's getting rid of him to Poland—probably hopes the poor bastard will get caught and spare the CIA the expense of putting him out to pasture." It brought back the old chill.

Life had settled into such a quiet pattern that she was startled when the suggestion came from John to alter it. It was obviously an effort for him, and he prefaced his request by saying, "Now, I'm not trying to involve you at all, but I wonder if you'd do something for me."

"Why, yes, of course—what?"

"Business is becoming so brisk that I need another safe rendezvous point. We can't overuse this place or it might draw attention to us. I'd like to set one up in Antakya— or, to be exact, several—but if I start making frequent trips over there by myself, that may also stir things up. So could you develop a sudden interest in the archaeology of the Amuq Plain? It would give me a great excuse to ferry you over, and then you could go look at antiquities while I do my thing on the quiet. The Turks would appreciate that no husband worth his salt would let his wife wander around these places by herself, so it'd be a perfect cover."

"Sounds harmless," she agreed cautiously. "Give me a week or so to bone up so that I can sound authentic, and I'm your woman."

"You don't mind?" he said uneasily.

"No, I don't," she assured him.

At her next Turkish lesson she put it to the enthusiastic Ahmet Ozguc, who had already shown her around the historic sites of the Iskenderun area. He was his usual efficient self. "Ah, the Amuq! Yes, very interesting. You go to Antakya Museum—very fine place. Antioch very big city in old times, you know. In museum one of your countrymen at moment—big wheel. He'll fill you in. He'll tell you what to see."

An eager John drove her across the Anti-Taurus mountains through the Belen Pass down to the wide valley of the Orontes and the sprawling city of Antioch and dropped her off before the museum. "Meet you back here about four," he stated, and roared off.

Her first sight of Ahmet's "big wheel" was not very inspiring. Ushered by an attendant into a small storeroom in the depths of the great museum, she found her target almost completely submerged in pots. He was a small, elderly man with a fringe of white hair surrounding a bald brown pate, and he was clad in very shabby khaki shorts and shirt and a pair of well-worn sneakers. His name, Herman Gross, was all she knew about him. "Er, Mr. Gross?" she ventured. "My name is Vanessa Bannerman, and I've been told you're the great expert on the Amuq.

I wonder if you'd be so kind as to give me some information about it—what to see, where to go, what to read. I'm very keen on archaeology."

A pair of very shrewd blue eyes under shaggy white brows looked up at her. "Oh, really now? Pretty young thing like you interested in all this old stuff? Well, then"— he looked at a white patch on his tanned wrist and clucked—"Damn! Put me watch down somewhere—what time is it?"

Vanessa looked at her own. "Almost one."

"I thought so—time for lunch!" he said with great satisfaction, and got up. "Right! We'll have lunch and I'll get you started."

He trotted her off to a nearby small restaurant, oblivious to the stares of the clientele—which was exclusively male—and, after ordering a large meal, started to gobble it down absentmindedly as he chattered on. "Well, first I'll take you around the museum, give you a general idea. Then I'll start you off on Antioch itself. Lots to see. The Amuq is crawling with stuff." He waved a hand vaguely to the north. "Woolley's Tell Atchana, Braidwood's Tell Judeideh, Garstang's Sakje-Geuze, me own Tell Murad— me own dig at last! Husband's a diplomat, you say? Then you'll know Russell Owen. Friend of mine from way back. Helped fix this for me. Too hot to dig now, of course. Waiting for fall to get back to it. Like to come digging, then? Anyway, time for that later." He rattled on in this staccato vein until his plate was entirely cleared, then patted his shabby pockets anxiously. "Now, what have I done with me wallet?"

Vanessa, who was half mesmerized, came to with a start and fumbled in her bag. "Oh, please—let me! You've been most kind to give me your time like this. Please, I insist!"

She looked up to see the old man's intelligent blue eyes soften. "That's very nice of you, m'dear," he said gruffly, "very nice indeed."

"It's nothing," she muttered, her color rising. "I find all you've told me fascinating. But I don't want to keep you from anything important."

"From now on, you're important. Not every day I get someone who wants to listen," he said firmly, and trotted her back at the same breathless pace to the museum. As they went in a guard came up and announced, a shade wearily, "I found your watch, Bay Gross, you left it on one of the exhibit cases again. Please to be more careful!"

"Oh, did I now," he humphed, and took the slim platinum watch. Vanessa's eyes widened a little: she had once seen its like in Tiffany's window with an astronomical price tag.

His all-seeing eyes caught her gaze and a twinkle appeared in them. "Next lunch is on me," he murmured. "Now, let's get to work."

She emerged from her first session in a daze, to find John waiting impatiently for her. "Well, how did it go?" he demanded when they were on the road home.

"Oh, fine. He's an amazing old man, a regular dynamo. I'm exhausted. He says he knows Russell Owen. He's called Herman Gross. Have you heard of him?"

John whistled softly. "My God, him! You're certainly moving in high circles."

"Why? Who is he?" she exclaimed.

"The Texas multimillionaire—got a fortune and an empire almost as big as Getty's."

"Oh, my God!" she said, her face flaming. "And I thought he was a poor old archaeologist—I stood him lunch!" John laughed all the way home.

The next trip, following the instructions of her mentor, she climbed up to the line of the ancient Roman walls, high above the city, and set herself to studying the map he had provided her, while John went about his business. She was so wrapped up in what she was doing that she was only vaguely aware of footsteps announcing the arrival of another on her high lookout, until a voice said, "Spectacular view from up here, isn't it, Mrs. Bannerman? Well worth the climb."

She looked up in startled amazement. A mustache now

covered the long upper lip, and the dark hair was now longer and wavy, but there was no mistaking the voice she had first heard a continent and a lifetime away: it was Richard Morse.

Chapter 21

All she could do was gape at him as he stood looking down at her, doubt slowly dawning in his hazel eyes. "Er—you *do* remember me, Mrs. Bannerman?"

"Of course I do," she managed to gulp out. "Richard Morse of OXFAM, isn't it? Johnannesburg."

"Ex-OXFAM." He grinned suddenly, the even white teeth in his lean brown face making him look even more like a young, debonair version of David Niven. He settled himself on the ancient wall beside her and looked out at the view. "You might say my ship came in, or my stars were in the right places, or something. A black-sheep colonial uncle died—a successful black sheep—and left me all his lovely lucre, so I have joined that steadily dwindling breed, the English leisure class, and will continue to lounge around the world until the money runs out."

"So what are you doing here?" she demanded. "This is such an incredible coincidence, meeting on a Turkish hilltop like this. I just can't get over it."

"Destiny's hand at work." He glanced sideways at her.

"I'm trying my hand at writing and I'm collecting material for a book. Very interesting part of the world, this, and nothing much has been done on it. I'll probably be around for some time. As to my finding you on this hilltop, I confess that's not so much of a coincidence. I saw your husband dropping you off at the museum, and after some devious inquiries I gathered from old Gross you'd probably be up here."

"You *know* him?"

"I've met him. Bizarre old character, isn't he?"

"I think he's marvelous," Vanessa said stoutly.

"*Chacun à son gout*," he murmured. "Anyway, you're looking a lot better than when I last saw you. Perfectly ravishing, in fact."

"You disappeared so quickly that I never had the chance to thank you for saving my life," she said stiffly. "Or for the lovely violets."

"I had to let you know it was '*au revoir*' and not good-bye—my magical Welsh blood, you see. I *knew* we'd meet again. As to saving your life, well, you know what the Chinese say about that. In this case I think it's a perfectly charming idea."

"What do the Chinese say?" she asked in spite of herself.

"That if you save a life, then you become responsible for that person's life forever after." He gazed steadily at her, and she could feel her color rising. "How did you come to pick out African violets?" she asked hurriedly. "They happen to be my favorite flower."

"Oh, I suppose some subliminal association between violets and chestnut hair. I've always had a great weakness for both," he returned, still gazing deeply into her eyes.

"You'd have a hard time finding the chestnut in my dark mop. I'm a brunette," she expostulated.

"Oh, I don't know." He looked reflectively at her hair. "Now, with the wind teasing your hair about your face and the sun shining through it, I can see nothing *but* chestnut; it all lies in the eyes of the beholder, doesn't it?" His voice took on a harder edge. "But I wish I didn't find you always in places where no man in his right mind would let a woman as attractive as you go by herself. Where is that husband of yours?" His eyes strayed to a Roman watchtower that loomed in the line of the walls above them. "Is he up there using you for tiger bait?"

"Don't be ridiculous!" she said hotly. "Of course not. I've become interested in archaeology, and John's sweet enough to ferry me over here because I don't much like driving on mountain roads. He's not interested in this sort of thing, so he wiles away the time while I do my thing. I believe today he's seeing our landlord, who lives in Antakya." The lie slipped out easily. "In any case, it's time I started back. It's a long walk down, and he'll be waiting for me."

He put out a lean brown hand to help her up but kept hold of hers after she was on her feet. "Have lunch with me next time you're over," he said, his voice husky. "I'm staying at the Hotel Daphne—all faded French glamour, but with the Orontes rolling merrily by at the foot of the garden. Unlike John, I *am* interested in archaeology, and I'd be delighted to squire you wherever your heart desires. I have a car." He looked at her intently. "No strings— honestly!"

She hesitated. "I don't know when I'll be over again," she evaded. "It all depends on John's schedule."

"No problem." He released her and, after searching in the pockets of his bush jacket, produced a pen and a scrap of paper and scribbled on it. "Here's the phone number of the hotel. Just leave a message, and I'll find you."

"You seem to be good at that," she murmured, storing the paper in her bag, and in spite of herself, she knew that she would do it. There was something about him that intrigued her, attracted her in a way she had no wish to analyze.

"Good, then that's settled," he said with a satisfied air, and on the way down the precipitous path that took them by the empty looted tombs of Roman aristocrats they talked gaily and amusingly of a host of unrelated things. At the bottom of the path they separated. "*Au revoir*, then, my dear Mrs. Bannerman—or may I progress to calling you Vanessa?" He smiled. "We've never been properly introduced, have we? Richard Vivian Morse, at your service. Age thirty-two, sound of wind, limb, and fortune, Oxford University by way of Rugby, and a drifter upon the ocean of life. There, now, we're all proper, at last. When we meet again, we shall meet as friends." And he was gone before she could think of an adequate reply.

She had every intention of telling John about her amazing afternoon, but when she got back to the museum it was to find him pacing angrily up and down. "Really, Van," he burst out. "The least you could do is keep track of the time. I've got an important appointment back in Iskenderun and I'm going to be damned late." The words died on her lips, and as they drove back in tense silence, so did her resolve; she said nothing to him about Richard, either then or later. Perhaps after the next visit, she told herself, she would just mention it casually when John was in a better mood and their relationship less strained than it was at the moment; then there would be no misunderstanding.

It did not turn out that way, for things changed rapidly—not for the better but for the worse. She arrived back from rehearsal late one afternoon, to find John already installed with a drink in his hand, a thunderous brow, and no sign of dinner. "I'm afraid dinner is up to you tonight," he growled as she came in. "Either that or we can go back into town."

"Why? What's happened? Where's Guzel?" she cried in sudden alarm. "Has something happened to the baby? It's not due for four months!"

"Baby?" He looked at her blankly. "I don't know anything about that. No, I sent them packing, bag and baggage. We'll have to find someone else."

"You did *what*?" She could not believe her ears. "Have you lost your mind? *Why*, in heaven's name?"

"I caught Mehmet eavesdropping at the guest house, and the man who was there at the time said his things had been gone through."

"But that's ridiculous," she cried angrily. "Mehmet doesn't even speak English, let alone read it! What possible harm could he have done? Anyway, what right have you to do such a thing without even *consulting* me? Good God, John, what's gotten *into* you? I could have found out what it was all about, and there was probably some very good explanation. Didn't you even consider that?"

"I can't afford to consider that. *If* you had been here, naturally I'd have consulted you, but you weren't—I am tempted to add 'as usual,'" he flared back. "There's no doubt he was listening at the door, and he had no explanation for it. In fact, he acted damned guilty. And we don't *know* he has not learned any English. What's going on is too damned important to risk any slipups, even if it does inconvenience you. So I'm sorry, but that's the way it is."

She tried to control herself. "I see. So, since I am so clearly redundant and obviously have so little grasp of what these great matters that make you judge, jury, and hangman require in the way of security, *you* do the hiring. I'll have no part in it. From now on it's your responsibility. I'll just transmit your orders, unless you'd like to do that as well. I really don't care."

"Oh, please, Van—don't go off the deep end on this!" he said wearily. "Of course I'll find you someone else, and of course I want you to go on doing the excellent job you've always done. None of this is any fault of yours; it's just a bad break, and I'm sorry about the crack I made. I'm happy that you've found so much to do; honestly I am." But it did little to mollify her.

Nor did the replacements he found do much to heal the situation. They were a typical middle-aged Turkish peasant couple, solid and silent and not very bright. The man had no other job and so was underfoot all the time, and unless Vanessa gave him a work schedule every single day he would sit at the kitchen table chain-smoking cigarettes while his wife, Meriban, did the major part of the work. She at least was willing, if not very able, and the standard of their meals deteriorated sadly, for Vanessa stubbornly stuck to her resolve of noninvolvement and did nothing to instruct her further. To make matters worse, the man, Bilger, had no means of transportation, so

Vanessa was forced to drive him into Iskenderun for supplies practically every day, and this she found both time-consuming and irritating.

John at least had the sense to hold his peace during their settling-in process, and it was several weeks before he diffidently suggested another trip to Antakya. The alacrity with which she said yes surprised him, as did her refusal of his tentative suggestion that they lunch there together. "I've made my plans for the next visit," she told him. "So you go your way and I'll go mine. What time do you want me back? Should we synchronize our watches? I would hate for you to miss another life-and-death appointment."

"Oh, Van!" he sighed. "Please spare me the sarcasm. I always seem to be on the defensive these days. I'm sorry about last time, and this time I thought we might just have a peaceful lunch together, that's all, but if you'd rather not, I understand. Anyway, I'm not in any rush today, so let's say five o'clock."

"I'll be there," she said coolly. She could hardly wait to make her phone call.

Herman Gross was as amusing and informative as always, and by lunchtime she was in a relaxed and happy mood when Richard arrived in a Jeep to pick her up. "Sorry it's not a Rolls, m'lady." He smiled as he handed her into it. "But I find this a lot more practical for bumping over the Turkish terrain. I'm taking you for a mystery tour and a picnic, so brace yourself!"

The day was glorious, her companion relentlessly charming, and as they lunched by the little cave that had housed the first Christian church in Antioch, she felt completely at peace. It was a wonderful lunch: cheese boreks that melted in the mouth, a crisply roasted chicken filled with a delicious, aromatic nut stuffing, Turkish dolmas and fresh-baked bread, and to top it off some rahat lokum, all washed down with two bottles of champagne.

"I must say you really do things in style, Richard," she said, sucking the powdered sugar from the sticky sweet off her fingers. "Usually I don't like sweets, but that Turkish delight is simply heavenly."

He was smoking a pipe, his eyes slitted against the lazily curling blue smoke. "Mm, yes, it is good. Not like the stuff they call Turkish delight in England—kind of a pink jelly and *quite* revolting. Having fun?"

"Oh, yes!" She stretched luxuriously. "This is wonderful—just the sort of break I needed."

He started to pick up the picnic clutter and dump it back into the basket. "Then it's time to get on with our mystery tour, or I'll never get you back by the witching hour. So hop back into Leaping Lizzie, m'lady."

"Where now?" she asked, lifting her face to the hot breeze as they roared northeastward beyond the confines of the city.

"Oh, just a preview of delights to come. Old Gross is opening up Tell Murad in a few weeks, and I know he's hoping to lure you up there. I may go myself for a bit. He thinks he's got another of these Bronze Age palace complexes like Woolley found at Tell Atchana—so that's where we're headed now, to Tell Atchana."

"Do we have time?" She was suddenly anxious.

"Oh, yes, plenty. It's not that far along the course of the Orontes, you'll see," he said, accelerating the car so that the speed took her breath away, and they drove in companionable and replete silence.

Shortly he drew up at the side of the road between a huge mound looming on the left and a much smaller mound on the right. "Here we are," he announced, and waved an explanatory hand. "That's Braidwood's Tell Judeideh—the big mound over there. Not much to see there, though. Here's Woolley's dig on the right. Doesn't look like much, but he hit the jackpot with it—palaces, temples, and lots of nifty finds."

"You seem to be very well informed," she murmured as he helped her down. "Don't tell me you're an archaeologist as well as a bon vivant!"

He laughed. "No, just a quick study. As I would become anything to please my lady fair." She let that pass.

He explained the layout as they strolled through the ruins and then excused himself with a rueful grin to disappear toward the river. She strolled on among the maze of walls that marked the ancient palace and on rounding a corner came face to face with two Bektashi crouching over what looked like a very sick camel. They came slowly to their feet, their hands straying to the long knives in their belts, their eyes searching the ruins behind her, then they exchanged delighted grins and began to advance on her, fanning out on either side and muttering to each other as they came. "Richard!" she called in sudden alarm. "Richard, I'm over here. We seem to have company, and they don't look friendly!"

This stopped them momentarily, but since there was no answering call, they came on again, their eyes hot and wild, their hands reaching out for her as she backed away. Suddenly a voice behind them rapped out, "*Impshi, y'Allah!*" and Richard stepped out from behind the shelter of a wall, his hand casually in his jacket pocket. They wheeled about and she could see their hands tightening on their knives. "The lady is with me, so go about your business," he said in Turkish, and then spat another angry phrase in Arabic as they started to sidle toward him, drawing their knives as they came. Richard's hand was out of his pocket in a flash, and with it came a snub-nosed revolver. "*Impshi!*" he shouted.

With an inarticulate cry they broke and ran off toward the river. He strode over to her. "You all right?"

"Oh, fine. A bit shaken, but otherwise fine." She was gazing in horrified fascination at the gun in his hand. "Do you always go around armed?"

"Only when I'm going to places that may be dangerous." He slipped it casually back into his pocket. "This just goes to show what I've said before—you simply can't go wandering about the world alone, particularly since you seem to have a positive flair for drawing danger to you." He took her arm and started to walk back toward the Jeep. "I think we'd be wise to get out of here. There must be a main Bektashi encampment around somewhere, and those chaps may decide to come back with reinforcements. Our meager dole of time is just about up anyway, so let our retreat be swift. We *do* see life together, don't we, m'dear?"

Firmly putting aside the doubts that stirred queasily in her mind, she gave herself up to his lively chatter as they drove back, and it was only when they were on the outskirts of Antakya that he became serious and said, "When may I see you again?"

She came out of her euphoria with a start. "Er—I just don't know."

"I could easily come in and pick you up anytime you say."

"No, that wouldn't do at all," she said hastily, and he looked sideways at her, knowingly. "So John doesn't know I'm around," he stated.

"The subject just hasn't come up," she said, staring straight ahead.

"I see." He was silent for a moment. "How about if you drove up to Belen and I picked you up there? Next week, same day, same time? Would that do?"

She hesitated, then a surge of frustrated anger shook her. Why shouldn't she? It was all perfectly innocent, and she enjoyed it. "Yes, that would be fine," she said.

It became part of the hidden pattern of her life that week, and the next, and the next; they explored, they enjoyed, and she realized she was becoming as attached to Richard as he was to her, although he gave no word or sign of wanting a deeper commitment. Where it was leading, what the end would be, she did not allow herself to think.

That she was not being honest with herself was brought home to her forcibly when John came home one day keyed up with excitement and some other emotion she could not analyze. "You'll never guess in a million years who we have in the neighborhood," he announced. "I just couldn't believe it myself."

Her heart pounding and her pulse jumping, she strove to appear casual. "Oh? Who?" she said with a quaver.

"The Wests are here! I had a call from Robin today. They're going to be in Adana. I was just bowled over by the news. He's just fine. Isn't that terrific? I said we'd be over to visit this weekend."

"Oh, just terrific!" she said in relief.

Chapter 22

*I*t was only after she had recovered from her own inner shock that she realized how odd the Wests' arrival was and, forgetting her determined noninvolvement, she asked, "You mean you didn't have any hand in this, didn't ask for Robin?"

John shook his head. "As I said, I was completely bowled over. He has nothing to do with me. He's a deep, deep cover man for Henfield, who set this whole thing up. The last I heard of Robin—well, I'm sure I showed you the letter—was that he was working in a low-stress job at Langley. He's almost as surprised as I am, but delighted nonetheless at being back in action. Of course, he couldn't say much over the phone, but presumably we'll hear all about it when we see them on the weekend." For the first time in months he sounded happy, although somehow the news had added to her own unease; it seemed to go beyond mere coincidence.

That Saturday they drove around the head of the Gulf of Iskenderun past the jewellike setting of the crusader's castle at Payas and then headed west, toward Adana, and she brought up the subject again. "So what exactly will Robin be doing in Adana?"

"Ostensibly he's a travel agent under the aegis of the Air Force, which has a big base just outside of Adana. He arranges air trips and sightseeing trips for the dependent families and so on. There's quite a demand for it, because it's a big base, and it'll give him a good excuse to travel himself. Knowing how Robin throws himself into things, he probably already knows more than we'll ever know about this whole area." This faintly irked her, because she felt she was becoming quite an expert on the Amuq Plain and the Hatay in general.

When they finally, after some misdirection and loss of temper on John's part, located the West's suburban villa on the outskirts of Adana, the reunion between the two men was warm and enthusiastic; that between the women less so. Bobby seemed guarded, a look of strain in her green eyes, and Vanessa saw streaks of white in her dark hair. Robin, on the other hand, looked better and more relaxed than Vanessa had ever seen him, although there was a gleam in his dark eyes that disquieted her. It was a gleam that verged on the fanatic.

The men, as soon as their glasses were charged, went off into the small garden, talking animatedly, leaving Vanessa in the kitchen with Bobby, who was diligently chopping up vegetables for a salad and who, after a short silence, started the conversation rolling with "So what are you doing with yourself nowadays? Do you like it here?"

"Oh, yes, just fine. I keep pretty busy." Vanessa was being equally guarded. "I belong to a small music group in Iskenderun and have developed a minor passion for archaeology. I'm learning a lot, and it's fascinating."

"Learning? Who from?" Bobby did not sound particularly interested.

"I was lucky enough to fall in with a wonderful character, an American, Herman Gross—have you heard of him?" Vanessa tried to sound casual.

Bobby stopped chopping and looked up in amazement. "Not *the* Herman Gross, the billionaire?"

"Well, yes, though I didn't know that when I met him."

Vanessa went on to relate their first meeting, which in retrospect she found hilarious. Bobby did not laugh. She resumed her chopping. "He must have thought you strictly from Hicksville," she snapped. "I mean, *everyone* knows about him. But he certainly sounds weird."

"I don't find him weird at all," Vanessa said tartly. "I think he's an absolute lamb and terribly clever."

"Oh, he's that all right!" Bobby snorted. "You don't get to be a billionaire unless you've got something on the ball. What in heaven's name is he doing in Iskenderun—buying up the Turkish oilfields?"

"He's not even in Iskenderun; he's in Antakya, and I'm not even sure he knows there *are* any Turkish oilfields. He is just absorbed in Tell Murad—that's his own dig on the Amuq, and he is *so* happy with it; it's really a joy to be with him." Vanessa's face softened into a smile at the thought.

"Humph. Probably a cover. I expect he's up to something," Bobby said, and turned her attention to seasoning the steaks and laying them on the charcoal grill.

"Can't I help you with something?" Vanessa said belatedly.

"You can keep an eye on them as they cook," Bobby said, opening up the oven to check on the foil-wrapped baking potatoes. "I decided not to have a live-in servant. There's a woman who comes in every day for the general cleaning, and I can do the rest. Henfield's okayed my being Robin's assistant on this, so I don't want any snoops around the house."

"You've met Henfield, then?" Vanessa said, with a little inward shiver.

"Yes, we stayed a week in Ankara on the way here."

"What did you think of him?" Vanessa asked cautiously.

"Seemed able and open to suggestions." Bobby was noncommittal.

"I found him"—Vanessa sought for an adequate word—"frightening."

"Bit of a cold fish, but at least he knows ability when he sees it. He was the only one to recognize that Robin was being wasted in that dead-end job at Langley and to give him a break." Bobby's tone was bitter. "Now we're rolling again, and about time, too."

"Robin is all right, then?" Vanessa asked.

Bobby gave her a cold stare. "Certainly, he's fine. All he needed was a good rest, as I said all along."

Further conversation was cut off by the arrival of the men for a refill of their drinks and general chitchat all around until luncheon was served. There was much bantering between the two men about college days, a certain amount of reminiscing about Vietnam, and a lot of "Whatever happened to old so-and-so," but Vanessa observed as she ate in silence that not one word had been said about South Africa or what had come after.

"My, that was good, Bobby!" John said, handing back his empty plate. "It has been a long time since I had a real American meal—we've gone all Turkish. The steaks were great! Where did you find them?"

"We've got commissary privileges at the base," Bobby said with a gratified smile. "I do all my shopping there— the local shops are frightful. Have you given up on your cooking, Vanessa?"

"I've given up on a lot of things," Vanessa said evenly, and was rewarded by a nervous glance from John and an acute one from Robin, whose brow furrowed.

"Van's been serving as a very useful cover for my Antakya activities," John said hurriedly.

"Oh, so you *are* keeping an eye on Gross!" Bobby looked at Vanessa in triumph. "I just knew there had to be something—archaeology indeed!" John looked puzzled.

Robin's presence appeared to have a soothing effect on Bobby, whose tongue had lost its waspish edge. "Vanessa has been moving in high circles, Robby," she informed him in a high glee. "A billionaire mentor, no less! Does he go around with a crowd of bodyguards, Van? Have you seen his local palace? Do tell us all about him. I think this is fabulous."

"If he has a bodyguard, I've certainly never seen him," Vanessa said uncomfortably. "And I gather he's staying

in a little hotel close to the museum until he goes out to
the dig. He appears to be a man of very simple tastes and
habits. We mostly talk about archaeology."

Robin began to ask some knowledgeable questions that
put Vanessa into a very real quandary. Although she had
already visited most of the places he was mentioning with
Richard, she could not admit to such personal knowledge;
John would wonder how she had gotten to them. So practically every statement she made was prefaced by "Well,
Herman says . . ."

Finally Bobby said with a roguish twinkle, "You'd better watch out, John! Herman Gross is a marrying man.
What is it, four or five wives, Robin? You'd better see
that he hasn't got his eye on Vanessa for number six,
since he's evidently impressed the hell out of her."

"Oh, I don't think I have to worry on that score," John
said heavily. "If I'm too old for her, he most certainly is."

There was a small surprised silence until Robin cut in
smoothly with another question, and he kept a firm hold
on the conversation from then on. Although she had never
lost the feeling that he had reservations about her and did
not particularly like her, Vanessa could not help liking
him. He had a charm about him that was almost poignant,
and she could well understand John's own devotion to
him.

The rest of the afternoon passed placidly enough and,
refusing an offer to stay for supper because of their long
ride home, they started to gather themselves up for the
return trip. "It's been great to see you both again," John
said. "And you're coming to us next weekend, right? In
any case, we'll be seeing you next Thursday in Iskenderun."

Vanessa had a twinge of misgiving—Thursday was her
usual rendezvous day with Richard. "What was all that
about?" she asked as they started homeward.

"You mean about Thursday? Henfield's coming down
and is going to meet us all for lunch at the consulate.
Robin won't be able to be in direct contact with him at
all, you see, so we're going to have to rig up some sort
of three-way relay for instructions—probably from Cyprus

to us to him. We'll work out the details then. But that commissary thing of Bobby's has given me an idea. I can arrange something with the Air Force and we can send Dick Fortescue in once a week to pick up supplies and rendezvous with Robin at the same time. It'll make an excellent cover, and we can enjoy some American goodies as well."

"I don't have to come on Thursday, then, if it's a business thing," she said quickly.

"Of course you have to come!" He looked at her in surprise. "It's supposed to be a normal luncheon party at the consulate. The last thing we want is for it to look like a gathering of the CIA clan. You and Bobby can chat with Mrs. Carson, and old Carson can go about his business while we huddle. I'm not asking you to coo at Henfield or sit in his lap—I know you can't stand him. All you have to do is act like an embassy wife for a few hours."

"Act is the operative word," she said, but put up no further protest. "When do you want to go over to Antakya again? We haven't been for some time."

"The Wests are coming Sunday, so I think I'll pop over on Saturday for a few hours. Will that suit you?"

"Yes, that will suit me," she murmured. "Tell me honestly, John. How do you think Robin is?"

He was silent for a while, staring straight ahead, and, looking at him, she saw the lost, vulnerable look that had always touched her heart. "I'm not sure," he said at length. "On the surface he seems fine, but ... well, there's something I can't quite put my finger on. . . . It's as if there's a spring inside him that, if tightened too much, will snap. I hope to hell Henfield isn't going to put too much pressure on him."

"Have you any idea of what he's got in mind?"

"No. Nor, for that matter, has Robin, except that whatever it is it's a very special mission. Anyway . . ." He looked at her sharply. "Why are you so interested all of a sudden?"

"Because I care about Robin," she said quietly. "And I don't want anything to happen to him."

He put his hand on hers and squeezed it. "I'm sorry," he said. "I know you do—as I do."

On Monday morning she called Richard about the change in plans, but his hotel informed her that he was away for a few days, and so she left the message "Saturday, not Thursday," and hoped he would understand it.

She was relieved on Thursday that the sharp-eyed Valducci was not included in the luncheon party, and on meeting Henfield she was struck again by the almost reptilian chill he emanated as he watched everyone with his flat gray eyes and contributed little to the general lunchtime conversation. His presence had a dampening effect on the ever-amiable Carsons, so that as soon as lunch was over the consul excused himself and Mrs. Carson, with almost visible relief, bustled Bobby and Vanessa into the garden for coffee and after-lunch drinks.

The afternoon stretched interminably on as Bobby, at her ebullient best, chattered away at Mrs. Carson, leaving Vanessa to her own thoughts. She wondered where Richard was and what he was doing, and she found her pulse quickening at the thought of their next meeting. Finally, Dick Fortescue emerged to announce that the meeting was over, his stammer so marked that Vanessa deduced Henfield had had his usual intimidating effect.

John was jumpy on the way home, so she asked no questions until he volunteered, "Well, we got the mechanics of the operation taken care of, but Henfield certainly plays his cards close to the vest. He gave no inkling of what the project was. I think Robin was irked."

She voiced a doubt that had been growing in her own mind. "You don't suppose Henfield got Robin out here specifically to keep tabs on you, do you?"

His hands tightened on the wheel. "Why on earth should you think that? What I'm doing has nothing to do with Henfield, and he knows it. This is not exactly a team sport, but I can't think of any reason he should *want* to know about my operation. And he wouldn't get it from Robin anyway. Although we're old friends, it doesn't mean we tell each other everything, and Robin would never dream of asking."

"I just thought that a peculiar character like Henfield might look on your independent operation within his own bailiwick as a kind of threat," she mused. "He strikes me as a man who likes to pull all the strings and who would be totally unscrupulous in going about it."

"If so, he certainly won't get anything from either of us," he snorted, and she let the matter drop.

She was secretly amused when, on the next trip to Antakya, John, instead of following his usual pattern of dropping her off at the museum, accompanied her inside, saying, "It's time I met this VIP of yours." They found Herman Gross poring over site plans, and after introductions had been made, he rattled on in his machine-gun style about the dig, his keen eyes appraising John all the while. A relieved John was at his most charming until Herman said, "I'd like to have Vanessa at the dig with me for a while—say a month or so—to show her what archaeology is all about. All the blood, sweat, and tears that go into collecting stuff like this"—he waved his hand around at the antiquity-crammed shelves—"that okay with you?"

John became wary. "Well, we do have rather a lot of other obligations," he muttered. "I'm not sure I can do without her for any length of time."

A knowing twinkle appeared in Herman's eye. "She'd have plenty of company besides me, y'know. One of my junior executives from Dallas—Ph.D. in archaeology— smart gal who thinks she knows everything"—he gave an expressive sniff—"which, of course, she doesn't. She'll be there helping me all the time." He twinkled an eye at Vanessa. "See, I'm an equal opportunity employer! Then there's this young English fellow, a writer—or so he says. He'll be there." Vanessa's heart skipped a beat, and she offered up a prayer that Herman would not say his name, but he rattled on. "And there are various other executives from my companies who suddenly have this burning interest in archaeology. I don't know who they think they're fooling, but I can always use some extra warm bodies, so they'll be coming and going. Anyway"— he clapped John on the shoulder—"think about it! Even a week or two. Make her glad to get back to all the comforts of home and a nice feller like you."

"Er, I suppose so. We'll see," John said a little dazedly. "When do you begin?"

"Already have," Herman chirped. "Got the crew doing the initial clearing of the site and putting up the camp and will be going out myself full time next week. Can't wait to get at it. Going to make this a dig to remember." He grinned fiercely and picked up his plans. "Glad to have met you. Knew a nice gal like this had to have a nice husband. Now I've got to show her what all this means." And with this firm dismissal John took his leave.

She found it hard to keep her mind on what Herman was telling her, wondering if Richard had gotten her message and if he would be out there waiting for her. When lunchtime came she could hardly wait to say her goodbyes to Herman and assure him she would do her best to get to the dig. "All you've got to do, m'dear, is get yourself to Antakya Airport, and one of my helicopters will be there to ferry you out," he told her. "They'll be making a couple of runs a day, and I'll put you down on the roster, so if you show up the crews'll know what to do."

Helicopters! she thought to herself as she scurried out of the museum. Herman's hidden might was definitely beginning to show. As she rounded the corner where Richard usually parked out of sight of the main entrance, she saw him pacing moodily by the side of the Jeep, and with a glad lift of her heart she ran up to him. "Sorry about the delay," she said.

To the amazement of the passersby, he gathered her in his arms and kissed her firmly; it was a breathless and very satisfying kiss. "Whoa! What was all that about?" she said shakily when he let her go.

"Just to show you how much I missed you." His tone was light, but his eyes were grave. "How much time do we have?"

"Not much. I'm supposed to meet John back here at three."

"Damn! Well, there goes our trip to Daphne. Only time for a quick lunch. We'll go back to the hotel." He seemed preoccupied, but when they got there he put himself out to be amusing. They were both a little tense, aware that a barrier had been crossed, but it was not until lunch was over and it was time to get back to the museum that he became serious again. As he let her off he took hold of both of her hands and looked at her searchingly. "I'm going off to Tell Murad next week, so I'm not going to be around. Please say you'll be there, too. It's very important. Please say you'll come!"

She was a little breathless with a sense of frightening inevitability. "It may not be easy," she said as calmly as she could. "But I'll do my damnedest to get there. Wait for me, Richard!"

"Forever, if need be," he returned.

Chapter 23

*I*t was her own commitments rather than any opposition from John that kept her from putting her plans into
immediate action. Her music group, in a show of solidarity
with their bass-playing major, was about to put on a recital
at the army base for the benefit of a visiting general whom
the Turkish major was hoping to impress. Their usual
leisurely pace had to be abandoned for some concentrated
rehearsing, and since the tugboat captain was on his usual
erratic schedule, she was elected first violin to carry them
through. They had carefully arranged their program to
give the major's bass as much of the limelight as possible,
and by the time of the concert they were almost as apprehensive about their impact as he was.

The night of the concert, the Turkish general, who was
built along the lines of a Sherman tank and was totally
impassive of mien, was very much in evidence in the
middle of the front row. His expression did not change
by one iota throughout the entire concert, which did nothing for their morale, and Vanessa found herself keeping
a nervous eye on the English secretary, who looked as if

she might burst into tears at any second. At the finale, however, the general rose to his feet, a huge smile splitting his leathery face, and began to applaud vigorously. The khaki-clad audience, taking its cue, surged to its collective feet and added thunderous applause. Weak with relief, the ensemble took their bows and were summoned to meet the general.

Things got off to a good start when he embraced his major with a bearlike hug, kissed him on both cheeks, and slapped him heartily on the back, causing the delighted major's knees to buckle slightly. He then proceeded to make a flowery speech about how good it was to see so many of his NATO allies in such complete and admirable accord, and how they were a shining example of what the entente cordiale was all about. Glowing with their heady success, they repaired to the French consul's for a champagne party, where they congratulated one another all over again at length, and then Vanessa, in a satisfied daze, hurried home to tell John all about it.

She had been initially relieved when he had begged off attending on the grounds of urgent business in Antakya, because she had been so uncertain of its outcome. Now she was irrationally disappointed that he could not have been there to witness their small triumph. When she got home there was still no sign of him, and so with a sense of dismal anticlimax she went exhaustedly to bed.

When she awoke the next day, his side of the bed was still empty, and the familiar sensation of panicky unease gripped her. She dressed hurriedly, determined to call Dick Fortescue to see what was going on, but when she got downstairs, she found John already installed at the dining room table, drinking coffee, bleary-eyed and unshaven, his expression grim and withdrawn. Her first feeling of relief was swamped by concern. "What's up? she asked. "What has happened? Are you all right? I was worried."

He came reluctantly out of his reverie. "Oh, some trouble." He was terse. "I had to spend the night at the office trying to repair the damage."

She waited for him to go on, but he lapsed back into

silence. "Well?" she challenged. "Would it help to talk about it? I'm not going to rush out and shout it from the rooftop, you know."

He gazed gloomily into the depths of his coffee cup. "One of my Arab operatives blew himself away with a car bomb in Damascus. God knows what he was thinking about—he wasn't even supposed to *be* in Damascus. Took thirty people with him, five of them children. Washington was irked, so I had to calm them down."

"*Irked!*" she exclaimed, sickened. "Just *irked*? Whatever happened to human feelings like compassion and horror? Oh, God, John, what are we doing here? Just when I had almost convinced myself that we do have a meaningful role, something as terrible and as senseless as this happens. How can you *live* with this?"

He looked across at her wearily. "As usual, you shouldn't have asked and I should have had more sense than to tell you. Senseless things happen all the time—not just in this job out everywhere. I can't undo what he did; I can't bring any of them back. All I can do is get on with my job and minimize the damage. So please, let's not have a scene, Van. I'm too tired, and I don't want to discuss this further. How did your concert go?"

"I don't want to talk about that either," she said, turning away, her brief happiness of the previous night like bitter ashes in her mouth. "I don't think this is the moment to talk of things like success and friendship and warmth. It would scarcely fit in with the normal tenor of our lives, would it?"

"No, I suppose not, especially since there no longer seems to be any place for me in your ivory tower," he said, and went heavily up to bed.

What came to her as a crowning blow happened the very next time they went to make love. It had been the one aspect of their lives that, in spite of all that had happened, had remained a constant and satisfying bond. True, she had been disconcerted and a little put off by John's increasing demands for oral sex, which she had never really enjoyed, but she had gone along with it, hoping it was just a passing phase of his need—and that the extended foreplay that she found merely frustrating herself was necessary to arouse his desire. Now, for the first time, in spite of a lengthy foreplay that had stretched her own nerves to screaming pitch, he could not get an erection, could not achieve an orgasm. He had finally flung himself away from her and out of bed with an angry exclamation. To her it was the ultimate rejection, the snapping of the last fragile bond that held their lives together. "Perhaps it would be better if I went away for a while," she said, tears of frustration pricking her eyes. "Down to Tell Murad. Maybe things will work out if we have some time off from each other."

He had lit a cigarette and was smoking it with short, angry puffs. "If that's what you want, I can't stop you. You evidently find the company down there more congenial than you find me. And I could certainly use a break from your constant, silent critical appraisal."

"That's not fair!" she cried. "This wasn't my fault and you know it. Maybe you should see a doctor. I mean, it does happen sometimes . . . and you have been working awfully hard lately."

"And particularly when a man gets over the hill—why not add that?" he snapped. "I'm sorry to be such a drag on your youthful ardor, but then that's what we're both stuck with, isn't it?" And he stalked out.

As she grimly packed her bags it was in the forefront of her mind that when she next entered this sheltered house with its fair views it would probably be to pack the rest of her belongings. She could not go on like this; the breaking point had come. She was not sure who had failed whom, but she knew she could no longer separate John from what he did, neither in reality nor in her own mind; she was no longer certain she even wanted to try. He appeared to have no need for her, and if that was so, there was no point in continuing the mockery their marriage had become. She was no longer a starry-eyed dreamer of twenty-two; next birthday she would be twenty-seven— and at the moment, she felt a very old twenty-seven.

She left a carefully worded note for John with instructions on how he could get in touch with her, should the need arise, but with no mention of dates or possible limits on her stay. Once free of the house and driving over the now-familiar route to the Belen Pass, she firmly put all the sorrows behind her and could feel her spirits lifting as she climbed, her pulse quickening with the sense of new vistas, new adventures ahead. At Antakya airport she made her way to the hangar on the outskirts of the small field that bore the impressive insignia "Gross Enterprises," and she presented her credentials to the bored-looking guard who was sitting in a little glass cubicle within the hangar's cavernous gloom. He brightened at the sight of another human being and volunteered, "Oh, yes, bayan, the helicopter will be here in half an hour." He waved a hand at a small pile of boxes topped by a crate of lugubriously clucking chickens. "Supply run, but plenty of space for passengers. No problem."

Feeling strangely tranquil now that she had taken the plunge, she sat down on the stool provided by the eager guard and during the short wait was treated to his entire life history, which included a wife, three children, and a mother-in-law with whom he did not get on. The large helicopter hove into view and settled heavily onto the ground like an overweight dragonfly. A lean, wiry, dark man emerged, flanked by two hefty men wearing Arab headdresses, and when Vanessa introduced herself he stuck out his hand. "Brannigan's the name. Yes, the boss was hoping you'd show up. Gave special instructions for VIP treatment if you did."

"Oh, dear! What does that mean?" she said.

He grinned at her easily. "It means you get to ride in the co-pilot's seat and not with the chickens." He hefted her bags as the Arabs scurried out to the helicopter with the boxes. "This all you brought? I hope that doesn't mean you'll only be here a short while—we could use some new blood. Digging in the middle of nowhere gets everyone a little antsy after a time. We thirst for someone else to talk to—or about."

"I've never been in a helicopter before," Vanessa confessed a little nervously as he helped her up into her seat.

"Not to worry—safe as a bus." He grinned, buckling her in. "The worst thing is the noise."

The vertical takeoff temporarily took her breath away, but as the airfield receded below she shouted, "How far is it?"

"By this bus, twenty-five minutes," he roared back. "By road, a good two-and-a-half hours, if you're lucky." He waved a hand at the Orontes that showed like a jade-green snake writhing through the mottled yellows and browns of the plain to their right. "It's right on the river, about twenty miles south of a little place called Islayhiya. Can't fly you along the river, though—too damned close to the Syrian border. Don't want a Syrian jet down our necks—they're so damned touchy these days, especially about anything with American markings."

She watched the passing scenery with fascination: the craggy flanks of the Anti-Taurus to their left and the greater, crenellated mass of the Taurus mountains heaving up directly ahead, while to the left the land flattened into an endless vista of desert. The chopper began to lose altitude and Brannigan yelled, "The site is directly beneath us. I'll come in slow to give you a good look at it from the air," and she looked down, to see a large, low, sprawling mound that looked for all the world like a tree stump surrounded by a fringe of fungi. The fungi took on definition as a horde of tents of all sizes and shapes nestled against the flanks of the mound, and she could make out the yellow dots of earth movers and bulldozers and the tinier dots of people like ants upon the tree stump's bole.

"I'd no idea it was such a large operation," she gasped.

"What else, with the boss around?" He laughed and then pointed. "That's the workmen's tent city over on the north side of the mound. The boss and his cohorts inhabit the tent city on the south side, and our landing pad is to the west, conveniently in between. Anyway, I'm sure he'll want to show you around himself, so as soon as I park this baby I'll take you right to him." He set it down gently in a a whirling cloud of dust, turned off the engines, and sat waiting for the sandstorm to settle. "How did you like your first helicopter ride?" he said in a normal voice.

Vanessa felt a sudden surge of elation. "It was just great! I don't know when I've felt so . . . free."

"That's the ticket!" He smiled, helping her down. "Well, anytime you want a bird's-eye view, I'm your man. Just whistle me up." His smile grew impish. "You know how to whistle, don't you?"

"Ah, another Bogey fan, I see." She smiled back. "Yes, I know how to whistle."

They ran Herman Gross to ground in one of the large squares that had been opened up in the mound. He was looking in cross-eyed fashion at a carved orthostat that was being carefully worked around by a squad of workmen under the eagle eye of a somewhat harassed-looking, middle-aged, honey-blond woman. "I think we've found the entrance gate," he greeted Vanessa. "Bang, right off! Late Hittite, by the looks of it, and a palace, or I'll eat my boots. Happened this morning. What luck!" His bushy eyebrows waggled furiously up and down. "You must have brought it with you. Good to see you, m'dear."

"I hope it's all right just dropping in like this," Vanessa said. "I had no means of letting you know in advance that I was coming."

"Of course it is. Wondered where you'd got to. Thought you'd forgotten us. Come and meet Mary Leroy and then I'll show you around myself. *Doctor* Leroy—she's very keen on that," he muttered in her ear, and sniffed.

The blond was introduced, and she looked positively relieved when her employer trumpeted, "Going to show Vanessa around before putting her to work. Sure you can manage this by yourself?" Mary Leroy, with a hint of acid in her voice, assured him that she could.

"Brannigan look after you all right?" Herman asked as he clumped down the mound with Vanessa in tow. He was looking even shabbier than when she had first laid eyes on him, his sandals having been replaced by a pair of battered army boots and his bald pate shielded from the sun by a fishing hat that was limp with age.

"Yes, he was very nice—gave me a bird's-eye tour of the site. He said he'd put my things in a guest tent, but I've no idea where that is."

"Oh, we'll get around to that. Brannigan's quite a character. Ex-mercenary, but a good pilot. How long can you stay?"

"Er—as long as you'll have me. I've no deadline," she said, and was aware of his keen-eyed scrutiny. She felt her color rising and said hastily, "I had no idea it would be on such a large scale as this. It's like organizing an army."

He brushed this aside. "Method and means, that's all it needs, method and means, and I've got plenty of both."

The tour took a long time, and the more she saw, the more impressed she became. The site even had its own electric generator, situated next to a tent that housed a bank of computers, carefully shielded from the omnipresent dust by clear plastic curtains. "Not only our own electricity but our own water supply," Herman said with a touch of pride as he showed her a tent housing a long line of shower stalls. "Filtered and pumped Orontes—but it's safe enough."

She was more than a little amused as they visited the excavated squares on the mound and saw the various young executives, who had been watching the workmen at their tasks with either boredom or bafflement, snap to instant, eager attention at the sight of Herman and try to explain in somewhat incoherent fashion what was going on. One young man, whose painfully fair skin was already seared with sunburn, said earnestly, "I think we've got something really important coming out here, sir. A coffin, by the looks of it."

Herman peered at what appeared to be the top of an ornate Greek sarcophagus. "Have ye, now! Splendid! Well, keep at it." As they moved away he chortled, "Coffin indeed! Little do they know that all they are good for is to keep the workmen from loafing or pilfering the small finds. Thank God I've got a good Kurdish foreman who knows what he's about—and, of course, there's always Mary." Again he sniffed.

Their tour finally brought them to a line of small individual tents. "The guest wing," Herman announced. "Your bags should be in one of those, so let's have a look-see."

They discovered the bags in the third one down. It was furnished simply with a neatly made army cot, a canvas director's chair, and two footlockers, one on top of the other, crowned by a small mirror. "This is what it's all about," Herman repeated. "Blood, sweat, and tears—roughing it. No frills here."

"It looks very nice," she said, testing the cot, and smiled up at him. "I'd say this was roughing it in style."

He grinned back. "What else? You want to rest up a bit or have lunch?" He consulted his watch, which for once was in the right place. "I'm going to have mine now. Going to keep me company?"

"Yes," she said promptly. "I'm ravenous. It must be the desert air."

"Good. I'll show you the ropes."

The mess tent was organized cafeteria-style, with tables and benches running around three sides and the food counter making up the fourth. When they had filled their trays with an impressive amount of food and settled at a table, he waved an explanatory fork at the thinly populated tent. "Meal times are flexible, so people eat at different times. Breakfast runs from six to eight. Lunch, noon to two. Dinner, six to eight. Eat when it suits you. Take the rest of the day to familiarize yourself with the site. I'll put you to work first thing tomorrow."

"Fine with me," she said, and applied herself diligently to her food, getting up the courage to ask the question that had been on her mind since her arrival. Although she had kept a sharp eye out for Richard, she had seen no sign of him either on the dig or in any of the many tents they had peered into. Finally she said casually, "By the way, I was wondering if an old friend of mine had turned up here—Richard Morse?"

"You know him well?" Herman was a little gruff.

"Oh, yes, we met a long time ago in South Africa." She kept her eyes fixed on her plate.

"Yes, he's been here. Strange fellow. He comes and he goes as he pleases—but then, I'm not paying him, so why shouldn't he?"

She looked up too see him staring at her. "So is he here?"

"No. Went off about a week ago. Didn't say when he'd be back, or even if."

So much for forever, she thought with a pang.

Chapter 24

*L*ong ago, when things had started to go bad between her parents, Vanessa had been shipped off to a girls' camp in New Hampshire, and after the inevitable first few days of homesickness she had enjoyed that summer more than any other she could recall. Although the terrain and the ambience were so different, Tell Murad reminded her of the camp and its atmosphere, and it amused her to continue the analogy in her mind. The dig, of course, was their organized activity, but apart from that the "school's out" atmosphere prevailed: the enormous appetites after a day in the fresh air; the swimming parties with shouting and splashing in the warm Orontes, to the mystification of the native workmen; the fierce Scrabble, Trivial Pursuit, and Monopoly games that went on in the recreation tent in the evenings, accompanied by much bickering and a certain amount of horseplay; and the early lights-out, for Herman was a stern taskmaster and expected everyone to be at his or her station on the site by eight at the latest, and the ones who made it sooner earned the brownie points of his approval. They were taken care of; they were secure; they were protected against the world.

As Brannigan had predicted, she was much sought after, though it amused her to note that it was not so much because she was a new face but because she was clearly an odd man out, and they were all intensely curious about her relationship with Herman. It aroused in her a sense of mischief, and she was deliberately vague as one young executive after another corralled her and tried to pump her for information. Apart from Mary Leroy and her, the camp was heavily masculine in composition, the only other woman being a company wife who had come along with her eager-beaver husband and who was palpably bored with the proceedings. Vanessa felt sorry for her in an irritated way, for, thanks to Mary Leroy, she herself was having a great time. That much put-upon and unappreciated woman had approached her the first evening in the mess tent, where she was eating dinner with Brannigan, and had said, a shade wearily, "Herman tells me you know a certain amount about all this. Do you have any special skills we could use? Photography, draftsmanship, computer programming—things like that? If not, you'll probably just have to oversee one of the squares, which is not the most thrilling of occupations."

Vanessa thought rapidly. "Art was my minor in college. I can draw pretty well. You mean for plans and so on?"

Mary Leroy's pale blue eyes brightened a little. "Well, if you can draw, that may be *very* useful. We seem to have a series of carved orthostats coming out in what Herman rashly calls the palace, and it would be very useful to have exact, detailed scale drawings made of them. Naturally, we have photographs as well, but with the difficulties of this harsh desert light, the photographs often miss the vital details."

"I'd love to try my hand at that," Vanessa said quickly, and so it was that on her first morning she was ensconced before the first orthostat with drawing board and chair, her eyes shielded by an old tennis cap, engrossed in putting the carving in exact scale on the paper in front of her. It showed a heavily armed and bearded man about to smite with a formidable-looking double ax a poor unfortunate soldier he was holding up by a topknot of hair; the expression on the victim's face reminded her for some reason of Robin. From time to time, Herman would shuffle up behind her, peer keenly at the stone and her rendition, pat her absentmindedly on the shoulder with a "Great, great!" and shuffle off again. He was clearly very excited about what the continuing excavation of the square was revealing: it was indeed an entrance to a large building of some kind and one that had clearly been burned, for as they advanced they found the stone-lined walls reddened and cracked from heat, and there were great areas of black carbonized wood, the residue from fallen beams. "An exact date!" Herman chirruped in triumph. "The Carbon-14 dating on those beams will give us an exact date for the destruction."

When she was on her third drawing, he came to her, literally trembling with excitement, and thrust a grimy hand under her nose. It held a small, very rusty iron arrowhead. "Look at that!" he squeaked. "Now we know the thugs that did the destroying—that's an Assyrian arrowhead. Can't you just see 'em pouring on over this place from the north, sacking, pillaging as they came?" And for a few seconds, fired by his enthusiasm, she could: the quiet site was filled with hoarse shouts in strange tongues, screams, and the crackling of flames.

"Do you realize there's some writing on this one?" she said, pointing to the stone. "There, right at the bottom. I found it when I was brushing away some loose dirt." She thought he was going to burst with excitement as he peered at it. "Mary!" he yelled, "over here, quickly. We may have the name of the poor bastard who got burned out." And so it went.

The days were so full that she hadn't time to dwell on her own problems. It was only at night, after she had put down the flap of her tent and flopped wearily into the small cot, that she had time for her own thoughts, her own life. She had quickly come to terms with the problem of Richard. She had just misread the whole situation, that was all, and she tried to tell herself it did not matter. Long ago she had read an old book about the games people play with one another, and now she recognized that Richard's game was "Cavalier"—a harmless game that made its object feel good and important without any deep commitment on the part of the player. She had just taken it too seriously because . . . because what? *That* was a problem. She had deliberately tried not to think of John until she herself was back in balance, but when she did, she found a curious thing had happened: she saw him as she had first seen him, charming, debonair, sensitive, and not the withdrawn, strained, and seemingly unfeeling man she had left in Iskenderun. Had she done that to him because she could not accept what he did or what he was? she wondered uneasily.

It was not a pleasant thought to deal with, and its implications sent her from her tent one moonstruck night to wander up to the ruins. Leaning against the cool stones of the ornate entrance, its air slightly acrid still from that long-ago conflagration, she tried to put her own worries aside and conjure up what had happened here, but the two intermixed in her mind. Senseless things did happen—in that ancient world, in this modern world. To the survivors—for there were always those who did survive—this must have been the ultimate senselessness, and yet they had gone on and coped. Some of their descendants might well be snoring in the tents on the north side of the mound at that very moment. Perhaps she should have had a child, she thought bleakly, the child John had so wanted. That would have been a commitment she could not have walked away from as she was doing now. Perhaps that would be an answer. They had loved each other so much; it could not all be gone. Or could it? She was no longer sure that John felt any need for her; perhaps the chasm between them had become too wide after all. With a weary sigh, she took herself off to bed to worry anew.

Despite the pain of her reflections, she began to feel she was making some progress, a progress that ran into an insurmountable obstacle two days later: Richard Morse came back.

She was intently scraping away at the bottom of one of the carvings when she sensed someone behind her, and she turned and found Richard grinning down at her. "Hi, there! Glad to see you made it. Have you a kind word for the returning prodigal, or am I in the doghouse?" His magnetism reached out and enveloped her, and she found herself smiling back. "Hi, yourself! No time for doghouses—far too busy and entertained."

"Oh, dear! As bad as that!" he exclaimed in mock dismay. "Out of sight, out of mind, eh? Well, we'll soon see about that." He offered no excuse, no explanation, either then or later, but contrived by his own brand of magic to cut her out from the crowd from that moment on. And again to her inward dismay, she let it happen. No one seemed to remark on this, save the all-seeing Herman, who appeared a little put out, and she wondered if that was not so much on her account but because Richard did not treat him with the awe he was usually accorded. It was he who pointed out to her a facet of the billionaire that had up to then escaped her. They were strolling past the computer tent and she was explaining enthusiastically to Richard, as Mary had explained it to her, how the computers were recording and reconstructing the site on a day-to-day basis and how the information was being fed directly back to the Dallas headquarters. "With the aid of these, Mary says it will be the most exact and fastest-published dig that has ever been done," she was saying fervently when Richard cut in. "All except that one," he said, jerking his head in the direction of a terminal that stood a little apart from the rest in a cubicle of its own. "And I see his highness is at it." There, sure enough, was Herman Gross, staring at a screen and tapping energetically away at a series of letters that made no sense whatsoever. "His own cipher—impressive, isn't it? Under our very noses he's probably cutting the ground out from under the feet of some poor sod half a world away. Hang around this place long enough and you'll learn how to be a billionaire, my sweet—and then what chance will I have?"

She never knew when to take Richard seriously. Most

of the time he was dancing at arm's length, fascinating her, amusing her, but then there would be a moment when he would make some loaded remark, some meaningful feint under her guard, that would set her to wondering all over again. One thing she was determined about was not to let it get to her. A week passed thus, and then another, and one evening they went for a solitary twilight swim in the river. When they emerged laughing and dripping, he suddenly gathered her in his arms and kissed her hungrily. When he drew away, his eyes were serious, and he said, "God, you've no idea how I've been longing to do that. Do you know how much I want you?" He moved toward her again; her own desire flaming, she yielded to his insistent lips until a slight noise from somewhere on the dusky mound behind them brought her to her senses and she pushed him away. "No, Richard, no," she panted. "No more! I'm not being a tease, but I'm not ready for this. Please try and understand. It was to be no strings, remember?"

He looked at her doubtingly. "That was long ago and far away. I thought things had changed. I thought you had left John. I thought—"

"Well, you thought wrong." She was abrupt. "I'm just trying to sort things out, and this doesn't help. I'm sorry, Richard, but that's how it is."

"I'm sorry, too," he said softly, "because I believe you want me as much as I want you. But if it's time you want, then it's time you shall have, my lady fair. I can wait for as long as it takes."

As she tossed in agonized frustration on her cot that night she felt she was back to square one; she was totally confused.

Her confusion was compounded by Herman's intrusion on the scene. The next day he called her to his tent with some question about her drawings, but after some hemming and hawing he got to what was really on his mind. "Sit down, m'dear," he said. "There's something I've got to talk to you about. You may think it's none of my damn business, but I've a good reason for asking. What exactly is Richard Morse to you?"

"Why, nothing," she stammered. "He's a friend."

He stared at her gloomily. "I was up on the mound last night," he stated. "I saw you."

"Oh!" she gulped. "That was nothing—nothing serious. It won't happen again."

"There's trouble in your marriage, isn't there?" he challenged. "I mean, a man as much in love as your husband obviously is with you doesn't let his wife go off indefinitely, without a word, without a sign from him for this amount of time, unless there's trouble. Tell me one thing. Is the trouble because of what he does?"

"I don't know what you mean," she gasped.

"I think you know very well what I mean," he growled. "The ambassador is a friend of mine, remember? And I've been sufficiently interested to find out about your husband—the truth, not the camouflage."

Vanessa's temper started to rise. "What right have you to pry into our affairs—" she began hotly.

He raised a placating hand. "Only the right of an old man who cares about you. Oh, don't get me wrong! Thirty years ago it might have been a different story, but now it's pure and simple: I *like* you—have done from that first meeting. You're no raving beauty, m'dear, but there's something about you, a warmth, a basic sort of innocent honesty, that makes you absolutely irresistible to a certain kind of man. Thirty years ago I'd have gone after you meself and that husband of yours could have gone to hell, but now it's different. He may still go to hell, for all I know, but I just don't want you getting out of one thing and into another that may be just as bad—*if* that's part of the problem."

"I haven't the remotest idea what you're trying to say," she cried.

"What I'm trying to say is that if you're thinking of getting involved with Richard Morse, you ought to find out a lot more about him. He's not all that he seems." He looked at her with troubled blue eyes. "You don't get to be what I am without being a good judge of people. In my book Morse is a hunter, a stalker. There's an edge of danger about him. I saw a little of it in your husband, too, but not to such a marked degree. Maybe I'm way out of line and that's what attracts you to them both, but if it *isn't* that..."

"No, it isn't that." It was out before she could stop it, and to cover her confusion she blurted, "But I don't see how you can possibly know anything about how John feels or what he is—you've only seen him once."

"True, but it was enough. I know a man in love when I see one. It's easy for a man to fake love when a woman is looking at him, but if he shows it only when a woman is *not* looking at him, when she is seemingly unaware of him, then you can spot it right enough. Not that that's an answer to everything..." He appeared to go off on a tangent. "You know, I expect, that I've had a lot of wives, but I'm going to tell you something I've never told anyone else. I've liked some of them, been passionate about others—at least for a time—but there was only one of 'em that I know I really loved: my second wife, the mother of my two sons. And despite that, I was a big enough fool to lose her. By the time I realized how much of a fool, it was too late—she no longer loved me. Life went on, of course, for both of us, but it left a void that somehow neither of us ever filled. She never did marry again, and I probably shouldn't have." He fell silent for a moment, then said simply, "I'd hate to see something like that happen to you."

Vanessa got up and looked at him levelly. "Well, thank you for your concern, but everyone's problems are different, and I'll have to solve mine for myself and in my own way. Don't worry about it."

He looked up at her and chortled suddenly. "That's right—come out fighting, m'dear, and keep your guard up! Just remember—if there is anything I can ever do, well, here I am."

He had given her much food for thought, much to think over, and Richard must have sensed this inner withdrawal, for a couple of days later he came up with a bombshell of his own. After work he asked her to go for a drive in the Jeep, and when she demurred, he said firmly, "You don't have to worry about a recurrence of the other

night. I just want to talk. It's important—to both of us,
I hope." So she accepted, none too graciously. He had
merely driven a little way along the river, out of sight of
the camp, and then he had parked. They sat in silence
for a while as the sun dipped below the mountains behind
them, then Richard said, "My timing on this may be lousy,
but I think it has become necessary to make my intentions
known, as the Victorians would say. I haven't been completely honest with you, Van"—a little chill tingled her
spine—"I'm not entirely the free and footloose fellow I've
pictured to you. In fact, I have roots, and now I have
every intention of becoming rooted. I own a small manor
house in Sussex—no stately home, just a glorified farm-
house, really—that hangs beneath the lip of the South
Downs and looks seaward over the Channel. It's a pretty,
peaceful place. I have one last obligation to fulfill and
then I'm through with all that has gone before. I intend
to go back home and settle down and live in peace and
plenty forever after. It won't be an exciting life, but it will
be a very nice life, a life that would be complete if you
were there and you were my wife. I want you to bear that
in mind, very much in mind, while you are sorting things
out. Will you do that?"

"Yes, I will," she said calmly. "This obligation you
were talking about, is that what keeps you here?"

"No, not exactly," he said uncomfortably.

She braced herself to ask the crucial question. "Tell
me, Richard. Are you in British Intelligence?"

"No." The answer was definite when it came, but he
had hesitated just a second too long; she knew she had
her answer, but it was not the one she wanted.

Chapter 25

For all Herman's brave words about her husband's love for her, and much as she would have liked to have accepted them, it was becoming increasingly difficult to believe in that love with every day that passed without any sign from John. She had written him after she had arrived with information about the mail arrangements—it was brought daily by helicopter from Antakya—and even about sending a message by the two-way radio that kept the camp in touch with Antakya, but it had elicited no reply, though a few personal letters from the States—mostly from her mother—had been forwarded. She had no idea whether he was angry, sulking, or merely indifferent. This did nothing to help her with her immediate problem. What is it about me that seems to attract spies like flies? she reflected dismally, and her thoughts turned fleetingly and a little wistfully to the single-minded Sam. At least he had been a simple, temperamental musician, and she knew how to deal with one of those. Looking back with unclouded eyes, she found that Richard's role now seemed so obvious, and she wondered briefly if his initial approach to her here had been some attempt to keep tabs on John; but even if that had been so, she was positive that the situation had altered and that he was quite sincere in the proposition he had made to her. She was certain he wanted her; not so certain she wanted him, although he was no whit less fascinating and attractive than he had ever been.

She began to wonder what she would do if the digging season ended and there was still no sign from John. Already she was a veteran in the camp, for the original complement of Herman's "warm bodies" had been completely replaced by a duplicate array. If the impasse lasted that long, the implication would be clear. She would have to return to Iskenderun for the rest of her things and keep on heading out—to where? She smiled grimly to herself. She could always go home to Mother, she supposed, or she could accept Richard's offer of peace ever after in a strange land, and her marriage would be over. What a sad end to such a glad beginning, she thought with a pang of anguish.

She was thankful that Richard put no pressure on her, although he now talked more openly, and in glowing terms, of his Sussex home. But her apprehensions both of him and for him returned in full flood when he said lightly one evening. "I may have to love you and leave you shortly. I hope it will not be for very long. But after that I'll be free as a bird, and I'm going to borrow old Herman's helicopter and take you for a night in Antakya that'll make your head spin. High time, too—you're starting to think more about these ancient Hittites than about me!"

It was true in a way, for she had caught Herman's infectious enthusiasm and was almost as avid about what the next day's digging would bring as he was. The large building was proving increasingly interesting and complex, and even the cautious Mary Leroy was beginning to talk of it as a royal hunting lodge—the summer palace of a late Hittite king, Padi-wa-la, who had seen his little kingdom and his fair life wiped out before his eyes by the marauding Assyrians on their way down to the conquest of Israel and Judah and the sacking of the Temple in Jerusalem. In one room of the palace they had found the skeleton of a woman huddled in a corner; under her protecting body had been the remains of two young children, one of whom, they learned from the small inscribed dagger at his belt, had been the crown prince of this little realm.

She was laboring over a drawing of this dagger, trying to get the cuneiform characters on it exactly right, in the tent that Herman had set aside for the plans and drawings of the site. Its flaps were fully open to catch the late-afternoon light, and when a shadow fell across the board, she looked up in annoyance to see who was about to bother her. John was standing in the opening.

She looked at him in shocked silence. He had lost a lot of weight, and the square lines of his jaw were so sharp that the bones showed, whitely outlined under the taut skin. His vivid eyes were cloudy and uncertain as he ducked into the low opening of the tent and came over to her. He cleared his throat and said huskily, "I've just dropped by to see if you were ready to come home. I hope so. I need you, Van. I need you very badly." He was so tense she could see the tremors in his bunched muscles as he brushed the dust of the road off his bush jacket.

"Just dropped by"—when he had to have been on this road to nowhere for hours. It was so absurd that it almost brought tears to her eyes. She was glad she was sitting down, because her own legs had begun to tremble, but she felt she had to appear calm and collected for both their sakes. "Well, this is quite a surprise—you've caught me right in the middle of something rather important." She gestured at the pathetic little bronze dagger sitting on the board. "Relic of the last crown prince of the kingdom of Ansawa, Melursis. He was all of six years old when he was killed."

Her matter-of-fact tone had the right effect, for she could see John relax a little. "Really? Well, if you want to finish this, maybe I should walk around a bit until you're through, and then maybe we can talk."

"Oh, I was just about to quit for today anyway—the light is almost gone. I'll finish it in the morning. Let's go and have some dinner while we talk. You'll have to stay the night in any case—it's too late to go back over that road tonight." She kept her casual tone.

Again he looked uncertain, as if this eventuality had not even occurred to him. "Will that be awkward?"

"Not a bit—there's always a guest tent available," she said, stowing away her drawing materials and the precious dagger. She stood up, face to face with him, and the look in his eyes was such that she could stand it no longer, so she put her arms around his neck and turned her face up to his. "I've missed you."

She was seized in an embrace so violent that she almost cried out as he crushed her to him and buried his face in her hair. "Oh, God, Van, and I you! You'll never know how much. I think I've been half out of my mind." He kissed her lingeringly, his lips trembling on hers. When he drew away, he said in a more normal voice, "Is there somewhere I could wash up? I can't disgrace you before the multitude looking like this."

"Sure, I'll show you." She took him by the hand and led him toward the showers, stopping by her own tent to pick up a towel. "Think you can find your way back here when you're through?"

He managed a tentative grin. "Like a homing pigeon."

She stowed the dagger away in one of the footlockers for safekeeping, and for the first time in over a month she put on some makeup and arranged her hair, studying herself thoughtfully in the wavy, hazy mirror. Now what was she going to do? Part of her was elated, the rest uncertain and a little apprehensive.

When John reappeared, he not only had showered but by some strange alchemy had also managed to exchange his bush shirt for a clean one, a silk scarf tucked into its neckline. "Will I do?" he demanded anxiously as she led him toward the mess tent.

"You'll do very well." She smiled.

None of the warm bodies paid them much attention as they settled at one of the tables, save Brannigan, who had just come in and who raised his eyebrows at her in mock dismay and inquiry, but he made no effort to join them. But they were not to be left to a peaceful tête-à-tête, for Herman shambled in and, after filling his tray, made a determined beeline for them. As he came up, John got up formally and said, "Well, sir, I've come to collect my wife. I hope you don't mind."

Herman settled himself with a grunt and looked up at him from under his shaggy brows. "Humph, taking away one of my most valuable assistants, are ye? Well, I don't know about that. What does she say about it? Lot of important stuff coming out now. Why don't you stay awhile and give us a hand?" Although his tone was gruff, Vanessa knew him well enough by now to realize he was alight with inward glee.

"I'm afraid I can't just now, but if there's a chance later, maybe we both could come back," John placated.

"Is this a family party, or can anyone join in?" Richard's voice broke in. He stood with a glass of beer in his hand and a smile on his lips, but his eyes were solemn as he and John eyed each other warily. It struck her forcibly that John was not in the least surprised to see him.

"Oh, sit down, sit down!" Herman said testily. "Seems this is a farewell party we're having."

"Farewell?" Richard looked directly at Vanessa.

"We really haven't had a chance to discuss it," she said, feeling a little helpless. "But in any case, I'm certainly going to finish the dagger drawing."

"That should take you all of two hours," Herman said pointedly.

A silence fell and, looking at the three disparate men, all of whom cared for her as she did for them, it was as if a veil had been torn from her eyes and she saw something clearly for the first time. Herman and Richard sat slouched casually, both grubby and unshaved—the gray stubble on Herman's face was three days old—their khaki work clothes rumpled and dusty, and yet they radiated, in their respective ways, a complete security and self-assurance. John looked as neat, elegant, and composed as always—and out of place. And suddenly she knew that this almost obsessive dressiness of his masked a raging insecurity within—an insecurity that made his frail ivory tower of appearance necessary to him. He needed an ivory tower to shelter him from the world of hunters; he needed *her* ivory tower; he *needed* her. That was the difference, the vital difference, and a sudden joy filled her. "Yes, I'll finish it tomorrow morning and then I'll be leaving," she said calmly. "I don't know yet if I'll be able to get back."

"That's all right. Always glad to see you—both of you—if you can make it," Herman said to his plate, disguising his satisfaction. "I'll be at it until Christmas. That's long enough for a first season." And that was that. From then on he firmly took control of the conversation and no one else could get a word in; after a while Richard quietly got up and went away.

Later, when John was gazing dubiously at the narrow cot in his tent, she asked, "Did you bring a sleeping bag in the car?" and when he nodded, she said, "Well, get it and we'll go to the palace—there's a lovely moon." He glanced at her with a faint grin and murmured, "Wow! Far out!" But did as he was bidden.

They settled in one of the smaller chambers opening out from what had been dubbed the throne room. Their pent-up desires made the first encounter swift, violent, and satisfying. Then, murmuring to each other the nonsense all lovers confide only to each other and their pillows, they settled into a long, languorous lovemaking that came to a slower and even more satisfying climax. "There's a lot to be said for palaces," John murmured at length. "I wonder where we'll ever find another one, my love."

"Not to worry," she murmured back. "We'll make our own." But before she fell asleep in his arms, she wondered briefly if in this place, where life had been cut short so savagely, perhaps a new life had been brought into being. That would be nice, she reflected sleepily, very nice—but I don't think we'd call it Melursis. . . .

The next morning, the drawing was finished and delivered along with the dagger to Mary Leroy, who seemed genuinely sorry to see her go. She said her brief goodbyes to all but Richard, who remained invisible, packed her gear into John's dust-smothered car, and they got under way. They did not talk much, both unwilling to dispel the rosy glow of their night of reconciliation. Only when they reached the Belen Pass did John volunteer, "You'll find some changes at home. I fired Bilger and, of course, Meriban. I never realized what a hopeless case he was until you left. You should have said something to me sooner. Anyway, this new couple, Sabit and Zehra, have a lot more on the ball. She's of Greek origin and a great cook, and he's got a motorbike, so that's one less chore for you. The house seems in pretty good shape now."

"How did you find them?"

"Oh, Bobby found them for me. She was the one who finally opened my eyes to what a layabout Bilger was."

"Have you been seeing a lot of the Wests?" she said casually.

He gave her a quick, uncomfortable look. "A fair amount. I stayed over there for a few weekends, and they've been over, too."

"How's Robin doing?"

"All right. A bit antsy from lack of action. He busted up a drug ring that had been operating on the base. Nothing to do with him, of course, and it didn't earn him any popularity points with the Air Force, who were a bit miffed he'd uncovered something right under their noses, but the dust seems to have settled now. He's hopeful that things are beginning to move at last. Recently Henfield has been showing some signs of life at long last, but he is as secretive as ever, so we're still in the dark."

"We?" Vanessa took up the word sharply. "You're not involved in this, are you?"

"Just a manner of speaking," he hedged. "His orders will come through me."

"Well, I'm glad you had plenty of company in my absence," she said, a little more tartly than she intended. "Or didn't they notice I was gone?"

"Oh, they noticed, all right—in fact, Bobby became quite a pain with her prying," he retorted, and the disloyal thought came to her that maybe it was this that had sent him in search of her. She quickly suppressed it.

After the Spartan rigors of the dig, the little house seemed the acme of comfort, and for the first few days at home she luxuriated in long, hot baths, soft beds, and the excellent food that Zehra produced in a steady stream. She and John were managing to maintain the atmosphere of a second honeymoon, though she sensed in him a deep disquiet that he was carefully suppressing, the cause of which she could not fathom. With her new-found commitment she was determined that she would not let things deteriorate again, and to this end she initiated something she had been thinking about that would also serve a purpose of her own. "How about taking a weekend off and coming with me on a trip to Izmir?" she suggested.

John looked at her with sudden, sharp suspicion. "Why Izmir?" he demanded.

"We've never been there. It's a nice city, lots to see, and I'd like to visit Eleanor Heitz. She's teaching there, you know."

"Oh." He appeared relieved. "Well, yes, fine! Let's do it. Nothing here that Dick can't handle for a couple of days. Matter of fact, there's one of our men there I'd like to touch base with. I can do that while you're having your hen party with Eleanor, whom I have no raging desire to see again."

"Fine," she said in her turn, for this suited her very well; she had things to ask Eleanor that could not be said before him.

It was a great success. The first day they wined and dined and saw the sights, wandering hand in hand through the city in a happy daze. The second day she had set up her meeting with Eleanor and John went off about his own business.

She was a little shocked at her first sight of Eleanor, who looked dowdy and uncared for, a far cry from the smartly dressed, intimidating woman she had first known; but her eyes were still serene, and to the inevitable question of how she was faring, Eleanor smiled resignedly and said, "Oh, some pluses and some minuses, but on the whole I'm content. In fact, now that I'm back in the swing of things, I may go even further than this. I'm thinking,

after my time here is up, of going home and joining the
Peace Corps—not such a heavily religious ambience as
this, but just as rewarding."

They chatted generally for a while, then Vanessa got
down to cases. "Eleanor, there's something I've simply
got to ask you. I asked you once before, but this is a little
different. John and I have been having problems, and most
of them stem from the hard time I have accepting the
CIA. As a long-term CIA wife, could you tell me honestly—was it better or worse after you had your children?"

"Who for?" Eleanor said promptly. "In my case, I'd
say it was better. I had three, and two of them, at least,
were and are the joy of my heart. In Armand's case, I'd
say it was worse, but then Armand was Armand: not a
fatherly type. If you are thinking of having a child, from
what I know of John, I'd say he'd be a good father, because
he's basically a very nice man. *Are* you?"

"I think we may be talking after the fact," Vanessa
murmured, although she had no idea why she was so
certain.

"Well, in that case, fine!" Eleanor studied her thoughtfully. "But you're never going to be able to shut the CIA
out, you know. Not like, say, Amanda Drake. Can you
live with that? I managed, but then after a while I didn't
much care what happened to Armand. You do care." It
was between a statement and a question.

"Yes, I do," Vanessa said dolefully. "And I suppose
I'll just *have* to live with it. Short of a miracle, I don't
see any hope of changing John's mind. He's such a
believer."

"We were all believers once," Eleanor murmured, as
if to herself. "But beliefs can be shattered—particularly
in this game. It could happen to John—and for your sake,
I hope it does."

Chapter 26

During their absence Dick Fortescue had retrieved her car from Antakya Airport, so three days after their return she drove down into Iskenderun to touch base with her musical group and take up the threads of her old life. She found that they had been contentedly resting on their laurels since the concert at the Army base, but all were delighted to see her back, and they spent a pleasant afternoon planning a Christmas concert, the proceeds from which, after some argument, they decided to donate to the local hospital. Vanessa took the opportunity to ask the English secretary about local doctors, for she did not want to go to the doctor normally used by the American consulate until she was sure that what she suspected was confirmed. The secretary, a little curious, supplied her with a name and address, and before she started home she dropped by the office and made an appointment for two weeks later. When she arrived home it was to find Zehra with a message for her to call John's office, and when she did so she reached an audibly excited Dick Fortescue. "John's gone to Adana and wanted me to let you know he won't be back tonight. I think you can guess why."

So it had come at long last, this mysterious assignment of Robin's. She wished she could feel excited about it, but all she felt was an uneasy sense of foreboding. I mustn't care, I mustn't get upset, she told herself fiercely. It's not John; it's nothing to do with him. But in spite of all her attempted self-discipline, she slept badly that night, with all the tensions and terror of the past roiling in her mind.

The lack of sleep left her jumpy and too lethargic to apply herself to anything, and when an obviously keyed-up John arrived home unexpectedly in the early afternoon she was relieved. He said, "Boy, I'm bushed! Stayed up all night with Robin talking things over, so I think I'll catch a nap before calling the office. I may even take the rest of the day off. Robin's on cloud nine! He never dreamt it would be this big an assignment—but if he brings it off...! Anyway, he's off and running. I'll tell you about it later, hon," and he went to bed, smothering a series of yawns.

She wondered if she ought to call and invite Bobby to stay over, then rejected that. If Bobby was playing anchor woman for this enterprise, she would have to stay put. Instead, she settled with a book on a chaise lounge in the peaceful garden, and after gazing unseeingly at it for a little, she slipped into a quiet doze from which she did not awaken until the shadows were long on the grass and the spicy aroma of dinner cooking percolated out of the open kitchen windows. She went in, to find a spruce John, his hair still damp from the shower, fixing a tray of drinks. He grinned at her. "Saw you sleeping out there, so I was going to surprise you awake with these. Zehra says dinner will be in twenty minutes, so we've time for a quick one. Here's to Robin!"

But they had barely clinked glasses and taken their first sip when the sound of a car drawing up in the driveway broke the twilight peace. "Who the hell can that be?" John muttered, going to the window and peering out. "Good Lord! It's Dick. Probably thinks I'm lost in the wilderness."

He went to open the door and admit his tall assistant while Vanessa sat trying to suppress her vague flutterings of unease. This was so unlike Dick, a very punctilious young man, who only had visited them on rare formal dinner occasions and had otherwise kept his distance.

"Come on in, Dick," John was saying heartily. "We were just having a drink. I should have called you to let you know all was well, but I was so bushed I put it off. What'll you have?"

"Nothing, thanks." Dick's prominent Adam's apple bobbed up and down as he nervously cleared his throat. He looked sideways at Vanessa in agonized uncertainty and said, "Something came up and I thought I'd better come rather than call about it. It may be nothing, but . . ." He trailed off.

"Well, at least sit down," John said, sitting down by Vanessa on the couch and putting an arm around her shoulders. "And don't mind Van; she's an old hand at excitement."

Dick sat on the edge of a chair, his thin hands kneading his bony knees nervously. "Something doesn't jibe," he blurted out. "Henfield said the first rendezvous was to be with the Druse leader, Al Ibn, and a representative of Khomeini's—right?"

John nodded, his hand tightening slightly on Vanessa's shoulder.

"Well, I was monitoring the stuff through Cyprus this afternoon"—Dick gulped—"and one of the items mentioned Al Ibn. He's in Libya consulting with Khadafi—something to do with arms."

"It must be a mistake, a planted story," John said. "Did you—"

"But I checked," Dick broke in. "He's there, all right. So if he's not in Syria, who the hell is going to be at that rendezvous?"

John removed his arm and leaned forward. "Did you contact Henfield?"

"I tried, but no one in Ankara seems to know where he is. He wasn't supposed to go, was he?"

John got up and started to pace up and down. "No.

Robin was to rendezvous just outside of Kilis with this agent who knows Al Ibn personally and who set up the meeting place just over the Syrian border, and they were both going in."

"You mean the British agent who was going to be the interpreter as well?"

Vanessa's throat closed over. "Richard—it has to be him!" It came out as a strangled moan.

John stopped dead and gazed at her, a nerve under his right eye jumping like a live wire. "Morse? How do you know?"

"He told me he would be going away soon—a final assignment, he said."

"I don't like it. If Al Ibn isn't there, it looks like a setup. They may be walking into a trap. We've got to head them off somehow—but how, in the name of God? We've got to get to the map in the office, Dick." John smote his fist against his palm. "I've got to get them out!"

"We could never do it in time," Dick exclaimed. "Robin should be almost there by now, and they were going in during the night. Even if you abort the whole thing and alert the Turks, it'll be too late!"

Vanessa came out of her paralysis of fear. "Brannigan—the helicopter!" she cried. "If we could get that, we could be there by dawn."

"But they'd never—" John started.

"Yes, they would," Vanessa said desperately. "Herman would okay it if I asked him, and Brannigan's an ex-mercenary. I *know* he would."

"Then let's go." John looked at Dick. "First we've got to get that map."

She sprang to her feet. "Let me go with you—*please*! It'll save time, and you'll need me in Antakya. Please!"

The tic writhed under John's eye. "Okay," he said thickly. "You have that right. Dick, you go get the map and follow us to Antakya. We'll rendezvous at the airport. If this idea of Van's works, doing it this way will save time. And bring the guns. If we can't get to them in time on this side, we may have to get them out by force."

As they sped up the mountain in the deepening dusk,

John said tightly, "Since you know this much, you may as well know it all, although I still hope this is a false alarm. The object of all this was to ransom our hostages from the extremist Jihad—eight Americans, two Britons, and a Frenchman. A three-way, top-secret deal, because it's going to step on so many toes. Robin was supposed to meet Al Ibn, who is the moderate influence in all this, as well as a representative of Khomeini and some of the Shiite leaders to negotiate the release. The terms were to be partly cash—hard currency to buy arms with—and our pledge to the Iranians to put pressure on Iraq to come to terms about the war, plus a pledge to the Shiites to get Israel to soft-pedal its support of the Christian militia in Lebanon. In return Khomeini's man was to order the Jihad to let the captives go. I just don't understand what could have gone wrong. It's not as if Robin was carrying any money with him this time. That was to come at the next meeting, when the hostages were supposed to be handed over at another place along the border."

"Where were they supposed to meet this time?" Vanessa queried, her lips stiff with fear.

"All I know is that it's a deserted khan—an old inn—across the border. It's why I need the map. It's somewhere between Kilis and a small place called Elbeyli, just across the border on a direct line south with the Syrian village of Suran. They picked it because the border patrols on both sides are a laugh in that area—virtually nonexistent. Khomeini's representative was to fly into Aleppo from Teheran, meet up with Al Ibn, and go on north from there with the rest. It has taken months to set this up."

"I can believe it," she muttered; it had been months since Richard had first reappeared so dramatically in her life.

"Morse told you, did he?" John said bitterly. "So much for security."

"Richard told me nothing but what I've told you," she retorted. "But it all adds up. He's been using Tell Murad as a base camp, coming and going on mysterious errands he never talked about—and he speaks Arabic. Herman was onto him, I'm sure of that. He may know more—he seems to have eyes everywhere."

"God, if Morse has blown this thing, I'll..." John's hands tightened on the wheel. He didn't finish his thought.

They drove in silence, the reckless speed at which John was negotiating the narrow mountain road demanding all his concentration. As they finally reached the valley and were hurtling toward the airport he said, "If this scheme of yours doesn't work out, as soon as Dick arrives I plan to keep going directly north. If Dick and I drive all night we might still make it by dawn."

"I want to go with you," she said stubbornly. "I'll be useful. I speak better Turkish than either of you, and I understand what people say to me. Besides, if need be, I can be your pipeline to Ankara. Even if Herman won't go for the helicopter, at least he'll let me use the radio."

John grunted but did not reject it out of hand. Screaming into the airport and up to the dark hangar of Gross Enterprises, they ran into their first obstacle. The radioman in his little shack by the side of the hangar was on the point of closing things down for the night and was unimpressed by Vanessa's desperate appeals to talk to Tell Murad. John had dropped her off and had returned to the main terminal to wait for Dick, and she was almost in despair when she spotted the Turkish guard whose life history she had listened to so patiently on her first arrival. She collared him and marched over to the radioman. "Tell him who I am," she commanded. "And tell him that it is vital I talk to Mr. Gross *now*. If I don't, there'll be hell to pay for both of you tomorrow."

He nodded and entered into an energetic parlay with the radioman, showing him the precious roster on which her name was heavily underlined. At length the radioman grudgingly unshrouded his equipment and made contact with the camp. "Vanessa Bannerman for Herman Gross. Very urgent message. Please contact immediately."

"Tell him this is a 'Mayday, Mayday,'" she urged, to his deep puzzlement.

There was a further agonizing wait before Herman was located, and when he came on the air his voice was brusque with concern. "Vanessa, is that you? What's the matter?"

She felt like bursting into tears. "Everything! I'm not kidding, Herman. This may be a matter of life or death. I need Brannigan and the helicopter here in Antakya as soon as possible. We've got to locate someone fast. He's to the north of here, heading into Syria. I can't spell it out, but it's a matter of national security, and it also concerns a certain party known to both of us who, unless I'm very wrong, is no longer with you."

There was a short silence at the other end, then Herman said, "Right. He left first thing this morning. Well, okay, I'll send Brannigan as soon as it gets light."

"That'll be too late!" she cried. "It's got to be *now*. Then he can gas up here and be ready to take off again as soon as it gets light."

"I can't ask that of him." Herman's voice was concerned. "It's damned dangerous to operate those things at night."

"But he knows this flight like the back of his hand," she pleaded desperately, "and he'll be coming into a lighted airport. Please! Ask him. Tell him what I've told you, but please ask him. If I know Brannigan, he'll do it, and it really is very urgent. Tell him I'll explain the rest of it when he gets here."

"Right. Well, hang on. I'll sign off now until I find him. But I'm not going to order him to do this, Vanessa—understood?"

"Understood," she said tightly, and there followed another agonizing wait as the radio operator glowered at her sullenly. The transmitter finally crackled into life. "He's on his way," Herman's voice stated. "I couldn't talk him out of it. Seems you pushed the right button. That husband of yours there with you?"

"He will be shortly. This is very good of you, Herman," she said belatedly.

"I don't like to think of you involved in something like this," he growled. "Why don't you come out here and wait? I'll send the other helicopter for you at first light."

"No, I'm going along. I'm *needed*. I speak Turkish

better than they do, and we're going to need every edge we can get in this."

"Well, then take care of yourself, m'dear," he muttered. "Anything else I can do on this end?"

"No, you've done wonderfully. We'll never be able to thank you enough," she said, choked with emotion, and the radio went dead.

John arrived back five minutes later; save for a bulky knapsack, he was alone. "Where's Dick?" she asked.

"I sent him back to Iskenderun. He's got a lead on Henfield, so I told him to keep trying for contact and to get him into the action fast," he said tightly. "What's the story here?"

"The helicopter is on its way," she reported, and from the north they could hear the steady throb of an engine. A pencil beam of light from a spotlight searched the ground in front of the hangar as out of the night the helicopter floated gently to the ground. The rotors were still in motion when a dark figure detached itself from the cockpit and came running toward them. As he came into the light, Brannigan was grinning broadly, his eyes sparkling. He stuck out a meaty hand to John, "Mr. Bannerman, Brannigan—had a Mayday from a lovely lady in distress. What's up?"

"What may be a false alarm," John said. "In fact, I'm hoping my assistant will get back here before dawn to say just that. But we have to go on the presumption that something is the matter and that one of my colleagues and Richard Morse may be heading into danger *if* they cross into Syria." At Richard Morse's name Brannigan gave them both a searching look, and John went on. "So here's what I'd like to do." He spread out the map on the hood of his car. "They'll be somewhere in this area between Kilis and Elbeyli—if you can fly us north and then along the border, we may be able to spot my colleague's car from the air and either buzz him to let him know something is up or—can you land this chopper easily?"

"I can set it down on any spot that's big enough to take the skids and where there's nothing to foul up the rotors." Brannigan grinned, still studying the map.

"Time's important. How soon can we get going?" John demanded.

Brannigan grimaced and looked at his watch. "Should start to get light around six. The thing is, I'm going to have to fly low to keep under the radar scan. I'm not too worried about the Turks, but I don't want to run into any Syrian jets out of Aleppo. I can fly the first bit north in the dark okay—I know it—but I'll need light for the rest of it. We could save some time, if you're willing to risk it, if we cut across Syrian territory by keeping in the shelter of that low mountain range there, which should blanket us from Aleppo"—he indicated with his finger—"and that'll land us directly at Kilis. It's one o'clock now. I've got to gas this baby up and then I suggest we try to get a couple of hours' sleep. If we set off at five, we'll be in the light by the time we get to this point. Should get us to Kilis by six. What do you say?"

"Any time we can save will be fine with me," John said tightly. "And sure, you rest up now. I have to wait for my colleague."

"Let me do that," Vanessa broke in. "You'll need to be fresh for what's ahead. It doesn't matter about me."

Brannigan loped off to fuel the helicopter and John looked at her. "I want you to stay here. We're going to be sticking our necks way out, and I don't want you involved."

"I *am* involved," she said quietly. "Please, John, don't shut me out on this. Please! I can be useful; I know it. For one thing, Robin will have transferred to Richard's Jeep for the last stretch—his car would never make it on this rough terrain—and I can spot Richard's Jeep among a hundred such." She did not look at him, although she could feel his eyes on her.

"All right," he said heavily. "But let's hope Dick gets here with news that'll take us all off the hook." He settled down on the floor of the radio shack and was shortly joined by Brannigan, and both men were soon heavily asleep as she kept her anxious vigil. But as the endless minutes ticked by toward zero hour there was no sign of Dick Fortescue, and a few minutes before five she shook them both awake, and then, to preclude any further argument, she went out and got into the helicopter.

They took off in somber silence and headed toward the unseen mountains. It was cold, and in her thin dress Vanessa began to shiver. John wordlessly took off his jacket and draped it around her shoulders, hugging her to him. She found herself willing the sun to rise, and as the blackness gave way to a dark gray that lightened by the second, the helicopter lunged northeastward at a greater speed to meet the dawn. They reached the outskirts of Kilis without incident by five-forty-five and circled low over the sleeping town. John, who was peering through the binoculars Brannigan had silently handed over, exclaimed, "There's Robin's car!" and then, "Hell! Not a sign of anyone. Keep going. That means we've got to scan for the Jeep." They drifted off toward Elbeyli. He handed the glasses to Vanessa. "Here, you said you know it. Take a look." He rubbed his tired eyes.

She was searching desperately for a telltale flash of red: Richard's cooler, which he always kept in the back of the Jeep. "Best equipped mobile bar in Turkey"—his words echoed in her mind, stirring bittersweet memories. In a little wadi, half hidden by bushes, she thought she caught the telltale flash and let out an exclamation. "Wait! Circle back. I think it's almost immediately below us." She handed the glasses to John. "See, it's a red cooler in the back of the Jeep. That's Richard's."

"Got it! Can you go lower, Brannigan?" The helicopter obediently sank down until John grunted, "No sign of life there either, so we'll have to go for broke. Brannigan, will you head directly south from here? We're looking for an old caravanserai. It should be just across the border."

The helicopter executed a giddy turn and headed south. "There it is!" John pointed directly below them, and Vanessa saw a dun-colored building that blended with the parched terrain around it. One of its mud brick walls was crumbled into ruin and stuck up from the plain like stumps of rotten teeth. "No sign of life there either. Head back and see if we can pick up anyone moving on the ground."

Again Brannigan circled. "Got the compass heading

between here and the Jeep," he reported tersely as John scanned the ground with feverish anxiety. Suddenly he let out a cry. "Hover and circle!" He looked desperately around, seized an orange flotation cushion, and hurled it out of the chopper. "Head back across the border and set it down," he ordered. "I'm going to have to go in on foot."

Vanessa grasped at his arm. "Why, John? What did you see? What's down there?"

In the gray light he looked at her, his face a grim mask. "I saw a man on the ground. I think he's dead. It's not Robin. It may be Morse."

Chapter 27

As the helicopter swept back toward the hidden Jeep John opened the knapsack and got out an M16 automatic rifle. "Got another of those?" Brannigan said. "I think you could use some help."

"You've done enough, Brannigan. This is my fight."

"If it's an American down there, it's my fight as well. Besides," the ex-mercenary went on with a faint grin, "I'm good at this sort of thing. I've been missing the action. I feel ten years younger already."

"You might never get any older," John retorted grimly.

Brannigan shrugged as the helicopter settled down and he switched off the engine. "Beats going gaga in some old people's home."

"In that case, help yourself." John tossed him the knapsack, into which he dived with all the enthusiasm of a small boy, extracting a duplicate M16 and a Biretta automatic. "Nice baby," he breathed. "Sixteen-rounder, right?"

They got out, and Vanessa could feel her legs trembling beneath her as she looked up at John. "Must you go?" she whispered miserably. "Isn't there any other way?"

John took her in his arms and held her tightly. "No," he whispered into her hair, "but I swear to you, Van, that if Morse is alive I'll bring him back to you somehow." And as he drew away she saw a bottomless anguish in his eyes.

Brannigan slung the M16 over one shoulder, a canteen of water over the other, and handed her the second Biretta. "Here, little lady, you mind the store. If any Turks come snooping around, play dumb. Say the chopper broke down and I went for help. Spin 'em a good yarn. If they get nasty, just keep this on 'em till we get back." Glancing at his watch-compass, he started to march away. "Take care, my love," John murmured, and started after him. Feeling utterly helpless, her heart in her mouth, she watched them walk out of sight. She started to pray as she had never prayed before; it was the only thing left to her.

As John caught up with him, Brannigan said, "What exactly *did* you see down there?"

"A dark-haired man in khaki drab on the ground in a small gully, partly hidden by bushes. He wasn't moving and there was blood on him. We should be able to spot that cushion. I got it fairly close to the place."

Brannigan grimaced. "Doesn't look good, does it? Maybe we'd better fan out a bit. I'll go left, so if you're going to do any shooting keep it off to the right."

"Stay close enough for voice contact. I'd rather not warn anyone that we're here," John said, silently indicating the knife at his belt. "But we may not have much choice. I've got to get Robin West out of there."

"They could have taken him off," Brannigan pointed out. "There wasn't a vehicle in sight, and I thought I saw some tracks going south. Still, here's hoping." And he slipped away.

A few hundred yards farther on, John caught a glimpse of orange. "Brannigan," he called softly, and started to sprint toward it. He was nearly upon it when he almost tripped over a body on the ground: a slight man wearing an Arab headdress and with a knife buried between his shoulder blades. He was very dead. By his side lay a Russian-made rifle.

"That what you saw?" Brannigan appeared from behind a bush and breathed in his ear. John shook his head and looked keenly around. A faint groan came from their left, and they advanced cautiously toward the screen of bushes. Parting them, they looked down into a little gully. Richard Morse was sprawled on his back beneath a bush, his entire left side dark with blood, a thin film of it on his bleached lips. With one silent bound Brannigan was at his side and examining him with an expert eye. "Alive and not gut-shot, thank God." He unhitched the canteen and started to dab water on the blood-crusted lips. "Looks as if he caught it in the back and it went clean through. Must've nicked his lung for him to have bled so. Lost a bucket, by the looks of it. We'll have to get him out of here fast, if he's going to make it."

John was kneeling on the other side of the prone figure, his hand on the neck pulse. "Still pretty strong. Morse, Morse!" He shook the uninjured shoulder. "Come out of it! You've got to tell us what happened. Where's Robin? Have they got Robin?"

The eyelids flickered, then opened a crack, and recognition came into the pain-filled eyes as the lips moved feebly. "Take it easy, Bannerman!" Brannigan muttered.

"Khan," Richard croaked feebly. "Knew something wrong. Robin went in first. They jumped him. Gave me time to get away. Bastard got me, but I got him." The eyes closed again.

"We've got to get him out of here," Brannigan repeated.

"Then you'll have to manage alone," John hissed. "I'm going on. There's still a chance Robin's alive." The look in his eyes told Brannigan there was no use arguing. "Right. Well, help me up with him," he growled. "Just as well I was a champion weightlifter in my class; as it is, I'll have to drag him. What'll I tell your wife?"

"She'll be too concerned about this to want to know," John said bitterly, and moved silently off.

To Vanessa's straining ears the dragging footsteps sounded like an army on the march, and, abandoning caution, she ran blindly toward the sound. Brannigan appeared, soaked in sweat, and at the sight of the burden he half carried, half dragged along, her senses began to swim. "Is he . . ." she gasped as Brannigan halted, panting heavily. "No, he's alive—just. Think you can get his feet? He needs blood. We've got to get him into the chopper and out of here fast."

She obeyed mechanically, and by the time they reached the helicopter, her arms felt dislocated and she, too, was streaming with sweat. As Brannigan propped him up against its side she hastily spread a blanket and more flotation pillows on the floor of the helicopter and helped heave Richard onto the makeshift bed. "All right, hop in and keep him steady while I get this revved up," Brannigan ordered.

She hung back. "Where's John?"

He looked at her curiously. "Went on after the other man."

"Then I'm staying right here," she said defiantly.

"But what about him?" Brannigan jerked his chin in the direction of the wounded man.

"You got him this far by yourself; you can get him the rest of the way," she flared. "That's my husband out there. Until he gets back I'm staying right here."

Brannigan unhitched the M16 from his shoulder. "With that look in your eye, I won't take the time to argue with you. Here—if you're set on staying, take this. If anyone you don't recognize comes in from the south, flip off this little latch and keep your finger pressed here. That should discourage 'em."

Van looked at Richard, who was moving slightly. "Where are you going to take him?"

"That's a tricky one." Brannigan's tone was heavy with concern. "The last thing we need is the Turks in on this, holding us up and asking a lot of questions. The big man has his doctor visiting the camp at the moment, and we've got medical supplies there, too. What I plan to do is fly him to Tell Murad, have the doc pump some plasma into him and get him stabilized, and then go on to the hospital at Antakya. I guess it'll have to be a hunting accident. Then I'll come back to pick you up."

"No!" She was definite. "You stay with him—go!"

"But I can't leave you stuck in the middle of nowhere!" he protested.

"There's the Jeep," she said evenly. "If John isn't in any shape to drive, I can get it as far as Kilis. For God's sake go—get out of here!"

A faint groan drew their attention back to Richard Morse, whose eyes were now open and fixed unseeingly upon her. She ran to him and took his hand. "Oh, Richard, it's going to be all right. Brannigan is taking you out of here. Hang on!"

He did not appear to hear her, though his eyes remained riveted on hers. "Oh, God, the screams," he muttered. "He never stopped screaming." Then the eyes fluttered shut and she thought he was gone. Brannigan felt for the carotid pulse. "It's there, but a hell of a lot feebler. Now or never?"

"Never," she said, and with a curt nod he leaped up into the cockpit. She backed away as the rotors started their slow circling. As it shot skyward in a pillar of dust she shielded her eyes and, shouldering the automatic gun, made her way back to the Jeep. The sun was now high, and it was very hot. She was parched with thirst, so she reached back to the red cooler and opened it up: a bottle of brandy, a bottle of white wine, and a bottle of Dimple Haig stood in a melting pool of ice together with some bottles of soda water. She uncapped one of these and sipped gratefully at its sparkling coolness. It was a touch of normalcy, a slight gesture from the world without in this terror-filled nightmare, and it steadied her. Was it only two days ago she had talked of Handel's Messiah and of Christmas, only yesterday she had dozed in a fragrant garden? And now it was as if all her fears over the years had come to a climactic crescendo and were being realized at this particular moment, leaving nothing but a cold, sick void of helplessness within her while the man of whom she was fond and to whom she owed her own life lay at the point of death, and the man she loved was somewhere out there in all the barrenness laying his life on the line to save another. And all she could do was wait and wait and pray some more.

As the sun rose toward its zenith she paced up and down along the invisible boundary between Turkey and Syria, her eyes fixed on the south, her ears straining for the least sound. At one point she thought she heard the faint crackle of faraway gunfire, but when she stopped, her heart pounding, she could hear nothing but her own blood singing in her ears. Out of the brazen sky three black dots appeared, and she crouched in the shelter of a bush, listening for the throb of engines; but as the dots took on clearer definition she could see they were huge birds sweeping toward the ground in cautious sweeps, circling and rising again and again, until one by one they dropped earthward out of sight and it dawned on her what they were—vultures! And that meant there was some-thing—someone—dead out there. She could stand it no longer; she had to know, and, abandoning caution, she broke into a frantic run toward them. The sound of her approach sent them wheeling upward again, marking her way, until she too almost stumbled over the body of the dead Arab. Her relief was so great that she did not even recoil at the sight of the bloody, tattered face. Instinctively she bent down and gathered up the rifle and the orange cushion that lay just beyond, then she hesitated, sorely tempted to continue on to the khan, the ruined walls of which she could just see; then she realized how foolish and futile that would be. But her brief spurt of action had started the adrenaline pumping and jolted her numb mind back into coherent thought, and as she walked slowly back to the Jeep she began to make plans. John had been gone almost three hours. She would wait one more hour and then, if there was still no sign of him, she would raise the alarm. At this point she did not give a damn about the consequences—all she wanted was John back, by whatever means.

Once back at the Jeep a reaction set in, and she was overwhelmed with a desire for sleep; willing her tired eyelids to stay open, she urged herself back to her endless pacing as the minutes dragged interminably by. A few minutes short of zero hour the sound of slow footsteps stopped her dead in her tracks, and she crouched down behind the Jeep, fumbling with fingers that shook at the safety catch. As she peered cautiously around her sparse cover a figure detached itself from the shimmering heat haze, and her heart almost burst with joy. "John!" she screamed, "Oh, thank God! John, darling!" And dropping the gun she ran toward him with open arms.

He was moving like an automaton, his eyes wide and fixed on some inner vision of hell; his clothes were blood-spattered, an ugly gash across his left arm oozed blood, and both his hands were bloodied and blistered. "Oh, God, darling, you're hurt! Here, let me help you," she cried, tugging the M16 from his unresisting hand. He looked vacantly at her. "What are you doing here?" he croaked, his eyes dazed.

"Where else would I be? Waiting for you, of course." She was pushing him toward the Jeep. "Here, sit down!" She got the brandy out of the cooler and held it out to him. "Drink this." He obeyed mechanically, and as he gulped down the fiery liquid he coughed and shuddered, but his eyes lost some of their fixity and he choked out, "Brannigan? The helicopter?"

"He took Richard back to the camp. He won't be back," she said, mopping at his wounds with the ice water. "As soon as I've cleaned you up a bit I'll drive you into Kilis and get that arm taken care of. Oh, darling, what happened out there? You're covered with blood!"

The vacancy vanished as his face twisted into a tortured mask, tears starting to stream down his haggard cheeks. "Not my blood," he cried in agony, "Robin's blood. Oh, God, Van, what they *did* to him! I can't bear it, I can't . . ." He buried his face in his mutilated hands.

Richard's incoherent mumblings took on a new, terrible meaning. "He . . . he's dead, then?" she whispered, aghast.

"He was still alive when I got to him," John sobbed. "Alive enough to know me. He looked at me, and he even tried to smile through what was left of his mouth, and he said . . . he said . . . 'They got nothing out of me, John, nothing. . . . Tell Henfield that,' and *then* he died.''

A sudden fear roused her and she grabbed the gun. "The men who did it—are they after you?"

He shook his head. "No. There were three of them there, and I took care of all the fiendish bastards, though shooting was much, much too good for them." His eyes steadied and he went on. "But we'd best get out of here. I think there were a couple more out there somewhere in a vehicle of some kind—I saw tracks. Maybe hunting for Morse." He put his hands on the hot steering wheel and winced in pain. "Damn! I'm afraid you'll have to drive until I can get some bandages on these."

She hesitated, loathing to ask but knowing she had to. "What about Robin?"

He looked at her in abject misery. "I knew I couldn't carry him back by myself, and besides"—he shuddered— "I didn't want anyone else to see what had happened to him. So I buried him there, where they won't find him, and left the rest to the vultures. I'm hoping whoever was behind this will think there was a successful rescue and leave it at that." He held up his hands. "There was nothing there to use. I had to dig the grave with my bare hands."

"Oh, darling," she whispered, her own eyes filling with tears as he moved over and she got into the driver's seat and started the car.

In Kilis they stopped at a small infirmary, and for the benefit of the mercifully incurious Turkish doctor, who cleaned up John's wounds without comment and bandaged them expertly, she concocted a story about a camping accident. She had found an old bush jacket of Richard's in the back of the Jeep, and this masked the bloodstained shirt, but there was nothing she could do about the trousers other than mask the blood with dust rubbed into the cloth. "I don't think I dare phone from here," John observed tautly. "I'm too damned conspicuous like this. We'd better drive through to Antakya. It'll be dark by then."

"Couldn't we stop at Tell Murad?" she said faintly. "I'm

not sure I can make it that far. I'm having a hard time staying awake."

"Of course, you didn't get any sleep last night. What a fool I am!" His face softened. "I can drive from here, my love. You get some rest. And I think we'd both better have something to eat and drink before we start, or I won't make it either."

She bought some bread, cheese, and fruit in the local market, and they drove beyond the town and parked in a small grove of trees to eat, washing the food down their reluctant throats with more of the brandy. As they ate, John said quietly, "Why didn't you go with him?"

She looked at him in surprise. "And leave you? Whatever for? Brannigan could cope."

"But I thought you and he . . ." he muttered, gazing at her.

"Then you thought wrong," she said. "I *like* Richard, whatever he may be, but it is you I *love*."

He put his arms around her and drew her to him. "Oh, Van," he murmured, "and I love you so very, very much— but I thought I had lost you. I know this is not the time or the place, and that I've said it all before, but let's make a fresh start when all this nastiness is over with and the two of us can really be alone and together again."

She hesitated a second and then made up her mind. "That may be a little more difficult than you think," she said, a little breathless. "I'm not absolutely certain, but I think that from now on it will be the three of us."

He drew away and looked at her in puzzlement, then realization slowly dawned. "You mean . . ."

"Yes, and baby makes three," she whispered. "Are you pleased?"

His face became radiant and he kissed her gently. "Oh, darling, pleased isn't the word—it's the most wonderful thing that's ever happened! I'm overwhelmed." Then his face tightened with concern. "But my God, what you've been through today is enough to—oh, no!—you must rest. Maybe we should go back and stay in Kilis—perhaps you should see a doctor. . . ."

"Oh, John, stop gibbering!" she chided. "I'm tired, but

I'm perfectly all right. Go on—I can curl up in the back, and when you get tired just wake me and I'll take over."

"You're sure?"

"Absolutely certain," she said, suiting the action to the word and climbing in the back of the Jeep. "Let's go, go, go."

Despite the jolting, she fell almost at once into the dreamless sleep of exhaustion, a comfortable void from which she did not stir until lights flickering across her eyelids caused her to waken, and she realized they were running on the smoothness of tarmac. "Where are we?" she muttered groggily, struggling up.

"On the outskirts of Antakya. I'm going to check us into a hotel, get you into a proper bed, and call Dick from there," John said, his voice husky from weariness.

In a sleepy daze she found herself following him up to a suite in Antakya's plushest hotel, their bedraggled state the object of tight-lipped disapproval from their hotel escort. As John made for the phone in the little sitting room, she staggered to the bathroom, stripped, and plunged luxuriously into a deep bath. Then, wrapped in a bath towel, she went in search of him. She found him sitting and staring, deep in thought, at the mute phone, his mouth tight with anger.

"What is it?" she asked.

He looked up at her, a curious expression in his tired eyes. "Dick found Henfield, and he's on his way here. According to Henfield, he never issued those orders, and Robin's death is entirely my responsibility. He had nothing to do with it."

Chapter 28

*T*o her horrified protest at Henfield's unexpected bombshell, John had returned cryptically, "It's a bad mistake to underestimate your enemy," and he insisted they go right to bed, saying, "There's nothing more to be done tonight, and I'll be able to deal a lot better with what's ahead after a good night's sleep."

He had slept long but restlessly, his dreams bringing forth little moans and cries of torment. Her long sleep in the Jeep had remedied her own fatigue, and after a few hours more of leaden sleep she awoke clearheaded and slipped quietly out of bed. She dressed and made her way out of the hotel. After a couple of cups of strong Turkish coffee to jolt her completely awake, she went shopping for a long-sleeved shirt, a pair of jeans, and shaving materials for John. She stopped at the hotel restaurant to order a large breakfast to be sent up to the room and went up herself to see how John was doing. After the horrors and terrors of yesterday, she found herself relishing all these small, everyday acts with an intense pleasure, though she knew full well the nightmare was far from over.

She found John stirring, his bandaged arm thrown across his eyes as if to blot out the threatening world, and she said matter-of-factly, "Breakfast is on its way, and I've been shopping. The best I could do on the spur of the moment and not up to your usual high standards, but enough to make you presentable." And she began to drape her purchases across his bare chest. He took his arm from his eyes, glanced down at them and then up at her with a faint grin. "What a jewel in my crown you are, my darling. Have I told you I love you?"

"Not since yesterday, but you had better get with it," she returned, "or I'll eat both our breakfasts. Want me to help you shave?"

"Thanks, but I'm not *that* feeble." He leaped out of bed, gathering up the clothes, gave her a hurried kiss on the forehead, and disappeared into the bathroom. He eventually emerged to the clatter of breakfast dishes, tucking his shirt into the jeans and announcing jauntily, "Behold the new man! Ready and willing to whip the world."

As she poured his coffee she asked, "What's the first order of business?"

He glanced up at her, the enigmatic expression back in his eyes. "I have a number of calls. While I do that would you mind taking Morse's Jeep over to the airport, parking it there, and picking up our own car? I'll know better what the next stop is when you get back with it."

"Yes, I can do that. Are you going to find out about Richard?" she said a little uncomfortably.

"Yes, that's item number one," he returned, but did not pursue the subject, and they finished their breakfasts, both deep in their own thoughts.

When she got to the airport she found the helicopter sitting silent and cold in front of the hangar and couldn't decide whether that was a good or bad sign, nor could she get any information from the guard, who was a stranger to her and had only just come on duty. Picking up John's car, she drove back to the hotel and saw John standing in front of it, looking expectant. As she drew up he poked his head in the window and, to her overwhelming relief, said, "Morse is okay. Critical but stable. Move over and I'll drive us to the hospital. They say we can have a few minutes with him, and I have to know what happened."

To their surprise, the first person they saw at the hospital was a bleary-eyed Brannigan, who was slurping a mug of coffee. He looked equally surprised and delighted to see them. "Well, you made it! Great!" He grinned. "Any trouble?"

"Plenty, but nothing I couldn't handle." John's tone was grim.

"Your friend okay?"

"Dead."

Brannigan sobered. "Sorry about that. Morse is going to make it. The old man thought it'd be a good idea if I stuck around until he was out of the woods. Besides"—his grin reappeared—"the little lady said to stick with him, so I bedded down here for the night."

"Is he in any shape to talk? It's important," John said tersely.

Brannigan eyed him. "He's conscious, but still pretty weak. Lucky the bullet went right through, so the wound was clean. Let's see." He led them down a corridor and into a semiprivate room with two beds. Richard lay in the one nearest the window, his eyes closed, hitched up to a transfusion apparatus. As they came to the bedside his eyes opened and Vanessa saw they were clear and steady as they fixed on hers, and he made a faint gesture with his hand.

"Morse, are you able to talk? I need to know exactly what happened out there," John said urgently.

"Yes." The voice was weak but clear. "What about West?"

"Dead," John repeated.

Richard sighed and closed his eyes for a second. "Poor devil!"

"You got one of them and I took out three others. Were there any more?"

Richard roused himself. "Five of them. One very big. The leader, I think—"

"Tell me what you can," John interrupted.

"Went in over the border about three o'clock. We didn't like the smell of things. Too many lights in the khan and no signal," Richard muttered. "West said he'd go in first, and if there was any trouble to get out fast. He was almost up to one of the windows when the headlights of a car came on and pinpointed him, and before he could get his gun into action four of 'em, including the big one, jumped him and hustled him inside. I heard him shout something about Al Ibn, and the leader knocked him down and laughed."

"Any idea who they were?"

"None. They spoke Arabic, but no sign of uniforms of any kind. Couldn't identify the headdresses, even." Richard closed his eyes again, grimaced, and went on. "They got right to work on West, so I thought I'd try a diversion. Get hold of their car, let off some shots and have them chase after me, circle around and try to get him out. Wasn't cautious enough. Thought they were all inside working on him. They had a guard on the car. Just as I got up to it I spotted him, but he spotted me. He got off a shot, yelled something, and came after me, but there was such a row going on inside I don't think they heard him. I knew I'd been hit, but didn't think it was much, so I took off, heading for the border, hoping to make it to the Jeep and maybe raise some help. Then I started to cough blood and knew that it was worse than I thought. I could still hear him coming, so I kept on until I felt my strength go, then I fell down and shammed dead. He came right up to me, kicked me over, saw all the blood, and was turning to leave when I got him in the back with my hunting knife. He went down without a sound. I knew they'd come looking sooner or later, so I tried to go on, but I was too weak by that time. I just hoped I'd go out before they found me." His voice was getting weaker and John was saying, "Okay, Morse, just one more thing. Who rang you in on this operation?" when the door opened and a highly incensed doctor bustled in and started to light into them in Turkish and in no uncertain terms. "I think we'd better go, John," Vanessa said hastily. "He says we're putting Richard's life in danger. Can't the rest of it wait?"

He hovered uncertainly for a moment. "All right, I guess so. Thanks, Morse." And he followed Brannigan out of the door. She was about to follow them when Richard put out a hand to her. "This is good-bye, isn't it, Van?" he whispered.

"Why, of course not. I'll be back to see you as soon and as often as I can," she said, taking his hand and squeezing it gently.

"That's not what I meant," he said. They looked at each other in silence as the doctor continued his tirade.

"Yes, I'm afraid in that sense it is good-bye," she said softly. "I'm sorry, Richard."

He summoned up a rueful grin. "Well, if you should ever change your mind, you'll know where to find me, my sweet. I shall live on in that hope."

Outside she found John and Brannigan in low-voiced conversation which they broke off as she came up to them. "So what now?" she asked.

"I guess I'll hang in here for a bit," Brannigan said easily, "in case there's any further trouble."

She looked at John in alarm. "You think there could be?"

He shrugged. "It's not very likely, but—well—one got away, so they may try to tidy up their loose ends. If Brannigan is willing, it may be a good idea until we find out more about it. We'd best get back to Iskenderun, where I can arrange for a relief." He cocked an eye at Brannigan. "You still have the Biretta?" The ex-mercenary nodded and patted the bulge under his shirt with lively satisfaction. "Right, then, I'll get word back to you as soon as I can."

On their way homeward Vanessa voiced a thought that had been troubling her. "What about Bobby? How on earth are we going to break all this to her? She'll be frantic with no word from Robin." John's jaw was grimly set. "First things first. I'm going to have to deal with Henfield and whatever he may be up to. And the sort of news I will have to bring Bobby won't get any worse with the delay. Even a carefully edited version is going to destroy her, and it's not something I'm exactly eager to do."

"Do you want me to do it?" she volunteered reluctantly.

"No way!" He was definite. "I won't have you further upset. God knows you've been through enough."

As they drove into the sheltered garden they saw two cars in the driveway: Dick Fortescue's and one she didn't recognize. "Ah, good!" John breathed. "Dick got him to come here—excellent!" She was startled by the venom in his voice. They went in to find Henfield, a glass in his hand, standing by the window, and Dick Fortescue at the other end of the room by the stereo. John looked over at him and Dick gave a slight nod as Henfield wheeled around and rasped, "What the devil have you been up to now, Bannerman? Getting one of my operatives involved and killed in some madcap operation of yours! Haven't you killed off enough of your own without starting in on mine? I'm going to have your head for this."

"Come off it, Henfield!" John was icy calm. "You know this was your baby from the start and all the orders were your orders, though I think I know what you're up to, now that it's all gone wrong."

"Oh, really? I suppose you have witnesses or *written* proof of it?" Henfield sneered.

"You know as well as I do that this type of operation is never on paper," John said as Vanessa looked at him, a cold fear squeezing her heart. He paused, and the antagonism between the men was like electricity in the air of the silent room. "But I do have proof," he went on softly. "I don't like you, Henfield, and I don't like your methods, so Dick and I took a few precautions. Granted, it's against company policy, but in this case . . ." He nodded at Fortescue. "You're on, Dick—the last one should be enough, I think." And Dick turned on the tape deck.

His voice came out of the speaker. "Unscrambled telephone conversation, eleven A.M., October ninth, between Henfield, chief of station Ankara, and Bannerman, chief of station Iskenderun." Then it was Henfield's unmistakable flat voice. "Bannerman, this is for your ears only, and you are to take these instructions to West personally. He is to proceed to Kilis tomorrow and rendezvous in the outskirts with the British agent to whom the meeting place is known. To proceed by Jeep, cross the border at the point specified, and, after exchange of signals at three-thirty A.M., deliver the terms agreed on to Al Ibn and set up exchange point for hostages. Return to station and report back to me. Understood, Bannerman?" And John's voice: "Understood." The tape went silent.

John looked over at Henfield, who, after an instinctive movement toward the tape deck, had remained frozen in place. "Well?" he hissed. "We have all the rest, if you're interested. Now, suppose we cut out this crap and you tell us what the *hell* went wrong. They walked into a trap; one is dead, the other badly injured. I don't give a shit whether the foul-up was your responsibility or someone else's. I just want to know *why* it happened."

Henfield showed his teeth in a travesty of a grin, his eyes snapping. "Well, it was worth a try," he muttered. "Two birds with one stone. I don't think any more of you than you do of me, Bannerman, and I don't like you on my turf. Still..." He seemed to become aware of Vanessa's presence for the first time. "I'll tell you what happened—in private." His flat eyes took in Vanessa and Dick.

"This is as private as you're going to get," John said tightly. "Without my wife's aid, we never would have known what happened out there—she has a right to know."

"And more witnesses, eh?" Henfield sneered. "I really do have you scared, don't I?"

"Like hell you do. Cut the crap, Henfield, and get on with it. You and I have a date with a widow in Adana as soon as this is over, and you'll have some more explaining to do. So make it fast and good. What went wrong?"

"Nothing," Henfield snapped. "All went according to plan. You nearly ruined everything by your interference. Thank God one of 'em got away, or it would all have to be done over again."

They looked at him in dazed incomprehension, and his lip curled into a sneer. "You didn't think the company would send a basket case like West on an *important* mission, did you? This was a feint, a diversion to draw off enemy attention from the real negotiations and the *real* exchange that will take place far, far from here. We knew Al Ibn's outfit was riddled with dissidents and informers and we had to have the setup look real. West would fall into their hands and spill his guts when they put pressure on him, and they'd be running off in the wrong direction with Al Ibn as the target. He's not really involved at all."

John had gone very white. "Oh, my *God*!" he exploded, "of all the *senseless*, diabolical... You sent him to his death deliberately, in cold blood—and for *nothing*! Your plan misfired, Henfield. Robin, God rest his tormented soul, didn't talk. He didn't tell them anything."

For the first time Henfield showed some emotion. "You're lying!" he blazed. "That fanatic fruitcake couldn't have held out under torture—it was the one thing I banked on."

"You'll die for that, you bastard!" John's sudden lunge took them all off guard, and before they could move, he had Henfield on the floor, his hands clamped on his throat, squeezing the life out of him. "No, don't, John!" Vanessa screamed as she and Dick tore at him, trying to pry him loose from his victim. Henfield kneed him in the groin and rolled free, choking and gasping, as they pulled John backward. "You fool!" he wheezed, "Langley'll destroy you for this. This wasn't *my* scheme; it was theirs. They set it up months ago. I just carried it out. West was expendable—useless. After that South African fiasco he staged, he wasn't any good to himself or anyone else. Surely you can see that."

John had slumped into a chair, looking at him with sick loathing, and Vanessa was trembling so much that she had to sit down herself, covering her face with her hands as the word "senseless, senseless, senseless" drummed in her ears. She felt her mind rocking with the horror of it all.

When John spoke again, his voice was strangely calm. "To think I have given years of my life blindly to a sewer like this, believing there was some sense, some plan to it all. Well, that's it. I'm through. Now I'll tell you exactly what we are going to do, Henfield. We are going over to Adana and *you* are going to tell Bobby West that her husband gave his life gloriously on a very important mission in the service of his country. Nothing is going to compensate her for this loss, but I'm going to make sure that the company is very, very generous, or I swear to God I'll go public with every bit of dirt I know—and I know plenty. After that they will have my immediate resignation—"

"M-m-mine, too," Dick's quiet voice broke in. "It makes me sick to think what other sick-minded deals I may have been party to in the name of the greater glory of the CIA."

Henfield's eyes narrowed as he stared at them. "Bobby West will be looked after. Don't you worry. The company knows what it's doing. And I don't threaten easily, so you two had better watch out. Getting out is not as easy as getting in, you know." His cold eyes fixed on Vanessa. "And accidents do happen along the way. But I'll go with you to Adana—we'll all go." He made for the door.

John looked down at Vanessa. "I'll be back as soon as I can, darling. Try to get some rest, and don't worry about this. I can handle Henfield." He bent down and kissed her, then he followed Dick out.

She sat frozen, torn between wild hope and bleak despair. John was getting out, not at her urging but of his own volition—a realization of all her fondest hopes. But would they let him go? She thought of the whispered stories she had heard over the years and shuddered. She had to help him; she had to find a way to ensure their escape, but where could she turn? What could she do? A plan began to form in her mind.

Chapter 29

A *sense of urgency drove her to immediate action on* her half-formed plan: she called Eleanor. As she outlined the ghastly sequence of happenings she realized she was babbling, but she could not stop the flood. At the end of the recital she said breathlessly, "So I need your help—yours and all the others. If the CIA knows a whole group of us are willing to stand up together and be counted, they aren't likely to try any of their dirty tricks on us as individuals."

Eleanor's reply when it came was cool and dry. "What you propose may be a good idea, but can you honestly see it working? Think about it. *I'd* be willing, but I am frankly a nonstarter; anything I said would be discounted as the venom of an unhappy ex-CIA wife. And can you really see Amanda Drake or Rose Ferraro rocking the boat of her husband's career on behalf of an ex-colleague? I'd say you hadn't a chance in hell."

"But there's Bobby, too," Vanessa said desperately.

"Oh, yes indeed, there's Bobby, the one with the best reason of us all to blow the whistle. But there, surely, if

John does as he proposes and shields her from the truth—and I think she *should* be shielded—well, there you've cut the ground from under your own feet. If I know Bobby—and I think I do—after the first paroxysm of her grief is past, she'll go to work for the company herself, firm in the belief that she is working for a glorious cause—and they'd let her. Besides, in order to be effective, your scheme would have to include all the details of the South African affair, and that would show Robin in a bad light. She'd never stand for that, and you know it. No, my dear, I'm afraid you must think again. We're no good to you."

"Then what am I to do?" Vanessa faltered. "What if they won't let John go? What if they crucify him on some trumped-up charge—or, worse, go after him?"

"Well, in the first place, I shouldn't pay too much mind to Henfield's threats," Eleanor comforted. "He's no fool. Too many people outside the company—this Englishman and the people at Tell Murad—know what's been going on, and he certainly can't shut all of *them* up. As to getting out with the minimum of fuss, what you need is someone with real clout to help you, not people like us. Maybe John knows someone in Washington who can help. I shouldn't worry too much—John knows how to protect himself, and the company *hates* any kind of bad publicity. Henfield might talk tough, but I don't see them making too many waves."

It was small comfort to Vanessa. "Thank you anyway for listening, Eleanor," she said forlornly. "I hope you're right." And she rang off.

Someone with clout: she had no idea if John had any such contacts, but she most assuredly had one. The question was could she, should she, involve him in something like this. She was still mulling this over when the phone shrilled. It was John, his voice tight and strained, and she could hear a woman sobbing in the background. "Darling, I hate to do this, but I think I'd better stay here overnight. Henfield did his part okay, but as you can probably hear, Bobby's in a pretty bad way, and I think I'd better stick around. I don't want you to be alone, so I'm sending Dick back to stay over."

She came to a decision. "No, don't! I'd like to go right down to Tell Murad—then you can stay as long as you need and do whatever is necessary, and I'll be quite safe there until you can come for me."

"But you can't drive that road alone in the dark!" he protested.

"I won't have to. If I leave now, Brannigan will still be at the hospital, won't he? If you can arrange someone to relieve him, he can fly me out."

John let out an exclamation. "Damn! I'd forgotten about that—yes, that's something I can do from here. And yes, you would be safer there. I'll tell him to wait for you at the airport. I'll be there as soon as I can, my love. And for God's sake, be careful—I love you."

"And I love you," she whispered, her resolve hardening.

She threw a few things in a bag, told the bewildered servants that she was off again, and started her trek back over the mountains. It was late afternoon by the time she once more rolled up to the Gross Enterprises landing pad, to find Brannigan contentedly dozing in the long shadows, a brandy bottle clasped to his chest.

At the sound of the car he opened his eyes, and he waved the brandy bottle as she emerged. "Well, here we go again," he called cheerfully. "Where to now, little lady? The old man is snorting like a prize stallion to know what's been going on." At the sight of her white, tense face he sobered and held out the brandy bottle. "Here, you look as if you need a snort of this. More trouble?"

She accepted it thankfully and took a swig. "Yes, you could say that," she said wearily, "though not quite as bloody as what we've been through—I hope. I have to talk to Herman. Can we get going?"

"Sure can. Baby is all set," he said, hoisting her bag and taking it out to the helicopter.

"How's Richard?" she asked as they buckled themselves in.

"Oh, they're keeping him sedated a lot, but in ten days or so he'll be as good as new. He's a pretty tough bird, you know." He looked sideways at her. "Where's your old man?"

"With Robin West's widow," she said bleakly. "Robin was his best friend."

"Tough!" he breathed, starting the engine. "Still, he's a pretty tough hombre, too, so don't you fret."

When they touched down on the pad at Tell Murad she felt a strange sense of homecoming; so much had changed in her own life during the short period she had been away that it came as a shock to find things exactly as they were, even to her guest tent, where she found a hairbrush she had left behind neatly aligned before the mirror. She just dumped her bag on the cot, hastily brushed her untidy hair, and went in search of Herman, whom she ran to ground emerging from the mess tent. He bristled at the sight of her. "So you're back, and about time, too! You send me a basket case and you're looking like one yourself. Would you tell me what the hell has been going on?"

"That's precisely why I'm here," she said grimly. "I have a long, involved, and very tragic story to tell—without interruptions, if you don't mind, or I might just collapse in my tracks."

"Humph. Like that, is it?" he growled. "Well, come along to my tent and we'll have a brandy. Looks to me as if you could use several. Graham!" His bellow made her jump. A young towheaded man came running, an eager smile on his face. "Make yourself useful. Stand outside my tent and see that no one—and I mean no one—interrupts us," Herman commanded, shuffling off. The young man looked askance at her and fell in behind them.

Herman waved her to a canvas chair, fixed her a large shot of brandy, and slumped into his own chair. "You've got the floor—shoot!"

She took a deep breath. "You once said that if I needed any help you'd give it. Well, I do need it—desperately. What I'm about to tell you probably violates every official secrets act in the book and John would murder me if he knew what I was doing, but I don't care anymore. This is how it is. . . ." She went on to relate the whole tragic series of events: her own involvment in Africa and Richard's rescue of her; Clara Zecco's murder and Robin's suicide attempt; and right on through to the ghastly events of the past three days. Herman listened raptly, his bright eyes fixed on her throughout the whole recital. "I don't want to end up like Clara," she finished breathlessly. "Or John to be wasted like Robin. All we want is to get out and be left in peace—but I don't think Henfield or the CIA will let us go that easily. You're a powerful man, Herman. Isn't there something you can do for us? The ambassador is a friend of yours—perhaps if you talked to him?" She paused hopefully.

"Oh, him!" he said absently. "A nice chap, but a light-weight. No, I can do better than that." Then he added, as if to himself, "Glad to know where Morse fits in. That had me puzzled." Then to her astonishment he asked, "Can you use a word processor?"

She gaped at him. "Why—er—a little."

"Good, good." He nodded briskly. "Well, I'll tell you what we're going to do. There's no point in starting tonight. You look tired, and it's too late for me to begin things in the U.S. First thing in the morning, while I'm doing my thing, you'll put everything you've told me into my computer. We'll have a printout here, and I'll relay a print to all my confidential assistants around the States."

"Put it on paper?" she queried uneasily.

"Yes, what you need is insurance, heavy insurance—and I need ammunition. When I tell someone I've got in mind to contact and tell 'em what we've done, I think I can guarantee you'll have no further trouble from any-one—ever."

"Oh, Herman," she cried, "That's wonderful! Are you sure it will work?"

"As sure as my name is Herman Gross," he said gruffly. "And just as well that husband of yours is getting out of such an outfit. I've suspected it for years, but if I had run my affairs in the stupid, slapdash way they seem to run theirs, I'd have been broke and out of business long since. Dirty tricks I can understand, even cruelty and violence, but sheer ineptitude? That's something else!" He wagged his head in disapproval. "Anyway, you look all in. Why don't you get a bite to eat and then get to bed early? We'll be hellishly busy tomorrow."

"I don't know how to begin my thanks," she said, getting up. "You're a truly remarkable man, Herman."

He grinned at her. "I know. Now, go get some rest, m'dear."

But she was too keyed up to obey him, and after a hasty snack in the mess tent she sat down and, to clarify her thoughts, wrote out what she intended to put into the computer on the morrow. After many crossouts and emendations she was satisfied with her efforts and, exhausted, tumbled into bed.

She was up early, feeling as if the weight of the world had been lifted from her shoulders, and as Herman put her to work at the computer he remarked, "There now, you look a different woman. I'm off to Antakya. Got to use the radio there to do what I have to do, and I'll drop in and see if I can have a word with Richard Morse. This thing is programmed to relay, so all you have to do when you're through is to push these two buttons. The computer will do the rest."

"When I'm finished, will it be all right if I stay on here until John fetches me?" she asked.

"Fine. Mary's been bitching at me like crazy. All sorts of work piled up—she'll be delighted. Stay as long as you can," he trumpeted. "And don't worry about a thing. You can leave the rest to me."

When he returned that evening he looked as smug as the cat that swallowed the canary, his eyes sparkling, but at her eager inquiries he only shook his head. "Everything's taken care of. Don't know when I've had so much fun. Twisted one hell of a lot of tails. But you've got to let me keep my little secrets, m'dear. Just rest assured that all is well. Your husband coming down here to pick you up, is he?"

"Yes, as soon as he can get free."

"Well, when he does come, be sure he has a few words with me," Herman muttered. "Get all your stuff in the computer?"

"First thing this morning." She smiled at him. "Since

then Mary's had me hard at work, and I'm enjoying every minute of it."

"Great, great. Did she show you the Greek sanctuary we've got coming out at the other end of the site? A shrine to Apollo, by the looks of it, just like the one at Daphne." He rubbed his hands together in glee, his eyes alive with delight. "What a first season! By the Lord, I'm not going to forget this year in a hurry!"

John appeared two days later. Once again she was hard at work at her drawing board. After the first rapture of kisses she drew away and examined him. "Was it very bad? How's Bobby?"

"Oh, I think she's over the worst of it." His voice was weary. "Henfield, damn him, did his part very well, and we spun her such a tissue of lies that she almost seemed relieved that Robin had found a heroic end. Henfield buttered her up so about her own abilities that I'm pretty certain she'll go back and work for the company in Langley. It's incredible, but there was little I could do about it under the circumstances."

So Eleanor had been right, she thought. "Herman wants to talk to you," she said. "Don't be mad at me, but I asked him for help to get us out of this. I thought we could use some."

"That's true enough, unfortunately," he sighed. "Though where we go from here I'm not sure. How's it feel to be hitched to an unemployed, middle-aged husband?"

"You're not having second thoughts, are you?" she asked in alarm.

"No." He was firm. "I'm through. Even if it means pumping gas for a living or being a security guard at a plant."

"That would be just fine with me," she murmured, kissing him again. "Just as along as we can live in peace and as far away from the CIA as we can get."

She was not included in the conference between John and Herman, and when he finally emerged, John looked more than a little dazed. "Well?" she said anxiously.

He shook his head in disbelief. "That man is simply incredible," he muttered. "But one thing we've both agreed on. Knowing the slow workings of bureaucracy, he wants to be sure that everyone has gotten the word, so we both think it would be safer for you to stay here while I go back and pack up and hand the operation over to the man Henfield is sending down pro tem as my replacement. It'll take me about two weeks. I hate to be away from you that long, but I do agree it's for the best."

"Are you sure you're going to be all right?" She was worried.

"Oh, yes. This is just the formalities. Henfield's going to be so delighted to get rid of me, he's not going to try anything now, and by the time he's ready for something else—well, if Gross's scheme works, he'll be damned lucky not to be on the job line himself."

And so it came about that she enjoyed a strangely tranquil period as their old life came to an end, consisting of work on the site punctuated by trips to Antakya to see the recuperating Richard, who, as predicted by Brannigan, was mending fast and who also had had a radical change of mind on Herman.

"He's really quite fantastic," he informed her grimly. "There's little doubt, now that I've put all the pieces together, that once I announced my intention of quitting, my people thought me as expendable as poor West. Of course, now they are saying it was all the fault of the Yanks and they had no idea what was really going on, but old Herman's long arm even stretches as far as England, and they are almost pathetically eager to see me out and quietly settled on my Sussex acres. The doc here thinks I'll be fit to travel in six days or so. Ah, the miracles of modern medicine! To think I was lying at death's door in the desert only a week ago, and here I am practically as good as new and heading for greener pastures. We're all even now—I saved your life, you saved mine, so..." He cocked an inquiring eye at her. "You wouldn't, by any chance, be in the mood to change your mind?"

"Richard," she interrupted him firmly, "no. Don't even finish the thought. I'm going to have a baby."

"That's not the reason you're staying with John, is it?" He was suddenly hopeful. "Because if so..."

"No, that's not the reason."

He sighed. "I was afraid not. Well, my sweet, I'm a rotten loser, so we'd better make this a final good-bye."

She leaned down and kissed him. "Good-bye, my dear," she said softly. "And thanks . . . thanks for everything."

John arrived on the helicopter shuttle four days later, complete with an overnight bag and two airline tickets for the States. "We're due to fly out of Iskenderun tomorrow, and from Istanbul the day after," he informed her. "The word seems to be out—at least, Henfield has been recalled to Langley. We'd better see Herman, clue him in, and say our farewells."

They found him sitting on a Greek tomb and gazing distractedly at the Orontes, puffing on a very large cigar. When John had delivered his news, Herman said, "So what are your ongoing plans?"

"First I have to return to Langley for final debriefing and separation, and then, I suppose, I'll have to put a résumé together and start on a job hunt."

"Hmm. Not too good, eh? Especially with a baby on the way. When's it due?" Herman barked.

They both gaped at him. "How on earth did you know that?" Vanessa said weakly.

He looked at her in surprise. "I've had seven of me own, you know. Always could tell—sometimes before even me wife knew. There's a sort of bloom that comes on a woman when it happens." His voice softened momentarily before he went on. "Interested in security work, are ye?"

"It's what I'm best fitted for," John agreed cautiously.

"Well, it's like this." Herman was puffing up a volcanic cloud of smoke. "One of my subsidiaries, Dynamex—got a lot of hush-hush government contracts. Need a security man with top-secret clearances. Lots of action. Industrial espionage by my competitors, spies, the works—should be right up your alley. My chief of security there is due for retirement in six months' time. Need a good replacement. Could go in right away and get the feel of things, and then in six months take his place. It'd mean living in

Dallas, but that's not bad. Do it myself on occasion. Interested?"

"Why"—John gasped—"Yes, very. It would be perfect."

"Good. Then that's settled," Herman got up. "Suppose I'd better fix you up with a double tent for the night, eh? Oh, and you can use my Dallas house until you're settled. Nobody there, except maybe some of the kids between marriages, but they won't bother you. Let me know when you're through in Langley and they'll be expecting you."

"Oh, Herman!" Vanessa cried, throwing her arms around his neck. "I love you, I really do."

"Ah!" he sighed. "If only I were thirty years younger, I'd take you up on that, m'dear. And there's no need for thanks. I know a good bargain when I see one."

She went to pack up her things and say her good-byes, and they wandered in a delighted daze up to the double tent that was theirs for the night. John looked at the twin cots nestled cozily together and turned to her with a grin. "Looks good to me. It isn't Venice, but 'twill serve, 'twill serve."

She put her arms around his neck and nestled close to him. "For me it will be far, far better than Venice," she whispered. "Oh, darling, am I dreaming all this, or is this really going to be happy ever after?"

"Yes, this time it's *really* going to be happy ever after, my love," he murmured as his lips found hers.

Extract from the Dynamex Monthly Newsletter: July, 198-

"Congratulations to new Chief of Security John Bannerman and his wife, Vanessa, on the birth of their son, Robin West Bannerman, 8 lbs., 2 ozs., at Gross Memorial Hospital, Dallas, on June 24. Mother and child doing fine. Father doing as well as can be expected."

27 million Americans can't read a bedtime story to a child.

It's because 27 million adults in this country simply can't read.

Functional illiteracy has reached one out of five Americans. It robs them of even the simplest of human pleasures, like reading a fairy tale to a child.

You can change all this by joining the fight against illiteracy.

Call the Coalition for Literacy at toll-free **1-800-228-8813** and volunteer.

Volunteer Against Illiteracy. The only degree you need is a degree of caring.

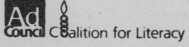

Ad Council Coalition for Literacy

LV-3